The McKennas: Finn, Riley & Brody

SHIRLEY JUMP

Published in Great Britain 2015
by Mills & Boon, an imprint of Harlequin (UK) Limited,
Eton House, 18-24 Paradise Road, Richmond, Surrey, TW9 1SR

THE MCKENNAS: FINN, RILEY & BRODY © 2015 Harlequin Books S. A.

One Day to Find a Husband, How the Playboy Got Serious, Return of the Last McKenna were first published in Great Britain by Harlequin (UK) Limited.

One Day to Find a Husband © 2012 Shirley Kawa-Jump, LLC
How the Playboy Got Serious © 2012 Shirley Kawa-Jump, LLC
Return of the Last McKenna © 2012 Shirley Kawa-Jump, LLC

ISBN: 978-0-263-25239-2

05-1115

Harlequin (UK) Limited's policy is to use papers that are natural, renewable and recyclable products and made from wood grown in sustainable forests. The logging and manufacturing processes conform to the legal environmental regulations of the country of origin.

Printed and bound in Spain
by CPI, Barcelona

New York Times bestselling author **Shirley Jump** didn't have the will-power to diet, nor the talent to master under-eye concealer, so she bowed out of a career in television and opted instead for a career where she could be paid to eat at her desk—writing. At first, seeking revenge on her children for their grocery store tantrums, she sold embarrassing essays about them to anthologies. However, it wasn't enough to feed her growing addiction to writing funny. So she turned to the world of romance novels, where messes are (usually) cleaned up before The End. In the worlds Shirley gets to create and control, the children listen to their parents, the husbands always remember holidays and the housework is magically done by elves. Though she's thrilled to see her books in stores around the world, Shirley mostly writes because it gives her an excuse to avoid cleaning the toilets and helps feed her shoe habit.

To learn more, visit her website at www.shirleyjump.com.

ONE DAY
TO FIND A HUSBAND

BY
SHIRLEY JUMP

To my husband,
who truly is my hero every day of my life.
Thank you for blessing me with your love,
and with our amazing children.

CHAPTER ONE

FINN MCKENNA wanted one thing.

And she was standing fifteen feet away, completely unaware of what he was about to do and definitely not expecting the question he wanted to ask her. He watched the woman—tall, blonde, leggy, the kind any man in his right mind could imagine taking to dinner, twirling around a dance floor, holding close at the end of the night—and hoped like hell his plan worked.

If he was his grandfather, he'd have been toting the McKenna four-leaf clover in his pocket, knocking three times on the banister and whispering a prayer to the Lord above. Finn McKenna's ancestors were nothing if not superstitious. Finn, on the other hand, believed in the kind of luck fostered by good research and hard work. Not the kind brought about by leprechauns and rainbows.

He'd put enough time into this project, that was for sure. Turned the idea left, right and upside down in his head. Done his research, twice over. In short, reassured himself as much as one man could that the lady he was going to talk to would say…

Yes.

"You're insane."

Finn turned and shrugged at his little brother. Riley McKenna had the same dark brown hair and sky-blue eyes as the rest of the McKenna boys, but something about Riley, maybe his grin or his devil-may-care attitude, gave those same features a little spin of dashing. Finn had inherited the serious, hard lines of his workaholic father, where Riley had more of their free-spirited mother's twinkle. "I'm not crazy, Riley. It's business. Risks are part of the job."

"Here." Riley handed him a glass. "I talked the bartender into pouring you and me some good quality Irish ale."

"Thanks." Finn sipped at the dark brew. It slid down his throat with smooth, almost spicy notes. The beer was dry, yet robust, the kind that promised a memorable drink in a single pint. A thick head of foam on top indicated the quality of the ale. Good choice on Riley's part, but Finn wasn't surprised. His little brother knew his brews.

All around him, people mingled and networked over several-hundred-dollar-a-bottle wines and martinis with names so fancy they needed their own dictionary. In this crowd, a beer stuck out like a dandelion in a field of manicured roses, but Finn McKenna had never been one to worry much about breaking the rules or caring what other people thought about him. It was what had fueled his success.

And had also been a part of his recent failure.

A temporary state, he reminded himself. Tonight, he was going to change all of that. He was going to rebuild his business and he was going to use Ellie Winston, interim CEO of WW Architectural Design, to help him do it.

She just didn't know it yet.

Eleanor Winston, known by those close to her as "Ellie," the new boss of WW, her father's company. Henry Winston Sr., one of the two Ws in the company name, had retired suddenly a couple weeks ago. Rumor was he'd had a major heart attack and would probably not return to the chair. The other W, his brother, had walked out in a family dispute eleven years prior, but his name remained on the masthead.

Finn ticked off what he knew about Eleanor Winston in his head. Twenty-nine, with a master's in design from a reputable college, three years working at a firm in Atlanta before moving to Boston shortly after her father's illness. Her design work was primarily in residential housing—the McMansions much maligned by the architectural world—and Finn had heard she was none too pleased to be spending her days designing hospitals and office supertowers. All the more reason for her to accept his offer with gratitude. He'd scoped out his competition for several weeks before deciding WW Architects was the best choice. A fledgling president, overseeing a sprawling company with multiple projects going at any given time—surely she wanted a…helping hand. Yes, that's what he'd call it. A helping hand. A win-win for her and him.

"So this is your grand plan? Talking to Ellie Winston? Here? Now?" Riley asked. "With you dressed like that?"

Finn glanced down at his dark gray pinstripe suit, crisp white shirt and navy blue tie. "What's wrong with the way I'm dressed?"

"Hey, nothing, if you're heading to a funeral." Riley patted his own shirt, as usual unbuttoned at the neck and devoid of a tie. "Make a statement, Finn. Get your sexy on."

Finn shook off that advice. Riley was the more colorful McKenna brother, the one who always stood out in a crowd. Finn preferred his appearance neat, trim and professional—the same way he conducted business. Nothing too flashy, nothing too exciting.

"This is the perfect environment," Finn said, nodding toward the woman. "She's relaxed, maybe had a couple glasses of wine, and best of all—" he turned to his brother "—not expecting the offer I'm about to make."

Riley chuckled. "Oh, I think that's guaranteed."

Finn's gaze centered on Ellie Winston again. She laughed at something the guy beside her said. A full-throated laugh, her head thrown back, her deep green eyes dancing with merriment. Every time he'd seen her, she'd been like that—so open, so exuberant. Something dark and deep stirred in Finn's gut, and for a split second he envied the man at her side. Wondered what it would be like to be caught in that spell. To be the one making her laugh and smile like that.

Damn, she was beautiful. Intriguing.

And a distraction, he told himself. One he couldn't afford. Hadn't he already learned that lesson from one painful mistake after another?

"A woman like that…" Riley shook his head. "I don't think hardball is the right way to play it, Hawk."

"I hate when you call me that."

"Hey, if the nickname fits." Riley grinned. "You, big brother, spy the weak, pluck them up and use them to feather your nest." He put a hand on Finn's shoulder. "But in the nicest way possible. Of course."

"Oh, yeah, of course." A magazine had dubbed Finn "the Hawk" a few years ago when he'd done a surprise buyout of his closest competitor. Then six months later, his next closest competitor. He'd absorbed the other businesses into his own, becoming one of the largest architectural firms in New England. At least for a while. Until his ex-girlfriend's betrayal had reduced his company to half its size, taking his reputation down at the same time.

Now he'd slipped in the rankings, not even powerful enough to make any lists anymore. Or to merit any other nickname other than "Failure."

But not for long.

A waitress came by with a tray of crudités and offered some to Finn and Riley. Finn waved off the food, but Riley picked up a smoked salmon–topped cucumber slice and shot the waitress a grin. "Are these as delicious as you are beautiful?"

A flush filled her face and she smiled. "You'll have to try one to see."

He popped it in his mouth, chewed and swallowed. Then shot her an even bigger grin. "The appetizer is definitely a winner."

The waitress cocked her hip and gave him another, sassier smile. "Perhaps you should try the other, too." Then she turned on her heel and headed for the next group.

"Perhaps I will," Riley said, watching her sashay through the crowd.

Finn rolled his eyes. Keeping Riley focused on the subject at hand sometimes required superhuman abilities. "Do you ever think about anything other than women?"

"Do you ever think about anything other than business?" Riley countered.

"I'm the owner, Riley. I don't have a choice but to keep my eye on the ball and my focus on the company." He'd had a time where he'd focused on a relationship—and that had cost him dearly. Never again.

"There's always a choice, Finn." Riley grinned. "I prefer the ones that end with a woman like that in my bed, and a smile on my face." He arched a brow in the direction of the waitress, who shot him a flirtatious smile back. "A woman like that one."

"You're a dog."

Riley shrugged off the teasing. His playboy tendencies had been well documented by the Boston media. As the youngest McKenna, getting away with murder had been his middle name almost since birth. Funny how stereotypical the three boys had turned out. Finn, the eldest, the responsible one, working since he was thirteen. Brody, the middle brother, the peacemaker, who worked a respectable, steady job as a family physician. And then Riley, the youngest, and thus overindulged by their mother, and later, by their grandmother, who still doted on the "baby" of the family. Riley had turned being a wild child into a sport…and managed to live a life almost entirely devoid of responsibility.

Finn sometimes felt like he'd been responsible from the day he took his first steps. He'd started out as a one-man shop right out of college, and built McKenna Designs into a multioffice corporation designing projects all over the world. His rapid growth, coupled with a recession that fell like an axe on the building industry, and one mistake he wished he could go back in time and undo, had damaged his bottom line. Nearly taken him to bankruptcy.

"Carpe diem, Finn," Riley said. "You should try it sometime. Get out of the office and live a little."

"I do."

Riley laughed. Out loud. *"Right."*

"Running a company is a demanding job," Finn said. Across the room, the woman he wanted to talk to was still making small talk with the other partygoers. To Finn, the room seemed like an endless sea of blue and black, neckties and polished loafers. Only two people stood out in the dark ocean before him—

Riley, who had bucked the trend by wearing a collarless white shirt under a sportscoat trimmed to fit his physique.

And Eleanor Winston, who'd opted for a deep cranberry dress that wrapped around her slender frame, emphasizing her small waist, and hourglass shape. She was the only woman in a colorful dress, the only one who looked like she was truly at a cocktail party, not a funeral, as Riley would say. She had on high heels in a light neutral color, making her legs seem impossibly long. They curved in tight calf muscles, leading up to creamy thighs and—

Concentrate.

He had a job to do and getting distracted would only cost him in the end.

"You seem to make it harder than most, though. For Pete's sake, you have a sofa bed in your office." Riley chuckled and shook his head. "If that doesn't scream lonely bachelor with no life, I don't know what does. Unless Miss Marstein is keeping you warm at night."

Finn choked on the sip of beer in his mouth. His assistant was an efficient, persnickety woman in her early sixties who ran his office and schedule with an iron fist. "Miss Marstein is old enough to be my grandmother."

"And you're celibate enough to be a monk. Get away from the blueprints, Hawk, and live a little."

Finn let out a sigh. Riley didn't get it. He'd always been the younger, irresponsible one, content to live off the inheritance from their parents' death, rather than carry the worries of a job. Riley didn't understand the precarious position McKenna Designs was in right now. How one mistake could cost him all the ground he'd regained, one painful step at a time. People were depending on Finn to succeed. His employees had families, mortgages, car payments. He couldn't let them down. It was about far greater things than Finn's reputation or bottom line.

Finn bristled. "I work long days and yes, sometimes nights. It's more efficient to have a sofa bed—"

"Efficient? Try depressing." Riley tipped his beer toward the woman across from them. "If you were smart, you'd think about getting wild with *her* on that sofa bed. Sleep's overrated. While sex, on the other hand..." He grinned. "Can't rate it highly enough."

"I do not have time for something like that. The company has been damaged by this roller-coaster economy and..." He shook his head. Regret weighed down his shoulders. "I never should have trusted her."

Riley placed a hand on Finn's shoulder. "Stop beating yourself up. Everyone makes mistakes."

"Still, I never should have trusted her," he said again. How many times had he said that to himself? A hundred times? Two hundred? He could say it a thousand and it wouldn't undo the mistake.

"You were in love. All men act like idiots when they're in love." Riley grinned. "Take it from the expert."

"You've been in love? Real, honest-to-goodness love?"

Riley shrugged. "It felt real at the time."

"Well, I won't make that mistake again." Finn took a deep gulp of beer.

"You're hopeless. One bad relationship is no reason to become a hermit."

One bad relationship? Finn had fallen for a woman who had stolen his top clients, smeared his reputation and broken his heart. That wasn't a bad relationship, it was the sinking of the Titanic. He'd watched his parents struggle through a terrible marriage, both of them unhappily mismatched, and didn't want to make the same mistake.

"I'm not having this conversation right now." Finn's gaze went to Ellie Winston again. She had moved on to another group of colleagues. She greeted nearly everyone she saw, with a smile, a few words, a light touch. And they responded in kind. She had socializing down to an art. The North Carolina transplant had made friends quickly. Only a few weeks in the city and she was winning over the crowd of their peers with one hand tied behind her back. Yes, she'd be an asset to his company and his plan. A good one. "I'm focused on work."

"Seems to me you're focused on her." Riley grinned.

"She's a means to an end, nothing more."

"Yeah, well, the only ending I see for you, Finn, is one where you're old and gray, surrounded by paperwork and sleeping alone in that sofa bed."

"You're wrong."

For a while, Finn had thought he could have both the life and the job. He'd even bought the ring, put a downpayment on a house in the suburbs. He'd lost his head for a while, a naive young man who believed love could conquer everything. Until that love had stabbed him in the back.

Apparently true love was a fairy tale reserved for others. Like kissing the Blarney Stone for good luck.

Finn now preferred to have his relationships as dry as his wine. No surprises, no twists and turns. Just a dependable, predictable sameness. Leaving the roller coaster for the corporate world.

He suspected, though, that Eleanor Winston and her standout maroon dress was far from the dry, dependable type. She had a glint in her eye, a devilish twinkle in her smile, a spontaneous air about her that said getting involved with her would leave a man…

Breathless.

Exactly the opposite of what he wanted. He would have to keep a clear head around her.

Ellie drifted away from her companions, heading toward the door. Weaving through the crowd slowed her progress, but it wouldn't be long before she'd finished her goodbyes and left. "She's leaving. Catch up with you later," he said to Riley.

"Take a page from my book, brother, and simply ask her out for a drink," Riley said, then as Finn walked away, added one more bit of advice. "And for God's sake, Finn, don't talk business. At least not until…after." He grinned. "And if you get stumped, think to yourself, 'What would Riley say?' That'll work, I promise."

Finn waved off Riley's advice. Riley's attention had already strayed back to the waitress, who was making her way through the room with another tray—and straight for Riley's charming grin. His brother's eyes were always focused on the next beautiful woman he could take home to his Back Bay townhouse. Finn had much bigger, and more important goals.

Like saving his company. He'd made millions already in architecture, and hopefully would again, if he could make his business profitable again. If not, he could always accept his grandmother's offer and take up the helm at McKenna Media. The family business, started a generation ago by his grandfather, who used to go door-to-door selling radio ad space to local businesses. Finn's father had joined the company after high school and taken it into television, before his death when Finn was eleven. Ever since his grandfather had died three years ago, Finn's grandmother had sat in the top chair, but she'd been making noise lately about wanting to retire and have Finn take over, and keep the company in McKenna hands. Finn's heart, though, lay in architecture. Tonight was all about keeping that heartbeat going.

Finn laid his still-full glass of beer on the tray of a passing waiter, then straightened his tie and worked a smile to his face. Riley, who never tired of telling Finn he was too uptight, too stiff, would say it was more of a grimace. Finn didn't care. He wasn't looking to be a cover model or to make friends.

Then he glanced over at his brother—no longer chatting up the waitress but now flirting with a brunette. For a second, Finn envied Riley's easy way with women. Everything about his little brother screamed relaxed, at home. His stance, his smile, the slight rumple in his shirt.

Finn forced himself to relax, to look somewhat approachable. Then he increased his pace to close the gap between himself and Ellie. He reached her just before she stepped through the glass doors of the lobby.

"Miss Winston."

She stopped, her hand on the metal bar, ready to exit. Then she turned back and faced him. Her long blond hair swung with the movement, settling like a silk curtain around her shoulders. The short-sleeved crimson dress she wore hugged her curves, and dropped into a tantalizing yet modest V at her chest. For a second, her green eyes were blank, then she registered his face and the green went from cold emerald to warm forest. "My goodness. Mr. McKenna," she said. "I recognize you from the article in *Architecture Today*."

"Please, call me Finn." She'd seen the piece about his award for innovative building design? And remembered it? "That was more than a year ago. I'm impressed with your memory."

"Well, like most people in our industry, I have an absolutely ridiculous attention for detail." She smiled then, the kind of smile that no one would ever confuse with a grimace. The kind of smile that hit a man in the gut and made him forget everything around him. The kind of smile that added an extra sparkle to her green eyes, and lit her delicate features with an inner glow.

Intoxicating.

Get a grip, McKenna. This was business, nothing more. Since when did he think of anything other than a bottle of single malt as intoxicating? Business, and business *only.* "If you have a minute, I wanted to talk to you."

"Actually I'm heading out." She gestured toward the door. A continual Morse code of headlights went by on the busy street outside, tires making a constant whoosh-whoosh of music on the dark pavement, even though it was nearing midnight on a Tuesday night. Boston, like most cities, never slept. And neither, most nights, did Finn McKenna.

"Perhaps you could call my assistant," she said, "and set up a meeting for—"

"If you have time tonight, I would appreciate it." He remembered Riley's advice and decided to sweeten the pot a little. Show her he wasn't the cold business-only gargoyle that people rumored him to be. Hawk indeed. Finn could be suave. Debonair even.

His younger brother could charm a free coffee from a barista; talk a traffic cop into forgetting his ticket. Maybe if Finn applied a bit of that, it might loosen her up, and make her more amenable to what he was about to propose. So he worked up another smile-grimace to his face—and tried another tack.

"Why don't we, uh, grab a couple drinks somewhere?" he said, then groaned inwardly. Casual conversation was clearly not his forte. Put him in a board room, and he was fine, but attempting small talk…a disaster.

Damn Riley's advice anyway.

"Thank you, but I don't drink. If you ask me, too many bad decisions have been made with a bottle of wine." Another smile. "I'm sure if you call in the morning—"

"Your schedule is certainly as busy as mine. Why don't we avoid yet another meeting?"

"In other words, get this out of the way and then I can get rid of you?"

He laughed. "Something like that."

"It's really late…"

He could see her hesitation. In a second, she'd say no again, and he'd be forced to delay his plan one more day. He didn't have the luxury of time. He needed to get a meeting with Ellie Winston—a private one—now. In business, he knew when to press, and when to step back. Now was a time to press. A little. "I promise, I don't bite."

"Or pick over the remains of your competitors?"

"That's a rumor. Nothing more. I've only done that… once." He paused a second. "Okay, maybe twice."

She threw back her head and laughed. "Oh my, Mr. McKenna. You are not what I expected."

What had she expected? That he would be the stern predator portrayed in that article? Or that he wouldn't have a sense of humor? "I hope that's a good thing."

"We shall see," she said. Then she reached out and laid a hand on his arm, a quick touch, nothing more, but it was enough to stir a fire inside him. A fire that he knew better than to stoke.

What the hell had been in that beer? Finn McKenna wasn't a man given to spontaneous emotional or physical reactions. Except for one brief window, he'd lived his life as ordered as the buildings he designed. No room for

fluff or silliness. And particularly no room for the foolishness of a tumble in the hay. Yet his mind considered
that very thing when Eleanor Winston touched him.

"I'm sorry, you're absolutely right, it is late and you
must want to get home," he said, taking a step back, feeling...flustered, which was not at all like him. "I'll call
your assistant in the morning."

Riley had said to say what he would say. And Finn
knew damned well Riley wouldn't have said that.

"No, I'm the one who's sorry, Mr. McKenna. I've had
a long, long day and I..." She glanced back in the direction of the closed double doors, but Finn got the sense
she wasn't looking at the black-tie crowd filling the Park
Plaza's ballroom, but at something else, something he
couldn't see. Then she glanced at her watch. "Midnight.
Well, the day *is* over, isn't it?"

"If you want it to be, Cinderella. Or you could continue the ball for a little while longer." The quip came out
without hesitation. A true Riley-ism. He'd been spending
too much time with his brother.

Or maybe not, he thought, when she laughed. He liked
her laugh. It was light, airy, almost musical.

"Cinderella, huh?" she said. "Okay, you convinced
me. It would be nice to end my day with some one-on-
one conversation instead of an endless stream of small
talk." She wagged a finger at him and a tease lit her face,
made her smile quirk higher on one side than the other.
"But I'll have tea, not tequila, while I hear you out on
whatever it is you want to tell me."

"Excellent." He could only hope she was as amenable to his proposal. Surely such an auspicious beginning
boded well for the rest. He pushed on the door and waved
Ellie through with one long sweep of his arm. "After
you...Cinderella."

"My goodness, Finn McKenna. You certainly do know how to make a girl swoon." She flashed him yet another smile and then whooshed past him and out into the night, leaving the faint scent of jasmine and vanilla in her wake.

Get back to the plan, he reminded himself. Focus on getting her to agree. Nothing more. He could do it, he knew he could. Finn wasn't a distracted, spontaneous man. He refused to tangle personal with business ever again. He would get Ellie to agree, and before he could blink, his company would be back on top.

But as he followed one of his biggest competitors into the twinkling, magical world of Boston at night, he had to wonder if he was making the best business decision of his life—or the worst.

CHAPTER TWO

She had to be crazy.

What else had made Ellie agree to midnight drinks with Finn McKenna—one of her competitors and a man she barely knew? She'd been ready to go home, get to bed and get some much-needed sleep when Finn had approached her.

There'd been something about his smile, though, something about him charmed her. He wasn't a smooth talker, more a man who had an easy, approachable way about him, one that she suspected rarely showed in his business life. The "Hawk" moniker that magazine—and most of the people in the architecture world—had given him didn't fit the man who had teasingly called her Cinderella. A man with vivid sky-blue eyes and dark chocolate hair.

And that intrigued her. A lot.

So Ellie settled into the red vinyl covered seat across from Finn McKenna, a steaming mug of tea warming her palms. So far they'd done little more than exchange small talk about the weather and the party they'd just left.

She'd never met the fabled architect, the kind of man talked about in hushed tones by others in the industry. She'd read about him, even studied a few of his projects when she was in college, but they'd never crossed paths. If she hadn't been at the helm of WW Architectural Design, she wouldn't even have been at the event tonight, one of those networking things designed to bring together competitors, as if they'd share trade secrets over a few glasses of wine. In reality, everyone was there to try to extract as much information as they could, while revealing none of their own.

"Was that your brother you were talking to in the ballroom?" she asked. Telling herself she wasn't being curious about the contradictory Finn, just conversational.

Finn nodded. "Riley. He's the youngest."

"He looks a lot like you."

Finn chuckled. "Poor guy."

"Is he in the industry, too?"

"Definitely not. He tagged along for the free drinks."

She laughed. "I can appreciate that. Either way, I'm glad that cocktail party is over." She rubbed her neck, loosening some of the tension of the day. "Sometimes it seems those things are never going to end."

"You seemed to fit right in."

"I can talk, believe me." She laughed, then leaned in closer and lowered her voice to a conspiratorial whisper. "But in reality, I hate those kinds of events."

"You and me both. Everyone trying to pretend to be nice, when really they just want to find out what you're up to and how they can steal that business away from you," Finn said. "I think of them as a necessary evil."

She laughed again. "We definitely have that in common." She'd never expected to have anything in common with Finn McKenna, whose reputation had painted him as a ruthless competitor, exactly her opposite. Or to find him attractive. But she did.

"I don't know about you, but I'm much happier behind my desk, sketching out a design. Anything is better than trading the same chatter with the same people in an end-less social circle."

"You and I could be twins. I feel exactly the same way. But…" She let out a sigh and spun her teacup gently left and right.

"But what?"

"But I stepped into my father's shoes, and that means doing things as he did." People expected the head of WW to be involved, interactive and most of all, friendly, so Ellie had gone to the event and handled it, she hoped, as her father would have. She had thought taking over her father's position would be a temporary move, but after the news the doctor gave her yesterday…

Ellie bit back a sigh. There were many, many dinners like that in her future. Henry Winston's heart attack had been a bad one, leaving him with greatly diminished car-diac capacity. The doctor had warned her that too much stress and worry could be fatal. A return to work was a distant possibility right now. If ever. It all depended on his recovery. Either way, Ellie was determined to keep WW running, and not worry her father with any of the details. He came first.

"Have you ever met my father?" she asked Finn.

He nodded. "I have. Nice guy. Straight shooter."

"And a talker. I inherited that from him." Ellie smiled, thinking of the father she'd spent so many hours with in the last few years, chatting about design and business and life. Her father had worked constantly when Ellie was young and been gone too much for them to build any kind of relationship. But ever since Ellie went to col-lege, Henry had made a more concerted effort to connect with his daughter. Although she loved her mother dearly, Ellie wasn't as close to Marguerite, who had moved to California shortly after divorcing Henry when Ellie was eighteen. "My father likes to say that he never knows where his next opportunity might come from, so he greets the cashier at a fast food place as heartily as he does the owner of a bank."

"People like that about him. Your father is well respected."

"Thank you." The compliment warmed Ellie. "I hope I can live up to his example."

"I'm sure you will."

The conversation stalled between them. Finn turned his attention to his coffee, but didn't drink, just held the mug. Ellie nursed her tea, then added more sugar to the slightly bitter brew.

She watched Finn, wondering why he had invited her out. If he wanted to talk business, he was taking his time getting to it. What other reason could he have? For all the joking between them earlier, she had a feeling he wasn't here for a date.

Finn McKenna was younger than she'd expected. Surely a man with his reputation had to be ten feet tall, and ten years older than the early thirties she guessed him to be? Heck, he seemed hardly older than her, but his resume stretched a mile longer. What surprised her most was that he had sought her out—her—out of all the other people in that room. Why?

He had opted for coffee, black, but didn't drink from the cup. He crossed his hands on the table before him, in precise, measured moments. He held himself straight—uptight, she would have called it—and kept his features as unreadable as a blank sheet of paper. He wasn't cold, exactly, more…

Impassive. Like the concrete used to construct his buildings. The teasing man she'd met in the lobby had been replaced by someone far more serious. Had that Finn been a fluke? Which was the real Finn McKenna?

And more, why did she care so much?

"I heard WW got the contract on the Piedmont hospital project," he said.

"We haven't even announced that hospital deal yet," she replied, halting her tea halfway to her lips. "How did you know about it?"

"It's my business to know." He smiled. "Congratulations."

"Thank you." She wanted to tell him the thought of such a big project daunted her, particularly without her father's valuable advice. She wanted to tell Finn that she worried the hospital design would be too big, too detailed for her to oversee successfully, and most of all, she wanted to ask him how he had done it for so long single-handedly, but she didn't.

She already knew the answer. She'd read it in the interview in *Architect* magazine. Finn McKenna wasted little time. He had no hobbies, he told the reporter, and organized his workdays in the most efficient way possible, in order to cram twenty hours of work into twelve.

And, she knew better than to trust him. He hadn't earned the nickname Hawk by being nice to his competitors. No matter how they sliced this, she was one of his competitors and needed to be on her guard. For all she knew, Finn was working right this second—and working an angle with her that would benefit his business.

At that moment, as if making her thoughts a reality, Finn's cell phone rang. He let out a sigh, then shot her an apologetic smile. "Sorry. I have to take this. It's a client who's in California right now, while we build his new offices here. I think he forgot about the time change. This should only take a second."

"No problem. I understand." She watched him deal with the call and realized that Finn McKenna had made himself a success by sacrificing a life. That wasn't what Ellie had wanted when she had gone into architectural design, but the more time she spent behind her father's desk, the more it became clear that was where she was heading.

That was the one thing her father didn't want to see. She thought back to the conversation they'd had this morning. *Don't end up like me, Ellie Girl. Get married. Settle down. Have a life instead of just a business, and don't neglect your family to protect the bottom line. Do it before...*

He hadn't had to finish the sentence. She knew the unspoken words—before he was gone. The heart attack had set off a ticking clock inside Henry and nearly every visit he encouraged Ellie to stop putting her life on hold.

The trouble was, she had quickly found that running WW Architectural Design and having a life were mutually exclusive. Now things were more complicated, her time more precious. And having it all seemed to be an impossible idea.

She thought of the picture in her purse, the dozens more on her phone, and the paperwork waiting on her desk. Waiting not for her signature, but for a miracle. One that would keep the promise she had made in China last year.

Nearly three years ago, Ellie had been on the fast track at an architectural firm in North Carolina. Then she'd gone to a conference in China, gotten lost on the way to the hotel and ended up meeting a woman who changed her life.

Ellie never made it to the hotel or the conference. She spent five days helping Sun Yuchin dig a well and repair a neighbor's house in a tiny, cramped town, and fallen in love with the simple village, and bonded with the woman who lived there. Every few months since, Ellie had returned. She'd been there to meet Sun's daughter, Jiao, after she was born, even helped feed the baby, and the following year, helped build an extra room for the child. In the process, Ellie had formed a deep friendship with Sun, a hardworking, single mother who had suffered more tragedies than any person should in a lifetime—her parents dead, then her husband two years later, and near the end of one of Ellie's trips to Sun's town, the woman finally confided the worst news of all.

Sun had cancer. Stage four. After she told Ellie, she asked her an incredible question.

Will you raise Jiao after I'm gone? Take her to America, and be her mother?

Finn ended the call, then put his cell back into his pocket. "The Piedmont hospital will be quite an undertaking for WW," he said, drawing her attention back to the topic.

Was he curious, or jealous? His firm had been one of the few invited to submit a bid. She remembered her father being so sure that McKenna Designs, clearly the leader in experience, would land the job. But in the end, either her father's schmoozing on the golf course or his more competitive bid had won out and McKenna Designs had been left in the dust.

Was this true congratulations or sour grapes?

Ellie gave Finn a nod, then crossed her hands on the table. "I'm sure we're up to the challenge." Did her voice betray the doubts she felt?

"I know a project of that size can seem intimidating," he added, as if he'd read her mind. "Even for someone with your experience."

The dig didn't go unnoticed. She was sure a methodical man like Finn McKenna would already know she'd built her career in residential, not commercial properties. He was expressing his doubts in her ability without coming right out and saying it.

He wasn't the only one with concerns. She'd gone into architecture because she loved the field, and chosen residential work because she loved creating that happy home for her clients, and had been rewarded well for that job. She'd never wanted to be a part of the more impersonal, commercial industry.

But now she was. And that meant she had to deal with everything that came her way, no matter what. And handle it, one way or another, because her father's company needed her to. She couldn't go to her father and risk raising his blood pressure. She'd muddle through this project on her own. No matter what, Ellie would hold on to what Henry had built.

"We have a strong, dedicated team," she said.

"Had."

"Excuse me?"

"You *had* a strong, dedicated team. As I hear it, Farnsworth quit last week."

Damn. Finn really did have his finger on the pulse of WW Architectural Design. Few people knew George Farnsworth, one of the oldest and most experienced architects at the firm, had quit. He'd butted heads with Ellie almost from the day she walked in the door, and eventually said he'd work for her father—or no one at all. Which wasn't quite true, because it turned out Farnsworth had had a lucrative job offer at a competitor waiting in the wings the whole time.

She'd been scrambling ever since to find a worthy replacement. And coming up empty.

"You seem to know quite a bit about my business, Mr. McKenna—"

"Finn, please."

"Finn, then." She pushed the cup of tea to the side and leaned forward. "What I want to know is why."

He gave her a half-nod. "What they say about you is true."

"And what, pray tell, do they say about me?"

"That you're smart and capable. And able to talk your way out of or into just about anything."

She laughed. "The talking part is probably true. My father always said I could talk my way out of a concrete box."

"Refill?" The waitress hovered over their table, coffee-pot halfway to Finn's cup. Then she noticed the two still-full cups. "Okay, guess not."

Finn paused long enough for the waitress to leave, then his sky-blue gaze zeroed in on hers. "You asked why I have such an interest in your business, and in you."

She nodded.

"I've done my research on your career, Miss Winston, and on WW Architectural Design because—" he paused a beat "—I have a proposition for you."

"A proposition?" Ellie arched a brow, then flipped on the charm. Two could dance in this conversation. Finn McKenna had yet to tell her anything of substance, and she refused to give away her surprise or her curiosity. He had likely underestimated her as a businesswoman, and after tonight, she doubted he'd do it again. "Why, Finn, that sounds positively scandalous."

He let out a short, dry laugh. "I assure you, Miss Winston—"

"Ellie." She gave him a nod and a slight smile. She had found that a little warmth and charm, accented by the slight Southern accent that she'd picked up in her years in North Carolina, often served her well in business dealings, and she used that tool to her advantage now. No giving Finn McKenna the upperhand. No, she wanted to know what he was after, and more importantly, why. "That's the least you can do, considering I'm calling you by your first name."

"Ellie, then." Her name rolled off his tongue, smooth as caramel. "I…I can assure you—" he paused a second again, seemed to gather his thoughts "—that my proposition is business only."

She waited for him to continue, while her tea cooled in front of her. This was the reason he'd asked her here—not for a date, but for business. A flicker of disappointment ran through her, but she told herself it was for the best. Despite what her father had asked of her, she didn't see how she could possibly fit dating, much less marriage, into her already busy life.

She had her father to worry about and care for, a company to run, and most of all, a home to prepare for the changes coming her way very soon. Getting involved with Finn McKenna didn't even make it on to that list. Heck, it wasn't even in the same galaxy as her other priorities.

"I know that without Farnsworth, you're in a difficult position," Finn continued. "He's the most senior architect on your staff, and you're about to undertake a major hospital project. The kind of thing WW has built its reputation on, and the kind of job that will bring millions into the company coffers."

She nodded. The Piedmont hospital was a huge boon for WW. Her father had worked long and hard to land that project. He was proud as punch to add it on to the company resume, and she was determined not to let her father down. This job would also firmly establish WW's place as a leader in medical facility design—a smart move in an era of increased demand from aging baby boomers.

"As the new CEO," Finn went on in the same precise, no-nonsense manner as before, "you're already at a vulnerable juncture, and losing this project, or screwing it up, could cause WW irreparable damage." He'd clearly studied her, and the company, and was offering an honest, if not a bit too true, perspective. He squared his spoon beside his cup, seeming to gather his thoughts, but she got the feeling he was inserting a measured, calculated pause.

She waited him out. A part of her was glad he'd gotten right to the point, avoiding the male-female flirting dance. She'd met far too many businessmen who thought they could finesse their way through a deal with a few compliments and smiles. Men who saw a woman in charge and took her to be an idiot, or someone they could manipulate over dinner. Finn McKenna, she suspected, was a what-you-see-is-what-you-get man, who saw no need for frills or extra words. Straightforward, to the point, no games. That brief moment in the lobby had been a fluke, she decided. This was the real Finn, aka the Hawk. He wanted something from her and clearly intended to stay until he had it.

"I have two senior architects on my staff who are more than capable of handling the hospital project for you," Finn said. "If you agree to this business proposition, then they would oversee it, sort of as architects on loan. You, Miss Winston—" he paused again, corrected himself "—Ellie, would remain in complete control. And myself and my staff at McKenna Designs would be there as a resource for you, as you navigate the complicated arena of medical facility design, and the troubled waters of the CEO world."

Troubled waters? Did he think she was totally incompetent? She tamped down the rush of anger and feigned flattery.

"That's a mighty nice offer, Finn. Why, a girl would be all aflutter from your generosity..." Then she dropped the Southern Belle accent from her voice, and the smile from her face. He'd made it all sound so smooth, as if the benefit was all to her, not to him. "*If* she hadn't been raised by a father who told her that no one does anything without a payoff. So, I ask you—" she leaned in, her gaze locking on his "—what's in this for you?"

He gave her a short nod, a brief smile, a look that said touché. And something that looked a lot like respect. "My business has struggled as of late. Partly the economy, partly—" the next words seemed to leave his mouth with a sour taste "—because of a project that had some unfortunate results. Although we have a few medical buildings on our resume, our work has primarily been in the retail and corporate world. McKenna Designs would like to move into the medical building field because it's a growing industry that dovetails well with our other corporate work. You would like to strengthen your position as the new head at WW by designing a hospital that puts a really big star in the company constellation, as they say." He spread his hands. "A partnership benefits us both."

"From what *I've* heard, McKenna Designs took a serious blow in credibility and finances over this past year and you've been reeling ever since." They worked in a small industry and people talked. The people who worked for Ellie had been more than happy to fill her in on the local competition when she arrived in Boston. Finn McKenna's name had come up several times.

"We've had our...challenges."

"As have we," she acknowledged.

"Precisely the reason I came to you." Now he leaned back and sipped at his coffee, even though it had surely gone cold long ago. He was waiting for her to make the next move.

As she looked at him, she realized two things. He didn't think she was capable of running the firm without his help and two, he was offering a deal that benefited him far more than her. She could hire another architect—maybe even, with the right incentives, steal Finn's best and brightest right from under his nose—and be just fine. He was just like all the other men she had met, and all the "concerned" colleagues of her father, who saw the little Winston girl as nothing more than a figurehead.

The Hawk was merely swooping in to try to scoop up an opportunity. This meeting had been a waste of time. The one luxury Ellie Winston didn't have.

She rose, grabbing her purse as she did. "I appreciate the offer, I really do, but we're just fine at WW, and we'll be just fine without an alliance with you. So thank you again—" she fished in her purse for a few dollars, and tossed them on the table "—but I must decline. Good evening, Mr. McKenna."

Then she left, hoping that was the last she saw of Finn McKenna.

CHAPTER THREE

ELLIE had vowed not to think about Finn's surprise offer. He was only out for number one, she had decided last night during the cab ride home, and she'd be a fool to even consider it. But as the morning's staff meeting progressed, she found her mind wandering back to that diner conversation.

You're at a vulnerable juncture.

Losing this project could mean irreparable damage.

A partnership benefits us both.

Had he meant what he said? Could it be a genuine offer? And if she accepted, would the benefits outweigh the drawbacks? Or was he trying to get in—and then take over her company? She'd heard how many times he'd done that to other firms.

She had floated Finn's name with a few of her colleagues this morning, trying to get more of a read on the man everyone dubbed "the Hawk." To a person, they'd urged caution, reminding her Finn "preferred to eat the competition for lunch rather than lunch with them."

That meant any sort of alliance with him required serious consideration. Was his proposal all a way for him to take over her father's company? Or would his proposal be a true two-way benefit?

She thought of what lay ahead for her life, about the

child about to become a part of her life, and wondered how she could possibly juggle it all. Was a partnership a good idea?

"I'm worried, Ellie." Larry, the most senior of her remaining architects let out a long breath. "We really need a strong leader on this project. Even though we have a lot of great architects here, without either your dad or Farnsworth to head this, well…"

"We don't have anyone with enough experience and that means we'll be in over our head from day one," Ellie finished for him. She'd known that going in, but had hoped that when she called the staff meeting someone would step up to the plate and produce a resume rife with medical design experience. Hadn't happened. "We have a great team here, I agree. But no one who has direct experience with medical institutions."

Larry nodded. "If we were building a bank, a resort, a hotel, we'd be fine. We could do those in our sleep. And I'm sure we could handle this project, too, but we'd be a whole lot better off with a good senior architect to oversee all those details. As it is, we're stretched thin with the new mall out on Route 1 and the condo project in the Back Bay."

Ellie knew Larry made sense. Between the integrated technology, clean environment requirements and strict government guidelines, a hospital build was so much more complex than an ordinary office building. Farnsworth's specialty had been in that arena, and without him, the team would be on a constant scramble to check regs, meet with contractors and double check every element. "I'll find someone."

"By the end of the week?" Panic raised the pitch in Larry's voice. "Because the initial drawings are due by the fifteenth."

Just a few short days away. "Did Farnsworth get anything done on them?"

Larry shook his head. Ellie's gut clenched. Farnsworth had lied and told her he'd done the initial work, but clearly his disgruntled attitude had been affecting his work for a while. Her father had designed several hospitals and medical buildings over the years, but Ellie certainly couldn't go to him for help, and no one on the current staff at WW had the kind of experience her father and Farnsworth had. She'd just have to hire someone.

But by the end of this week? Someone who could step right in and take the project's reins without a single misstep? And then produce a plan that would meet the critical eye of the hospital owners? She needed someone with years of experience. Someone smart. Someone capable, organized. And ready to become the team leader at a moment's notice.

"I'll find someone," she repeated again. "By the end of the day. I promise."

Ellie gave her team a smile, and waited until everyone had left the room before she let the stress and worry consume her. She doodled across the pad in front of her. It was a good thirty seconds before she realized she hadn't sketched a flower or a box or a stick figure. She'd written a name.

And maybe…an answer. The only problem was right now, this was more of a win for Finn, who would reap the benefits of a partnership, the prestige of the project and a cut of the profits, than for Ellie, who risked looking like a company that couldn't do the job and had to call in outsiders.

She tapped her pencil on the pad. There had to be something Finn could give her that would make a part-

nership worth the risk of an alliance with the predatory
Hawk. It would have to be something big, she mused.

Very big.

Finn sat at his massive mahogany desk, the same one he
had bought ten years ago at a garage sale, refinished by
hand then installed on his first day at McKenna Designs.
Back then, he'd had an office not much bigger than the
desk, but as he'd moved up, the desk had moved with
him. Now it sat in the center of his office, his headquar-
ters for watching the world go by eleven stories below
him. Friday morning had dawned bright and beautiful,
with a spring sun determined to coax the flowers from
their leaf cocoons. It was the kind of spring day that
tempted people to call in sick and spend the day by the
Charles River, picnicking and boating and jogging on
the Esplanade. The kind of day that drew everyone out
of their winter huddles, spilling into the parks and onto
the sidewalks, like newly released prisoners.

But not Finn. He had called an early meeting this
morning, and had been snowed under with work every
second since then. Sometimes he felt like he was just
plugging holes in a leaky water bucket. They'd lost another client today, a corporation that said they'd "lost
confidence" in McKenna Designs after hearing of the
defection of two other major clients. Apparently Lucy's
betrayal was still hitting his bottom line, even more than
a year later. He sighed.

He'd turn this company around, one way or another.
He'd hoped that Ellie Winston would hear his offer and
jump at the opportunity for some help. She was out of
her league on the Piedmont project, and definitely didn't
have anyone on her staff who could handle something

of that magnitude. When he'd considered his offer, he'd seen it only as a win-win for her. Yet still she'd said no.

It was a rare defeat to a man who had won nearly everything he put his mind to. The refusal had left him surprised, but not for long. He would regroup, and find another way to convince Ellie that his proposal was in her best interests.

Could she be thinking of hiring someone else? He hadn't heard rumors of anyone considering a job at WW, but that didn't mean there wasn't a prospective candidate. Finn had always prided himself on having an ear to the ground in Boston's busy and competitive architecture world, but that didn't mean he knew everything.

"Knock, knock. Time for lunch."

Finn glanced up and saw his brother standing in the doorway, grinning like a fool. Every time he saw Riley, his brother looked as happy as a loon. Probably because he didn't have a care in the world. Or maybe because things had gone better for Riley with women last night than they had for Finn. "Sorry. Maybe another time. I have a ton of work to do."

"Yeah, yeah." Riley waved that off. "And last I checked you were human…"

Finn dropped his gaze to his hands, his feet, then back up to Riley. "It appears so."

"And that means you need to eat on a regular basis. So come on." Riley waved at him. "Hey, I'll even treat."

Finn chuckled. "Considering that's almost a miracle in the making—"

"Hey." Riley grinned. "I resemble that remark."

"You're the poster child for it." Finn shook his head. Then his stomach rumbled and overruled his work resolve. "All right. You win. But let's make it a quick lunch."

"You know me. I'm always ready to get my nose back to the grindstone. Or rather, ready to get *your* nose back to *your* grindstone, and mine back to lazy living." Riley laughed at his joke, then walked with Finn down the hall to the elevator. "You know it wouldn't hurt you to take a day off once in a while. Maybe even enough time off to have a date or ten."

The doors opened with a soft ding sound and Finn stepped inside, followed by Riley. "We've had this argument before. Last night if I remember right."

"Yep. And we're going to keep having it until you admit I'm right and you're lonely."

"I'm fine." Finn punched the button for the lobby.

"You tell yourself that enough and you might even start to believe it someday, big brother."

Finn ignored the jab. "So how's the waitress?"

"I don't know." Riley shrugged. "I ended up leaving with the brunette."

Finn rolled his eyes.

Riley grinned. "What can I say? The world is filled with beautiful women. Like the one you were supposed to talk to last night. How'd that go?"

"It didn't go quite the way I expected." Had he come on too strong? Too weak? He found himself wondering what she was doing right now. Was Ellie having lunch at her desk? With a friend? Or alone in a restaurant?

She'd been on his mind almost every minute since she'd walked out of the diner. That alone was a clear sign he needed to work more and think less. He wasn't interested in Ellie Winston on a personal basis, even if his hormones were mounting a vocal disagreement.

"What, you struck out? Didn't get her phone number?" Riley asked.

"Her office number is in the yellow pages. I didn't need to ask for that."

Riley shook his head. "And the Hawk strikes again. Always business with you."

The elevator doors shimmied open. Finn and Riley crossed the lobby and exited onto Beacon Street. In the distance, rowers skimmed their sculls down the rippling blue river.

The Hawk strikes again.

Maybe it was the too sunny weather or maybe it was the rejection last night, but Finn found himself bothered by that phrase. He'd never much liked the moniker, but he'd always thought that he, of all people, combined humanity with business. He had never seen himself as quite the cold fish the media depicted.

His brother didn't understand what drove Finn. What kept him at that desk every day. What monumental weights sat on his shoulder, even as he tried to shed them. The one time he'd tried to live a "normal" life, he'd been burned. Badly. More than enough reason not to make that mistake again.

A slight breeze danced across the Charles River, tempering the heat of the day with a touch of cool. They walked for a while, navigating the rush of lunchgoers, heading for the same place they always went, in unspoken agreement. That was one good thing about lunch with Riley—the kind of common mind that came from being siblings. Even though he and Riley were as different as apples and oranges, Finn had always had a closer relationship with him than with Brody. Maybe because Riley was easy to talk to, easy to listen to, and the one who— though he kidded often—understood Finn the best. Even if their minds often moved on opposite tracks.

They reached the shadowed entrance to McGill's. Finn

paused before tugging on the door. "Do you ever wonder..."

Riley glanced at his brother. "Wonder what?"

"Nothing." Finn opened the door and stepped into the air-conditioned interior. The last person he needed to ask for personal—and definitely business—advice was his brother. Riley's standard answer—get a girl, get a room and get busy.

He wanted to ask Riley how his little brother could give his heart so freely. And whether doing so was worth the cost at the end when his heart was broken. He'd seen how much it hurt when the one you were supposed to love no longer felt the same. He had watched that pain erode the happiness in his mother's face day by day. As the youngest, Riley had missed those subtle cues.

Finn shrugged off the thoughts. It had to be the spring weather—and the overabundance of lovey-dovey couples out enjoying the sunshine—that had him feeling so maudlin. He liked his life just the way it was. He didn't need anything more than that.

It took a second for his eyes to adjust to the dim room, and to take in the space. McGill's had a warm interior—dark, rough-hewn plank walls, sturdy, practical tables and chairs and a worn oak floor that had been distressed by thousands of customers' shoes. The food was hearty and good—thick sandwiches, hand-cut fries, stout beer. Finn and Riley came here often, and were waved over to the table area by Steve McGill himself, who was working the bar this afternoon.

Finn waved off the waiter's offer of beer, opting for water instead. "The usual, Marty."

Marty MacDonald had been there for as long as Finn could remember. He had to be nearing seventy, but he moved twice as fast, and had twice the memory of the

younger waiters at McGill's. Marty nodded, then turned
to Riley. "For you?"

"I'll have my beer, and his. No sense in wasting it."
Riley grinned. "And a corned beef sandwich on rye."

Marty chuckled. "In other words, the usual?"

"You know me well, Marty." Riley waited until their
server had left, then turned back to Finn. "So what do
you think went wrong with the grand plan last night?"

Finn's phone rang. He signaled to Riley to wait a second, then answered the call. "Finn McKenna."

"I wanted to update you on the Langham project,"
Noel, one of Finn's architects, said. "I heard that Park
came in twenty percent lower than us. The client said
they're going to go with him instead. Sorry we lost the
job, Finn."

Joe Park, a newcomer to Boston's crowded architectural playing field, and someone who often underbid just
to get the work. Finn suspected it was the cost savings,
and some residual damage to McKenna's reputation that
had spurred the client's defection. Finn refused to let another client go.

"No, they won't," he said. "Let me give Langham a
call. In five minutes he'll see the wisdom of sticking with
us." Finn hung up with Noel, then called the client. In a
matter of minutes, he had convinced the penny pinching
CEO that working with the established McKenna Designs
was a far smarter choice than a rookie newbie. He soothed
the worried waters with Langham, and assured him that
McKenna Designs would be on top of the project from
start to finish. He didn't say anything outright bad about
his competitor, but the implication was clear—work with
the unproven Park, and the work would be substandard.

After Finn finished the call and put away the phone,

Riley shot him a grin. "I'm glad I'm not one of your competitors."

"It's business, Riley."

"That's not business, that's guerilla warfare." Riley shook his head. "Tell me you didn't treat that gorgeous lady the same way?"

"No, in fact quite the opposite. I think I might have been too nice."

Riley snorted.

"She turned me down. But I'm going to regroup, find another way." Finn reached into the breast pocket of his suit. "I've got a list of pros and cons I'm going to present to her—"

Riley pushed Finn's hand away. "For a smart guy, you can be a complete idiot sometimes."

"This is logical, sound reasoning. Any smart businessperson would—"

"I'm sure you're right. And if you have a month or three to go back and forth on pros and cons and heretofores and whatevers, I'd agree with you." Riley leaned in closer. "But you don't have that kind of time."

Apparently Riley had been listening to Finn's worries over the past year. Finn was impressed with his little brother's intuitiveness. Maybe he didn't give Riley enough credit. "True."

"So that means you need to change your tactics."

Finn had an argument ready, but he bit it back. Riley had a point. Negotiations took time, and that was pretty much what his list was. He was an expert when it came to the art of the business deal, but this was different—and he'd struck out with Ellie Winston in a big way. He needed a new idea, and right now, he'd take ideas from about anyone and anywhere. "Okay. How?"

Riley grinned and sat back. "Easy. Do what I do."

"I am not sleeping with her just to get what I want." Finn scowled. "You have a one-track mind."

Riley pressed a hand to his heart. "Finn, you wound me. I would never suggest that. Well, I might, but not in your case." Riley paused. "Especially not in your case."

"Hey."

"You are way too uptight and practical to do such a thing."

"For good reason." Nearly every move in his life was well planned, thought out and executed with precision. Even his relationship with his ex had been like that. He'd chosen a partner who was a peer, someone with common interests, in the right age range and with the kind of quiet understated personality that seemed to best suit his own.

It had seemed to be the wisest choice all around. The kind that wouldn't leave him—or her—unhappy in the end. He'd been stunned when she'd broken up with him and worse, maligned his business and revealed she'd only gone out with him to get information.

But had that been real love? If he could so easily be over the relationship, at least emotionally? Was real love methodical, planned?

Or a wild, heady rush?

The image of Ellie in that figure-hugging maroon dress, her head thrown back in laughter, her eyes dancing with merriment, sent a blast of heat through him. He suspected she was the kind of woman who could get a man to forget a lot more than just his business agenda. For just a second, that empty feeling in his chest lifted. Damn, he really needed to eat more or sleep more or something. He was nearly a blubbering emotional idiot today.

Wild heady rushes didn't mix with business. Wild

heady rushes led to heartache down the road. Wild heady rushes were the exact opposite of Finn McKenna.

"The secret to getting what you want, especially from a woman, is very simple," Riley said.

"Flowers and wine?"

Riley laughed. "That always helps, but no, that's not what I meant."

Marty dropped off their drinks, so quietly they barely noticed his presence. Marty knew them well, and knew when he could interrupt and when to just slip in and out like a cat in the night.

"You find out what the other party wants most in the world," Riley said, "then give it to them."

"That's what my list—"

"Oh, for Pete's sake, Finn. Women aren't into lists and pros and cons. Hell, who is?" Then he paused. "Okay, maybe you. But not the rest of the world. Most people are driven by three needs." He flipped out his fingers and ticked them off as he spoke. "Money, love and sex."

Finn chuckled and shook his head. Riley's advice made sense, in a twisted way. Hadn't Finn done the same thing in business a hundred times? Find out what the other party wants and offer it, albeit with conditions that benefited both sides. "Let me guess. You're driven by number three."

"Maybe." Riley grinned. "One of the three is what drives that pretty little blonde you met with last night. Figure out what it is she wants and give it to her."

"Simple as that?"

Riley sat back and took a sip from his beer. "Simple as that."

The room closed in on her, suddenly too hot, too close. Ellie stared at the woman across from her, letting the words echo in her mind. For a long time, they didn't make sense. It was all a muddled hum of sounds, rattling around in her brain. Then the sounds coalesced one syllable at a time, into a painful reality.

"Are you sure?" Ellie asked. She had walked into this office on a bright Monday morning and now it seemed in the space of seconds, the day had gone dark.

Linda Simpson nodded. "I'm so sorry, Ellie."

She'd know Linda for months, and in that time, Linda had become Ellie's biggest supporter as well as a friend. All these weeks, the news had been positive.

Operative words—*had been.*

Ellie pressed a hand to her belly, and thought of all she had given up to be a woman in a male-dominated field. Relationships...children. Children that now she knew would never happen naturally. Adoption, the obstetrical specialist had told her, was the only option.

Maybe it was her father's illness, or the approach of her thirtieth birthday, but lately, she'd been thinking more and more about the...quiet of her life. For years, she'd been happy living alone, making her own hours, traveling where she wanted. But in the last year or two, there'd been no louder, sadder sound than the echo of her footsteps on tile. She had no one but her father, and if the doctors were right, soon she wouldn't even have him.

And what would she have to show for it? A few dozen houses she'd designed? Houses where other people lived and laughed and raised children and shooed dogs out of the kitchen. Houses containing the very dreams Ellie had pushed to the side.

But no more. Jiao was waiting for her, now stuck in a limbo of red tape at an orphanage in China. Jiao, an energetic two-year-old little girl with wide eyes and dark hair, and a toothy smile. Everything Ellie had dreamed of was right there, within her grasp.

Or had been, until now.

Had Ellie heard wrong? But one look at Linda Simpson's face, lined with sympathy and regret, told Ellie this was no joke. The adoption coordinator sat behind her desk, her dark brown hair piled into a messy bun, her eyes brimming with sorrow.

"I need..." Ellie swallowed, tried again. "A husband?"

"That's what they told me this morning. Countries all over the world are tightening their adoption policies. The orphanage is sticking to the government's bottom line. I'm sorry."

A spouse.

Ellie bit back a sigh. Maybe it was time to pursue another adoption, in a more lenient country. But then she thought of Jiao's round, cherubic face, the laughter that had seemed to fill the room whenever Ellie had played with her, and knew there was nothing she wanted more than to bring that little girl home. She had promised Sun, and Jiao.

But how was she going to do that *and* run her father's company? And who on earth could she possibly marry on such short notice? There had to be a way out of this. A workaround of some sort.

"But they told me, *you* told me, I was fine. That because Jiao's mother asked me specifically to raise her daughter and endorsed the adoption before she died, that I wouldn't have to worry about the other requirements."

"The government is the ultimate authority." Linda spread her hands in a helpless gesture. "And they just feel better about a child being placed in a home with two parents."

Ellie tamped down her frustration. Being mad at Linda

didn't help. The coordinator had worked tirelessly to facilitate this adoption, working with both the U.S. and Chinese governments, as well as the orphanage where Jiao was currently living. Ellie had contacted the agency where Linda worked shortly after returning from that fateful China trip. She'd explained the situation to the woman, who had immediately helped set everything up for a later adoption, easing Sun's worries during the last days of her life.

Ellie had expected some delays, particularly dealing with a foreign government, but already three months had passed since Sun had died and Jiao was still in China.

A husband. Where was she going to get one of those? It wasn't like she could just buy one on the drugstore shelf. Getting married took time, forethought. A relationship with someone.

"What happens now?" Ellie asked. "What happens to Jiao?"

"Well, it would be handy if you had a boyfriend who was looking to commit in the very near future. But if not…" Linda put out her hands again. "I'm sorry. Maybe this one isn't meant to be." Linda didn't have to say anything more. Ellie knew, without hearing the words, that her child would go back into the orphanage system and maybe languish there for years.

Ellie couldn't believe that this wasn't meant to be. Not for a second. The entire serendipitous way she had met Sun, the way the two of them had become instant friends, despite the cultural and language barriers.

And Jiao…

She already loved the little girl. Ellie had held Jiao. Laughed with her. Bonded. During her trips to China, Ellie had become a part of Jiao's little family. A second mother, in a way, to Jiao, who had curled into Ellie and clung to her when they had buried Sun. It had broken Ellie's heart to have to go back to the United States without the little girl. She'd only done it because she'd been assured the next few steps of the adoption were merely a formality.

And now Jiao was all alone in the world, living in a crowded, understaffed orphanage, probably scared and lonely and wondering why she had no family anymore. Ellie thought of Jiao's pixie face, her inquisitive eyes and her contagious smile. Desperation clawed at Ellie. *Oh, God, Jiao. What am I going to do?*

Ellie took a deep breath. Another. She needed to be calm. To think.

Damn it. Ellie had made a promise. Jiao deserved to be raised with security and love, and Ellie would find some way to make that happen. "Let me think about this," she said. "Can I call you later?"

Linda nodded, her warm brown eyes pooling with sympathy. "Sure. I have a day or two to get back to the orphanage."

The unspoken message, though, was that after that, Jiao would slip out of Ellie's grasp like wind through the trees. Off to another family or worse, stuck in the system. Ellie needed a miracle.

And she needed it now.

CHAPTER FOUR

FINN MCKENNA was not a man easily surprised. He'd heard and seen a great deal in the past ten years of running his own company. But this…offer, if that was what he could call it, from Ellie Winston was a total shock.

"Marriage? As in a church and a minister?" he said. The words choked past his throat.

"Well, I was thinking more like city hall and a judge, but if you insist…" She grinned.

"But…w-we don't even know each other." The words sputtered out of him. He, a man who never sputtered.

Ever since she'd walked into his office five minutes ago and announced she had a counteroffer to his, that was what he had done—sputtered. And stammered. And parroted her words back at her. He couldn't believe what he was hearing. *Shocked* wasn't an adequate adjective.

Marriage?

He had expected her to ask for more autonomy with the project or a larger cut of the fee. Something…practical.

Instead she'd said she would allow him to be an equal partner in the Piedmont hospital project, if he married her.

Marriage.

"I think I need a little more time to…think about this."

Or find a counteroffer that could possibly overrule her insane request. "Perhaps we could table this—"

"I'd rather not." She was perched on the edge of one of the visitor's chairs in his office. The late morning sun danced gold in her hair. She had on another dress, this one in a pale yellow that made him think of daffodils.

For Pete's sake. Every time he got close to Ellie Winston he turned into a damned greeting card.

"If you're free for a little while," she added, "how about we go someplace and talk?"

He considered saying no, but then realized this was his best opportunity to get what he needed from Ellie Winston. In the long run, that would serve him better than staying at his desk. It wasn't the fact that he wanted to see more of her. Not at all. He glanced out his window. "We could do lunch, and be stuck in some restaurant or…the weather is gorgeous. How about a stroll on the Esplanade?"

"Sure. I can't remember the last time I walked along the river." She reached into her purse and pulled out a small bag. "I even have flats with me."

"Practical woman."

She laughed. "Sometimes, not so much, but today, yes." She slipped off her heels, tucked them in her bag, then slid on the other shoes.

Finn told Miss Marstein that he was leaving, then shut down his computer and grabbed his phone. A few minutes later, they were out the door and heading down a side street toward the Esplanade. Finn drew in a deep breath of sweet salty air. "I definitely don't get outside enough."

Ellie sighed. "Me, either. When I was younger, I used to be a real outdoorsy girl. Hiking, canoeing, bike riding. I tried to keep up with that after college, but the job takes up way too much time."

He arched a brow at her dress and the spiky heels poking out of her purse. "You hiked?"

Ellie put a fist on her hip. "Do I look too girly for that?"

His gaze raked over her curves, and his thoughts strayed from business to something far more personal. Damn. "Uh, no. Not at all."

"What about you?" she asked. "Do you hike or bike or anything like that?"

"I used to. I ran track in high school, was on the swim team, you name it. And during college, I biked everywhere. Now I think my bike's tires are flat and there are spiders making webs in the frame."

She laughed. "All the more reason to get it out of storage."

They crossed to the Esplanade, joining the hundreds of other people outside. A few on bikes whizzed past them, as if adding an exclamation point to the conversation. "Maybe someday I will," Finn said, watching a man on a carbon fiber racing bike zip past him. "I do miss it."

"Someday might never come," Ellie said quietly. "It's too easy to let the To Do list get in the way. And then before you know it, another year has passed, and another, and you're still sitting behind the desk instead of doing what you love."

He heard something more in her voice. Some kind of longing. Just for more outdoor time? Or to fill another hole in her life? He wanted to ask, wanted to tell her he knew all about using work to plug those empty spots.

But he didn't.

The bike rider disappeared among a sea of power walkers. Finn returned his attention to Ellie. She looked radiant in the sunshine. Tempting. *Too* tempting. He cleared his throat. "It's hard to keep up with the personal To Do list when the business one is so much longer."

"Isn't part of your business taking care of you? After all, if the CEO ain't happy…" She let the words trail off and shot him a grin.

For a second, Finn wanted to fall into that engaging smile of Ellie Winston's. Every one of her smiles seemed to hit him deep in the gut. They were the kind of smiles that Finn suspected—no, knew—would linger in his mind long after they were done. And her voice… her years of living in the South gave her just enough of a Southern tinge to coat her words with a sweet but sassy spin. It was…intoxicating.

Hell, everything about her was intoxicating. It wasn't just the dress or the smile or the curves. It was everything put together, in one unique, intriguing package.

She had him thinking about what it would be like to take a hike through Blue Hills with her, to crest the mountain and watch the busy world go by far beneath them. He imagined them picnicking on a rock outcropping, while the sun warmed their backs and the breeze danced along their skin.

Damn. What was it about her that kept getting him distracted? He needed to focus on business, and more importantly, on why she had proposed marriage a few minutes ago. No wild, heady anything with her.

Finn cleared his throat. "About your…proposal earlier. No pun intended. Were you serious?"

Her features went from teasing to flat, and he almost regretted steering the conversation back. "Yes. Very." She let out a long breath, and for a while, watched the people sitting on the grass across from them. It was a family of four, with a small dog nipping at the heels of the children as they ran a circle around their parents. "I need something from you and you need something from me. Marriage is the best solution all around."

"We could always do a legal agreement for the businesses. This is just one project, you know."

"For me, it's much more." Her gaze returned to his. "I have to have a husband. Now."

"Why?"

"First, let me lay out the advantages to you." She slowed her pace. "For one, our lack of familiarity with each other is what makes it a perfect idea and a perfect partnership, if you will."

"Partnership, perhaps. Not a marriage."

"I may not know you very well, Mr. McKenna," she went on, "but I know your life. You work sunup to sundown, travel half the year and have all the social life of a barnacle."

She could have opened up his skull and peeked inside his brain. Damn. Was he that transparent? And put that way, well, hell, his life sounded downright pitiful. Riley would have put up two enthusiastic thumbs in agreement.

Perhaps she was joking. He glanced at her face. Saw only serious intent in her features.

"But don't you think it's wiser to work out a business arrangement instead? More money, more prestige, a reciprocal arrangement with my next project?" Something he could quantify, put into those neat little debits and credits columns. Not something like *marriage*, for Pete's sake.

"Perhaps to you it would be. But a business arrangement isn't the number one thing I need right now." She gestured toward a small grassy hill that led to the river, away from the crowds out walking, and the energetic in-line skaters rushing past them. He followed her down to the water's edge. In the distance, a rowing team called out a cadence as they skimmed across the glassy blue surface.

Her green eyes met his, and a thrill ran through him. Damn, she had beautiful eyes.

"Not to mention, you're probably as tired of the dating game as am I," she said. "And maybe you've looked ahead to the future, and wondered how on earth you're going to fit the American Dream into your schedule."

He gave her a droll smile. "Actually I had that down for next year, on Tuesday, March 30, at two in the afternoon."

She burst out laughing, which also surprised him and stirred that warmth again in his gut. Those who knew Finn would never have described him as a man with a sense of humor. But apparently Ellie Winston found him funny. That pleased him, and had him wondering what else Ellie thought of him.

Damn. He kept getting off track. It had to be her proposal which had knocked the normally unflappable Finn off balance.

"I was hoping to fit it into my planner a little sooner than that," she said. "Actually a lot sooner."

"Why? Why now? And…why me? I mean, you are a beautiful woman. Smart, charming, sexy. You could have your pick of any man on the planet."

"I…well, thank you." Now it was her turn to sputter. A soft pink blush spread over her cheeks. Then she paused, seeming to weigh her answer for several moments before responding. He got the distinct impression she was holding something back, but what, he didn't know. He thought again about what he knew about her. Nothing pointed to "desperate to get married," no matter how he looked at the details he knew about her. Yet, there was an ulterior motive to her proposal—he'd bet a year's salary on it.

"There's a child in China who needs a mother. I promised her that I would adopt her, and everything was in place for me to do so. Until this morning." She bit her lip and turned to him. "The agency told me I need a husband to complete the adoption."

"Whoa, whoa." He put up his hands. "I'm not interested in becoming an instant father."

"I'm not asking that of you. At all."

"Then what *are* you asking?"

"A marriage based on commonality, not passion or lust or infatuation. We'll stay married for a short time, long enough for me to get the adoption finalized, then get a quiet divorce. Painless and fast."

In other words, no real strings attached and he'd be out of this nearly as fast as he was in it. He should be glad. For some reason, he wasn't. "Sounds so…clinical."

"Mr. McKenna…Finn. We're both detail oriented—clinical in a way—people. I'm not interested in losing my head in a relationship, or wasting a lot of time dating Mr. Wrong, not when I'm concentrating on running my father's company. I need a spouse, in name only, and you need a business partner."

He looked in Ellie Winston's eyes, and saw only sincerity, and a quiet desperation to help a child halfway around the world. He knew she wouldn't have come to him, with this insane offer, if she didn't have to.

Find out what she wants most in the world, Riley had said, and give it to her.

But this?

"I don't know if I agree with this," Finn said. "The child will undoubtedly be hurt when her father disappears after a few weeks."

"You don't have to be a part of Jiao's life at all. Just be there for the home visit and the adoption proceedings. And in return, we can work together on the Piedmont project. That will keep my father's business growing and help yours. It's a win all around."

Pigeons picked at the grass before them, looking for leftover crumbs. In the distance, there was the sound of children's laughter. The swish-swish of rolling cycle tires on the paved walkway. The continual hum of traffic, punctuated by the occasional horn. The world went on as it always did, swimming along beneath a sunny sky.

"It would be a platonic marriage," she said. "Nothing more."

"A purely impersonal alliance?" he asked, still not believing she had suggested this. When he'd made his list of possible ways to convince Ellie a strategic partnership was a good idea, marriage hadn't even come close to being in the mix. "A marriage based solely on like minds and like goals?"

Though when he put the marriage idea like that, it sounded cold. Almost...sad.

He shook off the thoughts. He was a practical man. One whose focus was solely on building his business back to where it had been. He wasn't going to get wrapped up in the foolishness of some romantic ideal—and that wasn't what Ellie was asking for. It was, in fact, the exact kind of relationship he had vowed to pursue. Then why did he feel as empty as a deflated balloon?

She nodded. "Yes."

"And in exchange, our companies partner as well?"

"Yes." She put up a finger. "However, we each retain ownership and leadership of our respective companies, in case...things don't work out." She dug in her purse and pulled out a piece of paper. "I took the liberty of having my attorney draw up a contract."

A contract. For marriage.

Finn skimmed the document and saw that it indeed promised everything she had talked about. The business arrangement, the annulment agreement. All he had to do was sign on the dotted line and he'd be a temporary husband, father in name only.

The businessman in him said it was an opportunity not to be missed. The partnership his business needed, and at the same time, the bonus of companionship. Not sex, clearly, but someone to talk to at the end of the day.

He thought of the nights he'd spent on the rooftop deck of his townhouse. Watching the city lights twinkle in the distance, while he drank a beer, and gathered his thoughts, wondered if he'd made the right choices. Lately those nights hadn't brought the peace they used to. More, a restlessness, a question of "is this all there is?" Except for the times he was with his brothers, his life was staid. Almost dull.

Riley was right. He was lonely, and tired as hell of feeling that way.

At the same time, he didn't want to pursue the empty one-night stands his brother did. He wanted more, something with meaning and depth. Something that was…sensible. Reliable. Practical. Something that wasn't foolish or wild or crazy—not the kind of whirlwind romance his parents had had, that had gone so horribly wrong after the children started coming and they realized that a quick courtship couldn't build a lifetime, not between such badly mismatched people.

Love—or any approximation of it—was a dangerous thing that left a man vulnerable. Not a position Finn

McKenna relished or welcomed. A marriage of convenience would be void of all those things.

Still, the cynic in him wondered if Ellie was proposing this as a way to knock him off guard, or maybe even an alliance that would allow her to gather facts about him and his business, facts she could use to take over his company later or eliminate him as a competitor. Hadn't Lucy done exactly the same thing?

But the man in him, the one standing beside a very beautiful, very intriguing woman with a smile that stayed with him, hoped like hell it was something more than that.

Was he truly considering this...this marriage of convenience? What choice did he have? He needed to be a part of that hospital project. Making it a joint venture with a company like WW would reestablish his company's reputation, and distract attention from that fiasco last year. And, as calculated as it sounded, a marriage to a charming woman like Ellie would also distract attention from the mess his company had been in lately, give the gossips something else to talk about. He'd be back on top before he knew it, and then he and Eleanor Winston could quietly dissolve the union, as she'd said. She'd have the child, and he'd have his business back. He could feel the old familiar surge of adrenaline that always hit him when he landed a big job, one that he knew could change the future of McKenna Designs.

"This contract looks pretty good," he said.

"I wanted to make it clear this was business only." Her gaze flicked to the water, and she let out a small sigh. Almost like she was disappointed. Which was crazy, because she was the one floating the idea in the first place. "But we don't have a lot of time to waste. Jiao is stuck in that orphanage, farther away from me with every passing day. And you, I suspect, would like to be on board from day one with the hospital project. The initial drawings are due the fifteenth so we have very little time to get everyone up to speed."

"The fifteenth? That does put a crunch on our time. By all rights, we should start right away."

"I agree. In the end, Finn, we're both decisive people, aren't we?" She smiled at him. "I'm not looking for a courtship with flowers and dancing and dinners out. What we are doing is more of a..."

"Partnership. Two like minds coming together."

"Exactly."

A part of him felt a whisper of...loss? Finn wasn't sure that was the right word to describe the yawning emptiness in his gut. Surely a deal like this—one that would benefit his company and at the same time, fill those quiet, lonely nights with good conversation, was a win-win all around.

Except...

No, he didn't need any more than that. As Ellie had said, a romantic relationship came with complications, emotional drama—all things he didn't have time for, nor wanted in his life. And clearly, not something she wanted, either. She saw him as a means to an end, and he saw her the same way.

Hadn't he learned his lesson with Lucy? A heady relationship would do nothing but draw his attention away from the business. In the coming months, the company would need more of his attention than ever, so the kind of relationship Ellie was proposing was perfect. With the addition of the legal contract, the risk to McKenna Designs would be minimal. He saw no downside to this.

Except the fact that it wouldn't be a real marriage. That it would be as faux as the wood paneling that still flanked his grandmother's fireplace, forty years after the house had been built, the same house she lived in because it was the one she'd bought with her late husband, even though she could now afford ten times the house.

A hummingbird flitted by, heading for a bright swath of flowers. Finn watched it for a while, as the world hustled by behind him.

"There's this bird in Africa," Finn said, watching the tiny hummingbird dart from bloom to bloom, "called a honey guide. Its whole job is to find beehives and lead the honey badger to them. When he does, the badger gets in there and gets the honey, clearing the way for the honey guide to eat the bee larvae." He turned to Ellie. "I guess that's sort of what this will be. Us working together to serve a mutually beneficial purpose."

"Not exactly the same as swans mating for life, but yes."

"Definitely not a partnership for life," Finn said. But even as he clarified, he felt a twinge of something like regret. He shrugged it off. Be smart, he reminded himself, like the badger and the bird. In the end, everyone wins.

"I don't want to rush you," she said. "But we need to make a decision. If you don't want to do this…I need to think of something else."

"Fine," he said, turning to her. "Let's go."

She blinked. "What…now?"

"Why wait?" he said, parroting her words back. "I have a friend at the courthouse. He'll take care of it. You can be my wife by the end of the day, Miss Winston."

"Today? Right now?"

"Yes, of course." He watched her closely, and wondered if, despite the contract she'd given him, she was as committed to this partnership as she had sounded. Only one way to find out, he decided. "You weren't expecting me to get down on one knee with some flowers or a ring, were you?"

"No, no, of course not." She swallowed. "Business only."

"My favorite kind of relationship." He gave her a smile, then turned to go back across the grass. He paused, turned back, waiting for her to join him. He had called Ellie Winston's bluff. The only problem...

He wasn't so sure she'd been bluffing.

"Are you ready?"

Was she ready? Ellie had no idea if she was or wasn't. The events of the last hours seemed surreal, as if it was some other Ellie Winston who had proposed to Finn McKenna, then hopped in his Town Car and headed to Rhode Island in the middle of the day.

Had she really just proposed to him? And had he really accepted?

She'd gone to his office right after leaving the adoption agency and then her lawyer's office, her mind filled with only one thing. She needed a husband and she needed one now. She'd do whatever it took to get that. She'd seen Jiao's trusting, hopeful face in her mind and thought of nothing else. Jiao needed a mother. Needed Ellie.

Linda had made it clear—marriage was the only sure route to bringing Jiao home. There was no one else that Ellie knew—not well enough in her short time living here in Boston—who would marry her on such short notice. No one who would go along with such a crazy plan, and not expect a real marriage out of the deal. So she'd gone to Finn, the only man she knew who needed her as much as she needed him.

A part of her had never expected him to say yes. But

say yes, he had, and now they were on their way to get married.

Married.

To Finn McKenna.

A man she knew about as well as she knew her dry cleaner.

This was insane. Think of Jiao, she told herself. Just think of Jiao. And as the miles ticked by, that became her mantra.

Massachusetts had a three-day waiting period for a marriage license, Finn had told her, as he got on I-95S and made the hour-long journey to Providence, Rhode Island, where there was no waiting period. The car's smooth, nearly silent ride and comfortable interior made the whole drive seem almost…romantic, even though it was broad daylight and the highway was filled with other cars. It was something about the cozy, dark leather of the car that wrapped around her, insulated them, drew them into a world of just the two of them, like lovers making an afternoon getaway. Which was crazy, because what they were doing was far from romantic. And they were definitely not lovers.

"How did you know there was a three-day waiting period in Massachusetts?" she asked.

"My brother." A grin slid across Finn's face. "Riley is a little…impetuous. We've had to talk him out of more than one crazy decision."

"We?"

"My younger brother Brody and me. We're the ones who received all the common-sense genes."

"Inherited from generations of common-sense McKenna men?"

He chuckled. "Exactly. Though my grandmother might quibble with how much common sense is in our DNA."

"So there are three of you altogether?" Ellie asked.

"Yep. All boys. Made for a busy life. Hell, it still does."

She tried to picture that environment, with three rambunctious, noisy siblings, and couldn't. The camaraderie. The joking. The warmth. "I'm an only child. I can't even imagine what it would be like to grow up with two sisters, or a bunch of brothers."

"It's loud. And sometimes things get broken." Finn put up a hand and pressed three fingers together. "Scouts' Honor, I had nothing to do with that antique vase or the missing coffee table."

Ellie heard the laughter buried in Finn's voice and craved those same kinds of memories for Jiao. She bit back a sigh. Adopting just one child as a single mother was proving to be difficult enough. Adopting multiple children seemed impossible. But maybe someday—

She'd have the warm, crazy, boisterous family Finn was describing.

Except that would mean taking a risk and falling in love. Ellie didn't need to complicate her life with a relationship that could end up hurting her—and in the process her daughter—down the road. This marriage, based on a legal contract and nothing else, was the best choice.

"Remind me to tell you the tree story sometime," Finn said. "And every year at Thanksgiving, we revisit the Ferris wheel one. That one was all Riley's fault. There's always an interesting story where Riley is concerned, and Brody and I try to exploit that at every opportunity."

Her gaze went to the city passing by outside the window, streaks of color in the bright sunshine. Thanksgivings and Christmases with a whole brood of McKenna men sounded like heaven, Ellie thought. Her childhood had been so quiet, so empty, with her mother gone all the time and her father working sunup to sundown. She envied Finn and for a moment, wondered if they would be married long enough for her to sit around the Thanksgiving dinner table with a trio of McKennas, sharing raucous stories and building memories over the turkey.

She pictured that very thing for a moment, then pulled away from the images. They were a bird and a badger, as he'd pointed out, not two swans in love. Besides, she knew better than to pin her hopes on some romantic notion of love. That happened for other people, not her.

"My parents weren't around much when I was a kid. Now my mother lives in California, so it's really just my dad and me." She shifted in her seat to look at him. "I guess you could say my life has always been pretty… quiet and predictable." Now that she said it, she wondered if that was such a good thing. For one, she wanted to add the chaos of a child. Would she be ready for it? She, who had never so much as babysat a neighbor's kid? Save for a few vacations spent in China with Jiao and Sun, she had no experience with children…what made her think she could do this? Heck, Finn, with all those younger brothers, was probably better suited to parenting than she was.

All Ellie had was a deep rooted conviction that she would love her child and be there for her. She wouldn't leave Jiao with an endless stream of babysitters or miss her third-grade recital or pay a tutor to help her with her homework so Ellie could work a few more hours. She would be there.

Somehow, she'd find a way to run WW Designs and be the mother that Jiao needed, the kind of parent Ellie had never had. Even though she knew it would be easier to do that if she had a real husband, one who was a plugged-in father, she vowed to make this work on her own. One attentive, loving parent was better than two inattentive, unavailable parents. And she had no intentions of forcing this marriage to limp along after the adoption was final. The worst thing for Jiao would be to have a distant parent, one who left her wondering if she was truly loved.

Finn turned on his blinker, then exited the highway. "Your life might have been quiet and predictable up until now, but I'd say getting married on the spur of the moment is pretty far from either of those adjectives."

She laughed. "You're right. No one would ever think I'd elope."

"That goes double for me." Finn paused at the end of the off-ramp. He turned to face her, his blue eyes hidden by dark sunglasses. "Still sure you want to do this?"

She thought of what he had just told her. About his brothers and his noisy childhood. Then thought of the quiet, empty life she led. She had her father, yes, but other than that, all she had was work.

"Yes, I'm sure," she said.

"Okay." Then he made the turn, following the signs that led to the downtown area. "Me, too."

He said it so softly, she wondered if there was more behind the words than a simple agreement. Was he missing something in his life, too? Was he looking to fill the empty spaces, add life to those quiet rooms? Or was this solely a business merger for him?

He said nothing more, just drove, and she let the silence fill the space between them in the cavernous Town Car. A little while later, they pulled in front of the courthouse, a massive brick building with dozens of tall windows and a spire reaching toward the clouds. The stately building resembled a church as much as it did a place for justice.

They parked in one of the many parking garages nearby, then walked the short distance to the court. Ellie noticed that Finn opened her car door, opened the garage's door, lightly took her elbow when they crossed a street. Such small gestures, but ones that Ellie appreciated. After all, this was a business deal. He didn't have to play the chivalrous man.

They went up the few stone steps to the entrance, with Finn stepping in front of her to open and hold the heavy courthouse door for her, too. "Thank you."

"It's the least I can do for my future wife."

She faltered at the word. She'd heard it twice already today, and still couldn't believe it was happening. "Are you planning on carrying me over the threshold, too?"

He paused. "We hadn't talked about that detail."

"Which one?"

"Where we're going to live after this."

The mirth left her. Oh, yeah.

She hadn't thought that far ahead. In fact, she'd just gone with this insane plan, clearly not thinking it through. The adoption agency would undoubtedly do its due diligence before signing off on Ellie's adoption. At the very least, they'd want a report from Linda on the living conditions.

It wouldn't take a genius to realize her marriage was a sham if she and new "husband" were living in separate homes. Ellie had never been much of an impetuous woman. Until today and now, she could lose it all by not thinking this through.

"We should live together," she said, all the while watching for his reaction, "or no one will believe it's real. We'll need people to believe we're together for more than just a business deal."

"We'll have to make it seem…real," he said.

"Yeah. We will."

Finn turned to her in the bright, expansive lobby.

People rushed around them, hurrying to courtrooms and offices, their shoes echoing on the marble floors, their voices carrying in the vast space.

But Ellie barely noticed. She stood in a world of only two, herself and the man who had agreed to marry her and in the process, change her life. And Jiao's, too.

"Maybe if people find out I eloped, it'll change their image of me as the Hawk."

She laughed. "And what, turn you into the Dove?"

"I don't think so." He chuckled. "I could get married at a drive-thru chapel in Vegas with Elvis as my best man and that still wouldn't be enough to do that."

"You never know. Marriage changes people. Relationships change them." Her voice was soft, her mind on one person a world away.

"Yes, I think it does. And not always for the better."

She wanted to ask him what he meant by that. Did he mean the ex-fiancée who had ruined his reputation? Or was he talking about something, someone else?

He cleared his throat. "You're right. Our marriage is going to need a measure of verisimilitude, and being in the same residence will do that. In addition, we can work on the hospital project after hours."

Even though Finn's voice was detached, almost clinical, the words *after hours* conjured up thoughts of very different nocturnal activities. Since the first time she'd spotted Finn in the ballroom of the Park Plaza, she'd been intrigued. She'd liked how he bucked convention by having a beer instead of wine, how he'd been so intent yet also charming. From a distance, she'd thought he was handsome. Up close, he was devastating. Her heart skipped a beat every time he smiled. Her traitorous mind flashed to images of Finn touching her, kissing her, making love to her—

Whoa. That was not part of the deal. At all. Keeping this platonic was the only—and best—way to ensure that she could walk away at the end. She didn't want to chance her heart on love, or risk her future with a relationship that could dissolve as easily as sugar in hot tea. Falling for him would only complicate everything.

And marrying him on the spur of the moment wasn't complicated? All of a sudden, a flutter of nerves threatened to choke her. Ellie opened her mouth to tell Finn this was crazy, she couldn't do this, when the door to the courthouse opened behind them and a slim, tall man hurried inside.

"Sorry I'm late. My day has been crazy." He chuckled. "As usual. Story of my life. And yours, too, huh, Finn?"

Finn patted the other man on the back and gave him a grin. "Charlie, how are you?"

"Just fine. Not as good as you, though. Running off to get married. You surprise me, old friend." He grinned, then put out a hand toward Ellie. "Judge Charlie Robinson, at your service."

Ellie gaped. "You said you had a friend in the courthouse. Not a judge."

"Charlie and I have been friends since we were kids. We roomed together at Harvard," Finn said, then shot Charlie a smirk. "To me, he's not a judge. He's the guy who sprayed whipped cream all over my room."

"Hey, I'm still pleading innocent to that one." Charlie raised his hands in a who-me gesture, but there was a twinkle in his eye.

Again, Ellie saw another side of Finn. A side that intrigued her, even as she pushed those thoughts away. She refused to fall for Finn. Now or later. She was here for a practical reason and no other.

Finn chuckled. "Well, we should get to it. I know you have a hectic day."

"No problem. I can always make time for a good friend, especially one who's getting married. So…" Charlie clapped his hands together. "You two kids ready to make this all legal and binding?"

Legal. Binding.

Now.

Ellie glanced at Finn. She could do this. She *had* to. There was no other way. Besides, it was a temporary marriage, nothing more than a piece of paper. But a union that would bring Jiao home and give Ellie the family she had always craved. She could do that, without getting her heart tangled in the process. "Yes," she said.

"Great." Charlie grinned again. "Okay, lovebirds, let's head up to my office and get you two hitched."

Finn turned to Ellie and put out his arm. "Are you ready to become Mrs. McKenna?"

Was she?

She lifted her gaze to Finn's blue eyes. She barely knew this man, but what she knew she liked. Respected. Trusted. Would that be enough?

She thought of Jiao again, and realized it would have to be. In the end, running WW would be fulfilling, but not nearly as fulfilling as coming home to Jiao's contagious smile and wide dark eyes.

"Why, Mr. McKenna, I can't think of another thing I'd rather do in the middle of the day." Then she linked her arm in Finn's and headed toward the judge's chambers.

CHAPTER FIVE

THE whole thing took only a few minutes—including Charlie's beginning jokes and closing quips. They called in his assistant and a court clerk to serve as witnesses, the two of them looking like they'd seen more than one impromptu wedding. Charlie thought they were getting married out of love, and in typical Charlie fashion, strove to make the event fun and memorable. Finn stumbled when Charlie asked him about rings, which Charlie racked up as bridegroom nerves. "I can't believe you, of all people, forgot a major detail like the rings," Charlie said. "No worries, but be sure you make it up to her later with a *lot* of diamonds," he said with a wink, then in the next breath pronounced them man and wife.

Man and wife. The words echoed in Finn's mind, bouncing around like a rubber ball. He'd done it. And no one was more surprised than Finn himself. He, the man who hadn't operated without a plan since he was writing his first research paper in fourth grade, had run off in the middle of the day and—

Eloped.

Holy cow. He'd really done it.

"And now for the best part," Charlie said, closing the book in his hands and laying it on his desk. "You may kiss your bride."

Finn stared at Charlie for a long second. Kiss the bride? He'd forgotten all about that part. He'd simply assumed a quick civil union in a courthouse would be devoid of all the flowers and romance part of a church wedding. "Uh, I don't know if we have to——"

Charlie laughed. "What, are you shy now? Go on, kiss her."

Finn considered refusing, but then thought better of it. Charlie would undoubtedly question a marriage where the groom didn't want to get close with his bride. And if they were going to pull off this fiction in front of their friends and colleagues, they needed to at least look the part. Finn turned to Ellie. Her green eyes were wide, her lips parted slightly. In shock? Anticipation?

She looked beautiful and delicious all at the same time in that simple daffodil-colored dress. In that instant, his reservations disappeared, replaced by a fast, hot surge of want. No, it was more than desire, it was a…craving for whatever inner happiness was lighting Ellie's features.

She stood there, looking as hesitant as he felt. A faint blush colored her cheeks, disappeared beneath her long blond hair. She looked like a bride—pretty, breathless, yet at the same time she possessed a simmering sensuality. He wanted her, even as he reminded himself this was a purely platonic union.

There would be no kisses. No lovemaking. Nothing but this moment. And right now, Finn didn't want to let this moment pass.

Her gaze met his and a curious tease filled the emerald depths. "Well, Mr. McKenna, are you going to do as the nice judge says?"

"I would never disobey a judge," Finn said, his voice low, hoarse. Just between them. Charlie, the witnesses, hell, the entire world ceased to exist.

He closed the gap between them, reached a hand to cup her jaw. Electricity crackled in the air, in the touch. A breath extended between them, another. Ellie's chest rose, fell. Her dark pink lips parted, her deep green eyes widened, and her light floral perfume teased at his senses, luring him closer, closer.

Damn, he wanted her. He'd wanted her from the minute he'd met her.

With one kiss he'd seal this marriage. But was that all this kiss was about? This moment?

No. He knew, deep in his gut, that there was something else happening here, something he wasn't sure he wanted or needed in his life. He could have been standing at the edge of a cliff, ready to plunge—

Into the cushion of water, or the danger of rocks? He didn't know.

All he could feel was this insistent *want*. For her. For just one taste. He lowered his mouth to hers, and at the instant that his lips met hers, he knew.

Knew that kissing Ellie was going to change everything.

Her lips were sweet and soft beneath his, her hair a silky tickle against his fingers. She leaned into him for one long, blissful second, and he inhaled, drawing in the scent of her, memorizing it, capturing the moment in Technicolor in his mind.

Ellie.

Then she drew back and the kiss was over, nearly as quickly as it began. The flush in her cheeks had deepened to a light crimson. Her gaze met his for one hot, electric second, then she looked away, and turned back to Charlie.

Platonic. Business relationship. The heady rush gone.

He told himself he was glad. That it was exactly what he wanted.

"There. It's official now." Charlie grinned, then he reached out and shook hands with both of them. The witnesses murmured their congratulations before slipping out the door. "Congratulations," Charlie said. "May you have an abundance of happiness and children."

Children. Or, rather, a single child. Half the reason they'd embarked on this fake union. Finn glanced over at Ellie, but her gaze was on the window, not on him, hiding whatever she might have thought about Charlie's words.

A few minutes later, they left the courthouse, a newly minted marriage license in hand. The paper weighed nothing, but felt heavier than a concrete block.

Married. To a near stranger.

A stranger whose kiss had awakened a roaring desire inside Finn. He had thought he was doing this just for business reasons, but that kiss was as far from business as the earth was from the moon. And he needed to remember his uppermost goal.

Don't get involved. Don't fall for her. Don't lose track of the priority. Don't get swept up in a tsunami that would leave him worse off in the end.

As they walked down the street toward the parking garage, Finn dug his car keys out of his pocket, then paused. They were married. And that meant the occasion, even if it was merely a professional alliance, deserved some kind of celebration. "How about we get some dinner before we head back to Boston?"

"I should probably get back to work. I left in the middle of my day and have a lot on my To Do list." She stepped to the side to allow a quartet of lunch workers to power past them. "But thanks for the offer."

His To Do list was probably just as long, but for the first time in a long time, Finn didn't want to go back to his office, didn't feel like sitting behind that mahogany desk, even as the sensible side of him mounted a vigorous objection. "It's not every day you get married, you know. We should at least have a glass of wine to celebrate. Or iced tea for you. I'll have the wine."

"Don't you have work to get to, too?"

"Always. But it's waited this long. It can wait a little longer. Regardless of why we got married, this is a big moment for both of us." He grinned. "Don't you agree?"

It was Finn's smile that swayed Ellie. There was something…disarming about the way Finn McKenna smiled. He had a crooked smile, curving up higher on one side of his face than the other. She liked that. Liked the way nothing about him was exactly what you would expect.

Neither was his kiss. She'd thought that he would just give her a perfunctory peck on the lips, a token gesture to seal the deal. But he'd done so much more. Kissed her in a way she hadn't been kissed in forever.

Their kiss had been short, but tender. When he'd touched her jaw, he'd done it almost reverently, his fingers drifting over her cheek, tangling in her hair. He'd leaned in, captured her gaze and waited long enough for her heart to begin to race with anticipation before he'd kissed her. When had a man ever taken such time for something so simple?

It left her wondering what it would be like to really be Finn's wife. Would he kiss her like that at the end of every day? Before he left for work in the morning? For just a moment, she wanted to hold on to that fantasy, to believe that this was real, and not just a means to an end.

Even if it was.

Finn was right—it wasn't every day that she got married, and she wasn't sure she was quite ready to go back to her ordinary world, and all the questions this was bound to raise. They still had to settle on their story, and deal with other practical issues, like where they were going to live afterward.

Whatever little thrill she might have felt faded in the light of reality. This wasn't a date, it wasn't a celebration. It was business, pure and simple.

And nothing more.

"You did what?" The shock in Riley's voice boomed across the phone connection. *"You got married?"*

"Uh, yeah, but it's not…" Finn was about to tell Riley it wasn't a real marriage, then he glanced across the sidewalk at Ellie, standing in the shadowed circle beneath an oak tree. She was talking into her cell phone with someone at her office, her hand moving to punctuate her words. Little bits of sunshine dappled her blond hair, kissed her delicate features and gave her a slight glow.

He had seen hundreds of beautiful women in his lifetime, but none that had that whole package of incredible looks and incredible personality. The kind of woman any man in his right mind would be proud to call his wife.

Except, this was merely a way to resurrect his business. Besides, he didn't need the complication of a relationship, the heady distraction of a romance. He liked his life as straight as a ruler. And he'd continue to keep it that way.

"It's unexpected, is what it is," Riley finished for him. "What were you thinking?"

"I wasn't." That was true. He'd thought he was challenging her offer, then once they were standing in front of Charlie, he'd stopped thinking about the pros and cons of what he was about to do and just…done it. Eloped. He, of all people. He hadn't thought about the incongruity of that when he was in Charlie's office. All he'd seen was Ellie's smile.

"I thought you were all antimarriage. Especially after the Lucy thing."

"I was. I am. This was…" Finn paused. "Different."

"Well, congratulations, brother," Riley said. "You'll be all the talk at the next family reunion."

Finn chuckled. "I'm sure I will be as soon as you get off the phone and call Brody. You spread gossip faster than a church picnic."

Riley laughed with him. "So, where are you guys going on your honeymoon?"

The word *honeymoon* conjured up images of Ellie's lithe, beautiful body beside his. He glanced at her across the way from him, and didn't see the daffodil-yellow dress, but instead saw her on some beach somewhere. Her skin warmed from the sun, all peaches and cream and pressed against him. Taking things far beyond a simple kiss in the judge's chambers.

Damn. That was not productive. At all. He shook his head, but the images stayed, chased by the memory of kissing her. The scent of her perfume. The feel of her in his arms.

Again, he forced them away and tore his gaze away from Ellie.

He'd come close to that kind of craziness when he'd dated Lucy. Granted, most of their relationship had been practical, staid…predictable. Then he'd had that moment of insanity when he'd rushed out to buy a ring, run over to her office to propose—

And found out she was stealing his clients behind his back.

No more of that. He'd gone off the rails for five minutes, and it nearly destroyed his business and his career. A smart man approached marriage like any other business deal—with clarity, sense and caution.

"Uh, we don't really have time for that right now," Finn said, reminding himself that there would be no honeymoon. Not now, not later. "Work schedules, meetings, that kind of thing gets in the way of the best laid plans, you know?" He made light of it because for some reason, he couldn't bring himself to tell Riley the whole thing was a temporary state. That most likely by the time their schedules opened up enough that they could plan a joint vacation, they would be filing for divorce.

"You *are* going to celebrate at least a little, aren't you? I mean, if any occasion screams having a party, this is it." Riley paused a second. "Hmm…I wonder if it's too late to throw you a bachelor party?"

"I don't need one of those, and yes, it is too late." Finn shifted the phone in his grasp. "Actually that's why I called you. I was thinking of taking her out for drinks and dinner. But…"

"You realized that idea sounds about as lame as a picnic in the park?"

"Hey!" Then Finn lowered his voice. "What's lame about a picnic?"

Riley laughed. "Don't tell me. That was your second idea."

Finn didn't want to admit that it had actually been his first idea, but then he'd thought about bugs and sunshine, and proposed a restaurant instead. Damn. He was a hell of a lot rustier at this dating game than he'd thought. Not that this was a date—at all—just his effort to make this business alliance a little more palatable. "It's a nice day. We could grab some sandwiches—"

"Last I checked, you don't get married every day. So

don't do an everyday thing to celebrate it. Here's what I would do," Riley said, then detailed a plan for Finn that far surpassed anything Finn had thought of. A few minutes later, Riley said goodbye and Finn ended the call. At the same time, Ellie tucked her phone away and crossed to Finn.

"Sorry about that," she said. "Duty calls."

Finn chuckled. "Believe me, I understand. It calls me all the time, day and night." At the same moment, Finn's phone began to ring. He fished it out of his pocket, about to answer, when Ellie laid a hand on top of his.

"Don't." Her fingers danced lightly across his, an easy, delicate touch, but one that sent a shock wave running down his arm. "Let's put our phones away. I don't want to deal with work for now."

"Me, either." He pressed the power button, turned the phone off, then slipped it into his jacket pocket. "Besides, I have plans for you, Mrs. McKenna."

Her eyes widened at the use of her married name. "Plans? What kind of plans?"

"You'll see," he said, then said a little prayer that he could execute Riley's plans as well as his brother would have. Because just for today, Finn wanted to woo the woman who was now his wife.

Tomorrow was soon enough to get back to business—and stay there. For as long as this practical, contracted arrangement lasted.

How he'd done it, Ellie didn't know. She stared in wonder at the tableau laid out before her. Chubby terra cotta pots held thick, lush flowering shrubs, lit from above by soft torch lights on bronze poles. A pair of squat white wicker chairs with fluffy striped cushions flanked either side of a matching table, already set for dinner with floral plates and crystal wine goblets. Candles flickered in the soft breeze, dropping a blanket of golden light over everything.

The sun had started setting, casting Boston's skyline in a soft purple glow. Lights twinkled in the distance, while the red and green bow lights of passing boats dotted the harbor.

She'd had no idea that Finn had been planning this while they were riding back from Providence. Or how. They had kept their phones off, as agreed, and spent the hour of travel talking about everything and nothing—from growing up in the city to the challenges of architectural design in a world going green.

She'd learned that Finn hated spinach but loved the Red Sox, that he had his one and only B in seventh grade Science and that his first job had been delivering newspapers. She'd told him that her favorite food was cake, and that she'd been the last on her block to learn to ride a bike. She told him about the time she'd gotten lost in the train station and the day she got her braces.

It was the most she'd shared with anyone in a long, long time, and it had felt nice. Then the car pulled up in front of Finn's building and Finn had turned to her and said, "All those details should really help when we meet with the adoption people," and Ellie had been reminded that her marriage was nothing more than a sham.

If that was so, why had Finn gone to all this trouble to set up such a romantic tableau?

"How...when..." She let out a breath. "This is incredible, Finn."

He grinned. "Thank you."

"How did you do it?"

"Remember that rest stop we went to on the way back from Rhode Island?"

She nodded.

"I made a few phone calls while you were…indisposed."

"A few fast phone calls. And clearly productive."

"I'm a man who likes to get things done." He reached for her hand, and she let that happen, wondering when touching Finn had become so easy or if she was just telling herself it was to preserve the mood, and then they walked forward onto the private terrace of his building, temporarily transformed into an outdoor dining room.

Just as Finn pulled out her chair, music began, a soft jazz floating from an unseen sound system. A waiter emerged from a door at the side, bearing a tray with water glasses and a carafe filled with two bottles—one a chilled white wine, the other a sparkling grape juice. He placed the water glasses on the table with merely a nod toward Ellie, then uncorked the wine and juice, pouring Ellie's nonalcoholic version first, then Finn's wine, before disappearing back through the door again. Finn had remembered she didn't drink, and had clearly put a lot of time and thought into the entire evening. Why?

He raised his glass and tilted it toward her. "To… partnership."

"Partnership," she echoed, and ignored the flutter of disappointment in her gut. In the end, they would go their separate ways, and for that, Ellie was glad. She didn't need the complication of dating Finn, of a relationship. Just enough information and time with him to effectively pretend…

Pretend they were in love. "And to business," she added, for herself as much as him. "Only."

CHAPTER SIX

THE glint of gold caught Finn's eye before he was fully awake. It took a second before he remembered why he had a ring on his left hand. And why he was waking up in a room he didn't recognize.

Last night. Marrying Ellie Winston. The rooftop dinner. The rings he'd given them—purchased earlier that evening by his assistant and delivered to the terrace before they arrived—so the two of them had the outward evidence of a marriage.

Then, after a dinner that alternated between tense and friendly, bringing her to her townhouse, and by mutual agreement, he'd spent the night. In the guest room.

Of his *wife's* home.

From outside the room, he heard the sound of music. Something upbeat…a current pop hit. He got out of bed, pulled on a pair of sweatpants from the bag he'd brought with him and padded out to the kitchen. Everything about Ellie's townhome was like her—clean, neat, bright. Lots of whites and yellows with accents of blue. It was the complete opposite of his heavy oak, dark carpet apartment. Softer, more feminine. Nice.

Ellie was standing at the kitchen sink, her hips swaying in time to the music as she filled a carafe with water. She was already dressed for work in a pale blue skirt and a short-sleeved white sweater. Her hair was curled, the tendrils curving over her shoulders and down her back in tantalizing spirals. Her feet were bare, and for some reason, that made him feel like he was intruding. It was such an unguarded, at-home kind of thing.

And oh, so intimate.

In the light of day, the reality of moving in with Ellie presented a bit of a dilemma. Like how he was going to resist her when she was right there every day, in bare feet, humming along to the radio. How was he going to pretend he hadn't felt anything with that kiss in the courthouse?

Because he did. He'd thought about it all last night, tossing and turning, a thousand percent aware she was also in bed, and mere feet down the hall. He'd made a concerted effort to keep their celebratory dinner more like a board meeting than a date, but still, a part of him had kept replaying that kiss. And had been craving another.

Hadn't he learned his lesson already? Getting distracted by a relationship left him vulnerable. Made him make mistakes, like nearly marrying someone who wanted only to destroy him. He saw where that kind of foolishness got a person—and it wasn't a path he wanted to travel.

So he forced his gaze away from her bare feet and her tantalizing curves, and cleared his throat. "Good morning."

She spun around, and nearly dropped the carafe. "Finn. Oh, hi. I almost forgot…" A flush filled her face. "Good morning. Do you want some coffee?"

"Yes. Please."

She busied herself with setting up the pot, then turning it on. When she was done, she pivoted back to him.

"I'm sorry I don't have much for breakfast. I'm usually running out the door with a muffin in my hand."

"A muffin's fine. Really. This whole...thing was unexpected." His gaze kept straying back to the ring on her hand. He was now the husband of Ellie Winston. No... Ellie McKenna.

Just a few days ago he'd been thinking how he wanted a relationship without any drama. One based solely on common interests, none of that silly romantic stuff that clouded his brain and muddled his thinking. Now, he had that—

And for some reason, it disappointed him like hell.

What was he thinking? He didn't need the crazy romantic notion of love. He needed something steady, dependable, as predictable as the columns in his general ledger. The problem was, there was a part of Ellie that Finn suspected, no, knew, was far from predictable. And that was dangerous.

The song shifted from pop to a ballad. The love song filled the room, stringing tension between them.

"I have, uh, blueberry and banana nut." She waved toward the breadbox. "Muffins, I mean."

He took a step farther into the kitchen. The walls were a butter-yellow, the cabinets a soft white. No clutter that he could see, merely a few things that added personality—a hand-painted ceramic bowl teeming with fruit, a deep green vase filled with fresh daisies, and a jade sculpture of a dragon, probably picked up in China. It seemed to suit her, this eclectic, homey mix.

Beside him, the coffeepot percolated with a steady drip-drip. The sun streamed in through the windows, showering those curls, those tantalizing curls, with gold. He wanted to reach up, capture one of those curls in his palm. "I'd love one."

"Which?"

It took him a second to realize she meant which flavor, not which he wanted—her or the muffins. "Blueberry, please."

"Sure." She pivoted away, fast. The breadbox door raised with a rattle. Ellie tugged out the plastic container holding the muffins, then spun back. The package tumbled out of her grasp and dropped to the floor. Muffins tumbled end over end and spun away, spinning a trail of crumbs. Ellie cursed.

Finn bent down, at the same time Ellie did, to reach for the runaway muffins. They knocked shoulders and Finn drew back. When had he become so clumsy? This wasn't his usual self. "Sorry."

"It's okay, it's my fault." She reached for the muffin closest to them, at the same time he did. Their hands brushed. She staggered to her feet, nearly toppling, and reached out a hand to steady herself. It connected with his bare chest, just a brief second, before she yanked her palm away.

A jolt of electricity ran through Finn. His gaze jerked to her face. Ellie's eyes were wide, her lips parted. "Sorry," he said again.

"No, I am." She looked away from him, back at the floor. "I can make toast, if you prefer."

Toast? Muffins? Had she been affected at all by that accidental touch? "I'm not hungry. I should get to work."

Yes, get to work, get to the office and get on with his day. Rather than indulge in any more of this craziness. Get his head clear—and back on straight.

"I'll clean this up," she said, gesturing to the mess on the floor. "If you want to hop in the shower and get ready."

"Sure, sure." He dumped the crumbs in his hand into the trash, then turned to go.

"Finn?"

His name rolled off her tongue, soft, easy. For a second, he wondered what it would be like to hear her say his name every day. Every morning. Every night. He turned back to face her, taking in those wide green eyes, the sweet smile that curved across her face, and yes, those bare feet. "Yeah?"

She shot him a grin. "Coffee's ready."

Coffee's ready.

A heavy blanket of disappointment hung over Finn while he got ready. Hell, what had he expected her to say? Stay? Kiss me? Take me back to the bedroom?

No, he didn't want that. He wanted exactly what he had—a platonic relationship that let him focus on work and didn't send his head, or his world, into a tailspin.

Except the image of Ellie in her kitchen, swaying to the music and doing something so mundane as making coffee, kept coming back to his mind. He had lived alone for too long, that was all. That was why the sight of her affected him so much.

He got ready, then headed out the door, leaving Ellie a note that he had to stop by his office and would meet her at WW later. He knew it was the coward's way out, but he'd been thrown by waking up in her place. It was all moving so fast, and he told himself he just needed some time to adjust.

Later that morning, he was heading up to the tenth floor of the building housing WW Architects, flanked by Noel and Barry, two of his best architects, who'd met him in the lobby. The team Finn brought in had been part of the bidding process, and was already familiar with the Piedmont hospital project, so the trio exchanged small talk until they reached Ellie's floor. A few minutes later, an assistant led them to a conference room where the WW staff had already assembled. Ellie stood at the head of the table. Her curly blond hair was now tucked into a tight bun, the bare feet were clad in sensible black pumps, and her curvy figure hidden beneath a jacket that turned the blue skirt into a suit.

She was all business now. Exactly what he wanted.

Then why did he feel a sense of loss?

"Thank you for coming today, gentlemen." Ellie made the introductions between her team and Finn's. Finn headed to the front of the room to stand beside Ellie. "Before we get started, we…I mean, Finn and I, have an announcement."

She exchanged a look with Finn. He nodded. They had talked about this last night, and decided the best way to spread the news was fast and first. "We…Ellie and I… we got *married.*"

Jaws dropped. People stared.

"You got married?" Larry asked. "As in…married?"

"Last night." Ellie nodded and smiled, the kind of smile that reached deep into her eyes, lit up her features. Just like the smile of a happy new bride. "It was an impromptu thing."

"You married her?" Noel scowled at Finn. "Is *that* why we're working together?"

Finn wasn't about to tell their employees the real reason he had married Ellie. If he did, it would taint the project. No, let them all think it was some act of passion. Cover up the truth with a lie.

A lie that a part of Finn wished was true. The part that was still thinking about coffee with Ellie and seeing her in the kitchen. "Not at all. Working together is just a…

fringe benefit," Finn said. "Ellie and I agreed to merge our companies for this project. After that, we go back to being separate entities."

Ellie leaned in and grabbed his arm. That same jolt of electricity rushed through his veins. "Separate business entities at least." She grinned up at him and for a half a second, he could almost believe she loved him. Damn, she was good at this.

"*You* eloped last night?" Noel let out a little a laugh. "I don't believe it. I'm sorry, Finn, but I just don't see you as the eloping kind."

Explaining that the practical, methodical Finn they all knew had done just that was suddenly much harder than he'd expected. "Well, I...I..."

"Blame it on me," Ellie said, pressing her head to his arm. "I didn't want the fanfare of a big event, and so I told Finn, let's just run to the courthouse and get it done. Then we can all get back to work." She peered up at him, her eyes soft and warm. "We'll take that honeymoon a little later."

"Uh...yeah," he said, his thoughts running rampant down the path of what a honeymoon with Ellie would be like. When she was looking at him like that, he could almost believe this was real. That at the end of the day, they were heading back to a little house in the suburbs with a fence and a dog and a dinner on the stove. And more—much, much more—after the dishes were done and the lights were dimmed. "We're, uh, planning on leaving as soon as this project is done."

"Well, then congratulations are in order," John said. He shook with Finn, then Ellie. "Best of luck to both of you." The rest of the group echoed John's sentiments. They congratulated, they shook and they beamed. And Ellie pulled the whole thing off with nary a blink.

"Okay, back to work. We have a major project ahead of us, and not a lot of time," Ellie said. "So as much as we'd love to take time for a celebration, we need to dive in and work until we have the particulars hammered out."

Larry, one of Ellie's architects, grumbled under his breath, but didn't voice any objections. The rest of the team seemed to be giving Finn's people the benefit of the doubt. "I appreciate you bringing us in on this project, Ellie," Finn said, rising to address the group. "I'm confident that by combining the experience of both McKenna Designs and WW Architectural Design, we can create a hospital that will outshine all others in the New England area."

Ellie shot him a smile. "That's our goal, too." She opened the folder before her. "Okay, let's get to work. Piedmont wants this design to be groundbreaking. One of the key elements that sold them on WW as the architects was our innovative approach. Rather than basing the design on existing models, WW talked about approaching the design process from the patient's perspective, from admission through discharge. The challenge is to create an environment that creates a healing atmosphere, one that offers warmth with minimal noise, while also keeping patient safety as the top priority."

"Excellent ideas," Finn said, nodding to Ellie.

"Thank you. Although I have to admit that one of the challenges we are having is creating that warm, healing atmosphere. WW specializes in corporate buildings, which aren't usually described as cozy." Ellie gestured toward Finn and his team. "I think if we combine our expertise in the safety arena, with yours in environment, we'll have a winner."

"I agree." Finn sketched out a drawing on the pad before him, then turned it toward Ellie and the others.

"We'll design standardized rooms, where every medical element is in the same place, no matter what floor or wing, yet also give each room its own flair. Install ambient lighting in addition to the harsher lighting needed for procedures, and soundproof the space so patients aren't bothered by constant pages and hallway traffic. Studies have shown that a warmer, quieter space speeds patient healing." Finn filled in another section of the drawing, sketching in fast movements, limited in details, focused on getting the bare bones on the page first. "We should also provide a small visiting area in each room for family members. Nothing huge, but something far superior in comfort and flexibility to the current models in today's hospitals."

"What about pricing? That kind of thing is going to raise the costs." Larry scowled. "Piedmont will not be happy."

"Easy," Finn said. "We call the vendors and tell them that they're going to be part of a groundbreaking new hospital. One that will have plenty of media coverage. They'll be jumping at the opportunity to be a part of that, and be very amenable to lowering their pricing."

"In other words, beat them up until they cave?" Larry said.

"I think it's a good strategy," Ellie said. "Thanks, Finn." She clapped her hands together and faced the room. "Okay, what else?"

As if a wall had been dismantled, the room erupted with ideas, people from both teams exchanging and brainstorming, no longer separated into an "us" and "them," but becoming one cohesive unit, brimming with creativity. Ellie got to her feet and jotted the ideas on the whiteboard behind her, quickly covering the wall-length space. Finn pulled out his computer to take notes, his fingers moving rapidly over the keys of his laptop. It occurred to him somewhere into the first hour that he and Ellie made a good team. Neither tried to outtalk the other or prove their idea the best. Their thoughts seemed to merge, with her suggesting one thought, and him finishing it. He was so used to being the one in charge, the one who had to pull the team together and take the lead, that suddenly sharing the job was…nice. When the group broke for lunch, Finn stayed behind in the room.

"We work well together," he said, rising and crossing to Ellie. He picked up a second eraser and helped her clean off the whiteboard.

She smiled. "We do indeed."

Out in the hall, the team was whispering and exchanging glances in the direction of the conference room. "Seems we've got people talking," Finn said.

"It was bound to happen. Though I thought we'd have a little more time to…"

"Work out our story?"

"Yeah. We should have talked about it more last night. I really didn't think that part through."

"Me, either. I was too focused on work."

She laughed. "I know what you mean. That's how my days have been, too." She moved away from him, then stretched, working out the kinks in her back. He was tempted to offer her a massage, but instead he kept his hands at his side. A massage was definitely not part of this…partnership.

"You pulled it off well," Finn said. "Hell, even I believed…"

She cocked her head. "Believed what?"

"That you were wildly in love with me."

She laughed, and that told him that there was no doubt she'd been acting earlier. Finn told himself he was glad.

"Well, I'm glad it worked. Anyway, I guess I'll see you back here in a little while."

"Wait. Do you have lunch plans?" he asked, then wondered what he was doing. Was he asking her on a date—a date with his wife—or a simple lunch meeting to discuss the project? He told himself it was just because people would expect them to eat together. He was keeping up the facade, nothing more.

"I have one of those frozen dinners in the office refrigerator." She gave him an apologetic smile. "I usually eat at my desk."

"So do I." Outside the sun shone bright and hazy, a warm day with the promising scent of spring in the air. Inside, all they had was climate controlled air and a sterile office environment. The same kind of place where he spent five, sometimes six, days a week. He thought of the calls waiting to be returned, the emails waiting to be answered, the projects waiting to be completed. Then he looked at Ellie, and wanted only a few minutes with her, just long enough to hear her laugh again, see her smile. Then he'd be ready to go back to the To Do lists and other people's expectations. "Let's go have lunch on the plaza. Get out of here for a while. I think both of us have spent far too many afternoons at our desks."

"Two days in a row, taking time off? My, my, Finn, whatever will people say?"

Damn. He was really starting to like the way she said his name. "Oh, I think we've already given them plenty to talk about, don't you?"

She looked up at him, and a smile burst across her face. It sent a rush through Finn, and he decided that if he did nothing else, he would make Ellie smile again. And again.

"Oh my, yes, I do believe we've done that in spades,

Mr. McKenna." Then her green eyes lit with a tease and she put her hand in his. "What's a little more?"

As time ticked by and the afternoon sun made a slow march across the sky, Ellie was less and less able to concentrate on her sandwich or anything Finn was saying. On her way into work that morning, Ellie had called Linda and left her a message telling her that she had gotten married, and now the wait for Linda's return call seemed agonizing. Thank God for the meeting, which had taken her mind off the wait, and for Finn, who had convinced her to leave the office and get some fresh air. Still, she had checked her cell at least a dozen times.

Finn had taken two calls, and she'd been impressed with the way he handled business. Efficiently, with barely a wasted word. He argued with a contractor who wanted to make a change that Finn felt would compromise the building's structure, and negotiated a lower price on materials for another project.

"I can see where you got the nickname," Ellie said when Finn hung up. "You're relentless."

"I just like to get the job done."

"Yeah, but negotiating a discount, while at the same time moving up the deadline, I'd say you pulled off a miracle."

"Just doing my job." He seemed embarrassed by her attention.

"You do it well. Does that come from being the oldest?"

"I don't know. I guess I never thought about that. Maybe it does."

"Well, it seems to be working for you." She felt her phone buzz and checked the screen, then tucked it away.

"Waiting on a call yourself?"

She nodded. "From the agency. I told my adoption co-ordinator that we got married. I'm just waiting to hear back."

He unwrapped the sandwich they had bought from a street vendor, but didn't take a bite. "How are you planning on doing this?"

"Doing what? The interview? It should be relatively straightforward."

"No, not that. This whole—" he made a circle with the sandwich "—raising a child alone thing."

"People do it every day."

"Not people who also happen to be CEOs of busy, growing companies."

"True." She glanced at the park across the street. It bustled with activity. Children ran to and fro, filling the small park with the sound of laughter. Dogs chased Frisbees and couples picnicked on the grass. "I'm sure it's going to be hard." That was an understatement. She'd worried constantly that she wouldn't be able to juggle it all. "But I'll figure it out somehow."

"Would it have been better if you had waited to marry someone who could...well, create a real family with you?" Finn asked.

Ellie watched a family of three pass by them, mother and father on either side of a toddler, who held both his parent's hands and danced between them. "Maybe. But honestly, I never intended to get married."

"Ever?"

"I guess I was always afraid to get married," Ellie said softly.

"Afraid? Of what?"

"Of being a disappointment and of getting my children caught in an endless limbo of...dissatisfaction." Ellie sighed. "I looked at my parents, and they were more roommates than spouses. They came and went on their own schedules, and we very rarely did anything as a family. I guess I never felt like I knew how to do it better."

"I think a lot of people feel that way," Finn said after a moment.

"Do you?"

He let out a short laugh. "When did this become about me?"

"I'm just curious. You seem the kind of man who would want to settle down. Complete that life list or whatever."

"Yeah, well, I'm not." He got to his feet and tossed the remains of his sandwich in the trash.

He had shut the door between them. She had opened herself to him, and he had refused to do the same. The distance stung.

Ellie glanced at the family across the park. They had stopped walking and were sitting on the grass, sharing a package of cookies. The mother teased the son with a cookie that she placed in his palm, then yanked back, making him giggle. Over and over again they played that game, and the little boy's laughter rang like church bells.

A bone-deep ache ran through her. Deep down inside, yes, she did want that, did crave those moments, that togetherness. She'd always thought she didn't, but she'd been lying to herself.

She watched Finn return to the bench and realized she wasn't going to find that fairy tale with the Hawk. He was going about their marriage like he did any other business deal—with no emotion and no personal ties.

It was what she had wanted. But now that she had it, victory tasted stale.

Because a part of her had already started to get very, very used to him being her husband.

CHAPTER SEVEN

AN HOUR on the treadmill. A half hour with the weight machines. And a hell of a sweat.

But it wasn't enough. No matter how much time Finn spent in the gym, tension still knotted his shoulders, frustration still held tight to his chest. He'd been unable to forget Ellie—or bring himself to go home to her.

Home. To his wife.

Already he was getting far too wrapped up in her, he'd realized. They'd had that conversation at lunch about marriage, and he had found himself wanting to tell her that he felt the same way. That he had never imagined himself getting married, either.

Then he had come to his senses before he laid his heart bare again, and made the same mistakes he'd made before. He'd watched his parents locked in an emotional roller coaster of love and hate, then repeated those mistakes at the end of his relationship with Lucy. No way was he going to risk that again with Ellie. She saw him as a means to an end—a father on paper for her child—and nothing more.

He pulled on the lat bar, leaning back slightly on the padded bench, hauling the weights down. His shoulders protested, his biceps screamed, but Finn did another rep. Another. Over and over, he tugged the heavy weight down.

It wasn't just the distraction of getting close to Ellie that had him sweating it out in the gym. It was the growing reality of the child she was about to adopt.

No, that *they* were about to adopt. He'd promised Ellie that he would go along with her plan, but now he was wondering if that was the right thing to do.

How could he be a temporary husband, temporary dad, and then, at the end of the hospital project, just pack up his things and go? If anyone knew firsthand what losing a parent suddenly could do to a child, it was Finn. He'd gone through it himself, and watched the impact on his younger brothers. They'd been cast adrift, emotional wrecks who took years to heal, even with the loving arms of their grandparents. How could he knowingly do that to a child?

He gave the lat bar another pull, his muscles groaning in protest, then lowered the weight back to the base. He was finished with his workout, but no closer to any of the answers he needed.

He showered, got dressed in jeans and a T-shirt, then hailed a cab and headed across town toward Ellie's townhouse. Night had begun to fall, draping purple light over the city of Boston. It was beautiful, the kind of clear, slightly warm night that would be perfect for a walk. Except Finn never took time to do that. He wondered for a moment what his life would be like if he was the kind of man who did.

If he was the kind of man who had a real marriage, and spent his life with someone who wanted to stroll down the city streets as dusk was falling and appreciate the twinkling magic. But he wasn't. And he was foolish to believe in a fantasy life. His mother had been like that—full of romantic notions that burned out when she saw the reality of her unhappy marriage. Finn was going to be clearheaded about his relationships. No banking on superfluous things like starry skies and red roses.

He paid the cabbie, then headed up the stairs to Ellie's building. He paused at the door and caught her name on the intercom box. Ellie Winston.

His wife.

Already, he knew they had a connection. It wasn't friendship, but something more, something indefinable. A hundred times during the meeting today, he found his mind wandering, his gaze drifting to her. He wondered a hundred things about her—what her favorite color was, if she preferred spring or fall, if she slept on the left side of the bed or the right. Even as he told himself to pull back, to not get any deeper connected to this woman than he already was. This was a business arrangement.

Nothing more.

As he headed inside, he marveled again at the building she had chosen—the complete opposite to the modern glass high-rise that housed his apartment. Ellie lived in one of Boston's many converted brownstones. Ellie's building sported a neat brick facade and window boxes filled with pansies doing a tentative wave to spring adorned every window. The building's lobby featured a white tile floor and thick, dark woodwork. The staircase was flanked by a curved banister on one side, a white plaster wall on the other. A bank of mailboxes were stationed against one wall, lit from above by a black wrought-iron light fixture that looked older than Finn's grandmother, but had a certain Old World charm.

He liked this place. A lot. It had a…homey feeling. At the same time, he cautioned himself not to get too comfortable. They weren't making this a permanent thing, and letting himself feel at home would be a mistake. He'd get used to it, and begin to believe this was something that it wasn't. He'd fooled himself like that once before.

Never again.

He found Ellie in the kitchen again, rinsing some dishes and loading them into the dishwasher. "Hi."

Kind of a lame opening but what did one say to a wife who wasn't a real wife?

She turned around. "Hi yourself. I'm sorry, I ate without you. I wasn't sure what your plan…" She put up her hands. "Well, you certainly don't have to answer to me. It's not like we're really married or anything."

There. The truth of it.

"I grabbed a bite to eat after the gym." He dropped his gym bag on the floor, then hung his dry cleaning over the chair. "Did you find out when the interview would be?"

"In a couple days. Linda's trying to coordinate all the schedules."

"Okay. Good." The sooner the interview was over, the sooner they could go their separate ways. And that was what he wanted, wasn't it?

"After this morning, I think we should work on our story," she said. "You know, in case they ask us a lot of questions. I don't want it to seem like…"

"We barely know each other."

She nodded. "Yes." She gestured toward a door at the back. "We can sit on the balcony out back if you want. It's not a rooftop terrace, but we'll be able to enjoy the evening a little."

They got drinks—red wine for him, iced tea for her—and Ellie assembled a little platter of cheese and crackers. Finn would have never thought of a snack, or if he had, it probably would have been something salty, served straight from the bag. But Ellie laid everything out on a long red platter, and even included napkins. The night air drifted over them, lazy and warm. "You thought of everything,"

She shrugged. "Nothing special. And it's not quite the evening you planned."

"No, it's not." He picked up a cracker and a piece of cheese, and devoured them in one bite. "It's better."

She laughed. "How is that? There's no musicians, no twinkling lights, no five-course meal. It's just crackers and cheese on the balcony."

"Done by you. Not by others. I don't have that home-making touch. At all."

"I'm not exactly Betty Crocker myself. But I can assemble a hell of a crudités platter." She laughed again. "So I take it you can't cook?"

"Not so much as a scrambled egg. But I can order takeout like a pro. My grandmother is the real chef in the family. She doesn't cook much now, but when I was a kid, she did everything from scratch."

Ellie picked up her glass and took a sip of tea. "Where are you parents? Do they live in Boston?"

The question was an easy one, the kind people asked each other all the time. But for some reason, this time, it hit Finn hard and he had to take a minute to compose the answer.

"No. They don't. Not anymore." Finn was quiet for a moment. "My parents…died in a car accident, when I was eleven. Brody was eight, Riley was just six."

"Oh, Finn, I'm so sorry." She reached for him, and laid a soft hand on top of his arm. It was a simple, comforting touch, but it seemed to warm Finn to his core. He wanted to lean into that touch, to let it warm the icy spots in his heart.

But he didn't.

"We went and lived with my grandparents," he continued. "I think us three boys drove my grandmother nuts with all our noise and fighting."

"I bet you three were a handful."

He chuckled. "She called us a basketful of trouble, but she loved us. My grandmother was a stern, strict parent, but one who would surprise us at the oddest times with a new toy or a bunch of cookies."

Ellie smiled. "She sounds wonderful."

"She is. I think every kid needs a grandmother like that. One time, Brody and I were arguing over a toy. I can't remember what toy it was or why. So my grandmother made us rake two ends of the yard, working toward each other. By the time we met in the middle, we had this massive pile of leaves. So we jumped in them. And the fight was forgotten."

Ellie laughed. "Sounds like you learned some of your art of compromise from her."

"Yeah, I guess I did. She taught me a lot." He hadn't shared that much of his personal life with anyone in a long, long time. Even Lucy hadn't known much about him. They'd mainly talked about work when they were together.

Was that because she didn't care, or because it was easier? Or was it because Finn had always reserved a corner of himself from Lucy, with some instinctual self-preservation because he knew there was something amiss in their relationship?

Was Ellie's interest real, or was she just gathering facts for the interview? And why did he care? On his way here from the gym, he had vowed to keep this impersonal, business only. Why did he keep treading into personal waters? He knew better, damn it.

"I think every person needs someone like your grand-mother in their lives," Ellie said softly.

"Yeah," he said. "They do."

Damn, it was getting warm out here. He glanced over at Ellie to find her watching him. She opened her mouth, as if she was going to ask another question, to get him to open up more, but he cut her off by reaching into his pocket for a sheet of paper. He handed it to her. "I, uh, thought you'd want to know some things about me for the interview. So I wrote them down."

She read over the sheet. "Shoe size. Suit jacket size. Car model." Then she looked up at him. "This doesn't tell me anything about you, except maybe what to get you for Christmas."

"That's all the particulars you would need right there."

She dropped the sheet of paper onto a nearby table, then drew her knees up to her chest and wrapped her arms around her legs. She'd changed into sweatpants and a soft pink T-shirt after work, and she looked as com-fortable as a pile of pillows. "What a wife should know about a husband isn't on that list, Finn."

"Well, of course it is. A wife would know my shoe size and my car—"

"No, no. A wife would know your heart. She'd know what made you who you are. What your dreams are, your fears, your pet peeves. She'd be able to answer any question about you because she knows you as well as she knows herself."

He shifted in his chair. The cracker felt heavy in his stomach. "No one knows me like that."

"Why?"

It was such a simple question, just one word, but that didn't mean Finn had an answer. "I don't know."

"Well, surely the woman you were engaged to got

to know you like that. Like the story about your grand-mother. That's what I want to hear more of. Or tell me about your fiancée. Why did you two not work out?"

"I don't want to talk about Lucy."

Ellie let out a gust. "Finn, you have to talk about something. We're supposed to know each other inside and out."

"That's why I gave you the list—"

"The list doesn't tell me anything more about you than I already knew from reading the magazine article." She let out a gust and got to her feet. For a while she stood at the railing, looking out over the darkened homes. Then she turned back to face him. "Why won't you get close to me?" Her voice was soft and hesitant. It was the kind of sound that Finn wished he could curl into. "You take two steps forward, then three back. Why?"

"I don't do that." He rose and turned to the other end of the balcony, watching a neighbor taking his trash to the curb. It was all so mundane, so much of what a home should be like. Between the crackers and the cheese and the sweatpants—

Damn, it was like a real marriage.

"What are we doing here, Finn?" Ellie asked, coming around to stand beside him.

When she did, he caught the scent of her perfume. The same dark jasmine, with vanilla tones dancing just beneath the floral fragrance. It was a scent he'd already memorized, and every time he caught a whiff of those tantalizing notes, he remembered the first time he'd been close enough to smell her perfume.

He'd been kissing her. Sealing their marriage vows in Charlie's office. And right now, all he could think about was kissing her again. And more, much more.

Damn.

"We're pretending to be married," he said.

"Are we?" He didn't respond. She lifted her gaze to his. "Can I ask you something?"

"Sure."

She let a beat pass. Another. Still her emerald gaze held his. "Why did you agree to marry me?"

"Because you said that's what it would take. To get on board with the hospital project."

"You are 'the Hawk,' Finn McKenna," she said, putting air quotes around his nickname. "You could negotiate your way out of an underground prison. But when I proposed this…marriage, you didn't try to negotiate at all. You agreed. What I want to know is why."

The night air seemed to still. Even the whoosh-whoosh of traffic seemed to stop. Nothing seemed to move or breathe in the space of time that Ellie waited for his answer. He inhaled, and that damned jasmine perfume teased at his senses, reawakened his desire.

Why had he married her? She was right—he could have offered something else in return for her cooperation on the hospital project. Or he could have just said no. "I guess I just really needed that project to help my business get back on track."

She took a step closer, and lifted her chin. "I don't believe you."

"Truly, it was all about business for me."

"And that was all?"

She was mere inches away from him. A half step, no more, and she'd be against him. Desire pulsed in his veins, thundered in his head. His gaze dropped from her eyes to her lips, to her curves. "No," he said, with a ragged breath, cursing the truth that slipped through his lips. "It's not."

Then he closed that gap, and reached up to capture one of those tendrils of her hair. All day, he'd wanted to do this, to let one silky strand slip through his grasp. "Is it for you?" he asked.

She swallowed, then shook her head. "No. It's not." She bit her lip, let it go. "It's becoming more for me. A lot more."

Finn watched her lips form the words, felt the whisper of her breath against his mouth. And he stopped listening to his common sense.

He leaned in, and kissed Ellie. She seemed to melt into him, her body curving against his, fitting perfectly against his chest, in his arms. She was soft where he was hard, sweet where he was sour, and the opposite of him in every way. Finn kissed her slow at first, then harder, faster, letting the raging need sweep over him and guide his mouth, his hands. She pressed into him, and he groaned, in agony for more of her, of this.

His cell phone began to ring, its insistent trill ripping through the fog in Finn's brain. He jerked away from Ellie, then stepped away. "I'm sorry." He flipped out the phone, but the call had already gone to voice mail. The interruption had served its purpose.

Finn had regained his senses.

Ellie stepped toward him, a smile on her lips, and everything in Finn wanted to take her in his arms and pick up where they left off. But doing so would only do the one thing he was trying to avoid—

Plunge him headlong down that path of wild and crazy. The kind of roller-coaster romance that led to bad decisions, bad matches, and in the end, unhappiness and broken hearts.

"We can't do this." He put some distance between them and picked up his glass, just to have something to do with his hands—something other than touch Ellie again.

"Can't do what?" A smile curved across her face. "Let this lead to something more than a contract?"

"Especially not that. We can't treat this like...like a real marriage. It's a business partnership. And that's all." He shook his head and put the glass back on the tray. The remains of their snack sat there, mocking him. Tempting him to go back to pretending this was something that it wasn't.

But Ellie wasn't so easily dissuaded. She stood before him, hands on her hips. "What are you so afraid of?"

"I'm not afraid of anything. I just think it's best if we keep this business only."

"So that's what that kiss was, business only?"

"No, that was a mistake. One I won't make again."

"And the rooftop dinner? The kiss in the courthouse? Also mistakes?"

He sighed. This was why he hadn't wanted to go down this path. He could already see hurt brimming in Ellie's eyes. He'd done this—he'd made her believe their fake marriage might be leading to something more—and he'd been wrong.

Was any project worth hurting Ellie? Seeing her crying, just like he had seen his mother crying so many times?

He exhaled, then pushed the words out. The words he should have said long ago. "After the interview, I don't think we should wait to annul this marriage." There. He'd said it. Fast, like ripping off a bandage.

Didn't stop it from hurting, though.

Her green eyes filled with disbelief. A ripple of shock filled her features. "What?"

"The business deal can be maintained if you want," he said. He kept his voice neutral, his stance professional. If he treated this like business as usual, perhaps she would, too. But the notes of her perfume kept teasing at his senses while the tears in her green eyes begged him to reconsider. Finn struggled to stick to his resolve. This was the best thing, all around. "Uh, if you like, I'll keep my team in place at WW, and help you through the project. It seems like they're working well together. No reason to break that up."

"That wasn't the deal. You were supposed to help me adopt Jiao."

"I'll do my part. When the interview is set up, just let me know and I'll be here for that."

"Pretending to be my husband."

"Wasn't that the arrangement?"

She didn't say anything for a while. Outside her building, a car honked, and a dog barked. Night birds twittered at each other, and the breeze whispered over them all.

"Was that all you were doing a minute ago? Sealing a business deal?"

She made him sound so cold, calculated. So like the Hawk nickname he hated. "You think that's the only reason I kissed you?"

"Isn't it? You wanted an alliance that would help your company. I wanted a child. We each get what we want out of this marriage. It's as simple as that. That's all this marriage is about. A simple business transaction." She took a step closer, her gaze locked on his. "Isn't it? Or did it start to become something more for you, too?"

She was asking him for the truth. Why had he married her if it wasn't about the business?

He couldn't tell her it was because he was tired of sleeping on that sofa bed. That he was tired of hearing nothing other than his own breath in his apartment. Tired of spending his days working and his nights wondering why he was working so hard. And that when he had met

Ellie he had started to wonder what it would be like to have more.

But he didn't.

Because doing that would open a window into his heart, and if he did that, he'd never be able to walk away from Ellie Winston. He'd get tangled up in the kind of heated love story that he had always done his best to avoid. No, better to keep this cold, impersonal. Let her think the worst of him.

He let out a gust. "This is anything but simple."

"Why? What is so bad about getting involved with someone, Finn? What makes you so afraid of doing that?"

"I'm not afraid of getting involved. We got married, remember?"

"In name only. That's not a relationship. It's a contract. And I know that's what I said I wanted when we started this thing, but…" She let out a long breath and shook her head. "You know, a few times, I've thought I've seen a different side of you, a side that is downright human. And that made me wonder what it would be like to take a chance with you. I'm not a woman who takes chances easily, especially with my heart. But in the end, you keep coming back to being the Hawk."

He scowled. "That's not true."

"You're a coward, Finn." She turned away. "I don't know why I thought…why I thought anything at all."

Why couldn't she understand that he was trying to be smart, to put reality ahead of a fantasy they would never have? Acting without thinking and living in a dream bubble got people hurt. Ellie needed to understand that.

"You think we can turn this fantasy into a real marriage?" he asked. "Tell me the truth, Ellie. Was a part of you hoping that maybe, just maybe, we'd work out and make a happy little family with two-point-five kids and a dog?"

"No." She shook her head, and tears brimmed in her eyes. Above them, a light rain began to fall, but they both ignored it. "Not anymore."

His gaze went to the glass balcony door. The reflection of the neighborhood lights shimmered on the glass like mischievous eyes. Droplets of rain slid slowly down the glass, and Finn thought how like tears the rain could appear. "I'm sorry," he said. "But I have to be clear. I can't give you any more than what the contract stipulated."

Ellie didn't see the ramifications that he could. He had been through this already, seen his parents suffer every day they lived together. Sure, he and Ellie could have some hot, fiery romance, but in the end, they'd crash and burn, and the child would be the one who suffered the most. She was already starting to head down that road, and if he didn't detour them now, it would go nowhere good.

Tears began to slide down Ellie's cheeks, and for a moment, Finn's determination faltered. "That's all I am? A contract?"

"That's what you wanted, Ellie. And it's what's best for all of us." Then he turned on his heel and headed out into the rain.

Before the tears in her eyes undid all his resolve.

CHAPTER EIGHT

HE WAS having a good day. The smile on Henry Winston's face told Ellie that, along with the doctor's tentatively positive report. They were on an upswing right now, and her father was gaining ground. For the first time, the doctor had used the words "when he goes home."

Gratitude flooded Ellie, and she scooted the vinyl armchair closer to her father's bedside. Happy sunlight streamed through the windows of his room at Brigham and Women's Hospital. Her father had more color in his face today. The tray of food beside him was nearly empty. All good signs. Very good.

After last night's bitter disappointment with Finn, Ellie could use some good news. She'd tossed and turned all night, trying to think of a way to convince Finn to help her with Jiao. If he didn't, how would she make this work? He hadn't said for sure he'd get an annulment, but she hadn't heard from him since the conversation on the balcony. She could pick up the phone and call him herself, but she didn't. Because she didn't want to hear him say he'd ended their marriage. And ended Ellie's hopes for adopting Jiao.

Maybe Linda could try appealing to the Chinese again. Perhaps if they saw how committed Ellie was to adopting Jiao, they'd relent on the marriage rule.

Ellie bit back a sigh. From all Linda had told her, that was highly unlikely. Ellie was back at square one, with Jiao stuck in the same spot. Finn had let her down. He'd accused her of wanting this to be a real marriage.

Was he right? Did a part of her hope, after those kisses and that dinner, and all the jokes and smiles, that maybe this was turning into something more than just a platonic partnership?

She glanced out the window, at the city that held them both, and at the same time separated them, and realized yes, she had. She'd let herself believe in the fairy tale. She'd started to fall for him, to let down her guard, to do the one thing she'd vowed she wouldn't do—entangle her heart.

Time to get real, she told herself, and stop seeing happy endings where there weren't any.

For now, Ellie focused on her father instead. One thing at a time. "How are you doing, Dad?"

"Much better now that you're here." He gave her a smile, one that was weaker than Henry's usual hearty grin. But beneath the thick white hair, the same green eyes as always lit with happiness at her presence. "They've got me on a new med. So far, it seems to be working pretty well." He lifted an arm, did a weak flex. "I'll be ready to run the Boston marathon before you know it."

She laughed. "And the Ironman after that?"

"Of course." He grinned, then flicked off his bedside television. His roommate had gone home yesterday, so the hospital room was quiet—or as quiet as a room in one of Boston's busiest medical facilities could be. "How are you doing, Ellie girl?"

"I'm fine, Dad. You don't need to worry about me."

"Ah, but I do. There's some things that don't stop just because your kids grow up."

She gave her father's hand a tight squeeze. She wasn't about to unload her problems on his shoulders. He had much more important things to worry about. "You just concentrate on getting better."

"How are things going with the adoption? I'd sure love to meet my granddaughter."

Ellie sighed. "I've run into a bit of a snag." Then she forced a smile to her face. Worrying her father—about anything—was not what she wanted. Henry didn't need to know about her marriage or her new husband's refusal to help. Chances were, Finn had already filed the annulment and Ellie's marriage was over before it began. For the hundredth time, she was glad she'd kept the elopement a secret from her father. "It'll be fine. It'll just take a little bit longer to bring Jiao home."

"You sure? Do you want me to call someone? Hire a lawyer?" Her father started to reach for the bedside phone, but Ellie stopped him.

"It'll be fine. I swear. Don't worry about it at all." She didn't know any of that for sure, particularly after Finn had told her he wanted nothing to do with the adoption, but she wasn't about to involve her poor sick father. "Just a tiny delay. Nothing more."

"Well, good. I can't wait to meet her. I've seen enough pictures and heard enough about her that I feel like I know her already." Her father settled back against the pillows on his bed, his face wan and drawn. "Hand me that water, will you, honey?"

"Sure, sure, Dad." She got her father's water container, and spun the straw until it faced Henry. She helped him take it, and bring it to his mouth, then sat back. "You sure you're up to a visit?"

He put down the water, then gave her a smile. "Seeing my little girl always makes me feel better. Now, talk to me about something besides doctors and medications. Tell me how things are at the company."

"Good." She hadn't told her father about any of the problems she'd encountered with Farnsworth quitting and the rush to get the Piedmont project underway. She wasn't about to start now. Maybe down the road when he was stronger and feeling better.

He tsk-tsked her. "You always tell me that things are good. I know you're lying." He covered her hand with his own. "I know you have the best of intentions, but really, you can talk to me. Use me as a sounding board."

Oh, how she wished she could. But the doctor had been firm—no unnecessary stress or worries. Her father, who had worked all his adult life, had a lot of trouble distancing himself from the job, and right now, that was what he needed most to do. Whatever she wanted—or needed—could wait. "You need to concentrate on getting better, Dad, not on what is happening at work."

"All I do is lie here and concentrate on getting better." He let out a sigh. Frustration filled his green eyes, and knitted his brows. "This place is like prison. Complete with the crappy food. I need more to do. Something to challenge me."

"I brought you a lot of books. And there are magazines on the counter. A TV right here. If you want something else to read—"

He waved all of that off. "Talk to me about work."

"Dad—"

He leaned forward. The strong, determined Henry Winston she knew lit his features. "I love you, Ellie, and I love you for being so protective of me. But talking about work *keeps* me from worrying about work. I'm not worried about you being in charge—you're capable and smart, and I know you want that business to succeed as much as I do—but I miss being plugged in, connected. That company is as much a part of me as my right arm."

She sighed. She knew her father. He had the tenacity of a bulldog, and now that he was feeling better, she doubted she could put him off much longer about WW Architectural Design. Maybe she could set his mind at ease by sharing a small amount of information, and that would satisfy his workaholic tendencies. "Okay, but if your blood pressure so much as blips, we're talking only about gardening the rest of the day."

He grimaced at his least favorite topic, then crossed his heart. "I promise."

"Okay." She sat back and filled him in, starting with a brief recap of Farnsworth's defection, followed by glossing over most of the setbacks on the Piedmont project, and finally, touting the positive aspects of her temporary alliance with Finn. She kept the news mostly upbeat, and left out all mentions of her elopement.

"You are working with Finn McKenna," Henry said. It was a statement, not a question.

She nodded. "He has the experience we need. I could hire a new architect but we don't have enough time to do another candidate search and then bring that person up to speed. The prelims are due the fifteenth."

"Finn McKenna, though? That man is not one you should easily trust. He's made an art form out of taking over small companies like ours. You know he's our competition, right?"

"Yes, and we have worked out an amicable and fair arrangement. His business got into a little trouble—"

"Do you know what that trouble was? Did he tell you?"

"He didn't give me specifics." Dread sank in Ellie's

gut. She could hear the message in her father's tone. There was something she had missed, something she had overlooked. Damn. She had been too distracted to probe Finn, to push him to tell her more.

She knew better. She'd rushed headlong into an alliance because her mind was on saving Jiao and nothing else.

"He got involved with the daughter of a competitor. In fact, I think he was engaged to her," Henry said. "And when things went south in the relationship, several of his clients defected to the other firm, taking all their business with them. I heard Finn raised a ruckus over at his office, but it was too late. A lot of people said he only proposed to her so he could take over her company and when it ended badly, she stole his clients instead."

Daughter of a competitor. Wasn't that what she was, too? Had Finn married her for control of the company?

Oh, God, had she made a deal with the devil? Her gut told her no, that Finn was not the cutthroat businessman depicted by the media. But how well did she really know him? Every time she tried to get close to him, he shut the door.

Wasn't this exactly why she had stayed away from marriage all these years? She'd seen how her parents had been virtual strangers, roommates sharing a roof. She didn't want to end up the same way, married to someone she hardly knew because she mistook infatuation for something real.

Ironic how that had turned out. Well, either way, the marriage would be over soon. She told herself it was better that way for all of them.

"Just be cautious, honey," Henry said. "I've heard Finn is ruthless. You know they call him—"

"The Hawk." The nickname had seemed like a joke

before, but now it struck a chord. Had she missed the point? Was this entire marriage a plan by Finn to get his company back—

By taking over WW Architectural Design?

Maybe his "help" was all about helping his own bottom line. "I'm sure Finn will be fine," she said, more to allay her own fears than her father's. Because all of a sudden she wasn't so sure anything was going to be fine. "He's really smart and has been a great asset on this project."

"I'd just be very cautious about an alliance with him," her father said. "He's one of those guys who's always out to win. No matter the cost."

"He's been very up-front with me, Dad. I don't think he has a hidden agenda." Though could she say that for a hundred percent? Just because she'd married Finn and kissed him didn't mean she knew much more than she had two days ago. Every time she tried to get close to him, he pushed her away.

"Don't trust him, that's all I'm saying. He's backed into a corner, and a dog that's in a corner will do anything to get out."

Anything. Like marry a total stranger.

And try to steal her father's legacy right out from under her.

CHAPTER NINE

RILEY and Brody dragged Finn out for breakfast. The two brothers showed up at Finn's office, and refused to take no for an answer.

"Why are you stuck in this stuffy office, instead of spending time with your hot new wife?" Riley said. "You've been married for almost a week now, and I swear, you spend even more time here than you did before you got married."

Brody gave Riley's words a hearty hear-hear. "Jeez, Finn. You'd think being married would change you."

He didn't want his brothers reminding him about his marriage—or lack of one. Or the fact that he hadn't seen Ellie in a couple of days. He'd gone home after that night on the balcony, and had yet to return to her apartment, or her office.

He'd sent his senior architects to most of the meetings at WW, and only gone to one when Ellie wasn't scheduled to be there. He conferred with his team back here at his office, and in general, avoided Ellie. Entirely. He used the excuse that the drawings were due in a few days, but really, he knew that was all it was—an excuse. An excuse to keep his distance. Because every time he was with her, he considered the kind of heady relationship he'd spent a lifetime avoiding. "I am changed."

Riley arched a brow. Brody outright laughed. "Sure you are. Prove it and leave the shackles behind for a little while."

Finn scowled. "I have work to do."

"Come on, let's get something to eat," Brody said. Like the other McKenna boys, Brody had dark brown hair, blue eyes and a contagious smile. As the middle brother, he had a mix of both their personalities—a little serious and at the same time a little mischievous.

Riley turned to Brody. "What do you say we kidnap him?"

Brody put a finger on his chin and feigned deep thought. "I don't know. He's pretty stubborn."

"We'll just tie him up." Riley grinned. "So there's your choice, Finn. Either come with us or we're going to haul you out of here like an Oriental rug."

Finn chuckled. "Okay. I can see when I've been beaten." He wagged a finger at them. "But I only have time for a cup of coffee, no more."

The three of them headed out of the office, and instead of going down Beacon to their usual haunt, Riley took a right and led them toward a small corner diner on a busy street. The sign over the bright white and yellow awning read Morning Glory Diner. It looked cheery, homey. The opposite of the kind of place the McKenna boys usually frequented. "Hey, I really don't have room in my schedule to go all over the city for some coffee," Finn said. "My day is very—"

Riley put a hand on his arm. "You gotta ask yourself, what do you have room for?"

"Because it's sure not sex." Brody laughed. "I can't believe you've been at work bright and early every morning. Haven't you heard of a honeymoon period?"

Finn wasn't about to tell his brothers that his was far

from a conventional marriage. A honeymoon was not part of the deal. Nor was he even living with his "wife."

"Take advice on marriage from you? The eternal bachelor twins?"

"Hey, I may not be interested in getting married— ever." Riley chuckled. "But even I know a newly married man should be spending all his time with his new bride."

"Yeah, and in bed," Brody added.

Damn. Just the words *bed* and *wife* had Finn's mind rocketing down a path that pictured Ellie's luscious curves beneath him, her smile welcoming him into her heart, her bed, and then tasting her skin. Taking his time to linger in all the hills and valleys, tasting every inch of her before making slow, hot love to her. Again and again.

He'd had that dream a hundred times in the days since he'd met her. He found himself thinking of her at the end of his day, the beginning of his day, and nearly every damned minute in between.

And that alone was reason enough to end this. He was a practical man, one who made sensible decisions. The sensible side of him said keeping his distance from Ellie was the wisest course. The one that would head off the disaster he'd created before. A part of him was relieved.

Another part was disappointed.

The part that dreamed about Ellie Winston and wondered what it would be like to consummate their temporary marital union.

Finn cleared his throat and refocused. He was in a platonic marriage, and there was no definition of that word that included having sex. "I'm not taking relationship advice from you two."

"Maybe you should, brother." Riley quirked a brow at him, as they entered the diner and sidled up to the coun-

ter. The diner's namesake of bright blue flowers decorated the border of the room, and offset the bright yellow
and white color scheme. "So, besides the fact that you
aren't in bed with her right now, how is it going with the
new missus?"

"Do you want to talk about anything else this morning?"

Riley glanced at Brody. "Not me. You?"

"Nope. Finn's life is my number-one topic of conversation."

He loved his brothers but sometimes they took well-
meaning just a step—or ten—too far. "Well then, you
two will be talking to yourselves." Finn ordered a black
coffee, then gestured toward Riley and Brody. "What do
you guys want?"

"Oh, you're paying?" Riley grinned. He turned to the
waitress, a slim woman with a nametag that read Stace.
"Three bagels, a large coffee and throw in some extra
butter and cream cheese. Can you pack it in to-go bags,
too? Thanks."

"Two blueberry muffins and a large coffee for me,"
Brody said.

"You're guys aren't seriously going to eat all that, are
you?" Finn fished out his wallet and paid the bill.

"Hell no. I'm getting breakfast for the next three days."
Riley grinned again.

"Yeah, and considering how often you offer to pay,
maybe I should have ordered a year's supply." Brody
chuckled.

Finn rolled his eyes. "You two are a pain in the butt,
you know that?"

"Hey, we all have our special skills," Riley said.
"Except for you, because you're the oldest. You get the
extra job of taking care of us."

"Last I checked you were grown adults."

"Hey, we may be grown, but some us aren't adults." Riley chuckled.

"Speak for yourself." Brody gave Riley a gentle punch in the shoulder.

Finn pocketed his change and followed his brothers over to a corner table. Since it was after nine, the breakfast crowd was beginning to peter out, leaving the diner almost empty. The smell of freshly roasted coffee and fresh baked bread filled the space.

"You know, I was just kidding," Riley said. "You don't have to take care of us. Or buy us breakfast."

"I didn't see your wallet out."

Riley grinned. "You were quicker on the draw." Then he sobered. "Seriously, sometimes you gotta take care of you."

"Yeah, you do," Brody said.

Finn looked at his brothers. "What is this? An intervention?"

Riley and Brody both grinned. "Now why would you think that?" Brody said, affecting innocence that Finn wasn't buying. His brothers clearly thought he was working too much and living too little. "This is just coffee, isn't it Riley?"

Their youngest brother nodded. A little too vigorously. "Coffee and bagels." Riley held out the bag. "Want one?"

Finn waved off the food. He glanced around the diner. Filled with booths and tables, the diner had a cozy feel. Seventies tunes played on the sound system, while Stace, apparently the lone waitress, bustled from table to table and called out orders to the short-order cook in the back. "What made you pick this place?" Finn asked. "I didn't even know you came here."

"Oh, I don't know. We thought it'd be nice to have

a change of scenery." Riley's head was down, while he fished in the bag.

"Change of scenery?" Finn tried to get Riley's attention, but his brother seemed to be avoiding him. "What is this really about?"

The bell over the door rang and Riley jerked his head up, then started smiling like a fool. He elbowed Brody. "Well, there's our cue to leave."

"What? We just got here."

Riley rose. Brody popped up right beside him, guilty grins on both McKenna faces. "Yeah, but someone much better company than us just showed up." Riley dropped the bag of food onto the table. "I'll leave these. Be nice and share."

"What? Wait!" But his brothers were already heading for the door. Finn pivoted in his seat to call after them. And stopped breathing for a second.

Ellie stood in the doorway, framed by the sun, which had touched her hair with glints of gold. She had on a dark blue dress today that skimmed her knees and flared out like a small bell. It nipped in at her waist, and dropped to a modest V in the front. She wore navy kitten heels today, but still her legs, her curves, everything about her looked amazing.

Finn swallowed. Hard.

Riley and Brody greeted Ellie, then Riley pointed across the room at Finn. Riley leaned in and whispered something to Ellie, and her face broadened into a smile. It hit Finn straight in the gut, and made his heart stop. Then Ellie crossed the room, and Finn forgot to breathe.

Her smile died on her lips when she reached him. "I didn't know you'd be here this morning."

"I didn't know, either." Finn gestured toward the door. "I suspect my brother is at work here."

"I think you're right. I've seen him in here a couple times. I recognized him from the cocktail party and we got to talking one day. I told him I'm here pretty often for my caffeine fix. I guess he figured he'd get us both in the same place."

"That's Riley." Finn shook his head. "My little brother, the eternal optimist and part-time matchmaker."

"He means well. And he thinks the world of you." She cocked her head and studied him. "Wow. You three do look a lot alike."

"Blame it on our genes." Finn wanted to leave, but at the same time, wanted to stay. But his feet didn't move, and he stayed where he was. He gestured toward the bag on the table. "Bagel? Or do you want me to get you a coffee?"

She glanced at her watch. "I have about fifteen minutes before I have to get to a meeting. I really should—" Her stomach growled, and she blushed, then pressed a hand to her gut, then glanced at the growing line at the counter. Despite the light banter, the mood between them remained tense, nearly as tough as the bagel's exterior. "Okay, maybe I have enough time for just half a bagel."

Finn opened the bag and peered inside. "Multigrain, cheese or plain?"

"Cheese, of course. If I'm going to have some carbs, I'm going all out."

"A woman after my own heart." Finn reached in the bag, pulled out a cheese-covered bagel and handed it to her, followed by a plastic knife and some butter. She laid it out on a napkin, slathered on some butter, then took a bite. When the high calorie treat hit her palate, she smiled, and Finn's heart stuttered again.

"Oh, my." Ellie's smile widened. "Delicious."

He watched her lips move, watched the joy that lit her features. "Yes. I agree."

"Oh, I'm sorry, do you want some?"

"Yes," he said. Then jerked to attention when he realized she meant the bagel. And not her. "Uh, no, I already ate this morning."

"Let me guess." She popped a finger in her mouth and sucked off a smidgen of butter. Finn bit back a groan. Damn. He wanted her. Every time he saw her, desire rushed through him.

"You had plain oatmeal," Ellie went on. "Nothing fancy, nothing sugary."

"No. Muffins."

Her brows lifted and a smile toyed with the edge of her mouth. "Not ones from the floor, I hope?"

The words brought the memory of that day in her kitchen rocketing back. Their first day as a married couple. The sexual tension sparking in the air. The desire that had pulsed in him like an extra heartbeat.

He cleared his throat. "Freshly baked and boxed," he said. "From a bakery down the street from my apartment. I rarely eat at home and usually grab something on the way to work."

"This bagel is delicious." She took another bite. Butter glistened on her upper lip, and Finn had to tell himself—twice—that it wasn't his job to lick it off.

Except she was his wife. And that was the kind of thing husbands did with wives.

Unless they were in a platonic relationship.

But were they? Really? How many times had he kissed her, touched her, desired her? Had he really thought he could have a friends-only relationship with a woman this beautiful? This intriguing? A woman who made him forget his own name half the time?

And that was the problem. If he let himself get distracted by Ellie, he'd make a foolish decision. Finn was done making those.

"Why not?" Ellie asked.

"Uh...why not what?" His attention had wandered back to the bedroom, and he forced it to the present.

"Why not eat at home?"

It was a simple question. Demanded nothing more than a simple answer, and Finn readied one, something about hating to cook and clean. But that wasn't what came out. "It's too quiet there."

Her features softened, and she lowered the bagel to the napkin. The room around them swelled with people, but in that moment, it felt like they were on an island of just two. "I know what you mean. I feel the same way about where I live. The floors echo when I walk on them. It's so...lonely."

Lonely. The exact word he would have used to describe his life, too.

A thread of connection knitted between them. Finn could feel it closing a gap, even though neither of them moved. "Have you always lived alone?"

"Pretty much. Even when I was younger, my parents were never there. My dad worked all the time and my mom..." Ellie sighed and pushed the rest of her breakfast to the side. "She had her own life. In college I did the dorm thing, but after that, I had an apartment on my own. I used to love it in my twenties, you know, no one to answer to, no one to worry about, but as I've gotten older..."

"It's not all it's cracked up to be." He wondered what had made him admit all this in a coffee shop on a bright spring day. He'd never considered himself to be a sharing kind of man. Yet with Ellie, it seemed only natural to open up. "Though it was nice to share your space for a couple of days."

Her face brightened. "Was it? Really?"

"Yeah. Really." The kind of nice he could get used to.

He ignored the warning bells ringing in his head, the alarms reminding him that the last time he'd allowed a woman to get this close, it had cost him dearly. He couldn't live the rest of his life worried that someone was going to steal his business. Riley and Brody were right. It was time for him to stop taking care of everyone else and focus on himself for a little while. Just for today.

"I agree." She toyed with the bagel. "I guess my priorities have shifted, too. I built all these houses for other people and after a while, I realized I wanted that, too."

"What?"

"You were right the other day." She lifted her gaze to his and in her eyes, he saw a craving for those intangible things other people had. "As scared as I am of falling in love, of having the kind of bad marriage my parents had, I really do want the two-point-five kids. The block parties. The fenced-in yard. Even the dog."

His coffee grew cold beside him. He didn't care. People came and went in the busy coffee shop. He didn't care. Time ticked by on his watch. He didn't care. All he cared about was the next thing Ellie Winston was going to say. "What…what kind of dog?"

"This is going to sound silly and so clichéd." She dipped her head and that blush he'd come to love filled her cheeks again.

"Let me guess. A Golden retriever?"

She gave him an embarrassed nod. "Yeah."

He shook his head and chuckled.

"What?"

"When I was a kid, I asked Santa for a dog. My mother

was allergic, so it was never going to happen, but I kept asking. Every Christmas. Every birthday. And the answer was always the same. No." He shrugged. "They got me a goldfish. But it wasn't the same."

"What kind of dog did you want?" Then her eyes met his and she smiled. "Oh, let me guess. A Golden retriever."

The thread between them tied another knot. What was it Ellie had said about a real marriage? That it was one where the two people knew each other so well, they could name their dreams and desires?

Were they turning into that?

Finn brushed the thought away. It was a coincidence, nothing more. "Billy Daniels had a Golden," he said. "It was the biggest, goofiest dog you ever saw, but it was loyal as hell to him. Every day when we got out of school, that dog would be waiting on the playground for Billy and walk home with him. Maybe because Billy always saved a little something from his lunch for a treat. He loved that dog. Heck, we all did."

"Sounds like the perfect dog."

"It seemed like it to me. Though, as my mother reminded me all the time, I wasn't the one dealing with pet hair on the sofa or dog messes in the backyard."

"True." She laughed. "So why didn't you get a dog when you grew up?"

"They're a lot of responsibility. And I work a lot. It just didn't seem fair to the dog."

"But every boy should get his dream sometime, shouldn't he?"

She'd said it so softly, her green eyes shimmering in sympathy, that he could do nothing but nod. A lump sprang in his throat. He chastised himself—they were talking about a dog, for Pete's sake. A gift he'd asked for when he was a kid. He was a grown man now, and he didn't believe in Santa anymore. Nor did he have room in his life for a dog.

What do you have room for? Riley had asked. And right now, Finn didn't know. He'd thought he had it all ordered out in neat little columns, but every time he was near Ellie, those columns got blurred.

"You know what I do sometimes?" Ellie said, leaning in so close he could catch the enticing notes of her perfume. "I go to the pet store and I just look. It gives me that dog fix for a little while."

"Maybe if I'd done that more often when I was a kid, I wouldn't have kept bothering Santa."

She got to her feet and put out her hand. "Come on, Finn. Let's go see what Santa's got in the workshop."

"What? Now? I thought you had a meeting to get to."

"It can wait a bit." To prove it, she pulled her cell phone out of her purse and sent a quick email. "There. I have an hour until they start sending out the search party."

He had a pile of work on his desk that would rival Mount Everest. Calls to return, emails to answer, bills to pay. He should get back to work and stop living in this fantasy world with Ellie. Instead he took out his phone and shot an email to his assistant. "There. I have an hour, too," he said.

"Good." She smiled. "Really good."

Finn took Ellie's hand, and decided that for sixty minutes, he could believe in the impossible.

CHAPTER TEN

ELLIE had been prepared to walk out of the diner the second she saw Finn this morning. To refuse the bagel, the offer of coffee, to just ignore him as he'd done to her for the last few days. Then Riley had leaned over and whispered, "Give him a chance. He's more of a softie than you know."

And so she'd sat down at the table, and wondered what Riley had meant. Was Finn the competitor her father had cautioned her against, or was he the man she had seen in snippets over the past days?

Today, he'd been the man she'd met in the lobby—complex and nuanced and a little bit sentimental. And she found herself liking that side of him.

Very much. Falling for it, all over again, even as her head screamed caution.

Then he'd gone and surprised her with their destination and she realized she didn't just like him a little. She liked him a lot. Finn McKenna, with his gruff exterior, was winning her over. Maybe doing a lot more than that. Even as she told herself to pull back, not to get her heart involved, she knew one thing—

Her heart was already involved with him. Ellie was falling for her husband.

The problem was, she wasn't sure he wanted to be her

husband anymore, nor was she positive she could trust him. Her father's words kept ringing in her head. *He's backed into a corner, and a dog that's in a corner will do anything to get out.*

Did Finn have a secret agenda to take over her company? Was that why he kept retreating to the impersonal? Or was he struggling like she was, with the concept of a marriage that wasn't really a marriage?

A contract, he had called it. The word still stung.

If that was all he wanted, then why was he here? What did he truly want?

"Are you two looking to add a dog to your family?"

The woman's question drew Ellie out of her thoughts. "No. Not yet. We're just looking."

Beside her, Finn concurred. He had a brochure from the animal shelter in his hand, and had deposited a generous check into the donation jar on the counter. The director of the shelter, a man named Walter, had come out to thank Finn, and engaged him in a fifteen-minute conversation about the shelter's mission. When Ellie had asked him to go to the pet store, she'd been sure he'd drive to one of the chain stores in the city. But instead he'd pulled into the parking lot of the animal shelter, and her heart had melted. Finn McKenna. A softie indeed.

Every time she told herself not to get close to him, not to take a risk on a relationship that could be over before it began, he did something like that.

"Well, we have plenty of wonderful dogs here to look at." The woman opened a steel door and waved them inside. "Take your time. I'll be right back. We're a little short-staffed today, so I need to get someone to man the phones, then I'll join you." She left the room, and as soon as the door clicked shut, the dogs took that as their cue.

A cacophony of barking erupted like a long-overdue

volcano. Down the long corridor of kennels, Ellie could see dogs of every size and breed. They pressed themselves to the kennel gates, tails wagging, tongues lolling, hope in their big brown eyes.

"Everyone wants to go home with us," Finn said as they started to walk down the row and the barking got louder. "We could be the people in *101 Dalmatians*."

We. Had that been a slip of the tongue? Or was she reading too much into a simple pronoun?

"I don't think so." Ellie laughed. "One dog would be plenty."

Finn bent down, wiggled a couple fingers into the hole of the fenced entrance and stroked a dachshund under the chin. The dog's long brown body squirmed and wriggled with joy. "Hey there, buddy."

Ellie lowered herself beside Finn and gave the little dog a scratch behind the ears. "He's a cutie."

"He is. Though…not exactly a manly dog."

"You never know. He could be a tiger at the front door."

Finn chuckled, then rose. They headed down the hall, passing a Doberman, some Chow mixes and a shaggy white dog that could have been a mix of almost every breed. Finn gave nearly every one of them a pat on the head and the dogs responded with enthusiastic instant love. Ellie's heart softened a little more. She kept trying to remind herself that she didn't want to fall for this man, didn't want to end up unhappy and lonely, trapped in a loveless marriage, but it didn't seem to work.

Finn walked on, then stopped at a cage halfway down on the right side. A middle-aged Golden retriever got to her feet and came to the door, her tail wagging, her eyes bright and interested. "Aw, poor thing," he said softly. "I bet you hate being here." The dog wagged in response. "She's a beautiful dog."

Ellie wiggled two fingers past the wire cage door and stroked the dog's ear. The Golden let out a little groan and leaned into the touch. Finn gave her snout a pat, then did the same to the other ear. The dog looked about ready to burst with happiness. Ellie reached up and retrieved the clipboard attached to the outside of the cage. "It says her name is Heidi."

"Nice name for a dog. Wonder why she's here?"

Ellie flipped the informational sheet over. It sported bright, happy decorations with lots of "Adopt Me" messages, along with a quick history of Heidi. "The paper says her owner got too old to take care of her." Ellie put the clipboard back. "That's so sad."

"Yeah. Poor thing probably doesn't understand why she's here." He gave Heidi another scratch and she pressed harder against the cage.

"Stuck in limbo, waiting for someone to bring her home." Ellie sighed. She grasped the wire bars of the cage, the metal cold and hard against her palm. The dogs in the kennel began to calm a little, their barks dropping to a dull roar, but Ellie didn't hear them. She looked into Heidi's sad brown eyes and saw another pair of sad eyes, on the other side of the world. "So tragic."

"You're not talking about the dog, are you?"

Ellie bit her lip and shook her head. "No."

Finn shifted to scratch Heidi's neck. The dog's tail went into overdrive. "Tell me about her."

Ellie glanced up at the clipboard again, scanning the information on the top sheet. "She's six years old, a female, spayed—"

"Not the dog. The little girl in China."

"You mean Jiao?" Ellie said, her heart catching in her

throat. Finn had never asked about Jiao, not once since the moment she had proposed the marriage of convenience. "You really want to know about her?"

Finn nodded. He kept on giving Heidi attention, but his gaze was entirely on Ellie. "Yeah, I do."

She wanted to smile, but held that in check. Just because Finn asked about Jiao didn't mean he wanted to be part of Jiao's life. He could be making conversation. "She's two. But really bright for her age. She loves to read books, although her version of reading is flipping the pages and making up words for what she sees." Ellie let out a laugh. "Her favorite animal is a duck, and she has this silly stuffed duck she carries with her everywhere. She's got the most incredible eyes and—" Ellie cut the sentence off. "I'm rambling. I'm sorry."

"No, please, tell me more." He got to his feet. "She's important to you and I want to know why. How did you meet her?"

Ellie searched Finn's blue eyes. She saw nothing deceitful there, only genuine interest. Hope took flight in her chest, but she held a tight leash on it. "I went to China for a conference a few years ago. But on the way to the hotel, my cabdriver took a wrong turn, and I ended up in a little village. His car overheated, and while we were waiting for it to cool down, I got out and went into this little café type place. The woman who served me was named Sun, and since I was pretty much the only customer, we got to talking. I ended up spending the entire week in that village."

"Is Sun Jiao's mother?"

Ellie nodded. Her gaze went to the window, to the bright sun that shone over the entire world. In China, it was dark right now, but in the morning, Jiao's world would be brightened by the same sun that had greeted Ellie's morning. "She was."

"Was?"

"Sun...died. Three months ago." Just saying the words brought a rush of grief to her eyes. Such a beautiful, wonderful woman, who had deserved a long and happy life. Fate, however, had other plans and now the world was without one amazing human being.

Finn put a hand on her shoulder. "Aw, Ellie, I'm so sorry. That's terrible."

She bit her lip, and forced the tears back. "That's why Jiao needs me. Over the years, I made several trips back to China and became close friends with Sun. On my last trip, Sun told me about her cancer. Because we were so close, she and I worked out an arrangement for me to adopt Jiao. And I've been trying ever since to bring Jiao home."

He turned back to the dog, and she couldn't read his face anymore. "That's really good of you."

"It's a risk. I don't know if Jiao will be happier here with me, or in China with another couple. I don't know if I'll be a good mother. I just...don't know." She wove her fingers into the fence again, and Heidi rubbed up against her knuckles.

Finn placed his hand beside hers. Not touching, but close enough that she could feel the heat from his body. "I'm sure you'll be fine. You have a certain quality about you, Ellie, that makes people feel...at home."

She met his gaze and saw only sincerity there. "Even when I drop muffins on the floor?"

"Even then." He looked at Heidi again, and gave the dog some more attention. "That's a valuable quality to have for raising a kid, you know. When your home is uncertain, it makes it hard to just be a kid."

She sensed that this was coming from someplace deep in Finn. They kept their attention on the dog, as the conversation unwound like thread from a spool. "Did you have a hard time just being a kid, Finn?"

He swallowed hard. "Yeah." He paused a moment, then went on. "I was the oldest, so I saw the most. My parents loved us, of course, but they should have never married each other. They knew each other for maybe a month before they eloped in Vegas. My mother was pregnant before they came home. My father always said he would have left if not for the kids."

"Oh, Finn, that had to be so hard on you."

"I wasn't bothered so much by that." Finn turned to Ellie, his blue eyes full of years of hard lessons. "It was that my father had fallen out of love with my mother, long, long ago, but my mother kept on holding on to this silly romantic notion that if she just tried hard enough, he'd love her again like he used to. If he ever did. So they fought, and fought, and fought, because she wanted the one thing he couldn't give her."

"His heart."

Finn nodded. "He provided money and clothes and shoes, but not the love my mother craved. I watched her cry herself to sleep so many nights. I've often wondered if…"

When he didn't go on, Ellie prodded gently. "If what?"

"If they got into an accident that night because they were fighting again." He let out a long breath. "I'll never know."

She understood so much more now about Finn. No wonder he shied away from relationships. No wonder he kept his emotions in check, and pulled himself back every time they got close. Was that why he buried him-

self in work? Instead of giving his heart to someone else?
"You can't let that stop you from living, too."

"It doesn't."

"Are you sure about that?" she asked. He held her gaze
for a moment, then broke away.

"Did you get a date for the home visit yet?"

He had changed the subject once again, pushing her
away whenever she got close. Why? "Yes. I was going
to call you today. Friday at eleven."

He nodded. "I'll be there."

"You will? I wasn't sure…" She bit her lip. "I didn't
think you would. After what you said the other day."

"I'll be there. Because—" his fingers slipped into the
thick fur on Heidi's neck again, scratching that one spot
that made her groan "—no one should have to be in a
place like this. No dog. No person."

She wanted to kiss him, wanted to grab him right then
and there and explode with joy. But she held back, not
sure where they stood on their relationship, if they even
had one. Doors had been opened between them today,
and Ellie was hesitant to do anything that might shut
them again. "Thank you."

"You're welcome." His gaze met hers, and for a long
heartbeat, it held. Then Heidi pressed against the cage,
wanting more attention, and Finn returned to the dog.
"You're a good girl, aren't you?"

If anyone had asked her if she had thought Finn "the
Hawk" McKenna would be a dog lover who would be
easily brought to his knees by a mutt in an animal shelter, she would have told them they were crazy. But in the
last few days, she had seen sides of Finn she suspected
few people did. And she liked what she saw. More every
minute. "You really like dogs, huh?"

"Yeah." He turned to her and grinned. "Don't tell Billy

Daniels, but sometimes I snuck his dog a little of my left-over lunch, too."

She laughed and got to her feet again. "My, my, Finn. You do surprise me."

He rose and cast her a curious glance. "I do? I don't think I surprise anyone."

"You're not what I thought. Or expected."

He took a step closer, and the noise in the room seemed to drop. The dogs' barking became background sounds. "What did you expect?"

"Well, everything I heard about you said you were business only. The magazine articles, the way the other architects talked about you." What her father had said about him. Right now, she had trouble remembering any of those words. "Everything you said, too."

"My reputation precedes me," he said, his voice droll.

"But when I first met you, well, not when I *first* met you, but that day in the office, you were like that. A cool cucumber, as my grandmother would say. You didn't seem like the kind of man who would have dramatic out-bursts or irrational thoughts. And from what I've seen, you're smart and good at your job."

He snorted. "That sounds boring."

"And then I see this other side of you," she went on. "This guy who makes corny jokes about Cinderella, and eats at fast food restaurants so he doesn't have to stay in an empty house, and has a soft spot in his heart for a dog he never even owned. A guy who takes a girl to an animal shelter instead of a pet store."

"I just thought, there are tons of unwanted dogs and why buy a puppy when…" He shrugged, clearly uncomfortable with the praise. "Well, it just made more sense."

"It did." She smiled, and leaned ever so slightly toward him. She wanted more of this side of Finn, more of him in general. Every moment she spent with him showed her another dimension of this man who was her husband, yet at the same time, still a stranger. A man who had been wounded by his childhood, and yet, seemed to still believe in happy endings.

The Finn she saw today—the one who pitied a dog in a shelter and realized how like Jiao's life the dog's was—that Finn was the man she was...

Well, starting to fall for. And fall hard. Damn. Every time she tried not to—

She did.

The thought caused a slight panic in her chest, but that disappeared, chased by a sweet lightness. Could she really be falling in love with her husband?

"You're a good man." Ellie smiled.

"Thank you," he said, his voice gruff, dark. He reached up a hand and cupped her jaw, and Ellie thought she might melt right then and there. God, she loved it when he touched her like that. She saw something in his eyes—something that said maybe this wasn't just a contract to him, either, despite what he'd said.

Ever so slowly, Finn closed the gap between them, winnowing it to two inches, one. His breath dusted across her lips and his sky-blue eyes held hers. Anticipation fluttered in her chest. The dogs, apparently realizing no one was interested in them right now, quieted. But Ellie's heart slammed in her chest, so fast and loud she was sure Finn could hear it.

"You are surprising, too," he said. "In a hundred ways."

"Really?"

"Really." Then he kissed her.

He took his time, his lips drifting across hers at first, tasting and tempting. Then his hand came up to cup the back of her head, tangle in her hair, and with a groan, his kiss deepened. His mouth captured hers, made it one with his, and Ellie curved into him. Finn's body pressed to hers, tight and hard, and their kiss turned breathless, hurried. Each of them tasting the other with little nips, shifting position left, right, his tongue plundering her mouth and sending a dizzying spiral of desire through her body.

This was what she had dreamed of in those nights since Finn had slipped a wedding ring on her finger. What she'd had a taste of at the courthouse, and then later on her balcony. This was what she had imagined, if the two of them had a real marriage. The heat nearly exploded inside of Ellie and she knew that if they hadn't been standing in the middle of an animal shelter, they would have been doing a lot more than just kissing.

Behind them, the dogs began barking again and Ellie drew back, the spell broken. "I can't do this."

"Why not?"

She looked into his eyes and saw the same hesitation as before. She wondered if it was true emotional fear on his part, or if her father's cautions were right. Or because she knew she was risking her heart, and he was keeping his to himself. When would she learn? "Because every time I kiss you, I only get half of you, Finn. You keep the rest of yourself locked away."

"I'm not—"

"You are. You told me yourself that you watched your parents suffer through a miserable marriage. I know that has you scared, because I saw the same thing when I was a kid, and I've done my best to avoid getting close to anyone ever since. But you know what I learned in China? What Sun taught me just before she died? That it's okay to love with your whole heart. It's okay to take that risk, even if it costs you everything. Because in the end, the people you love will be better off for having you in their hearts."

He shook his head and turned away. "Sometimes all you end up with is a broken heart."

"Just like in business, huh? Sometimes you win, and everything works out perfectly. And sometimes you lose and take a dent to the bottom line. But you can't do either if you don't take a risk."

She waited a long time for Finn to respond. But he didn't.

Because the truth hurt or because he was keeping his distance, and stringing her along just to grab the business out from under her later? The part of her that had seen Finn take pity on a shelter dog wanted to believe otherwise, but the part that had read the news reports and heard about how he nearly married another competitor's daughter, wondered.

Was she letting herself get blinded by her emotions? The very thing she'd vowed not to do?

Behind them, the door opened and the woman from the shelter stepped inside. "Did you two find anything you wanted?"

Ellie glanced back at Finn one more time. His features had returned to stoic and cold. The man she thought she'd seen earlier today was gone. If he'd ever really been there at all.

"No," she said. "There's nothing I want here. I'm sorry for wasting your time."

CHAPTER ELEVEN

FINN drove back to his office alone. By the time he reached the sidewalk—after being detoured by Walter, who stopped a second time to thank Finn for his donation—Ellie was gone. She'd either walked or taken a cab. It didn't matter. The message was clear.

She was done with him.

He should be glad. For a minute there in the shelter he had lost his head, and let his hormones dictate his decisions. He'd kissed her, allowed himself to start falling for her, and stop thinking about the smart decision. The one that would leave everyone intact at the end.

Ellie had accused him of being afraid of repeating his parent's mistakes. Hell, yes, he was afraid of that, and afraid of doing it with Jiao caught in the crossfire. The already orphaned girl had been through enough. She didn't need to watch the marriage of her new parents fall apart.

He thought of the orphaned dogs he'd seen earlier. They were all so sad, yet at the same time so hopeful. Their tails wagged, tongues lolled and their barks said they were sure these two visitors would be their new saviors.

All it required was saying yes, and opening his heart and home.

Then why had he never done that? Never adopted a dog. Never settled down, never had children. Ellie was right. He'd taken risks in everything but his personal life. And where had it gotten him?

He stepped into his office and looked at the towering stacks of work sitting in his IN box. Everything was in its place, labeled and ordered, easy to organize and dispense. This was where he felt comfortable, because here he could control the outcome.

With a marriage or with a child...there were so many opportunities to make a mess of things. Finn excelled here, in the office, and even that had turned into a disaster in the past year. What made him think he could handle a dog, or a child? Heck, except for that goldfish, he'd never even had a pet.

And even the goldfish had gone belly up within a week.

He dropped into his desk chair, and let out a sigh. He dove into the piles of papers stacked beside him and spent a solid two hours whittling it down from a mountain to a molehill but work didn't offer the usual solace. If anything, the need to be in the office grated on him, and made him feel like he was missing out on something important.

"Hey, Finn, how's married life?"

Finn looked up and grinned at Charlie, then waved his friend into his office. "What are you doing here?"

"Had some business to take care of in Boston." He thumbed toward the street. "Remember my aunt Julia, who lived here?" Finn nodded. "Well, she died last month, and her will's just been a mess over at probate."

"I'm sorry to hear that."

"It's no big deal. It gives me a chance to come back and see some of the guys from the old neighborhood."

Charlie settled into one of the visitor's chairs and propped his ankle on his knee. "I miss having you guys around. The four of us got into a lot of trouble."

Finn chuckled. The McKenna boys and Charlie had been the neighborhood wild children, whooping it up until their mothers called them in for supper. "We did indeed."

"Then we all grew up and got serious. Well, all of us except for Riley."

"I don't think Riley's ever going to grow up. He's the perpetual kid."

"Sometimes that's good for us." Charlie gestured toward Finn. "Besides, who are you to talk? You *eloped*, my man. If I didn't marry you myself, I never would have believed it."

Finn waved it off. "Temporary moment of insanity."

"I met your wife, remember? I gotta say, I think that was the smartest decision you ever made in your life."

"Smartest, huh?" It hadn't felt so smart lately. He had married a woman, thinking he could keep it all about business. Considering how many times he'd kissed her, he'd done a bad job of business only. It was as if he was drawn to the very thing that scared him the most—an unpredictable, heady relationship fueled by passion, not common-sense conclusions.

"She's perfect for you, Finn. Intelligent, beautiful, funny. And willing to marry *you*."

"Hey. I'm not that bad."

"No, not *that* bad." Charlie grinned. "But, I've known you all your life and you can be a bit…difficult."

"Difficult?"

"Yeah, as in a mule in the mud. In business, that's served you well. You put your head down, plow through any obstacles and don't take no for an answer. And look where you are today." Charlie waved at Finn's office. "Up on top of the world, overlooking the city of Boston. Doesn't get much better than that."

"I don't know. I had a bad year last year."

Charlie waved it off. "Lucy did her damage, yes, but in the end, it toughened you up, made you a better business-man. If you never had any failures to knock you down, you'd never be able to appreciate the successes that bring you back up."

Finn took in the city below him, then thought of the company he had built from the ground up. Sure, he'd suf-fered a pretty bad setback last year, but overall, he was still in business and still doing what he loved. "True."

"And really, you didn't fail. You just met someone who is exactly like you." Charlie chuckled. "A Hawkette."

Finn thought about that for a second. Was that where all his careful planning, detailed lists and sensible dat-ing got him? He'd tried so hard to find someone who was similar to him in personality, career and goals, and it had backfired. He'd tried to mitigate the risk by being smart—

And in the process, made an even bigger mistake. "I did, didn't I?"

"Yep. That's why I think this Ellie is good for you. She's sunshine to your storm clouds."

"I'm not that bad. Am I?"

"Nah. But you could use someone who rounds you out, Finn. You've always been a practical guy and when you're running a business based on straight lines, that's impor-tant. But when it comes to the heart, man—" Charlie thumped his own chest for emphasis "—you gotta fol-low the curves."

"Maybe you're right."

"Hey, I'm a judge. I'm always right." Charlie grinned.

"So, how are the kids?" Finn asked, just to change the subject.

"Perfect, as always." Charlie beamed. "But then again, I'm a little biased."

Finn could see the joy and pride in Charlie's face. He'd known Charlie since elementary school, and had never seen his friend this happy. He seemed to have it all—a great career, a wonderful wife, incredible kids. He and Finn had started in the same place, grown up side by side, followed similar paths—college, then starting at the bottom and working their way up—that it made Finn wonder if maybe there was some secret to having it all that he was missing. "Don't you worry about messing it up?"

"Of course I do. Being a husband and a father is the biggest risk of all because you have other people's lives in your hands. But in the end, it's so worth it." Charlie had pulled out his wallet and was flipping proudly through the pictures of his kids. "This is what it's all about, my friend. Sophie just lost her two front teeth, and she goes around whistling everywhere. Max signed up for T-ball…"

Finn wasn't listening. He was looking at the clear love in Charlie's face, the determination to do right by his kids, and realized where he had seen that look before.

On Ellie's face. When she talked about Jiao.

She was scared to take the risk of being Jiao's parent, but she was doing it anyway. Clearly Ellie loved this little girl. Finn had no doubt she'd be a good mother. For a second, he envied her that love, that clear conviction that she could raise a child she barely knew. He was sure she would be a terrific mother. Any child would be blessed to be raised by a woman as amazing as Ellie Winston.

As Finn watched one of his oldest and best friends talk about the wondrous joy a family could bring to a man's life, he felt a stab of envy. Ellie was his temporary wife, and after all this was over, there would be no pictures or bragging or stories to tell.

He glanced at the clock and realized there was one thing he could do before they got divorced. He could help her bring that child home.

And make sure Ellie's floors would no longer echo.

CHAPTER TWELVE

ELLIE had spent the better part of Friday morning scrubbing her house from top to bottom. Cleaning helped distract her, helped take her mind off the worries about work, the home visit today, and the worries about Jiao. She had called the orphanage earlier and been assured that Jiao was fine and healthy, but that didn't help set Ellie's mind at ease when it came to her daughter's future. Every hour that ticked by with Jiao stuck in adoption limbo was undoubtedly hurting her emotionally.

When she wasn't worrying about the adoption, her mind was on Finn. For a while there, she'd thought they were building something. She'd thought...

Well, it didn't matter what she'd thought. Finn had made it clear over and over again that he wasn't interested in a relationship with her. There was the home visit today, and then the hospital plans were due to be delivered to the client on Tuesday, and after that, she was sure their alliance would end. Probably a good thing, she told herself.

Tears rushed to her eyes but she willed them back. Finn was the one losing out, not her. She told herself that a hundred times as she scoured the shower walls. But the tears still lingered.

A little after ten-thirty that morning, her doorbell rang.

Ellie peeled off her rubber gloves, dropped them into a nearby bucket, then ran downstairs to answer it. Finn stood on the other side.

"You came."

"I promised you I would." He was wearing a light blue golf shirt and a pair of jeans that outlined his lean, defined legs. The pale color of his shirt offset his eyes, and made them seem even bluer. Her body reacted the same as always to seeing him—a nervous, heated rush pumping in her veins—even as her head yelled caution.

"Thank you."

"No need to thank me." He gave her a grin, that lop-sided smile that made her heart flip. "I'm here to help you get ready. Not that I'm a whole lot of help in the home department, but I figured you'd be a wreck, and need a hand getting things done."

He could have been reading her mind. Joy bubbled inside her, but she held it back, still cautious and reserved. This was everything she'd ever wanted. Finn would be a temporary husband, just as she'd planned, he'd do the home visit with her, then go back to living his own life, leaving her and Jiao alone, to form their own little family of two. She should have been happy.

Then why did she feel so…empty? *Focus on Jiao. On bringing her home. Not on what will never be with Finn.*

"That sounds good," she said. "Thank you."

"We don't have much time before they arrive," Finn said. "And a lot to do. So let's get to work." Finn grabbed a box that she hadn't noticed beside his feet. "I brought a few more of my things to put around the house, so it looks more like I'm living here. I didn't bring enough before."

"Good idea."

"I was just trying to think through all possible angles.

People will expect us to have commingled belongings. I brought some clothing, the two photographs I have of myself, and a six-pack of beer."

She laughed at the beer. "That sounds like a typical male."

"That was my intent. I want to make sure we have maximum plausibility."

Disappointment drowned out her hope. This whole thing wasn't about Finn being thoughtful, it was about him being methodical and thorough, covering all his bases. Just when she thought the Hawk had disappeared…he came to the forefront again. She wondered again if this was true help, or a calculated move to help his business.

She'd focus on the adoption, and worry about the rest later. Linda would be here soon and Ellie only had this one shot to convince her and the social worker that Jiao would be happy here.

"You should probably put your things in my bedroom," she said.

"Yeah." His gaze met hers in one long, heated moment. She turned away first, sure that if she looked at him for one more second, she'd forget all the reasons she had for not getting involved with him.

"Why don't I help you?" She turned on her heel and led Finn up the stairs, trying not to think about how surreal this all was. She was taking her husband to her bedroom, for the sole purpose of pretending she shared the room with him. In the end, he'd pack up his things and be out of her life. Forever.

"I already moved the things you left behind in the guest room into here," she said. "I didn't know if you'd be here today and I guess I wanted to set up maximum plausibility, too."

"We think alike." He grinned. "Maybe that's a good thing."

"Maybe." She opened the door to the master bedroom, then followed Finn inside. Then she turned back and laid a light hand on his arm. "If I don't get a chance to tell you later, thank you."

He shrugged, like it was no big deal. "You're welcome."

"No, I mean it, Finn. This is huge for me, and I really, really appreciate you helping with this."

His eyes meet hers, and she felt the familiar flutter in her chest whenever he looked at her. "You're very welcome, Ellie."

The moment extended between them. Her heart skipped a beat. Another.

Behind her, Ellie was painfully aware of the bed. The wedding rings on their hands. If this had been any other marriage, they would be in that bed together, every night, making love. If this had been any other marriage, she would have stepped into Finn's arms, lifted her face to his and welcomed another of his earth-shattering kisses.

If this had been any other marriage...

But it wasn't. And she needed to stop acting like it was.

She spun around and crossed to the closet. "Uh, let me shift some of my clothes over, and we can fit yours in there." She opened one of the double doors and pushed several dresses aside, the hangers rattling in protest, then she turned back to Finn. He was smiling. "What?"

"Hootie & the Blowfish." He pointed at her closet.

She turned back and saw the concert T-shirt hanging in her closet. It had faded over the years, but still featured the band's name in big letters on the front. "Oh my. I forgot that was in there. That was oh, almost fifteen years ago." She pulled out the hanger and fingered the soft cotton shirt. "I don't know why I hung on to it for so long."

"Did you hear them in concert?"

"Yep. Me and two of friends went. We were both hoping to marry Darius Rucker. They were my favorite band, and I figured I could hear Hootie songs every day if I married the lead singer."

He chuckled. "I guess that didn't work out."

"Kinda hard to catch his eye when we're in the fortieth row." She laughed, then clutched the shirt to her chest. "Do you like Hootie & the Blowfish?"

He nodded. "I went to a concert, too, one of their last ones before Rucker branched out on his own."

She propped a fist on her hip. "Yes, but do you have the T-shirt to prove it?"

He dug in the box and pulled out a threadbare brown T. Laughter exploded from Ellie when she read the familiar name on the front.

"I saw them at the Boston Garden," he said.

"Providence for me." She flipped over her shirt to show the concert information. "We could go out as twins."

"Uh, yeah…no." He laughed. "I think that would be more damaging than anything. People would think we're crazy."

"Oh, it might be fun. And get people talking."

She remembered the first time she'd said that. It had been back in the office, on their first day as a married couple. They'd shared lunch in the outdoor courtyard, and for a little while, it had felt so real, as if they were any other couple sneaking in an afternoon date. And the time they had spent in her house, had seemed real, too. Had they been pretending? Or had a part of it been a true marriage? And why did she keep hoping for the very thing she told herself she didn't want?

Finn moved closer to her, and the distance between them went from a foot to mere inches. Ellie's heart began to race. Damn, this man was handsome.

"They already are talking," he said.

"Really? And what do you think they're saying?"

His gaze locked on hers. Ellie's pulse thundered in her head and anticipation sent a fierce rush through her veins. She held her breath, waiting on his words, his touch.

A slight smile curved across his lips. "I think they're saying that they can't believe I married you."

"Because I'm such a bad match for you?"

"No. Because you are such an amazing woman." He reached up and drifted his fingers along her jawline, sliding across her lips. She nearly melted under that touch, because it was so tender, so sensual. "Smart and funny and sexy and a hundred other adjectives."

"Finn..." She drew in a breath, fought for clarity. Every time she thought she understood Finn and his motives, he threw a curveball at her. Was he here for business, or something more? Was there anything between them besides an architectural alliance? A *contract*? Because right now, it sure as hell felt like something more. A lot more. And oh, how she wanted that more. She was tired of being afraid of falling in love, afraid of risking her heart. She did want the whole Cinderella fantasy, damn it, and she wanted it with Finn. The trouble was, she didn't know what he wanted.

"Every time I see you, I stop thinking—" he leaned in closer, and her heart began to race "—about anything but how much I want to kiss you again."

"Really?" The hope blossomed again inside her. Lord, she was in deep.

His fingers did a slow dance down her neck. Her nerves tingled, chasing shivers along her veins. "Really." Then finally, when she thought she could stand the wait no longer, he kissed her.

This kiss started out slow, easy, sexy, like waltzing across the floor. Then the tempo increased, and the spark between them became an inferno, pushing Ellie into Finn, searching, craving, more of him. She curved her body into his and the inferno roared down every part of them that connected. His hands roamed her back, sliding along the soft cotton of her T-shirt, then slipped over the denim of her jeans, sending a rush of fire along her back, her butt. Oh, God, she wanted him. She arched into him, opening her mouth wider, her tongue tangoing with his. Insistent, pounding desire roared through her veins. *More, more, more,* she thought. *More of everything.*

"Oh, God, Ellie," he said, his voice a harsh, low groan. Then, one, or maybe both of them began to move and in tandem, they stepped back, two steps, three, four, until Ellie's knees bumped up against the bed and they fell onto it in a tangle of arms and legs.

Finn covered her legs with one of his, never breaking the kiss. His mouth had gone from easy waltz to hot salsa, and Ellie thought she might spontaneously combust right then and there if she didn't have more of Finn. Of his kiss, his touch, his body. Damn, his body was hard in all the right places, and on top of hers, and sending her mind down the path of making love. His hand slid under her T-shirt, igniting her bare skin. She moaned, rose up to his touch, then gasped when his fingers brushed against her nipple. She gasped, arched again, and his fingers did it again. Oh, God. Even through the lacy fabric of her bra, she could feel every touch, every movement.

She murmured his name, then wrapped a leg around

his hips, pressing her pelvis to his hard length. God, it had been so long since she had been with a man, so long since she had been kissed. She wanted Finn's clothes off. Wanted his naked body against hers. Wanted him inside her.

Finn seemed to know everything about her. Every touch stoked the fire inside her, every kiss added to the desire coursing through her veins, clouding her every thought. Then as she shifted to allow him more access, the clock downstairs began to chime the hour.

Ellie jerked back to the present. What was she doing? Where was she going to go with this? Was she letting her hormones overrule her brain again? She shifted away from him and scrambled to her feet. "Why are you doing this?" she asked.

"Because I want you. Because you're the most beautiful woman I've ever met. Because—"

"No. Why are you helping me? Why are you here today for the home visit?" The clock downstairs chimed ten, then eleven times, and fell silent.

"Because I made you a promise." His sky-blue eyes met hers and when he spoke his voice was quiet, tender. "And because when you were telling me about Jiao at the animal shelter, I saw how much you loved her. Every child should have a parent who loves them like that. Who would move heaven and earth to provide them with a safe and loving environment."

"Is that all there is? No hidden agenda to steal WW out from under me?"

He looked surprised. No, he looked hurt, and she wanted to take the words back. "You think that's why I did all this? Really? After everything?"

"You told me yourself that your company has had a bad year and that you were desperate to recoup the business you had lost. Desperate enough to marry the daughter of your competitor?" She bit her lip, and pushed the rest out. She didn't want him here if in the end he was going to take away the very thing her father treasured. Nothing was worth that price. "Like you almost did before?"

"Is that what you think? That I go around town marrying the competition to try to build my business up? That the Hawk swoops in and drops engagement rings to lure them in?"

She crossed her arms over her chest. "I don't know, Finn. You tell me."

"I don't. The fact that you and Lucy both work in the industry is a coincidence."

"Is it? Because it seems to me that marrying me has given your business an advantage and I want to be sure my father's company is protected."

He cursed. "Ellie, I didn't marry you for your father's company. And I have no intentions of stealing it."

"Is that what you told Lucy, too?"

The doorbell began to ring. Linda was here. Ellie cursed the timing. "We'll have to finish this later."

"Okay." He turned to the box and quickly stowed the rest of his clothes in her closet. Finn finished hanging up his clothes, then turned to the dresser and nightstand to put out a few of his personal items. Ellie crossed to the door of the bedroom and took one last look at the closet that held the incongruity of her life. Finn McKenna's dress shirts and pants hung beside her dresses, making it look like her husband was truly a part of her life.

When that was as far from the truth as could be.

Two hours later, Linda and the social worker finished their visit at Ellie's house. As they were heading out the door, Linda leaned her head back in and shot Ellie a smile. "This went great. Thanks to both of you for being available on such short notice."

"You're welcome. It was our pleasure," Finn said. He shook hands again with Linda, then took his place beside Ellie, slipping an arm around her waist. Still playing the happy couple, and after a couple hours of it, it was beginning to feel natural. Hell, it had felt natural from the minute he'd said "I do."

"We'll get the report off to the orphanage in China and from there it should only be a few days." Linda beamed. "I'm so excited for the two of you. I'm sure Jiao will be very, very happy in her new home."

Ellie thanked Linda again, then said goodbye. After the two women were gone, she closed the door and leaned against it. Finn stepped back, putting distance between them again. The charade, after all, was over. He should have been relieved.

He wasn't.

He realized that this was it. They had finished the preliminary drawings for the hospital project and save for one more meeting to go over a few details, the business side of their alliance was done. And now, with the social worker gone and the home visit over, the personal side of their partnership was over, too. He had no other reason to see Ellie again.

And that disappointed him more than he had expected.

"Thank you again," Ellie said. "You were fabulous. Really believable."

"You're welcome."

"I loved how you managed to slip in that thing about us sharing the same favorite band, and the stories about how we both saw them in concert. I think it's the details that really make a difference."

"Yeah, they do." That damned disappointment kept returning. Was it just because they'd shared an amazingly hot kiss—and a little more—back in the bedroom? Or was it because they'd been pretending so well, it had begun to feel real, and now he was mourning the loss of a relationship that had never really existed? One that he had been doing his best to avoid? "I, uh, should get going."

Her smile slipped a little. "Okay. I'll, uh, see you Monday. At the meeting."

"Sure, sounds good." He picked his keys up from the dish by the front door—another realistic touch that he had added—and pressed the remote start for his car.

"Do you want to take your stuff now?"

"Maybe I should leave it. In case they come back."

"Oh, yeah, sure. Good idea." She paused. "Are you sure there isn't anything you need?"

"No, I'm good. Oh, wait. I left my wallet on the nightstand." He thumbed toward the stairs. "Is it okay if I go up and get it?"

"Sure. This is your house, too. At least for show."

He chuckled, but the sound was empty, the laughter feigned. This wasn't his house and even though he'd pretended to for a little while, he wasn't living here anymore. He headed up the stairs and into her room.

He paused inside the doorway and took in the room one last time. A fluffy white comforter dominated her king-sized bed. Thick, comfortable pillows marched down the center of the bed, ending with a round decorative pillow in a chocolate-brown. Sheer white curtains hung at her windows, dancing a little in the slight breeze. In one corner a threadbare tan armchair sat beside a table with a lamp. Close to a dozen books stood in a towering stack on the table. Finn crossed to them, smiling at the architectural design books, then noting the mysteries and thrillers that filled out the pile. Two of them were on his own nightstand.

They listened to the same music. Read the same books. Worked in the same field. Everything pointed to them being perfect for each other.

Except...

His gaze skipped to the bed. There was a fire between them, one he couldn't ignore. It made him crazy, turned his thoughts inside out and made him do things he had never done before—like elope.

Risk.

That's what marrying Ellie had been. A huge risk. And Finn, the man who never made a move that wasn't well thought out and planned, had taken that risk with both eyes wide-open. He glanced at a picture of Ellie posing with a smiling, gap-toothed two-year-old girl with dark almond eyes and short black hair. Jiao. The two of them looked happy together, already resembling the family they would soon become.

A part of him craved to be in that circle, with Ellie and Jiao. Wanted to form a little family of three. That was the biggest risk of all, wasn't it?

He'd taken it in the last few days and realized that every time he was with Ellie, he felt a happiness he'd never known before. A lightness that buoyed his days. Was he...falling for her?

And was he doing it too late?

Finn grabbed his wallet and turned to leave. Ellie stood in the doorway, watching him. "You never answered my question."

He sighed and dropped onto the bed. Did she really think the worst of him? That he was the Hawk, through and through? "I didn't propose to Lucy with the intention of stealing her company. I proposed to her because I thought she was the right one to settle down with."

Ellie hung back by the door. "The love of your life?"

He snorted. "Far from it. She was the one who met all the mental pros and cons I had listed in my head for a relationship. She fit my little checklist, so I told myself we'd be happy. And you know what?" He shook his head, and finally admitted the truth to himself. "I was never happy with her. I was content."

"Is that so bad?"

"It's horrible. Because you never have that rush of joy hit your heart when you see the person you love." His gaze met hers, and a whoosh ran through him. "You never hurry home because you can't wait to see her smile. You never catch yourself doodling her name instead of writing a contract. You never feel regret for leaving her instead of staying to the very end." He rose and crossed to Ellie. "The most impetuous thing I did was propose to Lucy—I rushed out and bought the ring at the end of the day. After I'd compiled a list of pros and cons." He shook his head and let out a breath. "Who does that? Pros and cons?"

"Some people. I guess."

"She didn't expect me to show up at her office, and definitely didn't expect me to propose. When I got there, I walked in on a meeting with her and my biggest client. In that instant, I knew that the whole thing had been a fraud. My gut had been warning me, but I'd been too busy being practical and sensible to listen."

"What was your gut saying?"

"That she didn't love me and I didn't love her, and that I was making the biggest mistake of my life. After I broke it off, she smeared my name all over town. Made it her personal mission to steal the rest of my clients." He looked deep into her green eyes. "You were right. I am afraid of risking my heart. But then again, so are you."

"Me? I'm not afraid." But her eyes were wide and her breath was quickened. He had hit a nerve, clearly.

"Really? Then why did you do your best to push me away?"

"This isn't going anywhere. You said so yourself."

He reached up as if he was going to touch her cheek, but his hand fell away. "And you accused me of being here to steal the company."

"Are you?"

"You know that answer already. Quit trying to put up walls that don't exist."

"I didn't…" She bit her lip.

"You did and so did I. It was all so easy, because we both kept saying this marriage had an end date. You did the same thing as me, Ellie. You got close, you backed away. Got close, backed away. I think you're just as scared as I am."

"I'm not."

"Really?" He leaned in closer. "Then what would you say if I said let's not end this?"

"Didn't…end the marriage? But that was the deal."

"I realized something today when I was here, in your house, pretending to be your husband for the last time." He caressed her check with his thumb. "The whole time I was wishing it was real. Because the time I've spent with you has been the best damned time of my life."

Fear shimmered in her eyes. Fear of being hurt, of letting go. Of trusting. When it came right down to it, Ellie was just as scared as he was of opening her heart. "Oh, Finn. I don't know what you want me to say."

"That you're ready to take that risk, too. That you want more than just the fiction."

She just shook her head. Finn released Ellie, then walked out the door, finally leaving behind a fairy tale that wasn't going to end with happily ever after.

CHAPTER THIRTEEN

ELLIE'S heart sang with the words the doctor had just said. *Great recovery. Going home soon. Should be okay to resume limited activities.* Her father had surpassed medical expectations and was going to be all right. He'd be on a limited schedule, of course, but he would be alive, and that was all Ellie cared about.

"You're doing fabulous, Dad," Ellie said. "The doctor is thrilled with your recovery." Henry was sitting up today, looking much heartier than last time. The color had returned to his face, and he appeared to have put back on some of the weight he had lost while he was sick. In the next bed, his new roommate was watching a reality show about wild animals.

"I'm just trying to do what I'm told," Henry said.

She laughed. "For the first time in your life?"

He chuckled. "Yeah." He patted the space beside him on the bed. "Come. Sit down and tell me how things are going for you."

"Good. Well, great." Except for the fact that she hadn't talked to Finn since that day at her house, things were great. She should have been relieved that the marriage was over, but she wasn't. A part of her wondered if maybe Finn was right—if she had let him walk away because it was easier than taking the risk of asking him to stay.

"The McKenna team worked with us to draw up the plans for the Piedmont hospital project. We submitted them to the client on time, and the initial review was really positive. But that's not the really good news..."

"What?"

"Well, you're about to be a grandfather." She smiled. "Jiao will be here in a few days."

A smile burst across his face. "Honey, that's wonderful! And while I'm excited to hear such good news about the business, I'm more excited about your addition to the family." He reached for the sheet of doctor's recommendations sitting on his end table and showed them to his daughter. "You can bet I'll be sticking to every one of these rules because I want to take my new granddaughter to the zoo and the park and wherever else she wants to go."

Ellie sat back, surprised at this change in her father, a man who'd never had time for those things before, a man who had stubbornly lived by his own rules—which was part of what had made him so unhealthy. "Wow. Really?"

"Really." His face softened, and he took her hand. "I missed all that with you, because all I ever did was work. Lying here in this bed has given me a lot of time to think, to regret—"

"Dad, I grew up just fine. You don't need to have regrets."

"I do. And I will. I want you to know how sorry I am that I missed out on your soccer games and band performances and prom nights." His face crumpled and tears glistened in his eyes. "Aw, Ellie, I should have been there more, and I...I wasn't."

She gave his fingers a squeeze and sent God a silent prayer of gratitude for this second chance with her father. "It's okay. We're building a great relationship now, and that's all that matters."

"No, it isn't." He let out a long sigh. "Once I'm out of this hospital, I have a lot to make up for with you, starting with asking you to move up here and take over the business. I never should have done that."

"Dad, I love architecture. I love this industry."

"But you don't love commercial buildings. I knew that, and still I asked you to take over my business." His green eyes met hers. So like her own, and filled with decades more of wisdom and experience. "You were happy designing houses."

She was, but she wasn't about to tell her dad that. She would never complain about stepping in for him at WW. It was a family business, and when your family needed you, you went. Simple as that. "You're my father. You were sick. You needed me. I didn't mind."

"I know you didn't, and that's the problem. You are too good of a daughter, Ellie girl." He sighed. "That's why I want you to quit."

"Quit? What? Dad, you're in no condition to run the company yourself. Not now." She didn't add the words *maybe never*. Because there was hope, and she wanted her father to hold on to that. "I'll stay until you come back and—"

"No." His voice was firm, filled with the strident tones people usually associated with Henry Winston. His heart might be weak but his personality and resolve remained as strong as ever. "You have a daughter to raise. You go do that."

She laughed. "Dad, I still need to pay my bills. I'll keep working and we'll work it out."

"No. I want you to quit WW Architectural Design... and start your own division. A residential division. Bring those beautiful houses you designed in the South to the Boston area. And hire lots of great people to work under you so that you don't have to put in the kind of hours I did."

"A residential division?" A thrill ran through her at the thought of getting back to designing houses again, to return to the work that had given her so much reward. "But who will run the commercial side?"

"Larry and...Finn McKenna."

Had she heard him wrong? When had Finn come into the mix? "Finn McKenna? Why? I thought you didn't trust him."

"You told me he was smart, and capable. So I gave him a call this morning," Henry said. "He told me all about how you two collaborated on the hospital project and how well it went for everyone. I never really got to know Finn before, only knew him by reputation, but now I realize I was wrong about him. He may be a tough businessman, but he's also a nice guy. Cares a lot about you."

She let out a gust at that. "He cares about his business."

"He cares about a lot more than that, but I'll let you find that out for yourself."

Was the Finn she had started to fall for the real man? Or was he the Hawk that had pushed her away a hundred times? She couldn't think about that now, she decided, not with her father to worry about, and Jiao arriving any day.

Her father shifted in the bed, and Ellie realized Henry looked a hundred times better now than he had when he'd first been admitted. It was as if having this taste of something to do had given him a new energy and it showed in his face.

"Are you sure about wanting me to quit?" she asked.

Working in residential design again, particularly if she didn't have to be there full-time, would give her the flexibility she needed to raise Jiao. She'd be able to have time with her daughter, something the little girl was going to need after such a traumatic year. It was a gift beyond measure, and she couldn't begin to thank her father enough.

He reached out and drew his daughter into a warm hug. "I don't want to see you make the same mistakes I did. I want you to watch your daughter grow up. And I want to have the time to watch her grow up, too. I didn't build this business just to watch you repeat my mistakes."

Ellie tightened her grip on her father. Tears slid down her cheeks, moistened the sleeve of his hospital gown. "You didn't make any mistakes, Dad. Not a single one."

Finn had stayed away for weeks. He'd told himself it was easier this way, that he could wean himself off Ellie Winston, and forget all about her. If that was the case, then why had he gone to see her father? Agreed to the idea of joining their companies? And heading up the new venture?

Because he was crazy. Doing that would put him in the same building as Ellie every day, and he'd known that going into this deal. He just hadn't been able to let go, even as every day he looked at his To Do list and saw "call lawyer" at the top. Procrastination had become his middle name.

Either way, it didn't matter. By the time he had the particulars in place and had set up a space in the more spacious offices of WW Architectural Design, Ellie was gone. On maternal leave, he'd been told. Her assistant went on for a good ten minutes about Ellie's trip to China, and her new daughter. Every day he heard another tidbit about Ellie and Jiao.

And every day it felt like someone had cut out his heart and put it on a shelf.

Now he stood at the entrance to a small playground carved out of the limited green space near Ellie's neighborhood. Bright red, yellow and blue playground equipment dominated the center of the space, flanked by matching picnic tables and chairs. Green trees stood like sentries inside the wrought-iron fence. The musical sound of children laughing and playing carried on the air.

Finn's gaze skipped over the mothers sitting in clusters, chatting while their children played. Past the kids playing tag in the courtyard. Past the tennis players working up a sweat on the court next door. Then he stopped, his breath caught in his throat, when he saw her.

Ellie, sitting on a blanket, with Jiao beside her, and Jiao's stuffed duck flopped against the young girl's leg. They were having a picnic lunch, the little dark-haired girl giggling as Ellie danced animal crackers against her palm. The two of them formed a perfect circle of just them. Beside her, Linda stood and watched, a happy smile on her face. The two women chatted for a moment longer and then Linda left.

As she headed for the exit, she saw Finn and stepped over to him. "Why hello, Finn."

He gave the dark-haired woman a smile. "Hi, Linda. Nice to see you again."

"How have you been?"

"Good." Finn's gaze kept darting toward Ellie and Jiao. He'd missed Ellie's smile. A hell of a lot.

Linda thumbed toward Ellie. "You know, you really should go over there and meet Jiao. She's a wonderful little girl."

Finn opened his mouth, shut it again. He wasn't sure what to say. If he admitted he'd never seen Jiao before, then Linda would know the marriage had been a farce and maybe that would cost Ellie. Maybe even undo the adoption Ellie had worked so hard to bring to fruition.

Linda put a hand on Finn's arm. "Don't worry. I already figured it out."

"You did? How? Was it because I didn't go to China with Ellie?"

Linda laughed. "No, it was something much more simple. Your shoes."

"My shoes?"

"When we came by the house, you had clothes in the closet and a wallet on the bedside table, but not a single pair of shoes anywhere. I had had my suspicions about Ellie's fast marriage, but I didn't say anything."

Damn. He couldn't believe he'd missed such a simple detail. He'd thought he'd covered everything. He'd almost ruined the most important thing in Ellie's life. "Why? I thought Ellie had to be married to adopt Jiao."

"She did. And she was. I told the Chinese orphanage that her husband had to stay in America for a family emergency, so they didn't wonder why you didn't come to China to pick up Jiao. Either way, I knew that with or without a spouse on paper, Ellie was going to be a fabulous mother." Linda glanced over her shoulder at Ellie and her daughter. "She loves that little girl more than life itself. That's a blessing."

"I agree." The two of them seemed to go together like peas and carrots. Envy stirred in Finn's gut. He had never felt more on the outside than he did right now. Ellie had everything she'd ever wanted, and it hurt to realize that didn't include him. Perhaps if he had handled things differently, they wouldn't be here right now.

Maybe he shouldn't have married her at all. If they'd kept things entirely on a business level, then he wouldn't have this deepening ache in his chest for a life he never really lived. This stabbing regret for a relationship that had slipped away.

"You know, it's a scary thing," Linda said.

"What is?"

"Giving your heart away. Ellie did that, not knowing if she was going to be able to bring Jiao home. But she took that risk, and put everything on the line, because she loved that little girl." Linda's gaze met his. "And I think you took a big risk, too."

"Me?" He snorted. "I didn't do anything."

"You married her and stood up as her husband when she needed you most. That's a risk. And you gotta ask yourself why you did it."

"Because she needed me." He watched Ellie with Jiao, their faces close together as they laughed over something. It was the perfect picture of maternal love. Yes, he'd done the right thing in helping Ellie. In that, he took comfort.

"Maybe," Linda said. "And maybe you did it for more than just that. Maybe if she believes that, she'll take that risk, too." Then she patted him on the shoulder. "I've got to get back to work. Enjoy your family."

Linda was gone before Finn could tell her that this wasn't his family. Not at all. And no amount of wishing would make it so.

He was about to turn away when a dozen kids from a daycare center came bursting into the playground, and Finn stepped aside to let them through. Ellie looked up at the sudden noise of the newcomers. Her eyes widened when she saw him. She'd seen him, and leaving was out of the question.

He crossed the park to Ellie. "Hi."

There couldn't possibly be a lamer opening than that. All these weeks, he'd thought of what he'd say when he saw her again. "Hi" wasn't on the list at all.

She looked up at him, sunglasses covering those green eyes he loved so much. "What are you doing here?"

"I'm…" He hadn't played that out in his head, either. "Looking for you."

Better to start with the truth than to make up something. Besides, his lying skills were pretty awful. And where had lying gotten him so far anyway? Still stuck in his empty apartment, staring at the wedding band sitting on his nightstand, wondering if he'd made a huge mistake by letting her go.

Beside Ellie, Jiao bounced up and down, saying something that sounded sort of like "cracker." Ellie smiled, then placed another animal cracker in Jiao's palm, keeping an eye on her daughter while the toddler ate the treat. "How did you know where I'd be?"

"The women at the office are always talking about you and your daughter. They fell in love with her, I think."

Ellie grinned and chucked Jiao gently under the chin. "That's easy to do."

"Anyway, they said you come here almost every day."

"Jiao loves to be outside. I think it's because she was inside for so many months at the orphanage. So we try to make it here every morning." Ellie gave her daughter a tender glance, then turned back to Finn. "Why were you looking for me? Is there something going on at the office we need to talk about? Because really, Larry is your go-to guy on the commercial side, now that I'm handling residential."

It stung that she thought the only reason he would seek her out was because of work. But then again, when had he ever made it about the personal? He'd always retreated behind the facade of the job. "I wanted to see how you were doing."

"We're fine. I should be back at work next week, but just part-time. Heading up the new division."

He'd heard all about Ellie's move into the housing sector from her father. He'd spent a lot of time talking to Henry Winston in the last few weeks, and found he liked Ellie's father a lot. He was becoming not just a friend to Finn, but also a sort of surrogate father. "I know."

"How are things going with the merger?"

"Pretty smooth. Your father had a phone conference meeting with all the employees to explain the changes. I think that helped set some minds at ease." They were still talking about business, and Finn knew he should reroute the conversation, but as always, he stayed in his comfort zone.

"How's the Piedmont project going?" Jiao, content with her cookie, climbed into Ellie's lap and laid her head on Ellie's shoulder. Ellie rubbed a circle of comfort onto Jiao's back. Finn watched, seeing the obvious love Ellie had for her new daughter. Jiao was clearly comfortable with Ellie, too, and snuggled against her adoptive mother as if they'd always been a family.

He started relating the details of the hospital project, all the while thinking that this was what they had become. Colleagues who worked at the same company. There was no hint of the woman he had been married to in her voice, no flirtation in her smile. It was just two co-workers having an ordinary conversation.

That was what Finn had said he wanted from the very beginning. How he had imagined things ending between them. They'd ally for the deal, work on the project, then split amicably and remain friends. But what he hadn't expected was how much that would hurt. He almost couldn't stand there and get the words out. Because he had fallen in love with her, and as much as he told himself he could be her colleague—

He couldn't. He wanted to be her husband, damn it.

He stopped midsentence and let out a sigh. "I can't do this."

"What?" Jiao had fallen asleep, and Ellie shifted to accommodate the additional weight.

"Stand here and talk about blueprints and city regulations as if there was never anything between us. As if we're practically strangers." Finn bent down, and searched for the woman he knew, but she was hidden behind those damnable sunglasses. "You took the coward's way out, Ellie."

"Me? How did I do that?"

"You didn't file for the annulment. Didn't call a lawyer. You just let us…dissolve."

"Finn, I have a child to raise. I can't be spending my time chasing—" She shook her head and looked away.

"Chasing what?"

She turned back to face him. The noise of the playground dropped away, and the world seemed to close in until it was just them. "Chasing something that will never be." Her voice shook a little. "We pretended really well for a while there, but both of us are too committed to other things to be committed to each other."

"Are you sure about that? Or is that just an excuse because you're just as afraid as I am of screwing this up?" Because he was afraid, scared as hell, to be honest. But the part of Finn that had been awakened by meeting Ellie refused to go away. And kept asking for more.

"I'm…" She let out a breath. "Okay, I am. But that's only because I have so much more at stake here." She nuzzled a kiss into Jiao's ebony hair. It fluttered like down against Ellie's cheek. "I can't take a chance that Jiao will be hurt again. She's already been through so much."

He'd said all this himself, hadn't he? Finn wanted to take the words back, to tell Ellie he was wrong. He understood Ellie's fear, because he'd felt it himself a hundred times before.

Was it fear, or was he trying to push for feelings she would never reciprocate? Was he repeating his past? "If you and I didn't work out—"

"You were right." She shrugged, but the movement was far from nonchalant. "She would be damaged. And I can't do that to her."

"But what about you, Ellie?"

"I'll be fine." But her voice shook again. "I am fine."

"Are you really?" He tried to search her gaze, but couldn't see past the dark lenses. What was going on inside her?

"Of course I'm fine." She cleared her throat, then got to her feet, hoisting Jiao onto her hip to free a hand to stuff their picnic things into the basket underneath.

She was leaving and he hadn't found the magic words to make her stay. "Ellie—"

"You know, Finn, you were right. I was afraid to fall in love. And so were you. It's a risk, maybe the biggest risk of all. But if you don't jump in with both feet, you'll never know what you were missing." She nuzzled her daughter's hair, and he saw the love bloom in Ellie's eyes. Then she bent down and buckled Jiao into the stroller. When she was done, she straightened and faced Finn with an impartial smile. "Anyway, I wanted to thank you for taking over the corporate side of WW. My father speaks highly of you."

"Is that what we're back to? Business only?"

She lifted her gaze to his and this time he could see the shimmer of tears behind her sunglasses. "When did we ever leave that, Finn?" Then she said goodbye to him, and left the park.

CHAPTER FOURTEEN

ELLIE told herself a hundred times that she had done the right thing by letting Finn go. That falling for him would only complicate things. Maybe he was right, maybe she was taking the coward's way out.

Okay, not maybe. Definitely.

She'd done one more cowardly thing after seeing him that day at the park—she'd contacted a lawyer of her own and put the annulment into motion. By now, Finn undoubtedly had received the legal papers from his lawyer. He hadn't called, hadn't stopped by, and her heart broke one last time. He hadn't been serious about them staying together—if he had, he would have fought the annulment. She'd been right not to risk her heart on him.

She dressed Jiao in a bright yellow sundress then strapped her into the stroller and set off down the sidewalk toward the park. The whole way, Jiao let out a steady stream of happy chatter, babbling in a jumbled mix of baby talk, Chinese and English. It was like music to Ellie's ears and she laughed along with her daughter. Jiao had adjusted pretty well to the changes in her life, and Ellie had great hopes for the future. Henry had been spoiling his new granddaughter mercilessly, with clothes and toys and visits.

"You wanna go to the park?" Ellie said, bending down to talk to Jiao.

Her daughter kicked her legs and waved her hands. "Yes, Momma. Yes!" Her English was improving every day. The little girl was bright and was picking up the second language quickly.

"Okay, let's go then." She pushed the stroller and increased her pace a little. "How about today I take you down the slide, and later we can go on the swings and—"

"Gou!" Jiao shouted, bouncing up and down. "Gou, Momma! Gou!"

Ellie's Chinese was minimal at best, and it took her a second to connect Jiao's enthusiastic words with the object of her attention. Across the street, a man was walking a little white poodle. Jiao kept pointing at it and shouting *"Gou!"* Ellie laughed. "That's a dog, honey. Dog."

"Dog," Jiao repeated. "Jiao dog?"

"No," Ellie said softly. "Not Jiao's dog."

"Jiao dog," her daughter repeated, reaching her fingers toward the white pooch, and Ellie pushed forward, putting more distance between them and the poodle. Jiao's voice trailed off in disappointment.

As Ellie walked, her mind went back to the day at the animal shelter with Finn. How he had opened up his heart, and let her see inside for just a little while. Every boy should have his dream, she had said. And so, too, should every girl.

Her dream had been the family in the two-story house. With all the laughter and the Thanksgiving dinners and the messes, and everything that came with that. She loved her daughter, loved her little home in the Back Bay, but a part of her still wondered—

What would it be like to have the kids and the house and the yard and the dog?

Had she made a mistake letting Finn go? Had she let her fears ruin her future happiness?

He had never left her mind, not really, though she had worked hard to forget him. She had come across the concert T-shirt the other day, and put it on, just because it reminded her of Finn. Then after a few minutes, she took it off and tucked it away in the back of her closet. Where she stored all the things that were memories now, not realities.

She'd buy a house in the suburbs and a dog, and have that dream herself. But the thought filled her with sadness.

If she did that, she'd be *content*. Maybe not ever truly happy.

Finn was right. She hadn't been brave enough to really push forward with this relationship when he'd offered her the chance. She'd backed off, so afraid of getting hurt again. She'd preached about risk, and not taken one herself.

She and Jiao rounded the corner and entered the park. Her daughter was practically bounding out of the stroller by the time Ellie stopped and unbuckled her. Jiao dashed over to the toddler-sized play area, complete with a rubber ground cover and a half dozen pint-sized puzzles and mazes for the little ones to play with. Jiao had already made friends at the park, and she toddled off with two other little girls she saw nearly every day. Ellie settled back on a bench and raised her face to the sun.

Something wet nuzzled her leg. Ellie jumped, let out a shriek, then looked down.

At the dark, moist snout of a Golden retriever. "Hey, you. What are you doing here?"

"Looking for you."

Finn's voice jerked Ellie's head up. "Finn." Then she

looked down at the dog again, and realized the retriever's leash was in Finn's hand. Her heart leaped at the sight of him and she knew that no piece of paper would ever make that stop. Damn. He still affected her. Maybe he always would. "Is this your dog?"

"Yup. Meet Heidi." Finn chuckled. "Wait. You already did."

She looked down again and realized it was, indeed, the dog from the shelter. "You...you adopted her?"

He nodded. "I did."

"Why? I mean, it's awesome, but I thought..."

"That I was the last person who would take on a dog?" He shrugged. "I am. Or I guess, I was. But something changed me recently."

She still couldn't believe she was seeing the shelter dog with Finn. He had gone back there, and given this puppy a home. It was one of the sweetest things she'd ever seen, and her heart melted all over again. "What changed you?"

He reached into his back pocket and pulled out a piece of paper. When he unfolded it, Ellie recognized it as the annulment agreement. Her heart sank. Had he signed it? Was it over?

"This came to my office the other day, and when I got it, it was like a slap across the face."

"Finn, I'm sorry, but we—"

"Let me finish. It hit me hard because I realized if I signed this, it was all over. I had lost you. Forever."

"You were right, though. I let this drag on, and I shouldn't have. Someone needed to pull the plug."

Finn bent down to her, his face level with hers, those blue eyes she loved so much capturing hers. Her heartbeat tripled, and she caught her breath. "Is this what you really want, Ellie?" His voice was low and quiet.

How she wanted to lie, wanted to just keep up the facade. All along, she'd been telling Finn to take a risk when she'd been the one too scared to do the same. She thought of the future that lay ahead. One where she was content, and never happy, and decided she didn't want that. Not anymore. "No." She shook her head and tears brimmed in her eyes. "I don't."

Finn reached up and cupped her jaw. Ellie leaned into that touch, craving it like oxygen. "Neither do I. Not one damned bit. You were so right about me. I picked Lucy because it was the practical decision, and told myself when it didn't work out, it was because love was too risky. But I was wrong. I never took that risk, Ellie. I never opened my heart. I made up this little list and tried to fit a relationship into a column, and then was surprised when it didn't work out." He ran a thumb along the line of her jaw, and caught her gaze. Held it. "Falling in love is risky. Riskier than anything I've ever done. So I came over here today because I couldn't let the most amazing woman I've ever met walk out of my life. Not without telling her one thing first."

"Tell her what?" It was the only word she could get out. Her breath caught in her throat, held, while she waited for his answer. Damn, this man had her heart. Maybe he always had.

Finn's smile curved across his face, higher on one side than the other, and filling her with a tentative joy. "I love you, Ellie. I fell in love with you the first time I saw you, but I didn't know it. I love the way you talk, I love the way you work, I love the way you smile. Every time I see you, I feel…happy."

Happy. Not content. "Oh, Finn—"

"Let me finish." He let out a long breath, and his gaze softened. "I've never been very good at relationships.

Give me a drafting board and a pencil and I can handle anything you throw my way. But when it comes to telling people how I feel…not exactly my strong suit. I guess it was because after my parents died, my little brothers looked to me for comfort. For answers. I couldn't break down and sob on their shoulders. I had to let them sob on mine. And as they got older, I kept on being the rock they stood on."

"They do. I can tell by the way they talk about you. They respect and admire you a lot."

He grinned a little at that, clearly surprised to hear his brothers speak so well of him. "Being a rock came with a price, though. I never wanted to rely on anyone, to be vulnerable to anyone, and most of all, I didn't want to let anyone down. Or take that risk you kept asking me to take." His fingers tangled in her hair and Ellie let out a little sigh. "I told myself I'd keep my heart out of it and then we could walk away and no one would be hurt. But that plan failed."

Across from Ellie, Jiao was standing at the edge of the toddler playground, watching them. Ellie sent her daughter a little wave. "How did your plan fail?"

"My heart got involved the very first day, even if I didn't want to admit it to myself or to you. And still, I wouldn't take that risk." His smile widened. "But then when I got the papers dissolving our marriage, I realized all I want to do is stay married to you, Ellie. Forever. I want to open my heart. I want to jump off that marriage cliff with you and trust that it's all going to work out for the next fifty, hell, hundred years. I want—" his gaze went to Jiao, and the smile grew a little more "—us to be a family. The question is whether you do, too. You took a risk adopting a little girl from halfway around the world. I'm asking you to take a risk and fall in love with me."

She looked into his eyes, and felt the fear that she had clutched so tightly for so long begin to dissolve. Right here was everything she'd ever wanted. All she had to do was reach out and take it. She could tell him no now and watch him walk away.

And regret it forever. She'd been given a second chance. She'd be a fool to throw it away.

So she took a deep breath, then tugged the annulment papers out of his hand and ripped them in two. "I don't want an annulment, Finn. Not now, not later."

She caught the glint of a gold band on his left hand. He'd never taken it off. And her cautious heart finally let go of the last guardrails and trusted. Her husband. The man she loved.

"I don't, either," Finn said then he drew her into his arms and kissed her, a tender, sweet kiss, the kind that would stay in her memory forever. She felt treasured and loved and…like a wife. "I love you, Ellie."

"I love you, too, Finn." She ran a hand through his hair and stared deep into his sky-blue eyes. How she knew those eyes, knew every inch of his face, every line in his brow. "I love you *because* you are the Hawk."

"The man who swoops in and buys up the competition?" He scowled.

She shook her head. "No. That's not what I mean. I looked up hawks one day when I took Jiao to the library. And yes, they're fierce predators, but they're also fiercely loyal and protective. They pick a mate and a nest and they stay there for life." She looked at Finn McKenna and saw the hawk inside of him, a man who would do anything for those he loved—he'd been doing it with his brothers ever since he was a child and he had done it for her simply because she had asked. He was a hawk—a man she could depend upon forever.

"So I should start to like the Hawk nickname, huh?" He grinned.

"Maybe you should." She smiled, then pressed a kiss to his lips. She thought of how close she had come to ending their relationship with a piece of paper. "I was so afraid to believe that you could be the kind of man I could depend on, count on to be there when I needed you. I never realized that the very traits I admired about you were the same ones that make you the perfect man for me. The perfect husband, and perfect father, if you want to be."

His gaze traveled to Jiao, and she saw his features soften as a smile curved across his face. "I want to be the kind of dad who pulls out pictures of my kid's band performance at a meeting and who hangs up their artwork in my office. I don't want to be content, Ellie." He swiveled back to face her. "Not anymore."

"Neither do I, Finn. Neither do I." She held his gaze for a long moment, then put out an arm, and waved over Jiao. "Then let me introduce you to your daughter."

Jiao hurried across the playground to Ellie's side. But when she saw the stranger, she hung back, biting her bottom lip, and giving Finn tentative, shy glances. "Jiao, I want you to meet Finn," Ellie said. "And Heidi the dog."

Jiao wiggled two fingers at Finn, then dropped back a little more. Her head popped up when she noticed the dog. Jiao looked at Ellie with a question in her eyes. "Dog?"

Ellie nodded. "Jiao's dog."

The little girl's eyes widened. She pointed at Heidi, then back at herself. "Jiao dog?"

"Yes," Finn said. He gave the leash a light tug, and Heidi scrambled to her feet, then pushed her furry head against Jiao's shoulder. The little girl laughed, exuberance bursting on Jiao's face. Heidi licked her face, tail wagging like a flag in the wind.

"Heidi, Jiao dog," the little girl said softly, happily. "Jiao dog!"

Then Jiao paused and took a step back, looking up at the man who was, essentially a stranger to her. "Momma?"

Ellie bent to her daughter's level, and waited until Finn did the same. "This is Finn," she said to Jiao. "He's your dad."

Jiao plopped a thumb into her mouth and hung back, studying Finn from under the veil of her lashes.

Finn put out his hand. "Hello, Jiao. It's nice to meet you."

Jiao paused a long moment, looking up at Ellie, then over at Finn. Her eyes were wide, wondering about this new development in her life. The little girl who had left China with nothing suddenly had a mother, a father, a dog. Ellie nodded. "It's okay," Ellie said.

Still, Jiao hesitated. The thumb wavered in her mouth.

"How about we start with Jiao dog?" Finn asked the little girl. "Would you like that?"

After a moment, Jiao nodded and gave Finn a shy smile. "Okay."

Finn ran his hand over Heidi's neck, and Jiao's smaller hand joined his. The two of them petted the patient dog for a long time, not saying a word, just bonding one second at a time while Heidi panted softly. Then Jiao shifted and stood closer to Finn. She looked up into his face. "Jiao...dad?"

"Yes." Finn nodded then met Ellie's gaze. Tears of joy glimmered in his eyes. "Yes, I'm Jiao's dad. And Ellie's husband."

"You are indeed," Ellie whispered, thanking the stars above for this amazing gift. "For real."

Then Finn reached out both his arms and drew all his girls into one great big hug. And on a sunny playground in the middle of Boston, a family was born. They laughed, and the dog barked, and the sounds of their happiness rang in the air, telling Finn and Ellie that from now on, the floors of their home would never echo again.

* * * * *

HOW THE PLAYBOY GOT SERIOUS

BY
SHIRLEY JUMP

To my readers.
You all are the best part of my job, and
I am humbled and honoured to write books you enjoy.

CHAPTER ONE

LIFE as Riley McKenna knew it was about to change.
And change in a big way. He sensed the change coming,
like the shift in the wind when summer yielded to fall.

"I love you, Riley, but I have to say this." Mary
McKenna looked her grandson straight in the eye, with
the steady light blue gaze that told him she was about
to say something he didn't want to hear. "It's high time
you grew up."

Gray-haired, elegant and poised, Mary sat in one
of two rose-patterned Windsor chairs in what was
called the morning room but that Riley and his brothers had long ago dubbed the "serious room," because
that was where their grandmother held all her serious
talks. When they were young, they knew getting called
into the morning room meant a long and stern lecture.
Even at twenty-six, Riley was occasionally summoned
to this space—and that was exactly what Mary did—
summoned—and given the familiar sermon about responsibility and maturity.

Mary had a presence about her, built over years of
helming first the family, then the family business. Truth
be told, she intimidated most people and even sometimes Riley, because she made no bones about her feelings—ever. So when Mary wanted to have a serious

talk, Riley knew enough to listen. But that didn't mean he wasn't going to try to escape the lecture about to come.

"Gran, it's my birthday." He shot her the grin that usually sweet-talked his grandmother into leniency. "That means I'm more grown up today than yesterday."

More or less.

He'd spent the night before his birthday in a bar, and had plans to hit a whole list of them tonight with his friends. He knew he should be looking forward to the night out, but for some reason, the thought of trading the same conversations with the same people over the same beverages sounded...

Boring.

He was just hungover. Or something. He'd be fine once he had a nice dark ale in his hands.

"That is not what I meant, and you know it." Gran sipped a cup of tea while the sun streamed in from the picture window behind her and kissed everything in the stately Victorian style room with gold. The house was over a hundred years old, a towering three-level clothed in dark paneling and the occasional modern touch. Mary could have afforded ten times the house but she had chosen to stay in the place where she had raised her children and loved her husband. To Riley, the house had a certain amount of dependability and comfort, which was half the reason he had yet to move out of the guest house that sat just down the driveway from the main house. He liked being here, liked being surrounded by his DNA's history. And he liked to keep an eye on his grandmother. She had a tendency to do too much, and to rarely listen to anyone who told her otherwise. The McKenna stubborn streak was alive and well in Mary McKenna.

Mary smoothed out a wrinkle that had dared to crimp her plaid skirt. "Your birthday is an occasion to rethink your priorities and focus on more mature pursuits."

More mature pursuits. Which to his grandmother, Riley knew meant getting married. Settling down. Something he avoided at all costs. He glanced out the window and saw a golden fur ball wandering the grounds. His oldest brother's adopted shelter dog, one of the nicest pets Riley had ever met. No wonder Finn spoiled her with treats and toys. "Finn drop his dog off here?"

"I'm watching Heidi for a few days while they take a trip together. She's a wonderful dog." Then Gran leaned forward. "I won't let you change the subject, Riley. This is serious business." She held up a newspaper. "Have you read this morning's *Herald*?"

Uh-oh. "Uh, no."

She laid it down again. "When you do, you will see that you have a starring role in the media. Once again." She sighed. "Really, do we need the world to know every single time you are caught in a compromising position?"

Oh. That. The woman he'd been with that night at the gala had been a little too eager, and he'd been a little too willing. He'd forgotten there'd be reporters skulking about. Before he could say stop, his date had her dress hiked up and her body pressed against his. There'd been a sound behind them, and the entire awkward moment was caught on film. Riley cringed. He hated seeing that look of disappointment on his grandmother's face. He'd let her down. Again. "It was a mistake. I had a little too much to drink—"

"No excuse. You are far past the age where you can act like a fool and get away with it. Your brother has just shipped off to Afghanistan, volunteering, I might add, to help the wounded. And instead of focusing on Brody's charity, the reporter has chosen to make the entire story about you and your…indiscretions." His grandmother leaned closer. "You do realize that you did this at a fundraiser for wounded veterans? The last thing the McKenna Foundation needs is publicity like this. From a family member, no less."

"You're right. It shouldn't have happened." He let out a long breath. "Sometimes I just don't think."

"This isn't the first time, Riley. I love you, but I can't have you smearing the family name." She shook her head. "You get swayed by a pretty smile and a nice pair of legs and forget that you're supposed to be a responsible adult."

Responsible adult. Those were two words no one had ever used to describe Riley. Finn and Brody, yes, but not Riley. Finn, the married CEO, and Brody, a general practice physician now volunteering his skills half a world away. For the hundredth time, Riley felt like he could never measure up to their examples. He excelled in one area—not being excellent.

For a long time that hadn't bothered him at all. He'd always been too busy seeking the next party, the next pretty face, as his grandmother said, to worry what anyone thought of him. But lately…

Well, lately he'd been thinking far too much.

Gran sighed. "I'm getting old—"

"You're decades away from old."

"—and I'm tired of waiting for great grandchildren."

"Finn just gave you one. And they have another on the way already." His oldest brother Finn had taken to marriage like a bear to salmon fishing. Married, one adopted child, and a baby due in a little over seven months. Riley had to admit that sometimes, when he saw how happy Finn and Ellie were, he felt a little…jealous. But only because Finn was so damned happy, it seemed like he'd caught a smiling disease.

"And now it's your turn," Mary said.

"Whoa, whoa. What about Brody? He's next in line for the yoke."

His grandmother pursed her lips at that. "Marriage is not chaining oxen together. Your grandfather and I—"

"Were the exception to the rule. Nobody stays married like that anymore." Even though his grandfather had died a little over three years ago, Mary still carried a torch for the man she had loved for more than five decades. They had been a loving, kind couple, the type that held hands when they rode in the car or walked the neighborhood. When Riley had been young, it had been nice to see, something that made him wonder if he'd ever have a relationship like that. Then he'd grown up, started dating, and realized his grandparents' lifelong love affair was about as common as unicorns in the zoo.

His grandmother took another sip of tea, then laid the china cup into the saucer. "You're just jaded. If you would settle down you might find love is a lot better than you think."

"I'm happy the way I am."

"Perhaps." She toyed with the teaspoon on the tray beside her, then lifted her gaze to her grandson's. Even at seventy-eight, Mary's mind was sharp and agile. She still ran McKenna Media, the advertising company started by her husband. She'd been grumbling about stepping down for years, but had yet to take even a day off. Riley suspected Mary kept working both to stay close to the husband she missed and to keep her days full. "You haven't really done anything with your life yet, Riley."

"I work, Gran."

She scoffed. "You show up at the office, goof off and collect a paycheck."

"Hey, we all have to be good at something. That's my area of expertise."

His grandmother didn't laugh at the joke, or even so much as crack a smile. The mood in the serious room tensed. "I have indulged you far too much because you are the youngest. I always treated you differently, because—" she sighed, and her pale blue eyes softened "—I felt bad for you. Losing your parents at such a young age, then being uprooted from the only home you ever knew to live with your grandfather and I—"

Riley waved that off. "I was fine."

Mary's gaze locked on his. "Were you?"

He looked away, studying the gilt-framed landscape hanging on the far wall. Painted sunlight dappled oil-created trees and brush-formed flowers, and caressed the roofline of a cottage nestled in a fictional forest. A perfect little world, captured in Technicolor paint. "I was fine," Riley repeated.

"I think if you tell yourself that often enough, you'll eventually believe it," Mary said softly.

Riley let out a long breath. He wasn't much for serious talks, or serious conversational topics, or, come to mention it, the serious room. Altogether far too stuffy and formal. And well, hell, *serious*. "I'm supposed to be meeting someone for lunch, Gran." He rose halfway out of the chair. "I really need to get going."

"Cancel your plans."

He cocked a brow. "Oh, now I get it. Are you planning a birthday party for me, Gran? You know you've never been able to surprise me."

"No party this year, Riley. In fact, I think it's high

time your party days were behind you." She steepled her fingers and brought them to her lips. "Sit back down please."

Uh-oh. Riley recognized that stance. It meant Gran had an idea—one he knew he wasn't going to like. He lowered his lanky frame back into the uncomfortable Windsor chair.

"I think you need a real wake-up call, Riley. Consequently—" Gran paused and her pale eyes nailed him like a bug on a board "—I'm cutting you off."

The words hung in the air for a long time before Riley processed them. "You're...what?"

"Effective immediately, you are fired from McKenna Media, not that you had a real job there as it was. And you will also be expected to pay a reasonable rent on the guest house. Every month, on the first. Which happens to be two weeks away."

Gran meant business. No mistaking that.

Riley opened his mouth to argue. To joke. To cajole. To employ any of a dozen techniques he'd used before to talk his stern grandmother out of punishments and edicts.

He didn't. Instead he considered her words and realized she had a point.

Gran had never approved of the way he lived his life. But what his grandmother didn't understand was that Riley didn't spend his days without any sense of commitment because he wanted to shirk responsibilities. It was because he had yet to find a direction that interested him.

He'd tried nearly every job at McKenna Media, and within a few days, been bored to death. He'd dated dozens of beautiful women, but not found a single one who dared his heart to take a risk.

Gran probably wanted Riley to go out and find yet another job in a field he could hardly stand, then settle down with one of her friends' single, available granddaughters. But what Riley really wanted was…

A challenge. Something that made him rush to get out of bed in the morning. Maybe he needed something—God help him—with substance.

Riley had always known this day would come, and for some reason, instead of being panicked by it, he felt…energized. For the first time in a long time.

Had his partying ways finally grown tiresome? No, he told himself. It was a minor bump, a moment of ennui, nothing more. He'd spend a few days doing things his grandmother's way, prove to her that he wasn't nearly as irresponsible as he looked, and then be back to his old life in no time.

"Okay," he said. "I'll do it."

She blinked her surprise. "Well, good." She reached into her pocket and handed him a slip of paper. "Your final paycheck. I'm kicking you out, and cutting you off, but I don't want you to starve the first day."

Riley gave his grandmother a soft smile, then leaned down and brushed a kiss across her wrinkled cheek. "I'll be fine, Gran." He pressed the check back into her hand, then said goodbye and headed out the door, and into a world he had never truly experienced.

He thought it would be easy, like everything else in his life had been.

He was wrong.

Stace Kettering had had enough. "I quit, Frank." She tossed her apron on the counter in emphasis, and slapped her order pad down beside it. The last of the breakfast crowd had left a few minutes earlier, giving Stace her first break since five in the morning. She grabbed a glazed donut out from under the glass dome on the counter and took a bite. "I'm serious. I quit."

Frank let out a laugh. His barrel belly shook with the sound, and his wide smile broke into an even wider grin. Frank Simpson had been the head chef and part owner of Morning Glory Diner for thirty years—almost as long as anyone could remember the burger that had made Frank's famous. Stace had worked there nearly all her life—almost as long as anyone could remember a Kettering offspring at the counter at Frank's.

"I've heard that before," Frank said, emerging from the kitchen to plant his beefy palms on the counter. He gave Stace a wink. "A hundred times. No, maybe two hundred." He picked up her apron and held it out to her.

"I'm serious this time. I'm done." She ignored the apron and took another bite of donut. The sweet glaze melted like heaven on her tongue.

"Is Walter giving you a hard time again? You know he means well."

"He is the grumpiest man in the city of Boston. No, the state of Massachusetts."

Frank chuckled. "I think the entire You-nited States."

That got a laugh out of Stace. "I think you're right." She plopped onto one of the counter stools and let out a sigh. "Why does he always pick my table?"

"He likes you."

Walter was a daily customer at Morning Glory Diner, though Lord only knew why he kept returning when all he did was find fault with everything from the forks to the fries. And every single time, he made sure he was seated in Stace's section, as if he was on a one-man mission to ruin her day. "He told me I was the slowest waitress in the entire solar system, complained that his water was flat—"

"Flat water?" Frank arched a brow. "Did he expect it to be round?"

"I think he ran out of things to complain about." Stace let out another laugh. She put down the donut, then reached for the apron and snatched it back, tugging it over her head before fastening the strings in the back. "Okay, so I won't quit today. But if you don't hire someone else soon, I will quit. On principle." It had been two weeks since Irene had gone on maternity leave, which had left Stace to single-handedly carry the weight of the diners at Frank's until she returned. The tips were great and much needed, but at the end of day, Stace was so tired she needed to be rolled to her little house eight subway stops away. And given the way things had been going at home lately, Stace needed to be alert. There wasn't just her to worry about anymore.

Frank gave her a smile. "You're exhausted, honey."

"I'm okay. Walter just stressed me out, that's all." She eyed the older man. "I'm more worried about how you are. I know business has been down for a while and I hate to see you working so hard."

He wagged a finger at her. "Nope, not falling for that. You know me, if I wasn't fine, I'd be complaining."

She laughed. "Frank, you never complain." Then her gaze softened and her hand covered his. "You keep talking about retiring, but never do. You deserve some time off, Frank."

He waved that off. "If I retire, who's going to make the famous Morning Glory burger?"

"Me."

Frank laughed. "No offense, Stace, but you can't even make grilled cheese. Your dad, God rest his soul, was the same way. Good at the books, good in the front of the house, but a nightmare on the grill." Frank's big brown eyes softened. "I know one thing, though. He'd be awful proud of you."

She glanced around the diner, at the building that her father had built. The morning glory border he had painted himself, the chairs and tables he'd picked out. Every wall in this place still seemed to beat with her father's heart. She missed him, but at least here, she could be close to him, and his memory. For a second, her father's presence filled her heart, surrounded her like a hug. "Thank you, Frank."

He shrugged, then fiddled with a spoon on the counter. "How's things with Jeremy?"

"We're getting there. He's a handful." Handful didn't even begin to describe her nephew, who was angry at his mother, angry at the world…just plain angry. He needed an outlet, something to help him work through the shock of his mother's abandonment, but Stace had yet to find anything the boy would stick with. She bit back a sigh. Later, she'd worry about that. For now, she'd focus on making enough money to handle the additional cost of an extra mouth to feed. While at the same time trying to find a way to increase business at the diner.

"Poor kid's been through a lot," Frank said. "You need anything, you come ask me. I'll be there for you."

Stace's hand covered Frank's beefy palm. The older man had already been a great presence in Jeremy's life, serving as a surrogate grandfather just as he'd served as Stace's surrogate father. Frank had given her a raise she hadn't asked for, quietly dropped off a new TV at her house when hers broke, and taken Jeremy school shopping when he'd refused to go with Stace. Even as she insisted she could handle it herself, Frank stepped in anyway. "I know you will."

Frank's eyes misted, but he let out a cough to cover for the momentary emotion. Frank was a man who loved well and hard, but rarely let that emotion show. Stace had only seen him cry once, and the sight of it had broken her heart because she knew the pain in Frank's heart lanced deep.

Frank cleared his throat. "Anyway, I promise, I'll hire the next person who walks in that door." He pointed toward the diner's glass entrance.

"Right." She laughed. "You've been promising to hire another server for two weeks now, and no one has even gotten past the application stage." Stace pointed at the Help Wanted sign propped in the window. "That thing is doing nothing but gathering dust."

He shrugged. "I'm picky. I can't find enough Stace clones."

"Now you're just buttering me up."

Frank grinned. "Did it work?"

"Yes. But just for today." She swiped the order pad off the counter, and tucked the pen into her pocket. Every time she reached the quitting point, Frank found a way to convince her to stay. Heck, he was right. She'd have stayed with or without the jokes and compliments. Her loyalty to Frank Simpson ran bone-deep, and always would.

"Good." He thumbed the straps of his apron and let out a long breath. "Back to the fryer for me. Those bloomin' onions don't bloom on their own, you know." Just as Frank turned back to the kitchen, the door of the diner opened, causing the overhead bell to let out a soft jangle. The two of them pivoted toward the sound.

Riley McKenna.

If there was a customer Stace dreaded almost as much as Walter, it was Riley. He was a handsome man— if one was the kind of woman who found blue eyes and dark hair appealing. And a charming man—if one liked a man with a ready smile and quick wit. But he was also a playboy, and if there was one thing Stace had no tolerance for, it was playboys.

Even if he took her breath away when he smiled. Damn, he was a good-looking man. Too bad he was all wrong for her.

She'd seen his picture in the papers with the girlfriend of the minute, heard other women talk about him with an actual swoon in their voice. As far as she could tell, the youngest McKenna hadn't followed in the family traditions of meaningful work or charitable organizations. Unless attending every party in the greater Boston area was considered giving back to society.

Stacey avoided men like Riley McKenna like the plague. She'd learned a long time ago that a nice smile and charming words were merely a cover for deeper flaws. Thank God she'd woken up before she married such a man. She'd known Jim for years, and fallen for his charismatic ways over and over again. He'd proposed on a Sunday and left town on a Tuesday—

With a girl he'd met the night before. She'd been fooled for so long, blind to his lies, because she'd wanted to believe in that smile. It had taken her a year to get over the betrayal, and from here on out, Stace would avoid men like that, thank you very much. And that meant avoiding Riley McKenna. And his smile.

Riley nearly always sat in her section and ordered an omelet. Not one of the dozen combinations on the menu, but always something of his own creation, which drove Stace crazy but didn't seem to bother Frank. She knew, from the lackadaisical way he ate his breakfast and the dozens of phone calls she'd overheard where Riley discussed the latest hot party or vacuous date, that his life was about as serious as confetti.

And on top of that, he seemed to think flirting was on the menu. He teased her, smiled at her, and had asked for her number once. Typical. Thinking every woman was just going to fall at his feet.

To her, perpetual flirt Riley McKenna was just another entitled bachelor in a city teeming with them. A man whom she suspected hadn't seen a hard day of work in his life, and never appreciated the hard work of others.

"How are you, Frank?" Riley shot them both a grin, then slid onto one of the counter stools.

"Good, good," Frank said. "And you?"

Riley's smile faltered. "I've had better days."

"Well, if it'll make you feel any better, I've got apple pie on the menu today," Frank said.

"Not today, thanks. Unless you're giving out free samples. I'm, ah, currently between funds right now."

"You?" Frank asked. "What, did you spend too much on a date last night?"

"Something like that." Riley gave Frank the cocky grin he gave everyone. The grin that said he'd probably spent his night bedding yet another in a long string of blondes. Stace kept on working. And ignoring him.

Stace soaked a cloth in disinfectant cleaner then started wiping down the pale yellow laminate counter. There wasn't much time before the lunch crowd began to filter in, and lots to do.

"I've been out looking for a job," Riley said.

"I take it the job search hasn't gone too well?"

Riley's grin raised a little on one side. "I'm not qualified to do much."

Frank laughed. Stace restrained herself from issuing a hearty agreement. "I'm sure you'll find something that works for you," Frank said.

"Actually…" Riley began.

Something white caught Stace's eye and she raised her gaze to see what it was. She froze.

"I thought I'd apply here," Riley said. He lifted the Help Wanted sign in his hands, the same one that had been in the window just moments before, and gave Frank a smile. "I figure I eat here enough, I might as well earn my keep."

Frank arched a brow. "You want to be a waiter? Here?"

"Yup. Consider this my official application." Riley slid the sign across the counter.

Frank sent Stace a glance. She mouthed "no," and waved her hands. Frank wouldn't dare. He'd said he'd hire someone, but surely he wanted someone with experience, someone who would be a help, not a hindrance. Someone who had a good work ethic. "Frank…"

Frank grinned at her word of caution, then turned back to Riley. "I told Miss Stace here that I'd hire the next person who walked through that door—"

He wouldn't.

"And since I'm a man of my word—"

He couldn't.

"You're hired, Riley McKenna." Frank reached over and clapped Riley on the shoulder. "Welcome to Morning Glory Diner. Stace here will be glad to show you the ropes."

He did.

Stace plastered a smile she didn't feel on her face, and faced her worst nightmare. An irresponsible womanizer who was going to make her life a living hell.

CHAPTER TWO

ONE day, two tops, Riley figured, and his grandmother would call him back to McKenna Media. Riley could have called in a favor with a friend, but that wouldn't prove he could do anything other than pick up the phone. Sure, waiting tables wasn't the ideal job, but it would do for now, and prove his point to his grandmother that he wasn't the irresponsible man she thought him to be. He looked around the bustling diner. He'd wanted a challenge, something a little different.

And this fit the bill to a T.

So Riley donned the black apron imprinted with Morning Glory Diner on the pocket, grabbed an order pad and pen, and crossed to the first set of customers he saw. Before he could even open his mouth, that waitress—Sally, Sandy—rushed over and nearly tackled him. "You can't take this table."

"I'm doing it. Watch me take their order, too." He clicked the pen, and faced the two construction workers whose broad frames nearly filled either side of the booth. Beefy guys in dusty T-shirts and jeans. "What can I get you guys?"

The first one, a nearly bald fiftyish man wearing a bright yellow hat emblazoned with Irving in thick black marker, gave Riley an are-you-an-idiot look. "Menus."

Riley glanced down and realized he had forgotten that important first step. No problem. He'd get it right the next time. This was waiting tables; it wasn't rocket science. "Right. Those would be helpful. Unless you just want to make up an order, and I'll zip it back to Frank in the kitchen." Riley thumbed toward the kitchen.

Sally/Sandy smacked his arm. "You can't just make up food. I've told you that a hundred times." Then she turned to the two men. "I apologize. He's new. Probably won't last long. Let me get you some menus." She turned on her sneakered heel, and started to walk away, then thought better of it, and grabbed a fistful of Riley's shirt and hauled him backward.

Riley's feet tangled and nearly brought him to the ground. "Hey, hey, hey! What are you doing?"

"Getting you out of there before you do any more damage." She stopped by the hostess station, snatched up two menus, then released Riley. "Stay." She punctuated the word with a glare. "And I mean it."

"Woof."

The glare intensified, then she stalked off, handed the menus to the customers, and returned to Riley's side. "Hey, all I did was forget menus. You're acting like I committed a federal crime," he said.

"Just stay out of my way and we'll get along just fine."

"I'm supposed to be making your life easier."

"Well, you're not."

She started to walk away, but he caught up with her and turned her to face him. "I was hired to help you."

"Well, you're not."

He eyed Sally/Sandy. He'd had the pretty blonde as a waitress a dozen times, and though he'd tried his best to get to know her, she'd resisted. Maybe she hated him. Why?

Maybe because he'd never learned her name, something he now regretted. And couldn't remedy because she didn't have on a name tag.

She was a beautiful woman with a petite, tight body and a smile that rarely made an appearance. She had wide green eyes, long blond hair that he'd only ever seen tied back, and a quick wit. He'd seen her friendly banter with other customers, and wondered why she'd always been cold with him on the dozens of occasions when he'd eaten here.

He'd asked her out a few times, flirted with her often, and she'd always resisted. Now he needed to get along with her—at least on the job. Ordinarily, he wouldn't care—he'd just avoid her at work or just avoid work, period. But this time, the job mattered, not just because he needed the paycheck, but because he wanted to prove himself, to Gran, to himself, and yes, in an odd way, to this angry waitress. "I admit, I have no idea what the hell I'm doing here," he said. "I'm on a steep learning curve, and that means I might get underfoot a little."

"A lot," she corrected.

"Okay, a lot. But I'm here to help, to take some of the burden off your shoulders. If you let me."

She let out a sigh. "What am I going to do with you?"

"Train me." He put up his two hands. "I can sit, stay and even beg."

"Just…stay," she said now. "You're no good to me out there. You'll just make my job harder."

"Why? You think I can't write down an order and deliver it to Frank?" He'd seen her do it a hundred times. It didn't look hard at all.

"Honestly, no."

"Why not?"

"Because a man with manicured nails and a thousand-dollar haircut is used to giving orders, not taking them."

Riley winced. Did people really see him that way? A useless playboy with nothing but time on his hands for mischief? And if they did, could he blame them? What had he done with his life up until now? But he was determined to change that, at least here, now, in this diner. "Frank hired me for a reason."

"Because he promised me he'd hire the next person who walked through that door. It could have been a monkey, and Frank would have given him a job just to prove his point."

"Which is?"

She let out a gust. "What do you care? You're only here because you needed something else to amuse you." The bell over the door jangled, and two more customers stepped inside the diner. She grabbed some menus out of the bin by the hostess station. "I don't want to be part of your little 'live like the common folk do' project." She put air quotes around the words.

"I'm not—"

But she was already gone, seeming to whoosh across the tiled floor like a tidal wave. In the space of thirty seconds, she had the second couple seated, given them their menus, then returned to the construction workers and taken their orders. She tore a page off the pad, slipped behind the counter and slid it across the stainless steel bar in the kitchen to Frank, calling off something Riley couldn't understand but sounded like "flop two, over easy" and "give it wings."

Frank garbled something back, and Sally/Sandy disappeared into the kitchen for a second.

Riley had to admit, he was impressed. He had watched her bustle around the diner, a tiny dynamo in a slim fitting pair of jeans, a hot pink Morning Glory Diner T-shirt, and a bobbing blond ponytail. Every time he'd seen her, she'd been like that, a human bee, flitting from one table to the next. She was fast, and efficient, even if her customer service skills with him were almost nonexistent. Maybe the job was more stressful than it looked. Many times, she'd been the only waitress in here when he stopped in for his morning breakfast, since lunch was almost always at McGill's Pub with his brother Finn.

Apparently help was hard to come by, because he'd seen that Help Wanted sign often over the years, and seen dozens of waitresses who worked here a few weeks, then moved on. The only constant was Sally/Sandy—he was sure it was something with an *S*—she had been here every day, and always with the same brisk, no-nonsense approach to the job.

"Hey, buddy, you just going to stand there?"

Riley leaned against the hostess station, flipping through one of the menus. He'd been given the menu before, but never really looked at it. He'd just ordered what he wanted and figured if they didn't have the ingredients, they would have told him. Now, though, it might be a good idea to get more familiar with it. Knowing Sally/Sandy, there'd be a quiz later.

"Buddy!"

Frank's offered a hell of a lot of food for such a small place. He'd started coming here in the mornings for breakfast because it was on the way between his subway stop and the offices of McKenna Media. Not to mention the Morning Glory's coffee was better than any he'd ever had. Riley scanned the pages of breakfast and lunch offerings, noted there was no dinner service. Working half days sounded good to him. He'd have his evenings free.

Except, the thought of spending an evening in yet another bar didn't thrill him anymore. Maybe it was being another year older. Maybe it was the shock of Gran's edict. Maybe it was a need for new friends. Whatever the problem was, he knew one thing.

He wanted more…depth to his days.

"Hey, moron!"

Riley jerked his attention toward the construction guys. "You can't talk to her like that."

"Her who? We're talking to you, Tweedledee." The two guys snickered, then the big one—the one with the hat that said Irving—wiggled his fingers like he was feigning sign language. "Two coffees. You know, the hot stuff in cups?"

"I know what coffee is."

"Good. Get us some. *Now*."

Bunch of Neanderthals ordering people around. Riley leaned against the hostess station and crossed his arms over his chest. Considered dumping the pot in the man's lap, just to prove the point. "No. Not unless you say please."

Irving's face turned red. His fist tightened on the table. Before he could open his mouth, Sally/Sandy came sailing past Riley, two cups in one hand, a hot pot of coffee in the other. The cups landed on the table with a soft clatter, and she filled them to just under the brim without spilling a drop. "Don't mind him. He's not really a waiter."

"What is he?" Irving said.

"I think you already called it. What was the word?" She put a finger to her lips. "Oh yes, moron."

The two men laughed some more at that. They thanked her, then sat back and started talking about work.

The waitress had an ease with smoothing the customers' ruffled feathers. He'd noticed that about her before—she'd turned more than one disgruntled frown into a smile. It was what had interested him about her before, and still did now. She was a contradiction. And that intrigued him. A lot.

Sally/Sandy returned, grabbed Riley's shirt again and tugged him around to the other side of the counter. She was surprisingly strong for such a petite woman.

"Hey, go easy on the manhandling," Riley said and gently disengaged her hand.

She snorted. "Manhandling. Right."

He leaned against the counter and eyed her. "Why do you hate me so much?"

"I don't hate you. You annoy me. There's a difference." He opened his mouth to ask a question but she put a hand up and stopped him. "Listen, I'd love to talk all day about your faults—"

"I don't have any faults." He grinned. "Okay, maybe one."

"But the lunch crowd will be here any second, and I have work to do."

"So do I. Are you going to let me do my job?"

"You can't handle this job."

"Let me prove it to you." He took a step closer. Wow, she had pretty eyes. They were the color of emeralds, a deep, dark green that seemed to beckon him in. "Listen, I've watched you work, and if you ask me, you work too hard."

"This job demands hard work."

"Not if you have readily available help to call on.

Something I've never seen you do, even when the other woman was working here. I can be useful, you know."

She let out a long breath, and Riley found himself wondering what was in that breath that she wasn't saying. What weights sat on her delicate shoulders. "I just feel better doing things myself."

"Asking for help doesn't make you weak. Just smart."

She cocked a brow. "And asking for *your* help, what does that make me?"

"Brilliant." He grinned.

She eyed him for a long, long time, while the coffee-pot percolated and the hum of conversation filled the air. "All right, I'll be better about letting you help. But stay out of my way and don't screw up. Don't flirt with the customers, and don't flirt with me. Just keep your head down and work." She narrowed her gaze at him. "Because when you screw up, it costs me, and I can't afford to let that happen. Got it?"

"Got it, captain." He gave her a mock salute.

She scowled. "And don't call me captain."

He leaned in, gave her another grin. "What should I call you?"

She held his gaze for a long moment. "Stace would be fine."

Stace. He liked that name. A short, no-nonsense name seemed to suit her.

"And you can call me Riley," he said, putting out his hand to shake hers. "I like it a whole lot better than moron."

Riley McKenna. The man had clearly been put on this earth—and in this diner—to drive her nuts. Stace had to stay on top of him for the entire lunch wave, which only complicated her job. He couldn't take an order,

couldn't remember the menus, didn't know where anything was, and delivered the wrong food to the wrong
table five times.

Not to mention he moved like a turtle on Valium.

He'd told her to let him help her, and she now regretted agreeing.

Worst of all, he kept attracting her attention. Tall,
dark-haired, blue-eyed, the kind of guy that wore a smile
like it was cologne. He had on dark wash jeans and a
golf shirt, with boat shoes, even though she doubted
he had been heading for a boat today. She had to force
herself more than once to concentrate on her job, instead of on him.

When the lunch demand eased, Stace slipped into the
kitchen. "What were you thinking?" she said.

Frank put a finger to his temples. "Uh, that my salsa
dancing days are behind me, but I can still cut a mean
foxtrot."

She laughed. "You are a pain in my butt."

"I know, and you love me for it." Frank grinned, then
wrapped an arm around Stace's shoulders.

She leaned into his embrace. Frank's thick arms
and broad chest enveloped her like a teddy bear. She'd
known Frank all her life, and even though he'd told her a
thousand times that she could get a better job than waitressing for him, she stayed. Not because she loved waitressing so much, but because she loved Frank and loved
the Morning Glory. Frank hadn't just been her father's
best friend, he'd been her father, too, in every way but
biology, and she couldn't imagine not seeing his familiar craggy face every day. Or this diner, which held so
many of Stace's memories in this one small building.
"Thanks for keeping me sane, Frank."

"Anytime." His voice was gruff. He turned to the

sink to wash his hands before he got back to work slicing tomatoes. "How's the new guy working out?"

"Terrible. He can't take orders, can't deliver food to the right tables, can't pour coffee without scalding someone."

Frank chuckled. "He'll learn."

"Why on earth would you hire him? He has no experience, no customer service skills and no—"

"Job. The guy needed a job." Frank shrugged. "So I gave him one."

Stace eyed her boss and friend. "You don't take pity on people like that. You're usually harder on the staff than I am. What's up?"

Frank paused and put the knife down. The blade seemed small next to his beefy palms. "Riley's been coming in here for a long time."

"Years."

"And he's been a bit of a pain."

"A bit? The man is an incorrigible flirt. And he's always asking for some custom thing or another."

"But at heart, he's a good guy."

"How do you know that?"

Frank considered her for a moment. "I just know. I'll let you figure that out for yourself. You'll see what I see."

She snorted. "I doubt it."

"Just have an open heart," Frank said. "You're a sweet girl, Stace, but your heart is closed off. Hell, you have a big old detour sign outside it."

"I have reasons why," she said softly.

"Don't you think it's past time you opened that road again?"

She glanced out the window, at the busy city that had once seemed to hold such promise, but then one day had stolen her biggest dream, and shook her head. Some days, being at the Morning Glory was so painful, she wasn't sure she could stay another minute. Other days, she couldn't imagine ever leaving. "Not now."

Maybe not ever.

She had her priorities now—a nephew who had been abandoned by his mother—and that meant she didn't have time or need for a relationship. It wasn't about not wanting to take that risk again—

Okay, maybe it was.

Either way, she didn't have time. Or room for a handsome, distracting man.

She pivoted toward the counter, took the two BLTs Frank had finished assembling, and hurried out of the kitchen, before the man who knew her better than anyone in the world could read the truth in her eyes.

That Stace wasn't so sure she had enough heart left to ever risk it again.

CHAPTER THREE

THIRTY minutes into the lunch rush, things fell apart. Riley had gone into the whole waiter job with a cocky, self-assured attitude, thinking this job, while busy, was relatively straightforward. Not easy, not once there was more than one table to juggle, but at least relatively manageable. More or less.

Then he'd been assigned Table Seven.

Stace had left him to his own devices. She'd hovered over him for the first couple of tables, but then the diner filled with customers, and she'd been too busy to supervise. "If you need something, don't be stubborn. Ask me," she'd said.

"I did. You turned me down."

She let out a gust. "Get your own orders, your own coffees. I'm not your personal servant."

He had asked her a few times to retrieve things for him. He'd thought she wanted to help him, not throw him into shark-infested waters without so much as a lifejacket. "I didn't—"

"You did. Treat this like a real job and we'll get along a whole lot better. And most of all, don't be an idiot."

He grinned at her. "You like me. Admit it."

"I despise you. Face it." But a smile played on her lips for a split second, before she spun on her heel and headed over to take care of two couples that came in and sat at one of the square tables. A four-top or something, she'd called it.

He watched her go, wondering why he cared that this one woman liked him. Riley McKenna had dated a lot of women. Proposed a few times, then found a way to wriggle out of the impulsive question. Though he entertained the idea from time to time, at his core, he wasn't much for settling down. He'd seen the American Dream at play in only a handful of the people in his life, and to Riley, that meant the odds that he could have the same were between slim and none.

Boston was an ocean with a whole lot of female fish to choose from, and yet, he found himself trying to make Stace smile. Trying to catch her eye. Trying to impress her with his skills. And failing miserably. He'd watched the diner's activity rise and fall, along with her irritation level, and wondered if perhaps the low income generated by the inexpensive food had her stressed.

He'd noticed the place struggling over the last few months, caught in the same bad economy as so many other businesses. What the diner needed was a new marketing approach, one that would give it some attention in Boston's crowded food industry. Riley pondered that as he crossed to Table Seven, another four-top, as Stace called it, which sat in the corner by the window. For whatever reason, Stace had seated this lone man at a table for four.

Before Riley said a word, the man put up a hand. He was tall, thin, with a thick graying beard that made him look like a human grizzly, a fact augmented by the thick dark brown plaid flannel shirt and the cargo pants he wore. For some reason, he looked familiar to Riley, but Riley couldn't place the face.

"You're new," the man said, "so I'm going to do this quick. I don't want a menu. I don't want advice, and I sure as hell don't want your opinion about the special of the day. I want a hot cup of coffee—hot, not luke-warm, not mildly hot, but *hot*—and a cheeseburger with fries. Don't skimp on the fries and don't eat any in the kitchen."

"I wouldn't—"

The man ignored Riley and barreled forward. "The cheeseburger better be well done. That means cooked through. Not so much as a hint of pink. Done, dead, and dark. You hear me? I don't need E. coli as a side dish."

Riley jotted down *burger, fries and coffee* on his pad. Wrote *well done* and underlined it three times. "Right away, sir."

"Don't call me sir or buddy or pal. I don't need a new friend. All I want is my damned food." The man eyed Riley up and down. "What the hell was Frank thinking when he hired you? You look about as much like a waiter as a walrus."

Riley started to answer. The man put up his hand again. "I don't need an answer. I'm not interested in your sob story. It'll be the same as every other one I've heard. Lost my job, lost my apartment, lost my damned dog. I don't care. Just get my food." Then the man shook out his newspaper and buried his nose in the Sports section.

Riley turned away and headed for the kitchen. Before he could give Frank the order, the older man was laugh-ing. "I see you met Walter," Frank said.

"If you're talking about Table Seven, yes." Riley ran a hand through his hair. "Is he always that pleasant?"

"Today he's in a good mood. Usually he yells his order at me from across the room." Frank plopped a fat burger onto the griddle, then turned to drop some fries into a fry basket. "You better go get his coffee. Walter doesn't like to be kept waiting."

On the way to the coffee, Riley got sidetracked by a customer who had to get to a meeting and wanted his order to go. Another who asked to add a salad to his lunch order and a third who wanted extra napkins. Riley dashed from place to place, trying to keep everyone happy, and wondering how Stace—who had twice the number of tables—managed to make it look so easy and he managed to feel like he was coming up short again and again. What he needed was an assistant, something he knew Stace sure as hell wouldn't approve. Hell, he'd had two assistants at McKenna Media. Now...none.

He wasn't used to being the gofer. Or the go-to anything. Riley had never expected the job to be this time-consuming or difficult. Yet Stace made it look effortless. She greeted every customer with a smile, seemed to sail from kitchen to table, and never missed a step. He caught himself watching her, more than once.

"New guy! Coffee!"

Riley jerked to attention and waved at Walter, then turned to the coffeepot and poured a hot cup of coffee. Just as he turned to bring over the mug, Frank dinged the kitchen bell. "Order up. Table Seven."

Riley pivoted back, grabbed the plate, and headed for Walter at a fast clip. The plate jiggled a little as he navigated the crowded diner, but he recovered his balance and delivered the lunch to Table Seven. "Here you go. One burger well done, side of fries, coffee."

Walter gave the entire thing a look of distaste. "I said hot coffee. This isn't hot."

"It's fresh out—"

"You poured it, then went to the kitchen. I don't care if it took you three seconds or thirty, my coffee is cooling while you dawdle and drool over your coworker. And as for my burger and fries—" he lifted the bun, grunted apparent approval at the charred beef, then ran a finger over the fries "—there are only twenty-one fries here. My order comes with twenty-two. No more, no less. I paid for twenty-two. I want that fry."

Across the room, Stace watched the exchange with a slight grin playing on her lips. She was clearly enjoying this.

"I'll get right back to the kitchen," Riley said, "and—"

"Start over. Bring me the whole thing again. From the top. Twenty-two fries."

"Sir, I can bring you more fries—"

"I don't want more fries, I want the ones I ordered." Walter leaned forward. "Did you eat it?"

Riley could swear he heard Stace let out a snicker.

"No, no. I would never—"

"You smell like fries. You ate my fry."

Out of the corner of his eye, Riley noticed a long pale rectangle on the floor. The missing fry, probably had taken a tumble when Riley had dodged a customer shoving back in his chair. "Sir—" A light, quick touch on his arm cut off Riley's words.

"Walter, you don't need to be giving the new guy such a hard time." Stace flipped out a coffee mug, and filled it with hot coffee. "Why, you'll scare him away before he finishes his first day."

Walter took a sip of the coffee. Something that approached a smile flitted across his lips. "Why'd you dump him on my table?"

"Because you're my best customer, that's why." Stace gave Walter a friendly look. "Now let me get you some new fries. And an extra pickle for your troubles."

Walter weighed the offer. "All right. But tell him—" he thumbed in Riley's direction "—to get his head out from between his—"

"Don't say mean things, Walter. It gives you indigestion." She flashed another smile, then turned on her heel and headed for the kitchen.

Riley caught up with her just inside the double doors. The movement brought them close together in the small space, so close, he could catch the vanilla and floral notes of her perfume. It danced around his senses. Sweet, light, enticing. "How'd you get Sir Surly there to smile like that?"

"Easy. I just feed into Walter's need to be right. And his addiction to pickles. Walter can be a pain in the butt—" she arched a brow in Riley's direction, and he wondered if that was a side reference to himself "—but he's all right. He just likes things the way he likes them."

He grinned. "Remind you of anyone you know?"

"Not at all." Stace blew on her nails and feigned indifference. That same slight smile teased at her lips again. "Why? Are you volunteering?"

Riley liked her. He always had. It had to be the way she stood up to him, and gave back as good as she got. She didn't fawn over him or gush compliments like a leaky faucet. She was straight, no-nonsense, what you see is what you get and if you don't like it, too bad.

And he liked that.

"Not at all," he said. A glint of devilish mischief danced in her green eyes, toyed with the corners of her smile. Maybe his being here had reduced the stress on her shoulders. "You gave me that table on purpose."

Stace turned and called back to the kitchen. "Frank, I need another order of fries."

He leaned around until she was looking at him again. "You know, and I know, that you set me up."

The grin playing at the corners of her lips rose a little higher. "Maybe."

"Part of the whole 'make the new guy's life miserable and maybe he'll quit' approach?"

She laughed. When she did, her features lit up, her eyes danced even more. "Did it work?"

"Not a chance." He took the fresh basket of fries from Frank's hands, then headed out the double doors. "You're stuck with me for a while."

"Don't bet on it," she called after him.

Riley was sure he heard Stace laughing as the door swung shut. Mission One accomplished. And it felt better than he'd thought.

He'd made dozens of women smile before, but never had it seemed like such a victory. And never had he worked so hard, nor cared so much about whether someone liked him. He was here for a job, nothing more, and getting distracted by the pretty and sassy waitress across the room would be a mistake.

Hadn't he learned that lesson already? When he let a beautiful face send him off course, it ended up in a disaster. And very often, that disaster made it into the papers. If he was going to do this, he was going to do it without dating his coworker.

An hour later, the lunch crowd had left, and the diner was empty. Frank stayed in the kitchen, cleaning up from that day and prepping for the next. Stace flipped the diner's sign to Closed, then turned the lock on the door.

Riley glanced at his watch. Just past three in the afternoon. He could probably catch up to his cousin Alec, and a few of his friends, see what they had cooking.

Alec, a day trader, often started his nights in the after-noon. Time spent with Alec was always memorable, if not a little beer-filled. Riley didn't have his usual bud-get to spend tonight, but he could make do with the tips in his pocket.

Riley headed to the back of the diner, pulled out his cell, dialed Alec's number and got the rundown on the evening's plans. As his cousin talked about the view from the bar, Riley glanced across the room at Stace, who was emptying the coffeepot. Even with her hair back in a ponytail and wearing an apron and jeans, she was beautiful. "Where I'm at has a pretty good view, too," Riley said. Alec started to make a joke, but Riley cut him off. "Hey, I gotta go. I'll catch up with you later."

He lingered a while longer in the back of the diner. Stace, unaware of him, had turned on the radio and was singing along. She had a light, lyrical voice, and she paused a moment to do a twirl, and toss a discarded napkin into the trash. For a moment, she looked…happy.

He crossed the room. Where did Stace go when her day was over? Why did she work in this diner when she seemed smart enough and determined enough to handle any job? And what would it take to make her smile like she was right now?

She jerked to a stop when she saw him. "Riley. Did you need something?"

He undid the apron, then draped it over one of the chairs. "I'm heading out." He almost said "home" then remembered Gran was charging him rent, a rent he'd only made a minuscule dent in paying, given the paltry tips in his pocket. He could have moved in with one of his brothers, but Finn was out of town and Brody was in Afghanistan. Riley could lean on one of his friends, but as he ran through a mental list, he realized there was no one he was close enough to to impinge on as a roommate.

What did that say about his life? That he didn't have one best friend to call during an emergency?

Riley shrugged off the thought. He'd figure it out, and he'd come out on top. He always did. "See you tomorrow."

"You can't leave yet," Stace said. "We still have to clean up."

He glanced around the diner. Most of the dishes had been cleared away, and the chairs sat square against the tables. "Looks clean to me."

"Right." Stace laughed, then slapped a rag into his hands. "I'll get the salt and pepper shakers off the table and you wipe. If we work together, we'll be out of here faster. Then we can argue over who mops the floor."

Wipe tables? Mop the floors? What was she going to have him do next, clean the windows? "Don't you pay someone to come in and do that stuff?"

She laughed. "Yeah. You. And me."

"Do you ever sit down?" he asked.

She laughed again. Damn, he liked her laugh. "If I do, then I'll fall asleep."

Her mood was lighter, and he liked that. It made the whole diner seem…sunnier. Still, the busy hours he had worked already had him dragging. The thought of staying longer—to clean, something Riley hadn't done since he was a kid and sentenced to kitchen duty for breaking the rules—made him feel even more exhausted.

He'd much rather be sitting in Flanagan's with Alec and Bill, knocking back a few.

"Sorry." He put the wet rag into her hands. "I have plans."

"No, you have a job. And that means you do what needs to be done. You don't just sponge it off on someone else."

He started to disagree. Then realized he'd been doing exactly that.

She pointed at the nearest table, then dangled the rag over his hand. "So get to work."

He leaned in close, searching her emerald gaze with his own. "Is this what you are, Stace? All work and no play? You don't ever blow off work?"

"No, I don't. Because I have priorities. And right now my priority is getting this diner clean so I can go home."

"Why?"

"What do you mean, why?"

"Why this place? It's just a diner."

"It's not just a diner. It's…special. And this job might be hard, but in the end, it's worth it. It's all worth it." Her gaze lit on the tables, the walls, the menus, then she shook her head, and the moment of vulnerability he had glimpsed disappeared. "Anyway, I have work to do."

She crossed to the table, and started clearing the last of the dishes, loading them into a big plastic tub nearby. A hit from the seventies played on the sound system, and Stace began to hum along, her hips swaying gently back and forth as she worked.

He thought of the guys, waiting for him down the street. There, they had beer and women, and—

And the same thing he had done every night for the past six years. He'd been there, done that, as the saying went, and wanted something else. What that something was, he didn't know, but maybe if he stayed here a little while longer with this woman who hummed while she worked a tough job, he'd figure it out.

* * *

After the third day, Stace had to give Riley some credit. Not a lot, and not easily, but she did. The playboy, who from what she'd seen and heard, had never seemed to be much good at anything other than goofing off, had put in several hours at the diner and stayed to clean up afterward. They'd been through a half-dozen waitresses in the past year, and few stayed after tangling with Walter, or getting Frank on a bad day.

But Riley, the last person in the world she would have picked, had stayed. Why? If this job was just a lark—the well-off spending a day in the shoes of the other half—then why was he still here? Did he really need the money?

What she'd heard and read of the McKennas suggested they weren't hurting in the cash department. Then why was the youngest McKenna hoofing it at a diner?

And why did she care? She didn't need a man in her life. She barely had enough room for herself.

Still, she liked that he had put in the hours, and she had to admit, she was beginning to like him. Look forward to seeing him. And his damnable smile. Even as she told herself to steer clear of his charm.

After working together for a few days, they'd worked out a system of partnership. They had cleaned half the tables already, and stacked the chairs to ready the floor for mopping—a big job, after two solid days of rain and muddy footprints. Frank was still in the kitchen, taking care of the dishes and next day's prep. Stace had offered to help, but stubborn Frank had insisted on doing the job himself. For a long time, he'd had a couple of helpers in the kitchen, but since the business had taken a downturn, he'd taken the entire kitchen load on his own shoulders. She sighed.

Frank had talked about traveling the world a hundred times, but never taken a step toward his dream. His health had been poor, something she was sure the stress of the diner augmented, and that just increased her determination to save her pennies and buy out Frank, something she'd offered a hundred times to do, and always he'd said no.

Maybe if she could increase sales he'd be able to hire back some help, and afford some time off. Either way, it wasn't something she could change today.

Stace paused to stretch her back and work out some of the kinks. She bent her neck right, left, then let out a deep breath.

"Tired?" Riley asked.

"Always." She tried to smile, but even that was too much right now. The day had been long, and had a long way to go yet. Jeremy would be leaving school soon and that meant her second shift as temporary mom to a difficult teenager was about to start. Frank had increased the volume on the radio, and his favorite oldies pulsed in the bright space. She cringed at the memory of Riley catching her in that unguarded moment a couple of days ago.

Riley studied her for so long she finally looked away, pretending that she was inspecting the diner. Why did his mere presence affect her so?

"Why don't you take a load off?" he said. "I'll get the rest of this."

"I really should—"

He jerked out a chair and waved toward the seat. "You really should sit, and let me help you."

"Why?"

"Because you're tired." He took the rag out of her hands, before she could protest. "And because I'm not nearly as bad as you think I am."

Exhaustion finally won the battle, and Stace dropped into the chair. "Just for a minute."

Riley grinned. "Take as many minutes as you need."

In fast, efficient movements, he tackled the rest of the tables. He removed all the salt and pepper shakers, then the sugar dispensers, before wiping them in quick but thorough circles. He'd paid attention to her instructions, clearly. Her respect for him inched upward another notch. Still, the pampered marketing exec didn't belong here, and she wondered for the hundredth time why he had taken the job.

"Tell me something," she said.

"What?"

"Why are you here?"

"I work here. Remember?" He flashed that grin at her again. The man smiled a lot, that was for sure. And if she'd been the kind of woman looking for a man who smiled like that, well, she'd be…tempted.

But she wasn't. Not one bit. Uh-uh.

"I know that. I meant why did you get a job here, as a waiter? Don't you work at an ad agency or something?"

"I used to. I got…fired. Sort of."

"How does someone get sort of fired?"

"I worked for my grandmother. She thought it was time I found other employment." He finished the last table, sent the rag sailing toward the bucket of dirty dishes, and waited for it to land with a satisfying thud before he returned to where Stace was sitting. He spun the opposite chair around and sat, draping his arms over the back. "She gets these ideas sometimes, and this was her latest."

"Ideas? On what?"

"On what's good for the McKenna boys." Riley chuckled and shook his head.

Stace's curiosity piqued. She told herself she didn't need to know anything more about this man than whether he would show up tomorrow. She knew his type. Knew better than to fall for a smile and a flirt. But that didn't stop the questions from spilling out of her mouth. "And what *is* good for the McKenna boys?"

"Hard work, beautiful women, and a good Irish stout."

She laughed. "Beer? Your grandmother really said that?"

"I might have added that one." Another grin. But Riley didn't expound on much more than that, and she realized even after three days, she knew little about him.

"And you have, what, two out of the three?" she asked.

"Right now, I have none. Unless Frank keeps some good, dark beer back there."

"No, definitely not."

"Then I'm batting a thousand."

"I don't know about that," she said. "You got the hard work over the last few days."

"True." He leaned forward, his blue eyes zeroing in on her features. "What about you? Why are you working here?"

She looked away. "It's my job."

"I know that," he said, repeating her words from before. "But what I want to know is why. You're smart and efficient. You could do a hundred things other than waitress."

She bristled and got to her feet. "We have a floor to clean. I can't sit around all day."

"Sorry." Riley rose, too. "I shouldn't have probed. I don't like people poking around in my private life. I shouldn't do it to you."

"Remember that, and we might just be able to work together."

It was her way of warning him off. She didn't want to get close to him, or to any man, right now. She had her priorities—working hard, saving money, and raising Jeremy—and there was no room in her life for a man like Riley, who'd just drain her heart and leave her empty in the end.

His gaze took in the glistening tables, the stacked chairs. "We did pretty good today."

"We did. Thanks for the help, and the rest. I needed it." She tossed him his apron. "I'll see you at five, playboy. And that's a.m., not p.m., so don't have too much of number three tonight."

"I was here at five this morning."

"No, you were here at five-fifteen today. Five-thirty yesterday." She worked another kink out of her neck. "That means I have to pick up the slack."

"Getting up early isn't exactly my strong suit." He made an apologetic face.

"You'll learn."

"Learn what?"

She shifted the chair until it was square against the table. "That you can't have it all, Riley."

He moved closer. "Speaking from experience?"

She turned away. "Just giving you friendly advice."

"Are you saying you never go out after work? There's no special guy who takes you out on the town?"

"I'm saying that I keep my life list in order," she said, turning back to him. "And my list is definitely different from—" The diner's door opened and Jeremy burst in the room. She could tell before her nephew even opened his mouth that bad news was coming.

"I'm never going back to that school again," Jeremy said. "It sucks. My whole life sucks."

Stace ached to put an arm around her nephew, to hug him, but she could see him already pulling back. The last year had been hard on him and whenever anyone got too close, he backed up. Years ago, her nephew had told her everything, come to her whenever he was upset. But lately...he'd been as distant as a man on the moon. "Jer, whatever happened today will be better tomorrow. I promise."

Jeremy snorted, then dumped his backpack on the floor. His mane of dark hair hung halfway over his face, obscuring his wide brown eyes from view. "I doubt that. Because I got expelled."

"Are you serious?" Stace's breath left her in a whoosh. "How? Why?"

He shrugged. "The stupid principal thought the drawing I hung in the hall was 'inappropriate.'" He waved air quotes around the word. "Whatever. I told him it was the First Amendment to express my opinion and he could go to—"

"Oh, Jeremy." Just when she thought things were improving, they took a serious detour toward Getting Worse.

Riley clapped Stace on the back. "Don't worry, Stace. I got expelled three times. And I turned out okay."

Jeremy's face perked up. "Really? What'd you do?"

"Do not talk to him," Stace said to Riley. "Not one word." She crossed to her nephew and stood between the two of them like a human shield for bad advice. But she was too late. Jeremy scooted around her and strode up to Riley, beaming up at the playboy like he was seeing a personal hero.

Stace had prayed for another male influence to come

into Jeremy's life. Someone who could speak to him on his level, maybe even take him to the amusement park or play football or any of the things that Frank didn't have the time or the energy to do.

Riley McKenna was the last person she would have picked for the job. And now, watching Riley and Jeremy talk—and her nephew smile for the first time in forever—Stace realized she was stuck with her worst nightmare. At work, and now, at home.

Somehow, Stace had to get rid of Riley. As she hustled her nephew out of the diner, she vowed to make sure the bachelor was gone by the end of the day tomorrow.

CHAPTER FOUR

RILEY had no business being here. He should have gone to his grandmother's house, to try to talk Gran out of her crazy idea. Or gone to hang out with his friends, who were undoubtedly several beers deep into their evening out already.

Instead Riley found himself flipping through a phone directory, then taking the train several stops down the Red Line until he arrived on the outskirts of Dorchester. Then a long, brisk walk to reach a neighborhood dotted with security bars over the store windows and battered No Trespassing signs nailed to the front of abandoned houses. He took a right, then a left, and another right before finally arriving before an aging one-story Cape with a sagging front porch and peeling white paint.

Riley checked the address he'd jotted down. Checked it again.

This was where Stace lived, according to the phone book. He thought of the guest house he lived in on Gran's property. It wasn't anything grand, but the Newton house and accompanying land were a far cry from the dilapidated building before him.

He wondered again how someone could work the job she did, for the pittance she received, and still be happy.

All those years of sports cars and women and parties, Riley had told himself he was happy.

But now he wasn't so sure that was true. Even though she faced the usual stresses involved in working a hard job, at the end of the day, when she was humming along to the radio, or giving him or Frank a good razzing, he saw something in Stace. A contentment, with her life, her job, herself. So he'd come here tonight, in part, to find a little of that for himself.

And maybe brainstorm a little. He'd been thinking about the diner's struggles over the last few days and had jotted down a few ideas, fiddled with some concepts. Maybe he could put something he'd learned at McKenna Media to work.

The front door flew open and Jeremy burst onto the porch. "Just stay out of my life!" he shouted, then gave the door a slam that threatened to bring down the entire structure. Jeremy stomped down the stairs, then halted when he saw Riley. "What are you, a stalker?"

"Nah." Riley gave the boy a grin. "I was in the neighborhood."

Jeremy looked him up and down, taking in the dress shirt, the pleated pants, the shiny dress shoes. "Sure you were."

"So, did you have a fight with your mom?" he asked Jeremy.

"She's not my mom. She's just my aunt." Jeremy wrinkled his nose in distaste. "All she does is ruin my life."

"By insisting you go to school?"

"Yeah. Like, who needs school? They don't teach me anything I'm going to use." Jeremy dropped onto the porch and rested his elbows on his knees. "School's stupid anyway. All I want to do is draw. Not learn algebra."

"Hey, I used to say the same thing." Riley waved to the space next to Jeremy and when the boy nodded, he sat down beside him. "I skipped school every chance I got, and got to know the principal on a first-name basis."

Jeremy let out a little laugh. "Yeah, me, too."

"Remind me to tell you about the time I smuggled in a chicken and let it loose. On the third floor. In the middle of schoolwide testing."

Jeremy's eyes widened. "You did? Man, what happened?"

"I got expelled. That was expulsion number three, by the way." Riley picked up a pile of grass that had landed on the stairs after a recent mowing and spun it between his fingers. "That was my wake-up call. Well, that and my grandmother's lecture."

"Your grandma? Man, that must have been harsh. What'd your mom and dad say?"

Riley flung the piece of grass at the sidewalk. It fluttered to the chipped concrete, a spiral of green, before slipping between the wide gray crack and disappearing. "My folks died when I was a kid. So me and my brothers went to live with my grandparents. And I gotta tell you, no one can lecture like my grandmother."

"You *have* met Aunt Stace, haven't you?" Jeremy said.

Riley chuckled. "Well, she's only lectured me a little. And I bet she only lectures you because she wants the best for you."

"Yeah, right." The boy got to his feet and leaned against the porch post. His gaze scanned the run-down neighborhood, the houses crying for some TLC. "If this is the best, I'd hate to see the worst."

"It'll work out," Riley said.

Jeremy snorted. "Oh yeah? How do you know that

for sure? You barely know me, man. My father's dead, my mother's a drug addict and all my aunt seems to worry about is whether I'm passing English. You have no idea how my life will work out."

Before Riley could respond, Jeremy thundered down the stairs and took off, a sullen figure in a dark sweatshirt disappearing into the gathering twilight.

The door squeaked behind him. Stace stepped out onto the porch and shot Riley a glare. "What did you say?"

"That you're the meanest woman in Boston."

"You did not."

"Nope, I did not." He got to his feet and tossed her a grin. "I was giving him advice."

She raised a skeptical brow.

"Ask him yourself."

She let out a long breath and her gaze went to the street that had swallowed Jeremy in the growing dark. "If he comes back."

"He will." Riley barely knew this boy, or this woman, so he wasn't entirely positive. Still, he'd had the feeling that underneath all the teenage anger, Jeremy loved his aunt and needed her. Riley stepped farther onto the porch, closer to Stace, and for the first time, noticed the dusting of shadows under her eyes, the lines of worry on her face. "Hey, you want to get something to eat? I had some ideas I wanted to talk over with you."

"Ideas? About what?"

"The diner. I thought if we sat down over some steaks…" Then he thought of the paltry pile of tips in his pocket, and realized he barely had enough to feed himself, never mind another human. "I forgot. I'm broke."

She snorted. "You? Right."

"Seriously."

She eyed him, her gaze penetrating his. "You really are serious."

He held up a palm. "As a heart attack."

"You're really broke?"

"Well, unless you count the coupled hundred dollars I've made so far this week, all of which has to go to rent, yeah."

He thought of his friends. He could hang with them, talk them into covering his dinner, but just the thought of it made him feel bored. Depressed even. He could go home to the guest house, but the space seemed so... empty right now. Hell, it always seemed empty, which was probably why he was more often at his grandmother's than at his own place.

"Anyway," he said, "I was in the neighborhood and thought maybe we could talk about some ideas I had for the diner. But you're busy, so I'll just see you at work." Then his stomach rumbled, like the punctuation to his sentence.

Stace chewed on her lower lip. She glanced down the street, then back at her house, before finally swinging her gaze back to Riley. "I've got a lasagna in the oven. You're welcome to stay."

"Lasagna?" His stomach growled in anticipation. "You're speaking my language, honey."

"Don't call me 'honey' and I might just let you have seconds." She laughed, then pulled open the front door. "I'm probably going to regret this."

He paused in the doorway to lean down close to her ear. "Probably," he whispered.

With the next breath Riley inhaled the sweet and spicy notes of her perfume, and wondered if he was the one making the mistake. But then the scent of lasagna caught him, like a breeze opening the door to the home he'd never really had, and he entered.

The man was a distraction.

Stace had always prided herself on being practical and smart. On making sensible decisions based on careful planning. *Impetuous* would be the last adjective anyone would use to describe Stace Kettering. Then why had she gone and invited a man to dinner on the spur of the moment? A man who was essentially a stranger? A man who was exactly the kind of man she knew better than to get close to?

Hadn't she learned her lesson with Jim? All those wasted years, thinking she was going to marry her childhood sweetheart, only to find out he was about as faithful as a bee in a rose garden. She'd steered clear of the same kind of self-centered man ever since.

Until now. Because every time she talked to Riley, she wondered if maybe there was more to him than the charming facade. Frank was a good judge of character, and if he said there was, there probably was. Riley had, after all, stuck it out so far this week, and that alone told her there might be more to him than just a handsome face. And darn if that handsome face didn't distract her all the time. Had her thinking about him when they weren't together and wondering what he was doing. So yes, a part of the invitation had been curiosity. That was all.

"Do you want something to drink?" She crossed to the fridge and pulled on the handle. "Lemonade? Iced tea?"

"Surprise me."

Surprise him? Like he'd surprised her by showing up here? She still wondered how and why he'd come, but instead of asking, she pulled out the pitcher of lemonade and poured two glasses. She handed one to Riley. "If it's too tart, let me know. Jeremy says I never add enough sugar."

"Tart? Like you?" He grinned.

"I'm sweet." Why was she arguing the point with him? Every time he was around, he brought out this other side of her. A lighter side. She didn't know if that was good or bad.

He laughed. "Of course you are."

"Hey, be nice. Or I won't feed you."

"Yes, ma'am." Riley grinned, then held up the glass. Lemon slices tangoed with ice cubes, and the pale yellow liquid shimmered in the overhead light. "Homemade?"

She nodded.

He took a long sip. "This is...perfect."

"Thanks. Frank says I'm only good at two things. Making drinks and making lasagna." Why was she telling him so much? Was it that she was nervous, having a man in her house, for the first time in...

Well, forever?

Or was some masochistic part of her interested in, and tempted by, Riley McKenna? She kept being lured into joking with him, befriending him...and telling herself she shouldn't do either.

He glanced around her kitchen, and for a second, she wanted to apologize for the outdated appliances, the worn countertops, the scuffed floor. The house had seen better days, many, many years ago, and as much as Stace knew she should move on—

She hadn't.

It was the house she'd lived in all her life, and a part of her couldn't give it up, despite its flaws. "The lasagna should, ah, be done in a couple minutes. Let me just, ah, set a place for you." She crossed to the cabinets again, withdrawing a plate, then silverware. She spun back to the table, but Riley blocked her path.

"You've waited on enough people today." He gently took them from her hands, and nodded toward the table. "You sit. I'll get this."

She let out a nervous chuckle. "I don't know if I should. I've seen you wait tables, remember?"

"Hey, that plate of spaghetti was slippery. And the woman I spilled it on was pretty understanding, considering."

'That's because you flirted with her."

"I did not."

Stace scoffed. "Riley McKenna, you are the biggest flirt I have ever met."

He cocked a smile at her, the same smile that had charmed the customer and made her forget all about the pasta on her skirt. "Hey, she left me a tip in the end."

"And her phone number?"

He grinned. "A gentleman never kisses and tells."

"Gentleman. Right." She reminded herself again not to fall for him. He didn't want her—she was merely a challenge he had yet to win. She was as far from his type as the earth was from Mars. Did he see her as a pity case? Or did he want to butter her up so she wouldn't complain when he slacked off at work tomorrow? Or worse, quit, and left both Frank and her in the lurch?

Because if there was one thing she suspected about Riley, it was that he didn't seem much for sticking. To anything. Or anyone.

He laid out the place settings. The oven timer began to beep, and before Stace could pop out of her chair, Riley had opened the door. He stood there for a second, looking at the hot pan. Stace laughed. "On the counter to your right. Unless you want to burn your hands."

He grabbed the oven mitts, then put them on his hands. "Did you pick pink just for me?"

"Of course." She bit back a smile at the incongruous sight of the tall, dark-haired man with the oversize bright pink mitts on his hands. For the second time, he'd insisted on doing all the work and letting her relax. She had to admit, it was nice, and had her intrigued. Who was Riley McKenna?

He pulled out the lasagna, laid it on the hot plate on the table, then shut the oven again and returned to the table with a spatula and the bowl of salad from the counter.

"Your dinner is served, miss."

"I could get used to this." Stace leaned back in her chair, while Riley dished salad into her bowl. "You're really getting the hang of waiting tables."

"It's a temporary situation. I have no intention of making that a permanent job," he said as he took his seat.

"Moving on to bigger and better things soon?"

Riley toyed with his silverware. "I can't exactly make a career out of working at a diner. I need to find something else."

"Something other than busing tables."

"I didn't mean there's anything wrong with your job—"

"It's okay. I get it. You're saying I should keep the Help Wanted sign in the window. And not depend on you."

"I'm not quitting tomorrow, you know."

"No, but you are quitting someday." All the more reason not to get attached to him. He was just like all the rest, and she'd do well to remember that. She'd feed him, then get back to her real goal—keeping the Morning Glory going and her nephew on track.

Stace cast a worried look down the hall. The front door had yet to open. Chances were good that Jeremy would stay out until it was time for bed. More and more, her nephew did his level best to ignore her. "He's not back yet."

Riley's hand met hers on the table, not touching, just…there. She didn't know how to read that. Every time she thought she had Riley figured out, he did something that didn't fit her definition of selfish playboy.

"Don't worry," he said. "If Jeremy is anything like I was at that age, he'll be here when his stomach is rumbling."

"I hope so." Riley didn't know Jeremy, though, or Stace, really. He couldn't predict the comings and goings of an angry teenager who felt betrayed by his parents and the world.

And neither, it seemed, could Stace. She sighed again, then reached for the dressing and poured some onto her salad, before passing the bottle to Riley. She cut a slice of lasagna, gave herself one, then repeated the action for Riley. The repetitive, ordinary actions of serving dinner kept the worry about Jeremy at bay.

"How did you end up raising Jeremy?" Riley asked. Then he cast an apologetic smile at her. "Sorry. I'm just curious. My grandparents raised me and my brothers after my parents died, and I always wonder when I find other kids in similar situations."

The personal tidbit surprised her. Since she'd met him, he hadn't exactly been Mr. Open about his personal life. Once again, she wondered if her perceptions of Riley—largely formed by overhearing his phone con-

versations or what she'd seen in the gossip columns—
might be a bit skewed. Or if this was merely a ploy to
get close to her—and into her bed. She thought of telling him it was none of his business, but didn't. She'd
been carrying this burden herself for so long. Maybe if
she just talked it out, she could relieve some of the tension of the last few weeks. "Jeremy moved in with me
a month ago after my sister left."

"Left?"

Stace's gaze went to the window, as if that would
suddenly show her a peek of where Lisa was and what
she was doing right now. "She couldn't handle it anymore," Stace said quietly. "So she left."

"Jeremy mentioned she was on drugs," Riley said,
his voice soft, concerned. And the sound opened a window in Stace's heart.

Stace nodded. Tears blurred her vision. "I've tried to
help her a hundred times, but it's never worked. She's
younger than me, and I think losing our mom when we
were young impacted her a lot more than me. Then after
my dad died, she fell in with the wrong crowd—and I
could never get her out of that. Then last month she got
into a car accident with Jeremy in the car, and I guess
that was the last straw for her. She hitched a ride out of
town and I haven't heard from her since."

In an odd way, it was liberating to talk about her sister, and her worries with Jeremy. She hated to burden
Frank any more than she already had, and having Riley
here to listen was…nice.

Riley handed her the basket of garlic bread. "Maybe
she'll come back."

"Maybe." It seemed all Stace did was wait for people to come back. She should have learned her lesson

by now. Staying in the same house, wishing the same wishes, didn't make them come true.

She was just starting to unwrap the towel keeping the bowl of garlic bread warm when she heard the front door open. Jeremy's heavy footfalls sounded in the hall. "I'm hungry. Did you make dinner, Aunt Stace?" he called.

Maybe they did, Stace thought. Maybe they did. She raised her gaze to Riley's and gave him a smile. "You were right."

He grinned, a grin as friendly and open as his words earlier. "It happens."

"I'm glad."

"Me, too." His blue eyes met hers. They seemed warm, comforting. Understanding. "Very glad."

CHAPTER FIVE

THREE voice mails, four texts, and two emails. All from Riley's friends, wondering where the hell he was. The general consensus—he must be dead, because he wasn't sitting in a bar, or out with the woman of the day.

Riley closed the phone and tucked it away. The siren call of his friends didn't speak to him this time. The invitations didn't lure him into the night. Instead, he stayed at Stacc Kettering's kitchen table and listened to her tell Jeremy an anecdote about a trio of female customers who'd come into the Morning Glory solely to eat one of every dessert on the menu, for breakfast. "That's how they celebrate their birthdays—dessert for breakfast, lunch, and dinner for the whole day, with lots of shopping in between," Stace said. "They were loud and funny, and a blast to wait on. They left me a Macy's gift card for a tip." Stace pulled it out of her back pocket. "I see some shopping in my future."

He watched the happy animation on Stace's face, while he ate the lasagna she'd baked, and wondered why he stayed here, in her house, and kept going back to the diner when he could have been scouring the classifieds for a better paying job.

His gaze went to the artwork hanging on the walls. Pictures of warriors, of landscapes, of military scenarios, all drawn by Jeremy, who had signed each one with a large, looping *J*. The boy had a good eye, a clear understanding of perspective, and an imaginative mind. He reminded Riley of himself at that age. A dreamer, always doodling and creating.

He glanced over at Stace, who was laughing and moving her hands as she talked, and wondered how she made it on her wages. No wonder she lived in this tiny house that shivered in the wind. Given how slow the diner had been, if she made even twice what he had today, heck, five times, she could hardly afford to eat, never mind pay rent in Boston.

And neither could he.

Granted, he could go to his grandmother, offer her a puppy dog face, and lots of apologies, and be back in Gran's good graces before the day was out. As paltry as those dollars in his pocket were, they were his. He'd earned them. He'd worked hard and he'd been rewarded for his labor.

Such a simple thing, really, to do some work and get paid for it. He'd gotten too used to just showing his face and collecting a paycheck he hadn't earned. Oh, sure, he tossed out an idea or two here and there, sat through a few meetings, and was called in to finesse a client from time to time, but he hadn't really worked at McKenna Media. Hell, the company got more productivity from the potted ficus in the lobby.

It was a new feeling, one that had his mind spinning in new directions. What if he had a job that challenged him? Made him feel productive, rewarded? He'd often heard his brothers talking about serving a purpose, and he'd always thought they were crazy.

Truth be told, Riley hadn't had anything close to a purpose in…well, in a long, long time. Maybe it was time to get that feeling back. The question was how. Maybe if he applied a little of what he'd picked up at McKenna Media at the Morning Glory, it'd be a start.

He glanced at Stace and realized why she loved her job. To her, it was a purpose. What purpose, he didn't know, but he could see the commitment and satisfaction in her every move at the Morning Glory. The problem with purposes, though, was that they made you get involved. Care. Connect.

And Riley made it a personal rule not to do any of the above. Not anymore.

Except, in this tiny little house in Dorchester, it was impossible not to connect. They were nearly elbow-to-elbow at the table, and it felt more like a family than at any dinner Riley had ever attended. The feeling both chafed and welcomed him.

"I'm not going back there," Jeremy said, interrupting Riley's thoughts. Clearly, the subject had changed at some point. The teenager got to his feet so fast, his chair let out a sharp screech and a thick black mark on the floor. "So stop asking me about stupid school. I'm leaving." He stomped out of the kitchen. A few seconds later, the door slammed and Jeremy was gone.

Stace sighed. She opened her mouth to say something, shut it again, then crossed to the sink with her dishes. Riley got up to join her. Outside the window, the skies had turned dark and ugly and a rumble of thunder shook the sky. "You okay?"

She nodded. "I was doing good until I mentioned school. He just doesn't understand the importance of an education."

"Want me to talk to him? I might be able to help. Sometimes the odd man out has a good idea."

She chuckled while she retrieved a plastic container from the cabinet. "Words of wisdom from you?"

"Nah, my grandfather. He was always spouting off some saying or another. It was like living with Confucius. And my father…" Riley shrugged. He didn't want to go there. "Anyway, just call it a bit of McKenna wisdom."

Stace laughed. Then she sighed. "Okay, if you think you can pull some rabbit out of a hat I haven't tried yet, you're welcome to try."

He considered making her a promise, then didn't. He hadn't come here to get more involved with the sassy waitress and her angry nephew. He was here to share ideas about boosting the diner's revenues. Trouble was, he kept forgetting to get around to the topic.

Together they cleaned up dinner, stowing leftovers in the fridge, then loading dishes into the soapy sink water. Riley thought how odd it was that this ramshackle place could feel so much more like home than the guest house he'd lived in since he was nineteen. Low-rent or not, it had a lived-in feel and a warmth about it that he liked.

And that was dangerous. He put his back to the counter. *Get back on track, stop letting this little house tempt you down the wrong path.* "Now that dinner's over, maybe we could sit down and brainstorm some ways to increase business at the diner. I've noticed it's been a little slow and—"

"Why are you doing this?" She crossed her arms over her chest. The easy mood between them arced with tension. "You're not staying. You told me yourself. So don't worry one bit about the Morning Glory. Frank and I have kept it running for a long time before you and we will after you leave, too."

He pushed off from the sink and studied her. "Why is it so hard for you to accept help?"

A second, louder rumble of thunder interrupted them, and then a rainstorm burst from the clouds, sending a fast rush of rain pounding onto the house, sounding like an invading army of ants marching across the shingles. The water slashed against the windows in wet, fast-moving highways. "Oh, damn!" Stace said.

She spun away, jerking open cabinet doors and tugging out two huge pots, and a trio of large plastic bowls. She thrust one of the bowls into Riley's hands. "To the right of the stairs with this one. And this one—" she shoved another bowl at him "—goes in the middle of the living room floor."

"What? Why?" But just as he said the words, he saw the reason—water had started dripping through the ceiling in the kitchen. Stace shoved a pan under the drip to catch the water, which hit the stainless steel bottom with a steady *ping-ping-ping.*

A couple of minutes later, they had the bowls and pots in place. The rain created a symphony inside the house, high-pitched pings and low bass plops. Riley glanced up at the massive polka dots of water stains on the ceiling. "You need a new roof," he said.

"And a new furnace. And new windows. And new appliances." She spread her hands and sighed. "There's not an inch of this house that doesn't need something or other. But the budget only goes so far, and right now, it's been eaten up by the leaky faucet I had to have repaired last week."

The rain continued outside, bolstered by a strong wind that seemed determined to blow the house down. The kitchen window shuddered, and the back door creaked. The symphony became louder, deeper, as the containers filled and the rain continued unabated.

"You should sell this place. It's damp and drafty and—"

"Mine. I happen to love it here. And it's not that bad. When the rain stops—"

A crash sounded down the hall, followed by two thuds and what sounded like a minor tidal wave. Riley and Stace ran to the sound, skidding to a stop outside of Stace's bedroom. Like the rest of the house, her bedroom was decorated in light, cheery colors—a sea blue, with white trim and a butter-yellow comforter on the bed. Or what used to be a butter-yellow comforter on the bed.

"I didn't know you were putting in a skylight."

She smacked his arm. "That is not even remotely funny. What am I going to do?"

He took in the scene before him—a gaping hole in the ceiling, open straight to the stormy sky. Broken shingles, crumpled Sheetrock, rotted framing, piled in a heap on the bed, in the middle of a growing pond. "You're going to have to go to a hotel or something tonight. You can't stay here now. I'll put something over the roof for tonight, and call a contractor in the morning."

Stace snorted. "You. Put something on the roof?"

"I'm handier than you think."

"No, I think *I'm* handier than *you* are."

"Are you saying I don't look the part of a handyman?"

Her gaze roamed over him. "Not at all."

"And why is that?"

"You're too…" She stopped talking. Her face colored. "Well, good-looking."

His grin widened. Did Stace Kettering like him? Or was he reading too much into a simple comment? "You think I'm good-looking?"

"I think *you* think you are." The fists went back on her hips, and her chin rose in defiance. "And well...you don't strike me as the construction type." She pulled one of his hands toward herself and turned it over. "Look. No calluses."

Her touch surprised him. Warm, soft, delicate, it sent a rush through his veins, and for a moment he forgot about the rain pouring into her bedroom. Hell, forgot his own name. He gently flipped over her palm, and ran his fingers down the tender skin. He wanted to do more, much more. Like kiss her. Hold her. Explore every inch of that peach-soft skin. "And this tells me you work too hard," he said quietly.

She glanced down at her hands, then back up at him, her green eyes wide. "I...I have to. I...have bills to pay."

"And that roof to fix." He ran his thumbs over her palm, his fingers over the back of her hand. The light floral notes of her perfume drifted up to tease his senses. Why had he never noticed how soft her hands were before? Or how her eyes were as bright and green as new spring grass?

"Yeah, the...the roof." She pulled away from him and turned back to survey the damage. The moment was gone. Disappointment washed over Riley. "Damn. What am I going to do?"

"Point me in the direction of the garage." He put up a hand to cut off her protest before she could voice it. "I'll take care of putting a tarp on the roof. You clean up the mess here. Anything you can't lift or do, I'll help you with. If we work together, we can get it done faster," he added, using her words from before.

She gave him another dubious glance, then finally nodded. "Garage entrance is in the hall outside the kitchen."

Riley headed out to the one-car garage, and flicked on the light switch. A small puddle in the corner pointed to another leaky spot, but overall, he found the space neat and clean. A compact older model two-door car sat to one side of the garage while a peg board and pair of shelves held assorted gardening and home repair tools on the opposite side. It took Riley a few minutes but he found a tarp, a hammer, some nails, and a ladder. He bundled several long, thin scraps of wood up with the tarp, then tied the whole thing in a bundle with a rope. Then he lifted the garage door and headed out into the rain.

He nestled the ladder against the side of the house, tucked the tarp under one arm, put the hammer and nails into his pockets, and reached out to climb the ladder with his free hand. He got four rungs up before he heard a voice behind him.

"What are you, Santa Claus now?"

Riley turned. Jeremy stood to the side of the ladder, shoulders hunched, his head tucked under a damp sweatshirt hood. Rain pelted his thin frame, darkened his gray sweatshirt.

"I'm fixing your aunt's roof," Riley said. "Temporarily."

"Why?"

"Because it's raining in her bedroom right now."

Jeremy scoffed. "That's because this house is a piece of junk."

"Yeah, well, instead of complaining about it, you could help me." Riley hadn't dressed for the weather, and the rain had already plastered his button-down shirt to his chest. The sooner he was out of the wet and into the house, the better.

"I'm not climbing up there. I could get hurt."

"Yeah, you could. Or you could help me and maybe learn a thing or two."

Jeremy stood there a moment, wavering. Then he reached for the ladder, and hauled himself up behind Riley. "If someone doesn't help you, you're going to break your neck, and then my Aunt Stace will be all upset."

"I'm not so sure about that," Riley said. "Okay, now be sure to hold on tight, and brace yourself on the roof. Okay?"

Jeremy scowled. "I'm not an idiot."

But Riley noticed the boy took his time climbing to the top, and then a moment to steady his feet on the slippery roof. Thankfully, Stace lived in a one-story house, so the drop wasn't as bad as it could have been. Riley tossed the tarp onto the roof, then gestured to Jeremy. "Go around to the other side. But be careful. This roof is like Swiss cheese."

Jeremy picked his way across the shingles, holding onto one corner of the tarp while using his free hand to help balance himself. He and Riley stood on either side of the hole in the roof, while the rain and wind buffeted them.

Stace looked up at them from down below in the bedroom. Through the hole in the ceiling Riley could see she'd already moved most of the mess off the bed, along with all the ruined bedding, and had placed a large cooler in the center of the bed to catch the falling rain. He bit back a laugh at her efficiency.

"Hey!" she shouted. "What is Jeremy doing up there?"

"Helping me. He'll be fine. And we'll get it done in half the time."

"But—"

"It'll be okay, Stace," Riley said. "Trust me. Now will you get out of that room before the rest of the roof caves in?"

"I can't. I have to rescue the teacups." She held up two delicate white China mugs, their fragile faces decorated with bright flowers and gold trim. "I keep meaning to put them on a shelf, and they're just sitting on my dresser. They're going to get crushed by the roof, if another piece falls in."

"Leave them. We'll get them later," Riley said. Beneath his feet, the roof bounced up and down like a sponge. "You gotta get out of that room."

"I will," Stace promised. "Just give me a minute. I can't leave them here."

"Stace—"

Jeremy laid a hand on him. "Let her get them. She's got this thing about those mugs. Her mom gave them to her or something."

So Stace Kettering was a bit sentimental. Clearly, she was about the diner, and now, the teacups. Riley smiled to himself about that, then refocused on saving the roof. Riley and Jeremy unfurled the rest of the tarp, then laid it against the roof. The wind argued and nipped at the edges, trying to tear the tarp out of their hands, but Jeremy held tight while Riley hurried to nail down the strapping. He came around to Jeremy's side and handed the young boy the hammer. "Here." Riley had to shout to be heard over the wind. "You can do this side."

"Me? I don't know how to do that."

"All the more reason why you should." Riley bent down and gestured to Jeremy to do the same. The rain protested even more. "Lay the wood over the tarp, a few inches in so it has something to hold onto. Place the nail between your fingers, then hammer. As soon as the nail has a bite, move your fingers out and send it home."

Jeremy hesitated. Riley nudged the hammer into his palm. "You can do it. I'll be right here."

"I've never done anything like this." Jeremy turned toward Riley. The falling rain ran down his face, soaked his hair. "What if I mess it up?"

The words rocketed Riley back nearly eighteen years. *But, Dad, what if I mess it up?*

You won't, his father had said. He'd laid a tender hand on his son's shoulder. *I'm right here to help you. Riley, if you're always afraid of messing up, you'll never try anything. So...try.*

"It's a tarp and some nails. You can't mess it up. Believe me." Riley handed Jeremy a nail, then laid a piece of wood on top of the blue plastic.

Jeremy hesitated. "I don't know."

"If you're always afraid of messing up, Jeremy, you'll never try anything new." The words his father had said to him so many years ago felt odd coming out of Riley's mouth. Odd, but right. "It'll be okay. I'm right here. Go ahead."

Jeremy did as Riley instructed. His first strike with the hammer was tentative, barely brushing the flat head. Then he hit it harder, and when the nail sank in, he flinched his fingers out of the way and hammered again. Once, twice, three times, until the nail head lay flush against the wood. He looked up at Riley, and a grin broke across his face. "I did it."

"Yep. Now do it a whole lot more. So we can get the heck out of the rain."

The two of them worked together for a few minutes

more, securing the tarp against the roof. When they were done, Riley helped Jeremy down the ladder first, then followed behind him. Stace was waiting at the bottom, bundled up in a bright red Red Sox rain poncho that dwarfed her small frame. She held the bottom of the ladder, worry etched in her features. "Jeremy, you shouldn't have gone up there. If you fell—"

"I was fine, Aunt Stace. I nailed down the tarp," Jeremy said. "Riley showed me how."

"You did? That's awesome, Jeremy." A smile broke across Stace's face. She put a hand on her nephew's arm. "Thank you. I appreciate you doing that."

The boy shrugged. "It was no big deal." He was doing his level best to affect the attitude of an surly teenager again, but it was conflicting with his clear satisfaction and self-pride for a job well done.

"It was a *huge* deal," Stace said, then mouthed a thank-you to Riley, too. "Come on, let's get you guys inside and dried off."

The three of them headed into the house, back to the symphony of raindrops. The temperature in the little house had begun to drop. The tarp would keep the rain out, but it was a temporary fix, and the wind still nipped beneath the plastic cover like an unwelcome visitor.

Jeremy headed to the bathroom to take a hot shower, leaving Riley and Stace alone in the kitchen. She pressed a hand to his shirt. His heart tripped at her warm, comforting…no, perfect touch. Delicate, yet also strong fingers, awakening parts of him that shouldn't be awake. Not when he was trying to keep this platonic. He was leaving, as he'd said.

"Thank you," she said. "You didn't have to do that."

"No, I didn't, but I did. To help you out."

The room closed in on them, tighter, smaller than

five minutes before. "You're, uh, soaked clear through," she said.

He covered her palm with his own. "It's raining outside."

"There's a storm out there," she said. Her green eyes met his, and her voice dropped into a softer, deeper range. "And in here."

Tension unfurled between them like a roll of twine. He watched her lips move, watched her eyes widen, watched her breath slip in and out of her mouth. He no longer felt the wet, cold fabric plastered against his skin. Instead a growing heat burned inside him. He lowered his head, until his lips were inches from hers. Damn. He wanted her. More now than before, when he'd barely known her. Now he'd tasted her cooking, heard her laugh, seen her smile, and that only quadrupled his desire. "Stace—"

"Here." She thrust a towel against his chest. "You... you should dry off before you get sick."

Riley backed away, took the towel—and the hint—from Stace, and rubbed the soft floral-scented terry cloth over his face, so she wouldn't see the disappointment in his features. For a man who didn't want to get involved, he kept doing that very thing. "Thanks."

"And...I'm sorry for not trusting you about the roof," she said.

He grinned. "Hey, what can I say? I have the hands of a man who does nothing all day."

"I shouldn't have said that. You did a great job with the roof, and my nephew. I appreciate it." She grabbed two cups of coffee from the counter and handed one to Riley. "Jeremy really needs a male influence. Frank is great, but it's nice for him to be around someone closer to his age. Someone who can teach him things." She gave him a self-deprecating grin. "I'm not exactly dad material."

Dad material? Riley McKenna didn't fit those words. Maybe he had made a small impact on Jeremy today, but Riley was sure it would probably be erased as soon as the subject of school or curfew came up.

If anything screamed "woman looking for a commitment," the words *dad material* were it. Riley knew he should stay away, walk out the door right now, and leave Stace and Jeremy to deal with their own lives. After all, he wasn't a man who got involved. Ever. He liked his life the way it was—unencumbered and easy. Except that way of life seemed so…empty lately.

What the hell was wrong with him?

He glanced around the run-down house again, at the half-filled pots of rainwater. And the urge to help just a little bit more roared to life. She wouldn't let him help with the diner but she had here. Jeremy and Stace were in trouble, and a helping hand didn't constitute involvement. It was just being…nice. "You can't stay here. It's freezing and wet, and who knows what will happen with the rest of the roof tonight? Come on back to my house, and then at least you and Jeremy will be warm and dry," he said. "Come on, I'll take you there."

"Please. I'm not…" She put up her hands, then cast a glance down the hall, and lowered her voice. "Interested in a…relationship."

Riley leaned in close. "Neither am I. This is about helping you. Not about sex." Then he took in a breath and caught the sweet floral fragrance wafting off her skin. And a part of him mounted a very vocal campaign for the idea of sex and Stace Kettering.

Stace worried her bottom lip again. "We won't stay more than a night."

"The roof won't be fixed that fast. And they're predicting rain for the next few days."

"I'll find somewhere else to stay. With Frank, or in a motel, or something. I don't want…"

"Want what?"

Her face colored. "We barely know each other."

"What better way to change that situation?" He tossed her a grin, and tried not to wonder why a man who was committed to staying uninvolved, kept getting involved with this woman. "I promise, I don't walk around nude or leave my dirty laundry on the kitchen floor. Most of the time anyway."

A smirk started on one corner of her mouth. "I don't know if it's a good idea."

"Come on, it'll be fun. I promise."

"Fun?" She let out a laugh. "The last time I had fun was probably 1998."

"Then all the more reason to start today. And who better to show you how to have a good time than the man dubbed one of Boston's most eligible bachelors?"

What had she been thinking?

Stace got out of the taxi, and stood in the driveway of the McKenna house. The main home was a stately dark green Victorian, complete with a spiraling turret, long, inviting porch, and crisp white trim. The brick driveway wound around the east side of the house, leading to a smaller version of the main house, a little one-story bungalow with a one-car garage. The guest house.

Where she and Jeremy would be staying with Riley. For at least one night.

How did she go from zero to sixty with this guy in mere days? One minute she was working with him, having dinner with him, and now, she was temporarily *living* with him. Last week, she barely even knew him.

Now she was sharing a bathroom with him.

"We're staying here?" Jeremy looked back at his aunt. "For how long?"

Stace jerked her suitcase out of the back of the car, then hauled Jeremy's bag up and handed it to him. "Don't get too comfortable. It's only temporary. A day or two." Riley opened the door to the guest house and waved at her from the front door. He really was a handsome man. The kind that made her forget all the reasons she had for not getting involved with anyone, and especially not involved with one of the most notorious bachelors in the city. *Especially* not with him. He had heartbreaker written all over him and she kept on overlooking that because he dished up her lasagna or fixed her roof. "We'll be gone before you know it."

"Of course," Jeremy grumbled. "Because why would we want to stay at a place with a pool?"

"He has a pool?"

Jeremy nodded, then pointed to the left of the guest house at a glass enclosure that wrapped around an inground pool. A hot tub flanked one corner, a barbecue and seating area on the other. The entire thing was designed to look like a private lagoon, with big faux boulders and lush greenery. In the middle of Boston, in the middle of fall.

The urge to dive into that sparkling water, to let it wash over her, take away the stress of the last year, rose up inside her. Then she glanced at Riley and an image of an entirely different sort sprung to mind. Him in that water with her, sliding against her body, hands running over her skin—

"We'll be moving out before you know it," Stace

said, more firmly this time. And before she could make a mistake.

The rain had abated—slightly—so she hurried toward the house, her suitcase bumping along the driveway behind her. Jeremy took his time, his hood up over his head, and his gaze roaming the grounds of the house.

A house with grounds. Space. The kind of house she saw on TV all the time, and dreamed about sometimes, but would never own. She wondered again why Riley McKenna had chosen to work at the diner, when clearly, he didn't need to work at all.

"Come on in," Riley said, taking Stace's suitcase from her before she reached the threshold. Jeremy ducked into the bungalow and dumped his bag right inside the door.

"Jeremy, don't leave that there," Stace said.

"He's fine. I'm not a picky housekeeper." Riley stood behind Stace and helped her off with her coat. He turned, hung it in a nearby closet, then gestured to a hall. "It's only a two-bedroom, so I thought you could sleep in the guest room and Jeremy could have the sofa bed."

"With that TV?" Jeremy said, pointing at the bachelor staple—a 50-inch big screen with surround sound.

Riley grinned. "Yep. All yours."

"Until ten," Stace added. "You have to get up in the morning for school."

"I'm expelled, remember? I don't have anywhere to go tomorrow. And nobody who cares where I go anyway," he added in a mumble. Then he flopped onto the couch, picked up the remote, and was flipping through channels in less time than it took Stace to say boo. For the hundredth time, Stace wished her sister was here—

and sober. Jeremy was clearly hurting, and there was so little Stace could do about it.

"Jeremy, you should ask permission before you turn on the television," she said. "This isn't your house."

"He's fine, Stace. Relax." Riley took her arm. "Come on, I'll show you your room. Let you get settled."

She glanced back at her nephew. "I should—"

"Listen to me. You work way too hard."

"Coming from the man who doesn't?"

"Hey, I worked today." He stretched the kinks in his back. "And I'm feeling it now."

She laughed. Apparently he was starting to realize that a day's work in the diner was harder than it looked. "Get used to it. Tomorrow will be worse."

"Why?"

"It's payday. We're always busier on payday than early in the week." She paused as he opened a door and waved her into a small, bright room. A double bed sat square in the center, flanked by two nightstands. The room was painted the color of a robin's egg. A soft beige rug anchored the room, and invited her to sink her toes into the thick plush. A pair of French doors on the far side opened onto a walkway that connected to the sparkling, bright blue waters of the pool. It all looked so inviting, comforting. Wonderful.

"It's not very big," Riley said. "Sorry about that."

"It's perfect." She turned and gave him a smile. "Thank you."

"You're welcome." His smile was warm, and just as inviting and tempting as the room.

The clock on the wall ticked by with the time. In the distance, she could hear the low murmur of the television. The rain pit-patted against the windows. But here, in this space, all she could see, hear, notice, was Riley

McKenna. His ocean-blue eyes seemed to hold her captive, and she stood there, inhaling the spicy notes of his cologne and wondering how those hands she had teased him about would feel against her skin. "Thank you."

"You said that already."

A flash of golden fur ran by outside. "You have a dog?"

"My brother's dog, Heidi. He and his wife are out of town for a couple days and my grandmother's watching her."

"Oh." Stace thumbed toward the closet. "I should probably unpack and get to bed. I mean, to sleep. Busy day tomorrow." God, now she was tripping over words and innuendos. Moving in here *definitely* wasn't a good idea.

He took a step back. Disappointment rushed in to fill the gap. "I'll leave you to it then." He stepped out of the room and shut the door, leaving Stace alone.

She should open her suitcase, hang up her clothes for work tomorrow, lay out her makeup, set up her nightly routine. It was after nine already, and four in the morning came early. She still had to find something to do with Jeremy tomorrow, and a way to get him into school again. Not to mention find the money to fix the roof. While still paying for groceries and electric and tuition.

The responsibilities weighed heavy on Stace's shoulders. She released the suitcase's handle and crossed the room, until she reached the glass doors. For a long while, she just watched the rain fall in shimmering lines.

Then she opened the door, stepped outside, and walked down the path to the pool area. The door opened easily, a wave of moist heat hit her, as comforting as an electric blanket. Stace kicked off her shoes and crossed to the tiled edge. She dipped one toe into the water, and let out a sigh.

"It's as warm as a bath, isn't it?"

Stace jerked away from the edge too fast, and lost her balance. Her arms pinwheeled at her sides and she wobbled on one foot. Before she tumbled into the water, Riley was there, one arm around her waist. He hauled her back onto the tile in a single fast, easy movement, as if she weighed no more than a feather."Riley! You scared me."

"Sorry." The lights overhead danced across his features, sparkled in his eyes. "You want to take a swim?"

"I can't. I didn't bring a swimsuit."

"My bad. I should have mentioned the pool. I'm hardly ever out here anymore, and sometimes I forget it's here."

"Really? If I had a pool, I'd be in it every day."

"You like to swim?"

"Very much." She sighed. "I was on the swim team and everything. A million years ago."

"Really?" He arched a brow.

"Yeah. It was back in high school. And then…" She wrapped her arms around herself, and turned away. Why had she started talking? She never talked about the past. Never revisited things that couldn't be changed. "Anyway, it was all a long time ago.

"It's been years since I've had regular access to a pool," she said. "I used to go to the Y and do laps in the pool there, but—"

"But what?" he asked, his voice as gentle as the ripples in the water. Urging, coaxing.

"I…I stopped after my father died." She let out a long breath. That was the truth of it. All these years, she told herself she'd quit swimming because she'd been so busy, but really, it was because she had been struggling to stay afloat in her life, and that had consumed all her energy. "I had to step in and work the diner, take care of my sister, my nephew, the house…" She put out her hands.

"And there wasn't any time to take care of you."

"I guess I just put me at the bottom of the list."

"Then today's the day you stop." Riley smiled at her.

Stace shook her head because if she spoke, she was sure tears were going to be falling.

Riley went on, undaunted. "My grandmother likes to bargain hunt so she has a bunch of swimsuits she's bought on sale in the changing room over there." He thumbed toward a door on the right. "I'm sure there's something in your size. Go get one and spend as much time in the pool as you want."

"I really shouldn't. The morning comes awful early." But she couldn't resist taking one look back at the pool, at the slight ripples kissed by pale white light. The water beckoned to her, like a friend.

"Nope, no excuses, Stace." He put a finger under her chin until she was looking at him. "Go ahead and enjoy yourself for once."

"Riley—"

"I'll go in if you will. And best of all the water's heated." Riley bent down, scooped up a handful of water, and drizzled it over her palm. The warm drops slid down her fingers, across her hand. "Now, how can you resist that?"

Two minutes later, Stace found herself standing on the deep end of the pool, dressed in a dark blue one-piece bathing suit that hugged her frame so snugly, there wasn't much left to the imagination. The water sparkled beneath her, and before she could think twice—

Stace leaped up and did a hard, fast cannonball into

the deep end. She plunged to the bottom, the water encasing her in a moment of silence before she popped back up.

"Bravo!"

She whirled around. Riley stood on the side, giving her a thumbs-up. "I'm sorry, I—"

"You had fun. And you did it well. Better than me, I think." He grinned. He was wearing a pair of red-and-black swim trunks, and carrying two towels. Wow. He was just as handsome and tempting unclothed as he was clothed. He had a broad, defined chest, narrowing in a *V* to a flat abdomen and tight waist. She curled her hands at her side because she had the strangest urge to place her palms on the muscled expanse of his chest.

She turned away and dove under the water, skimming down to the bottom then halfway across the pool. The minute the water enveloped her, a sense of peace settled on her shoulders, eased through her body. It was like…

Like coming home.

She forgot about Riley. Forgot about Jeremy. Forgot about the roof. She emerged for one quick breath, then went down again, gliding through the pale blue silent world under the surface. She swam from one end to the other, then rose up for another breath before making the journey a second time.

At the deep end, she came up for air again, and found Riley treading water beside her. "You are a hell of a swimmer," he said.

She shifted to tread water, too, pausing to wipe the hair out of her eyes. She told herself she didn't care how she looked wet—she never had before, and she wasn't going to start now. But a part of her did worry if there was mascara racooning under her eyes, or a tangled birds' nest of hair on top of her head. "Thanks."

His arms slid through the water in easy, practiced moves. His legs moved with a steady rhythm that didn't waste energy. "When I was younger, I spent a lot of hours out here."

"Pool parties with the girls in the neighborhood?"

"Nah. My football coach recommended we swim in the off season to build up our cardio and endurance. My grandfather heard that and put in a pool. I wanted to be the next Joe Namath, so I swam my butt off every winter. My grandfather thought it would build character, and he was right. I was in the water every morning by five, swimming for an hour and a half before school."

"Really? That's commitment."

He leaned in close. "I'm not as awful as you think I am."

"I don't think you're awful. At all." The words were out before she could stop them. What was it about Riley that had her confessing all her deepest thoughts?

"What *do* you think, Stace Kettering?"

"I...I think it's time to get out of the pool. Jeremy—"

"Is asleep. He passed out on the couch earlier. So stay, have some fun."

The water swished over her shoulders, trickled down her back. Droplets spiked on Riley's eyelashes, darkened his hair. "I, ah, should probably get out anyway. Early day tomorrow."

"I know. You keep saying that." He shifted closer to her, so close that she could feel the underwater currents created by his hands and legs. One of his legs brushed against hers, and she told herself to pull back. But she couldn't move. "If I'm not that awful then why do you do your best to avoid me?"

"I'm not avoiding you. I'm just not interested."

"Really?"

She swallowed. Tried not to look at his chest. "Really."

"So if I kissed you right now, you'd feel...nothing?"

Kiss her? A hot rush of anticipation flooded her. "I...I don't think we should do that."

"Why not? We're two consenting adults. Alone. In a pool. At night."

"I know that." Heck, every nerve in her body knew it. To her very core, Stace was hyper-attuned to Riley. To his bare skin, so close she could touch him with a whisper of movement, to his long legs, his hard chest, his broad shoulders. To everything.

"Then what's holding you back?" He shifted again, and now his legs were sliding against hers, and everything inside her melted.

She opened her mouth to speak, and couldn't. Every sensuous stroke of his skin on hers sent her mind skittering. Made her forget how she'd sworn off men like him.

"I want to kiss you, Stace," he said, his voice dark, low, tempting.

"I..." Her mouth opened. Closed again. "Okay." The word escaped her in a breathless rush.

Riley closed the gap between them. He wrapped one arm around her body. Their legs tangled, their torsos met, and every inch of her skin that connected with his seemed to light on fire. His blue eyes connected with hers, and held for one long heated second before he leaned in to kiss her.

At the same time, their two pairs of legs kicked, and tangled. The kiss became a knocking of chins, and the moment of unbalance sent them both bobbing under the water. Stace came up first, sputtering the unexpected wave out of her face and mouth, then Riley did the same. He looked like a wet puppy, and Stace started laughing. "Well, that wasn't exactly the moment of romance I was expecting," she said.

"Me either." He took her hand, and gave a big kick, dragging them both to shallower water. When they were both standing, he released her hand and cupped her jaw with both his hands. "Let's try that again."

This time, the anticipation roared through her like a train. Desire pooled in her gut, and she knew—knew without a shadow of a doubt—that this would be a kiss she would never forget. But most of all, she knew that letting Riley McKenna kiss her would be the biggest mistake of her life.

A mistake she couldn't afford to make.

CHAPTER SIX

For a busy diner, the silence could be deafening, Riley thought.

Stace hadn't talked to him since last night in the pool. She'd scrambled out of the water before he could kiss her, then sputtered something about needing to get to bed and hurried into the house. This morning at the diner, she'd done her job, kept her head down, and done her best to avoid him.

He'd gone out after the pool incident, headed off to barhop with Alec and Bill, staying out way too late, before coming home to collapse on his bed. He'd wasted half the money he'd earned on drinks that had done nothing to help him forget a woman with dancing green eyes. A woman who sang like a bird and did cannonballs like the best teenage boy.

When Riley woke up, Stace had already left for the morning. Jeremy was still asleep on the couch, so Riley had tiptoed around his house. On the kitchen counter, he had found a note from Stace to Jeremy, sitting beside a covered plate of pancakes.

Riley hadn't even known he had pancake mix. For a second, he envied the teenage boy who had someone who loved him enough to make him pancakes before the sun even had a chance to rise. Riley stared at those pancakes for a long, long time, and wondered about the woman who had intrigued him more than any he had ever met before. A woman who had already added a feminine touch to his home with the vanilla-scented pancakes, a floral makeup bag in the bathroom, and a bright yellow sweater draped over the back of a chair. A woman he told himself he didn't want, even as his gaze strayed to her again and again and desire pulsed inside him.

She bustled between the tables with the same efficiency as always, but with a decided distance from Riley. He missed her being at his shoulder, checking on his service, making sure he had the right order in place. He'd gotten used to her being nearby. And to her smile, her banter.

The morning rush passed quickly, though Riley found himself lagging behind several times. By his fourth cup of coffee, he was awake enough to handle the customer influx, and his hangover had abated to a tolerable level. By nine, the diner was empty and Riley heard Frank head out the back door for a bit of fresh air.

Across the room, Stace wiped tables in fast, concentric circles. No humming under her breath this time. Riley snatched up the salt and pepper shakers and held them out of her way. "How long are you going to avoid me?"

"I called a roofer this morning. He'll be out to give me an estimate later today. I'm going to move back to the house and just sleep on the couch until the roof is done and I can replace that mattress."

"You know, you shouldn't have been on the swim team."

She stopped cleaning and looked up at him. "What are you talking about?"

"You should have been on the track team because you are a master runner."

She scowled and went back to work. "I'm not running. I'm being realistic. I don't live with you, Riley. I live in that house in Dorchester, with all its flaws and problems. And I'm not going to date you and become another notch on your bedpost."

"Is that what you think last night was about?"

She straightened and propped a fist on her hip. "Are you going to try to tell me it wasn't?"

Disagreeing would mean telling her he had briefly considered something more. Something like the happiness Finn had found with Ellie. The same happiness his grandparents had enjoyed. But if there was one thing Riley had learned early in life, it was that depending on another person to be there when you needed them most was a foolish thing. So he retreated to his default position. "Well, you know me. Not the kind of guy who speaks the *M* word. Or the *L* one or any of the others in that alphabet of commitment."

A flicker of disappointment ran across her features. "Now that I believe."

For some reason, her assessment stung him. Riley had never been a man who wanted to settle down. Or sought a relationship that lasted longer than the expiration date on a block of cheese. He might envy Finn and his grandparents, but just the thought of those kind of ties made him feel choked.

The problem? Those were the kinds of ties that left pancakes on the counter in the morning.

So he decided to take the easy route. And change the subject. "Did you hear back from Jeremy's school?"

Stace plopped into an empty chair and dropped the rag onto the table. "Yes. I talked to them twice this

morning. They're not going to budge on the expulsion.
He can't just stay home all day, and the other school
in our district is…well, the lowest ranked in the state,
and not the safest or best learning environment. I really
don't want to send him there." She let out a long sigh.

"Have you thought about Wilmont Academy?"

"Wilmont Academy? I can't afford that." She dropped
her head into her hands. "I don't know what I'm going
to do."

He laid a hand on her shoulder. The touch was meant
to be comforting, friendly even, but it seared Riley's
palm and rocketed his mind back to the pool. To the
kiss that had ended before it started. He should have
followed her last night, damn it. Finished what they
barely began. But she'd made it clear she wasn't interested, and he had to accept that. Instead, he could at
least help take one worry off her shoulders. "Wilmont
might be the perfect thing for him. I went there, and it
was a great option for me. I was like Jeremy, creative,
a little ornery—"

She laughed. "Perfect adjective for you."

"I saw Jeremy's artwork at the house. I think he'll
love it there. And hey, maybe there's a scholarship or
something he could get."

"That would take a miracle," she said.

"You never know," Riley said, before turning to wipe
the last table. "Miracles have been known to happen."

The last of the lunch crowd began to peter out. Stace's
mind went to the pool at Riley's house. How nice it
would be to slip into the water, and lose herself for an
hour or so, in the mindless strokes of a good swim.

Thinking of the pool led directly to thinking of him.
Of how close they had come to kissing. How for a little

while, she really, really wanted him to kiss her. Riley McKenna, with his lopsided grin and piercing blue eyes, had gotten under her skin.

And that was trouble.

Stace didn't have time or room for a relationship in her life. She had Jeremy to focus on, then the balance in her bank account, and finally, Frank. She'd been working too hard and too long to save enough money to buy out Frank, and finally get him to retire and take some well deserved time for himself, to get sidetracked now. The roof repair, even with the amount covered by insurance, would take a chunk out of her savings, but if she worked hard, she could make that up.

And that meant staying away from trouble. Particularly trouble that came in a six-foot-two, dark-haired, blue-eyed package. She'd been down that road before and knew it led to heartbreak.

The bell over the door chimed, and a stately elderly woman entered the Morning Glory. She was tall, reed-thin, and had gray hair styled in a soft wave across her head. She wore a long plaid skirt, short heeled shoes, and an oatmeal-colored twinset. She looked like she'd just walked out of a church, or a bridge club. Stace crossed to her, lifting a menu out of the hostess station as she did. "Welcome to the Morning Glory, ma'am," Stace said. "Table for one?"

"For two." The older woman smiled and her gaze went past Stace. "Though I think someone is going to insist on making it for three."

Riley slipped in between them and pressed a kiss to the older woman's cheek. "Gran. You didn't have to make the trip down here."

"I'm not bed-ridden, Riley. I can still get around this city."

He chuckled then he gestured to Stace. "This is Stace Kettering, the best waitress in the city of Boston. Stace, meet my grandmother, Mary McKenna. And in the kitchen is Frank, who can cook you a burger with one hand tied behind his back and his eyes closed."

Mary put out her hand, and when she shook with Stace, her grip was firm and strong. "Pleasure to meet you, my dear."

"You too, Mrs. McKenna." Now that they were together, she could see the family resemblance between Mary and Riley. They had similar bone structure, the same blue eyes, and the same smile.

Riley put out his arm and waited for his grandmother to slip her hand into the crook. "Come on, Gran. Let me show you to the best table in the diner."

"And where is that?" Mary asked.

"Why, the one I'm sitting at, of course." He laughed, and she swatted him, but went along and sat at a corner booth. Windows fronted either side of the table, which made it a favorite among customers who liked to people-watch. It was indeed, as Riley had said, the best table in the Morning Glory, and the one Stace often sat at when the diner was empty and she had a chance to eat a meal or take a break. Riley waited until his grandmother was settled, with her clutch purse seated on the bench beside her. "Do you want some coffee?" he asked.

She arched a brow in surprise. "You're taking my order?"

"That's what they pay me to do." He gave the table a tap. "I'll be right back."

"Here you are, ma'am." Stace handed Mary a menu, and started to turn away when Mary put a hand on her arm.

"Please, sit. I'd like to get to know you." Mary gave

her a kind smile, then waved to the opposite seat. "Tell me. How's my grandson working out?"

Stace slid into the cushioned booth, and let out a sigh of contentment. After a long day of being on her feet, the mere act of pausing was like heaven. "He's doing great. He's learning. I think he's realized it's a harder job than it looks."

"He's a good man." Mary smiled. "And yes, I'm biased."

"That's okay. That's how it is with family." For a second, Stace envied Riley this connection with his DNA. She'd lost her grandparents when she was little, and with both her mother and father gone, there was no real Kettering connection for her anymore. Her sister had checked out long ago, and God only knew where she was now. That left just Jeremy and Stace. She missed family dinners and noisy Christmases. Riley still had that, and had two brothers to add to the mix. She wondered if he realized how lucky he was.

"Speaking of family," Mary said, "is your nephew here? I'd like to meet him. Riley says he deserves a McKenna scholarship."

"He did?"

Mary nodded. "He called me and said you were interested in Wilmont, but couldn't afford it. He told me a little about Jeremy, and said he'd be perfect for the scholarship."

Riley had said maybe a scholarship would come along to pay for the tuition. She'd never thought he meant he'd make that happen. "He said that? Really?" She glanced across the diner, where Riley was pouring three coffees. He'd stepped in to help, even when she'd told him not to. And for some reason, that pleased her. But still, she didn't want Mary to feel obligated to help.

"You don't have to do this just because Riley called. I'm sure we can find a way to handle it ourselves."

Mary laughed. "If there's one thing Riley will tell you about me, it's that nobody forces Mary McKenna to do anything. I'm sure Jeremy will love Wilmont Academy."

'He's not much of a student, I'm afraid."

"Neither was Riley, and that's why that school was perfect."

Riley deposited the coffees on the table. "Gushing about me again?"

"Of course not." Mary's voice was stern but her features soft. "You were a handful, and still are."

"You must be talking about Finn." Riley grinned, then thumbed toward the kitchen. "Are you hungry, Gran? Frank can make anything you want."

"A turkey sandwich would be nice," Mary said.

"Coming right up. With twenty-two fries, not twenty-one." The last he directed at Stace, with a grin, then he was gone.

"Twenty-two fries?" Mary asked.

"Inside joke." Stace found herself smiling. When had she and Riley gone from combative coworkers to friends with inside jokes? She thought of their almost-kiss the night before. Friends? Or maybe…something more?

No, nothing more. A moment of insanity.

After all, hadn't he just made it clear he hated responsibility? His whole life, or at least what she'd seen chronicled in the papers, had been about being irresponsible. The last thing she needed was one more person depending on her to be the grown-up. Jim had done that and it wasn't until he was gone that she'd realized how much she'd been the one to hold everything together.

"I'm glad to see Riley so happy," Mary said, drawing Stace's attention back. "Might I assume that has something to do with you living in the guest house?"

"Oh, no, no, that's a temporary thing. There's a hole in my roof and Riley insisted Jeremy and I stay with him until it's fixed." Stace made sure to emphasize her nephew's name, to remind herself and Mary that it wasn't a living together situation at all, merely a favor. "It's temporary."

"You said that already." Mary smiled and Stace wanted to shrink into the chair and disappear.

Why did she stumble every time she talked about Riley? She wasn't interested in him. At all. He'd gone out last night—which of course was his right, because they were coworkers, not husband and wife—and probably ended up with one of those pretty blondes she'd seen pictured beside him in the paper before.

And Stace wasn't jealous. Not one bit.

No, she was just glad it hadn't been her on his arm. That she'd resisted his kiss. Very glad. Uh-huh. Sure.

As if on cue, Jeremy emerged from the kitchen. He often came in the back door after school to hang with Frank and get a snack, before coming out to greet his aunt. Stace waved him over. Thank God. A reason to change the subject away from Riley McKenna. "Jeremy, this is Riley's grandmother, Mrs. McKenna."

"Hi," Jeremy said. Stace gave him an arched brow. "Uh, nice to meet you."

"She runs the McKenna Foundation," Stace reminded him. "And she told me that they give out a scholarship to the Wilmont Academy."

"That's a really cool school," Jeremy said, his interest piqued now. "I was just talking to one of my friends who goes there. He does photography and he sold a picture to the *Globe*. He's, like, famous now."

Mary patted the table. "Come, sit down, young man. Let me get to know you."

Jeremy did as he was asked, and after a few minutes of easy chatting between Jeremy and Mary, Stace took the cue from Mary and left the two to talk alone. She glanced back over her shoulder at her nephew, who was talking fast, his hands moving in animated excitement. Every time the subject turned to art, Jeremy's entire demeanor shifted from angry to eager and creative. Maybe Riley was right, and this new school would be the right thing to turn her nephew's life around.

She met up with Riley on the other side of the counter, where he was waiting for Frank to finish assembling Mary's sandwich. "Your grandmother is really nice."

"Thanks. And I know she means well when she does things like cut me off financially."

The pieces fell into place. Riley saying he was broke. Applying for jobs. Taking the one here. "That's what happened?"

Riley nodded. "Yup, that's why I'm here. She told me to get out there, pay my own way and truly earn my keep."

"But I thought you worked for the family business."

"Used to. And I didn't really do anything much." He gestured to the diner, and a measure of respect filled his features. "*This* is work. I don't know how you do it."

"I just do." She shrugged. "I have bills to pay, and I just suck it up and work hard."

"Well, I admire you."

Heat rushed to her cheeks, and she had to look away. "Thanks." His praise pleased her, more than she wanted to admit. Every minute she spent with Riley revealed another dimension to the man. Was he the fun-loving rich kid who shrugged off the word *responsibility* like a horsehair shirt? Or this Riley, who recognized hard work, loved his family, and helped out people he barely knew?

Riley leaned in close. "I have to tell you that I'm sorry for not being a good customer. If I'd gotten me, I'd have dumped a hot pot of coffee in my lap."

She laughed. "I was tempted. Many times."

"Well, next time, feel free." Then he glanced at the percolating pot. Steam rose from the brewing coffee. "On second thought, ice water might be better."

"I'll remember that."

"I bet you will." He laughed.

She gave Riley a light slug in the arm. "I'm kinda getting used to you being around here. You're becoming part of the Morning Glory Diner." And a part of her liked that, whether she wanted to admit it or not.

His gaze went past her, to the street outside, or to something else, she couldn't tell. "Well, before you know it, I'll be out of your hair, and back to being just a customer." He took the sandwich that Frank had laid on the counter and turned toward his grandmother's table. "So keep that ice water handy."

She watched him go. He lingered only a moment, exchanging a few words with Jeremy, and then his grandmother before he returned to where Stace was standing.

"Looks like Jeremy's got a new school to attend," Riley said.

"Really? Your grandmother approved him for the scholarship?"

He nodded. "It lasts as long as he attends. He does have to keep his grades up, though. Gran added that stipulation after I graduated. Apparently I set a bad example for the other kids." Riley grinned. "But you won't have to pay for anything."

"That's just…too much. I can't—"

"You can." His hand lingered on her back for a moment more.

Tears welled in her eyes, and before she could think twice, she flung her arms around him. "Thank you. You have no idea what this means."

He held her tight and thought of the pancakes, then he smiled into her hair and inhaled the scent of vanilla, lavender and a sweet goodness that he had never known before. "I think I do."

It also meant Riley was in deep. And he had a feeling he was going to be able to tread water for only so long.

CHAPTER SEVEN

ALL it took to trip the switch in Riley was a quartet of needy, demanding customers who complained loudly and often about the service, the food and even the napkins. They left Riley with a quarter for a tip, and an attitude.

He watched them leave, and the old familiar urge to run rose inside him. He'd left a half dozen jobs…no, more…because he hadn't found one he loved. And he sure as heck didn't love this one. What had Stace said earlier?

He was becoming part of the Morning Glory Diner.

When she'd said that, he'd realized she was right— he'd been connecting with the diners, to her, to her nephew. He was *bonding,* for Pete's sake. He'd gone and involved his grandmother, and helped not just Stace, but her nephew, too.

All Riley had wanted was a job. With no attachments.

This was a temporary position, a transition of sorts, not a permanent place for him to settle down. He bristled at the thought of being part of anything. Riley didn't do attached, and he wasn't about to start now. The whole thought of being here in a month, a year, heck, a decade, threatened to suffocate him.

So when Alec called with an invitation to lunch at

the club, the urge to return to the fancy, devil-may-care life he'd had before nagged at Riley. Shrug off these responsibilities and expectations for an hour. And away from Stace Kettering, who drew him in like a magnet every time he said he wanted distance.

Stace passed by him, a loaded tray balanced on one shoulder. "Don't worry about those customers. We all get bad apples from time to time."

"Yeah." Riley glanced at the clock, then the nearly empty diner, and had the apron strings undone and the yoke of his job tossed onto a nearby chair in the next second. "Hey, I'm going to go out to grab a bite to eat," he said to Stace. "Is that okay?"

"Sure. Just be back soon. I was hoping to get out of here early. Remember, I have the roofer coming by to give me an estimate."

"No problem." Relief surged in his chest, like loosening a set of chains.

Stace sent him a smile, and a ribbon of guilt ran through him. He shrugged it off. He had a right to a social life. He wasn't married to Stace, or to this job. And he sure as hell wasn't "responsible" or purposed or committed or any of the other things his grandmother and everyone around him seemed to think he should be. He deserved a lunch out with Alec. Some time where no one wanted coffee or checks or anything from him.

Responsible men settled down. Had families. Built stuff in the garage. He'd done enough of that in the past few days, and it was leading him down a dangerous path of doing more.

He wasn't going to be that kind of man. Ever. And the sooner Stace realized that, the better.

* * *

Stace refused to talk to him. Riley had returned to the diner a little after three, and found her finishing the cleanup alone. She didn't greet him when he walked in the door, and brushed him off when he offered to stack chairs. The afternoon's meal with Alec, in an overpriced club eating an overpriced sandwich accompanied by an overpriced beer, no longer seemed as satisfying.

"You're in trouble, boy," Frank said, when Riley headed into the kitchen.

"Sorry, Frank. Time got away from me." He reached for the apron he'd left behind earlier. It now sat folded on an empty shelf in the kitchen. Stace's doing? Or Frank's?

Frank put a hand on Riley's arm. "Leave it. Come back tomorrow. When you're ready to work, not pretend to work." The rebuke sounded clear and strong.

"All I did was take a long lunch. I apologized." Riley had taken dozens of long lunches when he worked at McKenna Media. So many, in fact, they had become a running joke.

Apparently, none of this was funny to Frank. "What, do you think we're all sitting here twiddling our thumbs all day? You want a job, you work. Not let the rest of us pick up your slack."

The sandwich Riley had had at lunch sat heavy in his stomach. He glanced back at the diner, at Stace working hard, and the guilt that had been nothing more than a whisper earlier became a full-out scream in his head. What had he been thinking, leaving her to handle this alone? He'd run out of here, thinking only of himself, of shedding the responsibilities that had become a second coat. Not of her.

He knew how hard the job was. This entire week, he'd found little ways to get out of working too hard. Asking her to refill customers' drinks. Leaving her to do the cleanup. And now, leaving her to handle the afternoon alone. No wonder she'd shot him that glare. He deserved it—and more.

He thought of all those long lunches. They weren't the joke—he was. God, what an idiot he had been. A lazy, irresponsible idiot.

"I'm sorry."

"I'm not the one you need to apologize to." Frank pivoted to face Riley again. "You know, it's okay to admit you ain't got it all together. People respect a man who's honest with himself and with others."

Riley didn't reply. He just slipped the apron on and tied it behind his back.

"I've known you a long time, Riley." Frank dumped in several cupfuls of mayonnaise, then started mixing the coleslaw, the spatula digging deep in the oversized stainless steel bowl. "You've always taken your time like you didn't have any place to get to."

"My other job was...flexible."

"Or maybe it's more you didn't have any place you *wanted* to go." Frank finished the coleslaw, wrapped it in plastic wrap, then stowed it in the refrigerator. "Once you find where it is you want to go, I think you'll be more inclined to have some staying power." Then Frank turned away and headed for the sink to wash his hands.

Any place he wanted to go.

Was that why Riley had jumped from job to job? Heck, woman to woman? He'd spent his whole life...

Searching.

And what had he found? Nothing. Not a damned thing. What on earth was he looking for?

The answer didn't magically appear, so Riley headed out to the diner, grabbing the mop and rolling bucket on the way. Stace kept working, her back to him, even though she surely heard the clatter of the bucket's wheels as he approached. He stopped beside her. "I'm sorry."

"I'm not talking to you." She crossed to wipe off the next table.

"Stace, I'm sorry. I just got overwhelmed by the job and—"

She spun back. "You think I don't get overwhelmed? Or Frank doesn't? You don't think most of the people who work a job have days when they just want to run for the hills, or lie in bed, for the fun of it?"

"I'm sure you do. I'm not arguing that."

"No, but what you're doing is letting us down. I don't need another man who's going to let me down, Riley, so if this is your M.O., the door is right there." She turned back to the table, and wiped in furious circles.

"Why do you do that?"

"It's called cleaning up at the end of the day."

"I meant, why do you lump me in with every other man you know?"

"Because I've dated you. Not you, but your kind. Heck, I almost married a man just like you. Selfish, irresponsible, answering to no one but himself. I wasted so many years…too many years, hoping he'd change. And he never did." She pivoted toward him, the wet rag raised in her hands like a weapon. "Tell me, how are you different? Are you looking for marriage? For commitment? For anything more permanent than a tan?"

The words stung. Was that how she saw him? Or who he had been? "I'm not here to stay, if that's what you're asking. You and me and Frank all knew this job was a temporary thing. A means to an end. I've told you that."

"Well, I'd appreciate it if you would work hard while you're getting your 'means to an end.' Because the rest of us have lives and responsibilities that depend on you being here and doing your share."

Then it hit him. The appointment she'd made. Her request to leave early. The roof. Damn. She was right. He hadn't been thinking about anyone but himself. And now he was staring right at the results of that choice. "Stace, I forgot all about your appointment."

"It's fine. I'll get another one." But her voice trembled when she said it, and she had returned to her table wiping.

He felt like a jerk. Was this what he'd become? A man who let other people down just to have lunch with a friend?

He put a gentle hand on Stace's shoulder. "I really am sorry about today. Why don't you let me make it up to you?"

She stopped working and turned to assess him. "I don't need you to do anything other than just show up when you say you're going to."

"Deal." He shook with her, which brought a ghost of a smile to Stace's lips. "Did you have another roofer lined up?"

She sighed. "I haven't had time to find one. I made six calls, and this guy was the only one who called me back. I think reliable handymen are harder to find than unicorns."

"Or responsible playboys?"

She laughed, and it sounded like sunshine. "I heard those are an endangered species."

Riley chuckled, then realized how true that was, even if they were joking. He flipped out his cell phone and scrolled through the numbers. Then he pressed Send and put the phone to his ear.

"What are you doing?" she asked.

"Calling a roofer. One of the guys I went to high school with—"

"Don't." She put a hand over his. "I can take care of myself."

He leaned in toward her. "I have no doubt that you can. But this is all my fault, and I feel bad about leaving you in the lurch today, so please, let me help you. The least I can do is clean up the mess I made." He was getting involved again, and even as his mind screamed caution, his gut countered.

Her gaze assessed him, and she worried her bottom lip. He could see the struggle in her eyes, the tough decision on whether to accept his help or throw it back in his face. "If I let you do this, it's only because I don't want to spend any more time than necessary in your guest house."

"Agreed." By making this call, Riley ensured Stace's departure. There'd be no more pancakes on the counter, or floral bags in his bathroom. The thought saddened him, but before he could figure out why, the man on the other end answered. Riley explained the situation, then set up an appointment and ended the call. "He'll be out tonight. And he'll be fair on price."

"Thank you."

He chuckled. "That was hard for you, I know."

It took a moment, but then a smile filled her face. "What will be harder is you getting back into my good graces again if you're ever late, or let me down."

The trouble was, Riley knew that answer already. Some day, and probably soon, he would let her down. It was what he did, after all.

Stace woke up in Riley's guest bedroom on the second morning and told herself not to get too used to the feel-

ing of the soft bed, luxurious linens, quiet grounds. But
here she was again.

She had told Frank she'd be in late, so she could get
Jeremy off to his first day of school okay. Riley had offered to cover, and Frank had called in Irene, the waitress who was on maternity leave. Stace glanced at the
clock, and realized she hadn't slept this late in months,
maybe years.

Then she glanced at the calendar and realized what
day it was. Her heart lurched, and she took a moment
to compose herself. Had she gotten so distracted in the
past few days that she hadn't noticed the calendar?

Stace tugged on a robe and padded out to the kitchen.
Jeremy was still asleep on the couch, looking so much
like his mother that Stace's heart broke. She missed her
sister with a pain that edged through her like a knife.
"Where are you, Lisa?" Stace whispered to the walls.
There was no answer, of course. There never was.

Almost her entire family, gone. Some days, the empty
echoes on the family tree hit especially hard. Like today.

So Stace did what she always did. She busied herself
with tasks that kept her mind from thinking too much.
Putting some hard-boiled eggs on to boil, making coffee, then showering and dressing while waiting for the
eggs to cook. When she was done, she woke Jeremy,
and prodded the reluctant teenager toward the shower.

While she waited, Stace took the time to glance
around Riley's home. She'd expected more of a bachelor pad, complete with overstuffed leather furniture,
sports memorabilia, and a year's supply of unhealthy
snacks. Riley's house was sedate, with tasteful decorations and comfortable furniture that beckoned guests.
The rooms were tidy, the carpets clean, and the faint
scent of chlorine from the nearby pool lingered in the

air. Did Riley clean up after himself? Had he done the decorating? Or let someone else do it?

And why did she care? She'd meant what she'd said about not getting involved with him, or anyone for that matter, but especially him.

Hadn't he proven yesterday that he was unreliable? In the end, Riley McKenna would run from responsibility like it was a forest fire. She needed to remember that—and not get tempted by his lips, his eyes, his words. It had taken her heart a long time to recover from being broken by Jim, and she didn't want to go there again.

The problem? Every time Riley looked at her, she thought of what they had started—and not yet finished. What if she hadn't jumped out of the pool? What if she had kissed him?

The door opened, and Stace pivoted, to find Riley standing there, as if she'd conjured him up simply by thinking about him. He was wearing jeans and a Morning Glory Diner T-shirt that was sporting a ketchup stain on one side, a coffee stain on the other. She felt a smile rush to her face, along with a hot rush of tears. Riley, of course, couldn't know what today was, but just having him here filled her with gratitude. "I thought you were taking my shift," she said. "Why are you here?"

"Things slowed down enough for Irene to handle it. Frank told me, in his exact words, 'to get the hell out of here and make sure Jeremy gets his butt to school. And that Stace doesn't cry when he leaves.'"

Stace laughed. "That's Frank."

"And I thought that since I'd gone to that school, it might make things a little easier on Jeremy to have me along."

Who was Riley McKenna? Every time she thought he

was an insensitive, self-centered playboy, he went and did something like this. Something sweet. Something that caught her off guard, and tangled her heart. "Well, thank you."

"No problem." His gaze caught hers, and for a second she had the crazy thought that he was going to kiss her. That same rush of anticipation roared to life inside her, then dropped away when Riley cleared his throat. "I'm just going to go change. I'll be back."

Then he headed down the hall, and Stace returned to her breakfast. But the eggs had lost their flavor and she tossed them out uneaten.

For the first time in a month, Jeremy smiled. Stace wanted to hug her nephew, but held back, afraid of breaking whatever magic spell had come over him when he walked into the Wilmont Academy.

"This place is so cool, Riley," Jeremy said as he spun in a slow circle around the lobby outside the principal's office. "Did you see all the artwork on the walls?"

"Yep. It's everywhere. They have classes in film and photography, too. And dance, though I don't know if that's your style."

Jeremy laughed. Actually laughed. "Me? No way, man."

"It's a good way to get the ladies." Riley patted his chest. "You're looking at a graduate of Ballroom Dancing 101."

Beside them, Stace stifled a smirk. Riley, ballroom dancer? That she'd pay money to see.

Jeremy's nose wrinkled as if he'd just eaten a lemon. "Didn't it make you feel...girlie?"

"Not one bit." Riley stepped over, swung an arm around Stace's waist, then spun her to the right with two quick movements. He stopped, leaned over, and gave her a quick, breathless dip. She tried to hold back her laughter, but it bubbled up all the same. "Is that girlie?" Riley asked.

"Not one bit," Stace said. In fact it was every inch manly, and had awakened some very heated hormonal responses inside her body. If they hadn't been standing in the lobby of a school…

But they were. She scrambled out of his arms and back to a standing position before she got too used to the feeling of being held by him, or started daydreaming about being in his arms for a whole lot more than a simple dance.

A door to their right opened and a woman emerged. She was tall, slender, and had long dark hair that flowed down her back. One of those women so beautiful they made everything around them, even the handmade art decorating the walls, pale in comparison. "What shenanigans are you up to in my hall, Mr. McKenna?"

Riley grinned. "None at all, Miss Purcell."

She laughed, then placed a hand on his arm and leaned in close. "Too bad." Her voice was husky, sexy.

To Stace, the two of them seemed overly familiar, and she could read the undercurrent of a past relationship in the air. There was too much of a smile, too close of a touch. As Riley introduced her to Merry Purcell, Stace tried very hard not to hate the woman on the spot.

After all, it wasn't her fault that she'd reminded Stace of all the reasons why she shouldn't be involved with Riley. Of the ex-boyfriend who had broken her heart by running off with another woman.

So Stace put on a smile she didn't feel and waited until Jeremy had been introduced and then sent on his way to his first class. The gorgeous Miss Purcell got back to work, and Riley and Stace headed out the door.

"I appreciate you coming along," she said.

"Just wanted to be sure his first day went off without a hitch." Riley thumbed toward his car. "I'm heading back to work. Do you want me to drop you off at home?"

The responsibilities for today had dropped away, and as Stace took in the bright day around her, she was reminded again of the date. She could have gone back to the diner, but for now, she wanted to be alone.

How she wished her father had been here to see his grandson enrolled in this school. He would have been the first one to offer Jeremy a hearty congratulations, and the proudest relative in the parking lot. Stace's gaze went to the skies, to the dark gray clouds that hung over Boston, and maybe, hung over wherever her sister was now. Did Lisa even know what she had left behind? And would she ever come back?

Stace ached to talk to her father. He'd always had some little snippet of wisdom that could turn any situation better.

"Stace?" Riley's voice pulled her back to the present. "Do you want me to drop you off somewhere?"

"Uh…no. I'll see you later." She turned away, and started to head down the sidewalk toward the train station. Above her, the sky rumbled. It was going to rain. Again.

An apt weather report, Stace supposed, and buttoned her sweater against the increasing breeze. A second later, the red sports car sidled up beside her and the passenger window descended. "Come on, at least let me give you a ride back to the house," Riley said.

"I'm not going home." Home? When had Riley's guest house become home? She cursed the slip of the tongue, and blamed it on her mind being on other things. Not this irrational, growing need to have him around.

"Okay," Riley said. "Then where are you going?"

She let out a long breath. "Listen, I'm sure Frank is expecting you back. Just go to the diner and I'll talk to you later."

"It's only ten. I have an hour until we start gearing up for lunch. And Irene's there right now." Above them, the skies opened up and the rain began falling in a steady sheet, soaking through Stace's sweater, and plastering her hair against her head. "Come on, don't be stubborn. Get out of the rain, Stace."

"I..." The rain cut off her argument. As much as she'd like to be stubborn, as he'd said, and just head off on her own, the darn subway station was three blocks away and she wasn't wearing a coat. And to be honest...

She didn't want to be alone right now.

So she opened the door and slid inside the car, settling against the soft black leather seat. For a sports car, the interior was decidedly roomy and nice. Riley pulled away from the curb, and started heading down the street.

"Where to?"

"Cedar Grove Cemetery. I can give you directions. It's over on Adams—"

"I know where it is." A shadow dropped over Riley's face. "Why do you want to go there?"

"You don't have to take me. I'll take the train." She reached for the door handle. The last thing she wanted to do was explain everything to Riley. If she did, she'd be letting him into her heart, and she'd just vowed five minutes ago not to do that.

Riley reached over and put a hand on hers. "I don't mind, Stace. Really."

She readied a reason again why she could do this on her own, but stopped it. Riley had accused her of never asking for help. Maybe he had a point. Right now, she needed…something.

Company at least.

She glanced at his face and saw earnest concern there. For the hundredth time, she wondered who Riley McKenna really was. The man who'd dated more women than she could count, or this tender man who wouldn't let her walk in the rain?

So she gave Riley directions, and within minutes, they'd reached the cemetery. She directed him through the wrought-iron gates, past the fish pond and the stone chapel, down the winding main path, then down a second smaller road on the right. As they got deeper into the cemetery and closer to her destination, Stace could feel emotion bubbling up in her chest. "Stop here."

He glided to a stop. "Stace—"

"I'll be right back." She tugged on the door handle and barreled out of the car and into the rain. The water sluiced down her face, blurring her vision, but it didn't matter. She knew her destination by heart. She climbed the small grassy hill until she reached a granite marker embedded in the ground. Grass had grown up around the edges, creeping onto the small gray slab.

KETTERING was carved across the top in block letters. Below that, two names in a smaller font. Karen on the left and David on the right, along with the dates of their deaths. Rain pooled in the etched letters of her parents' names, bubbling over into tiny ponds.

A sob hitched in Stace's throat. The rain fell hard on her head, her back. Above her, storm clouds rumbled with discontent.

"Oh, Dad, I miss you." She barely remembered her

mother, who had died when Stace was little. Almost all her memories centered around the burly David Kettering, who had a kind word for every person he met, and a joke for every friend he made. He'd been her rock, and then he was gone, and she'd been doing her best to stay strong ever since, and felt like she was failing.

There was a sound beside her, then the rain stopped falling on her shoulders. She turned, to find Riley standing there with an umbrella opened over her head. She gave him a weak smile. "Thanks."

He gestured at the granite marker. "Your father?"

She nodded. "He died eight years ago today. The Morning Glory was his baby, his and Frank's."

"I knew that place was special to you for more than just a job."

She stared at the grave while the rain pattered on the umbrella like a thousand fingers. "God, I miss seeing him there. I've been at the Morning Glory since the day I was tall enough to sit at one of the counter stools. At first, my sister and I were just there after school so my dad didn't have to get a babysitter. We'd sit at the counter, and Frank would spoil us rotten with French fries and ice cream sundaes, and all the pancakes we could eat." She smiled at the memory, and could almost see herself back there again, fingers all sticky with syrup, belly sloshing with milk. "Then when we got older, we started helping out. Wiping the tables, sweeping the floor. My sister never really liked the work, but I stuck with it. By the time I was in high school, I was waitressing over the summer."

"And after college, working there full-time?"

"I didn't go to college." She bent down and traced the letters of her father's name, feeling for the thousandth

time like she had let him down for not following the
dreams he'd had for her. How many times had she sat at
the kitchen table, discussing her dream of going to business school? Of making it big in the corporate world?
Fate had had other plans for Stace and even though she
wondered if she'd missed anything by skipping college,
she knew her heart would never have been in the corporate world. It was right there in the Morning Glory.

"I didn't go to college, because…" She paused, her fingers catching the raindrops that pooled on the stone
like tears. "My father was hit by a car outside the diner
a month after I graduated high school. I went to work
full-time at the Morning Glory and have been there ever
since." She gave the stone a final touch, then rose. "It
was a way of staying close to him. And helping Frank,
who was just devastated when my dad died."

"Stace, I'm so sorry. That had to be really hard on
you."

She shrugged, but the tears in her eyes belied the
show of nonchalance. "I got through it. By doing what
my dad did. I went to work, and took care of others." She
let out a long breath. "My sister took his death so much
harder than I did, and that's when she fell into drugs.
She was a great single mom to Jeremy before that, but
it was as if this was one more burden she couldn't carry.
For a while she lived with me, then she'd disappear,
come back, disappear again. Until she finally left for
good last month and left me a note asking me to take
care of Jeremy."

"Through all this," Riley said, "who took care of
you?"

Stace turned away. This was why she rarely opened
up to people. Because when she did, they asked the

tough questions, the ones she avoided at all costs. "I am fine…as long as I'm working."

"And when you're not?"

Damn this man. He seemed to have a bead on the very things she didn't want to think about. "I'm always working," she said instead of the truth. That when she paused to think about how her life had been upended, and how she had put everything on hold—college, marriage, children—that it allowed regret to crawl in and make itself at home.

"Maybe it's time you did something other than work."

She shook her head and started heading down the hill. There was no solace to be found here today. No voice of wisdom, no comforting hugs. Just a cold, wet stone. "You don't understand, Riley. I can't. The Morning Glory was my dad's business, and it needs me to be plugged in, to keep it running. Especially now that it's struggling. Frank can't do it on his own."

"No one said he had to. But the job doesn't all have to fall on your shoulders."

They had reached the path beside his car. She wanted to just get in the car and drive away, and not have this conversation, but it was Riley's car and he had the keys, and he wasn't making any move to leave. "Stop trying to question my life and my choices, Riley."

"I'm not. I'm just telling you there are other options."

"Like what? Living off my family? Because unlike you, I don't have one that has scholarships and guest houses at their disposal. There's me, and that's it. If I don't go to work, I don't eat." She saw that her words had hit close to home, and she reached out a hand to him. Her mouth had gotten away from her and regret filled her. "I'm sorry. I shouldn't have said that."

"No, you're right." He brushed a tendril of wet hair

off her forehead. "If there's one thing I've learned in the few days I've worked at the Morning Glory, it's that you have to work hard for what you want. I've gotten by for too many years on the bare minimum. And I don't want to do that anymore."

She let out a little laugh. "Well, I wouldn't mind a few days of the bare minimum."

A grin curved across his face. "Maybe we can work out a compromise. I had some ideas to increase business. I'd love to run them by you."

"Okay." She echoed his smile for a moment. "When I'm working at the diner, sometimes I really miss my dad. He made every day there one to look forward to."

"He sounds like he was a wonderful guy."

"He was." The smile hurt her face now, and tears threatened the back of her eyes. The rain kept up its steady patter, as if urging her to cry with it. She had been strong for so long, never showing an emotion, just putting in the hours at work, and lately, helping to raise Jeremy. Before that, it had been taking care of her sister, being the one that Lisa turned to when she was lost or cold or hungry. In all that time, Stace had put her own needs on hold. And now here was Riley, the one man she kept trying to resist, standing in the rain with an umbrella and an understanding smile, and in the process, opening her heart a little at a time. She swiped at her face and looked back at the hill that held her father's grave. "I wanted to come here today to tell him about Jeremy getting into that school. My dad would be so proud." She rolled her eyes and wiped away a tear. "It's silly. I mean, he's not even there. But I still like to talk to him."

"Aw, Stace." Riley put an arm around her shoulders

and drew her against his chest. He was warm and hard and smelled like soap. "It's not silly at all. Not one bit."

She looked up into his gentle blue eyes, and in them, saw a mirror of her own sorrow there, a peek inside the depths of Riley. For a long while, neither of them said a word. The rain pattered on the sidewalk, while Riley held onto Stace, and Stace held onto Riley.

"I come here a lot, too," he said softly. "My parents are buried just over the hill. For me, it's been twenty years since they died, but there are times when it feels like yesterday. And you know, all the scholarships and guest houses in the world don't make up for that."

"No, they don't." She'd never have expected that Riley, of all people, would understand. Would empathize. "I'm sorry I said that stuff about money."

"It's okay. If it had been me, I probably would have said the same thing." He sighed. "I come here sometimes for answers," he said. "But they aren't here, are they?"

She shook her head. "No. I sure wish they were." A long, shuddering breath escaped her.

Then she gave up the fight and leaned the rest of the way into Riley, pouring her tears into his soft shirt, and her grief into his broad shoulders. He just held her, his chin resting gently on the top of her head, and the umbrella shielding them both from the storm. She told herself not to get so close, not to care so much. But she did, oh, how she did.

After a long while, the rain began to ease and Stace's tears dried up. Riley pulled back. "You okay now?"

She nodded. "Thank you. I'm sorry for—"

He pressed a finger to her lips. "Don't. Don't ever apologize for needing someone."

"I don't…" She shook her head. He was right. "Okay, I won't. Thank you, Riley."

"You're welcome. Anytime." His hand slid down and cupped her jaw, turning her face up to meet his. His blue eyes were soft, caring, yet filled with as many mysteries as the stormy skies above. "I have never met a woman like you."

She shrugged. "I'm a waitress from Dorchester, Riley. I'm nothing special."

"Oh, you are wrong, Stace. Very, very wrong." He leaned down until his gaze was riveted on hers, and the only thing she could hear was the rapid beat of her own heart. He tipped the umbrella away from them, letting it fall to the ground. The rain had slowed to a mist, and it dusted them both with a soft blanket of wet.

Time slowed. The world stopped. And then Riley McKenna leaned in and captured Stace's mouth with his.

He kissed her tenderly at first, a long, slow caress across her lips that seemed almost reverent. Two kindred souls, seeking comfort, solace, connection. She leaned into him, and the kiss deepened, became a concert of sensations on her mouth. She closed her eyes, and for the first time in forever, allowed herself to do nothing but feel. Feel Riley's firm body against hers. Feel Riley's strong palm on her jaw. Feel Riley's lips moving against hers, his tongue dancing with hers.

And most of all, feel Riley McKenna becoming an indelible part of her heart.

CHAPTER EIGHT

RILEY had not intended to kiss Stace Kettering. To do anything other than offer her comfort, a shoulder to lean on. But then she had looked up at him with those sad eyes and that sweet smile, and he'd wanted nothing more than to make her his.

That was a dangerous thing. He was beginning to crave her presence, to think about her all the time and to wonder about what would happen next. It was as if he was falling for her, and that was one thing he couldn't do. She deserved a man who wanted to settle down in that little house in Dorchester, patch her roof, and fix her plumbing. Not a man who had all the sticking power of wet glue. He'd always excelled at short-term relationships because they were a hell of a lot safer than the kind where a man settled down for the rest of his life. Did he need a bigger reminder of why, than he had right here, standing in this cemetery?

Nothing lasted. And pretending otherwise only led to pain.

So he had pulled away, even as a large part of him didn't want to let go. He knew better, though, and knew deep inside he wasn't interested in the white picket fence life.

They both opted to go back to the diner, and relieve

the harried Irene, who thanked them up and down for letting her go home early. "The baby isn't letting me sleep yet," Irene said. "If I'm lucky, I can get a nap in before she needs to eat again."

After Irene was gone, and it was just Riley and Stace in the front of the diner again, the reality became clear to Riley. More dishes, more customers, more orders to take and fill. The prospect suffocated him, and he chafed at the thought of putting in several more hours here.

Because they'd gotten close earlier, and that had knocked him off-kilter again? It was like a push-pull in his chest. Every time expectations were heaped on Riley, all he wanted to do was...

Escape.

Riley McKenna didn't get close. Didn't form long-term relationships. Didn't do anything other than find one more way to amuse himself. That's what he needed to focus on, instead of his mind circling back to one tender moment in the rain.

The rest of the day's shift passed quickly. Stace left early to meet Jeremy outside the school, and Riley followed once the cleanup was done, to gather them from the train station and drive them back to the guest house. It was all beginning to feel a lot like...

A family.

So ordinary. Like peanut butter and jelly sandwiches.

Jeremy talked nonstop the whole way home about his day at school, and as soon as they got in the door, he started in on his first homework project, spreading out paper, pencils, and paints on the kitchen table.

"Is it okay if I use the pool?" Stace asked.

"Sure. Make yourself at home." He thought of offering to go with her, but then remembered the last time he had done that. Seeing her in her swimsuit, feeling her slick, wet body against his—

He'd be right back to doing what he swore he wouldn't do again. Kissing her.

Stace changed, then headed out to the pool. Riley stayed in the kitchen, loading dishes into the dishwasher—it was amazing how domesticated he'd been forced to become now that he wasn't paying for a maid service—and watching Stace from the kitchen window. She sliced through the water with a pro's precision, in long, easy, slow strokes that barely made a splash.

His phone rang. He glanced at the caller ID and for a second, considered letting the call go to voice mail. Instead, he answered it. "Hey, Alec."

"Are you sick? Dead? What the hell are you doing home, Riley? It's Friday night."

He hadn't even realized it was the weekend already. That alone showed how much Stace had gotten to him. Riley forced out a chuckle. "I'm just letting you guys get a head start."

"Oh. We have a head start, and then some." Alec laughed. "We're down at Flanagan's. I'll hold a seat for you."

Riley glanced at Jeremy, doing homework at the kitchen table, while nibbling from a plate of cookies from the diner that was sitting beside a cold glass of milk. A homey, cozy, suffocating scene.

"Give me twenty." Riley hung up, then headed into the shower. In a few minutes he was ready. He grabbed his car keys from the table. "Tell your aunt I went out for a while."

Jeremy arched a brow. "You go out a lot."

"No, I don't."

The teenager shrugged and went back to drawing. "Whatever. I'll tell Aunt Stace."

Riley leaned against the counter. "Does she go out a lot?"

"Aunt Stace? Heck, no." Jeremy scoffed. "She has, like, zero life. When I get old, I'm not going to be like that."

"Doesn't she date?"

"If you can call it that." Jeremy put down his pencil. "The last guy Aunt Stace went out with said he'd take her out to dinner. He showed up on her doorstep with a pizza and a six-pack."

"Oh, that's lame." Riley had a lot of other adjectives in mind, but he kept them to himself. No wonder Stace was gun-shy.

"Yeah. I felt really bad for her," Jeremy said. "I wasn't living there then but Aunt Stace told my mom about it." Jeremy's gaze went to a space in the distance. "Aunt Stace used to come over a lot to kinda check on my mom and me. Then when my mom started…being gone a lot, I just started staying at Aunt Stace's. And then one day my mom dropped off all my stuff, and she left, and I stayed behind."

Riley's heart went out to the boy. Riley's parents had died, not abandoned him. It was a car accident, not a choice, that took them out of his life. "That had to be tough on you."

"It is what it is, whether I like it or not." Jeremy shrugged but the pain still shone in his eyes and the hunch of his shoulders. "My aunt is pretty cool, I guess. Sometimes I feel bad about giving her a hard time."

"It's hard to grow up so fast."

The boy doodled on a scrap of paper. "Yeah."

Riley dropped into the chair beside Jeremy. "When

I went to live with my grandparents, I gave them a hard time, too. I guess I blamed them for what happened to my parents, even though it wasn't their fault. I wanted to be mad at somebody, because I felt robbed."

"I guess I did the same thing." Jeremy toyed with the pencils, rolling red over green, over yellow, over purple. "I still miss my mom."

"I hope she's back soon."

Jeremy shrugged as if he didn't care. Red went over green, over yellow, over purple, again and again. "Hey, uh, Riley, can I ask you something?"

"Sure."

"It's, uh, about girls. And I don't want to ask my aunt. You know it's like…"

"A guy thing."

"Yeah."

"Well, you've asked the right person. Girls are my specialty." Even as he joked about it, Riley sent up a silent prayer that whatever the boy asked him, he'd dispense good advice. He'd never been a father figure, in any sense of the word, to anyone, and the thought that Jeremy already looked at him as someone he could go to for advice both pleased and terrified Riley. "So, uh, what do you want to know?"

"There was this girl in my class today." A red blush filled Jeremy's cheeks. "She's, like, into art, too, although her stuff is more deco. She's really good, too, but she kept asking me what I thought. Like, if she should use a charcoal or an HB pencil, if she should color this part red or orange. I didn't know if she really didn't know or if she…well…you know."

"Liked you."

A shy smile curved across Jeremy's face. "Yeah."

Riley grinned. He remembered those days when he'd

first noticed girls. How he'd worked so hard to impress little Amanda Wilson in his seventh-grade English class. He'd stammered and blubbered and struck out. Time and experience had taken him from that awkward stage to one with slightly more finesse. "If a girl keeps asking for your help with a problem she can solve herself, chances are she likes you."

What did it say when a woman *refused* his help over and over again? Riley glanced at the glass doors. All he saw of Stace was the flash of her arm—up, down, up, down, like a piston.

"You think she likes me?" Jeremy asked.

"Definitely."

The shy smile on Jeremy's face morphed into a beam. "Cool. Maybe I'll send her an email or something tonight."

"Just take it slow, Jeremy. Don't rush into—"

But the boy was already gone, off to the computer in the corner of the living room. Riley got to his feet and turned toward the door, then pivoted back. Stace was still slicing through the water in controlled, even movements. Alone, in control, and so typical of Stace. She gave off the impression that she was an island unto herself, but Riley suspected it was all a cover.

He thought about what Jeremy had told him, and decided Alec could wait another night. Stace Kettering deserved a night out. And if anyone knew how to romance a woman on a date, it was Riley McKenna.

He just had to be smart enough to take his own advice and not rush into anything. No matter how tempting the race might be.

"How fast can you get dressed?"

At the same time Stace had come up for air, she'd

heard the door open. She stopped swimming, shook the water out of her ears, and stared up at Riley. "What did you say?"

"How fast can you get dressed?" Riley asked. He looked impossibly tall standing above her on the pool's edge, and impossibly sexy in a pair of jeans and a black button-down shirt. His hair was dark and wet from the shower, punctuating the blue in his eyes.

She stood up in the shallow end of the pool. Water cascaded down her back, over her face. She swiped it away with her palm and brushed her hair out of her eyes. "Uh, I don't know." She paused, caught her breath. "A half hour?"

"How about twenty?"

"What am I getting dressed for?"

"A date. In the city. With me."

Stace shook her head. "Riley, I'm just going to go to bed early and—"

"The diner opens two hours later on Saturday mornings, so you can go out tonight. And besides, I think you deserve a night out. One where the guy treats you to more than a six-pack and a pizza in your own living room."

She laughed. "You've been talking to Jeremy."

"As a matter of fact, I have. He asked me for some advice, and I gave it to him."

"You?" Stace cringed. Riley giving advice to her nephew? She wasn't sure she liked that. At all. "About what?"

"Women. And don't worry, I ended with the words 'take it slow.'"

She breathed a sigh of relief. "Good."

The advice surprised her, too. She'd thought Riley was all man's man, the kind of guy who would kid another about dating widely, and encourage her nephew to do the same. Dispensing the whole "don't get roped into marriage ever" talk. But he'd handled it well, from what he'd said, and she appreciated that. If there was one thing Jeremy needed, it was a steady male influence.

Riley surprised her every time she turned around, both with the way he'd handled Jeremy and the impromptu date. That both intrigued her—and scared her—because this Riley, the one who surprised her, was someone she was starting to like. A lot.

He held out a towel to her. "So come on, let's go out tonight." She hesitated. "I promise, I'll take it slow, too."

She tried to hold it back, but a laugh escaped her all the same. "Okay, you convinced me." She placed her hands on either side of the pool ledge and hoisted herself out. Riley wrapped her in the towel, and paused, just a moment longer than necessary. His hands wrapped around her arms with gentle strength, and his body provided the hint of heat behind her. She glanced over her shoulder. "Thanks."

"Anytime," he said, and she knew he wasn't talking about towels.

She swallowed. Did she want more than this? Or did she want to maintain the status quo, stay coworkers, and nothing more?

"I, ah, better get ready," she said.

"Okay." He released her, then stepped forward to hold the door as they headed back to the guest house. The cool night air made Stace shiver. Or maybe it was the anticipation of a date—a real date—with a handsome man. How long had it been since she'd been out on the town? So long, she couldn't even remember the last time.

Twenty minutes later, Stace had showered and

changed. She didn't have much to choose from for clothes, just a few things she had hurriedly thrown into a bag before she left the Dorchester house. Thankfully, one of the items was a short dark brown jersey dress that always looked good and never wrinkled, sort of her standby outfit for any occasion—party, date, church. She paired it with the lone set of heels that had been hanging on the hook with the dress—nothing special, just some strappy black heels she'd bought on sale a couple years ago. She took time drying her hair, getting it smooth and straight, then spent a few extra minutes on her makeup, telling herself it was just because she was excited to be going out.

Not to impress Riley McKenna. At all.

When she came out of the bathroom, Riley looked up from the newspaper he was reading and let out a low whistle. "You look amazing."

She smoothed a hand down the soft fabric of the dress. "It is a little prettier than the Morning Glory Diner T-shirt."

"Oh, I think you look pretty hot in that, too." He grinned, then rose. "Are you ready?"

"Where's Jeremy?" She'd been in such a rush to get ready, she hadn't even thought about leaving her nephew home alone. Granted, he was old enough to handle it, but still, she worried.

"I sent him over to the main house," Riley said. "He wanted to show my grandmother what he was working on for school, and she needed some company, even if she won't admit it. She's got the dog, but she likes human companionship. And I think Jeremy wanted to spoil Heidi while he was over there."

She was touched that Riley had thought of something to keep Jeremy busy—and in the process, given him a babysitter of sorts, one who clearly held a soft spot in Riley's heart. "You really watch out for her, don't you?"

He shrugged, as if it was no big deal. "She did it for me when I needed someone."

"Why Riley McKenna, you sound positively dependable. Not at all like your public image."

"I have a public image?"

"Yep." She tossed him as a smile as they walked out the door and down the walkway to the car. "Charming playboy, with nary a care in the world, is how I believe they characterized you in the gossip columns. Though the reporters might need to come up with some new adjectives. Like…good with a coffeepot, never disappoints on the fries and always…"

He paused in opening her door. "And always what?"

The dark night wrapped around them, and the quiet grounds left them in solitude. It was intimate, cozy, sexy. "Always…leaves them wanting to come back." The words escaped her in a soft rush.

Did she mean the diner?

Or herself?

He leaned in to her, and she caught her breath. Oh, what was she doing? She kept forgetting that she didn't want to get involved with him. Then he'd make her laugh or turn that irresistible grin on her, and Stace would fall for him all over again and forget her vow to not get too close.

"And how about you? Do you want to come back?" he asked, his voice as dark and intimate as the night.

Yes, she wanted to say, but instead she gave his chest a light jab, inserting distance between them. "I want my promised night on the town."

"Well, I'd hate to disappoint you." He pressed a quick kiss to her lips, which sent her heart racing all over again, and had her craving something more, something deeper, something…

Lasting.

But then she remembered that *lasting* and *permanent* were not adjectives used to describe Riley. He'd made that very clear, over and over again, and just because he was close to his grandmother or been nice to Jeremy didn't change anything. She'd do well to enjoy this night out, and take it as just that—a night out. Nothing more.

Nothing that would last longer than tonight.

They drove through the city, with its twinkling white lights and exclamation points of red taillights. Boston hummed with life, as busy at night as it was during the day. Riley had put down the windows, and Stace soaked up the sights, sounds, and smells. She had worked in this city forever, but never really experienced it, and barely ever at night. Getting up for work at four in the morning had put a serious crimp in her nightlife.

They stopped at a nightclub, where a valet came out for Riley's car. Riley greeted the man by name, then pressed a few bills into the man's hand. "Be nice to my car, Jimmy."

"I always am, Riley," the valet said with a grin, then he pulled away from the curb. The doorman pulled the door open for them, also greeting Riley by name, then the hostess, who led Riley to a table deep inside the club.

Stace sat down across from him, while the music pounded and pulsed around them and a rainbow of lights flickered across the dark room. The club was filled with bodies—a crush of people dancing, talking, laughing. She tapped her foot, and shifted her weight to the beat.

"You want to dance?"

"Oh, I'm not very good."

"You are. I've seen you, remember?" He rose and

waited for her to take his hand, then when she did, he led her to the dance floor. The music pounded, while Riley twirled her to the left. She stepped quickly with him, then stepped back when he moved forward.

She let the music sweep over her, like the water in the pool, until all she heard was the beat, all she felt was Riley's touch, all she knew was the movement of her own body. Inch by inch, she relaxed and allowed herself to let go, to forget everything in her life except this moment. Riley's smile widened, and he closed the gap between them, until her hips were shimmying against his pelvis, and the world became the two of them. The heat increased between them, the beat seemed to hasten, and Stace became very, very aware of every inch of Riley's body. About how it felt to touch him, be held by him, be close to him. Then the song ended, and they broke apart, as if someone had turned off a switch.

She stepped off the dance floor and Riley followed. "That was fun," she said.

"I'm glad you enjoyed it."

"I did." The song shifted again, and Stace itched to return to the floor. To his arms. Instead, she nodded toward the bar. The club had filled with even more people, until it was standing room only. "How about a drink?"

"How about we go someplace quieter? It's too crowded now."

A few minutes later, they were outside on the sidewalk, waiting for the valet to return with the car. Riley glanced back at the nightclub. People streamed in and out of the front door, like a tide ebbing and flowing on the beach. "You know, I used to really enjoy that place. But it's funny. I don't so much anymore."

"Why?" He was still holding her hand, and she realized she liked that. Too much.

"Guess my tastes are changing," Riley said. "Anyway, there's another club over on Boylston I like to hit, and there's always a party down in Southie. We could—"

"Riley..." She put a hand on his arm. "You don't need to impress me with clubs and valets and fancy drinks for us to have a nice time out. We can do something else."

"I'm not doing that. I'm..." He gave her a grin. "Okay, maybe I am. And I'm sorry it's not the Ritz or something like that. If I could have afforded it, I'd have taken you to the Top of the Hub."

"I don't need the Top of the Hub." He really didn't know her, did he? Or was it that Riley, a man who kept on going to places he didn't even like, didn't know himself that well, either? "You can have a lot of fun for free, or nearly free in this city."

The valet brought up their car. Riley tipped him, then held Stace's door before he slid into the driver's seat. "Where to now?"

"Do you trust me?"

His gaze held hers for a long, hot moment. The world dropped away, and the busy space closed in to be just the two of them. "Yes."

A delicious shiver chased down her spine, every time Riley looked at her in that intent, soul-seeking way. It was as if he could see inside her, see everything that she was thinking.

Did he know how much she wanted him to kiss her? How she melted every time he smiled? How she used to think she had it all together, in control, and had realized that with just one look, Riley McKenna could turn all that control upside down?

Yeah, it was probably a good thing he wasn't a mind reader.

She cleared her throat, and gestured toward the road. "Then let's head for Rowes Wharf. And I'll show you *my* definition of a good time, Riley."

CHAPTER NINE

RILEY had never been in a position like this. The roles reversed, with the woman planning the date. He had to admit, he kind of liked it.

They parked in a city garage, then headed up to the sidewalk. Stace turned to Riley, a knowing smile on her face. She had something planned, but what it was, he couldn't tell. "Can you wait here a second?" she asked. "I'll be right back." She dashed into a market beside them, and returned a few minutes later, holding a paper bag emblazoned with the market's name.

"What'd you buy?"

"That is a surprise. For me to know, and you to discover." A grin curved across her face. She was teasing him, and he liked it, very much. This was another side to Stace, something light and fun. He'd loved seeing that back in the club, watching her loosen up, pry off the bonds of her life. It was as if being away from the diner and her nephew had given her permission to peel back a layer of herself for him to see. Every moment he spent with Stace showed him another dimension.

"Let me carry the bag for you. I promise not to peek." He held up three fingers. "Scouts' honor."

"If you do—" she wagged a finger at him "—there will be dire consequences."

"Dire? What kind of dire? Hmm…almost makes me want to peek."

"Don't you dare." She laughed, then folded down the top of the bag and handed it to him. They walked down a brick pathway that ran alongside Rowes Wharf. Boats bobbed quietly in the water, and people strolled back and forth, enjoying the ocean breezes. The entire atmosphere offered a peaceful comfort, far removed from the city, even as traffic buzzed along a little way away.

And it was as far from what Riley normally did on a Friday night as one could get. He watched one of the boats pull away from the dock, embarking on a harbor dinner cruise. "If this was an ordinary date," he said to her, "I'd take you onto one of those boats and we'd have dinner out on the water. A waiter at our beck and call, and an unlimited supply of wine." He paused and turned to her. "I really did have plans to show you an incredible night on the town, or at least as incredible as I can get on my budget."

She stopped walking, cocked her head and studied him. "Maybe that's the problem."

"What? My lack of funds? I agree, but—"

"No, not that. You doing what you normally do." She shrugged. "I saw you back at the club. You didn't look happy."

A couple of lovebirds strolled past them, giggling into each other's faces and holding on so tight, it seemed they were one, not two. For a second, Riley envied their obvious love for each other. Then he looked away and the feeling was gone.

"Well, that's because it was loud and busy and…" He let out a breath, and finally faced what had been bothering him back at the club. The club scene no longer fit him. For years, it had been the only place he'd gone, but now, with Stace, he realized it wasn't what he wanted anymore. "I've gone there a hundred times over the years, but you know, I guess I never realized how much I didn't enjoy it."

"Then why do you go?"

"Because that's what us playboys do." He gave her a grin.

But in that smile, Stace detected something she had rarely seen in Riley. Vulnerability. She wondered what he was hiding, keeping to himself. There was something there, she'd bet a month's pay on it. Yet Riley had yet to fully open up to her. He kept retreating behind that grin.

"True," she said. "But is it what former playboys turned waiters at diners do?"

"Maybe not. It's expensive to go out like that." His gaze, and even though the night was dark and the lights were dim, she could see the connection in those blue depths. It made her shiver with anticipation.

"Then maybe learning to live on a server's salary will teach you a thing or two." She gestured to a bench that sat along the waterfront. Few people had ventured this far down the dock, and they had the space mostly to themselves. "Like how to have a romantic date on a budget."

He waved an arm toward the bench. "After you, madam."

She laughed, then settled on one end, and he settled on the other, with the bag between them. The stars glowed steady in the sky above them, punctuated by the occasional moving light of a departing or landing plane. The water lapped gently against the pier, sloshing up the dock posts, then down along the sides of the boats moored nearby. Far in the distance, the sound of boat engines purred on the water, while the muted steady song of highway traffic sang behind them.

"A small budget does force you to be creative. That's something I haven't been in a long time." His gaze went out to the water. "I guess that's what I really need to do—put my creativity to work. Like at the diner."

"You're going to start concocting recipes now?"

He laughed. "No. Just a marketing campaign to increase business. I think you need an event. Something that will get people talking about the Morning Glory."

"That'd be nice. But those kinds of things take time to plan. And getting exposure in such a big city is tough."

She had a point. He needed to mull this over some more. He didn't want to just throw out an idea just to say something. "We'll think of something."

"And until then, let's have dinner." She reached into the bag. "Date element number one. Wine." She handed him a bottle of white wine, followed by a set of plastic cups to drink from. "Date element number two. Cheese."

He laughed at the package of sliced cheese. It was a variety of flavors, in different hues of yellow and white. "Looks good so far."

"Date element number three. Bread." She tugged out a loaf of bread. The fresh-baked scent filled the space between them. "Date element number four. Grapes."

He held up the wine. "I thought we had plenty of them in here."

"We do, but we can always use more." A teasing smile played on her lips, lit the green in her eyes. "And finally, date element number five. Lots of napkins." She pulled out a stack of paper napkins and plopped them on the bench, then stowed the bag underneath.

"You've thought of everything. I'm impressed."

"It's just wine and cheese. Nothing big."

But to Riley it was. Not because of the beautiful setting of the Boston Harbor Hotel's famed lighted archway behind them. Or the quiet solitude of the oceanfront. Or the mild, cloudless night that dotted the sky with stars.

It was Stace Kettering. The way she had adapted easily to their two vastly different dates and made a nighttime picnic on Rowes Wharf seem like the most romantic place she'd ever been. On the water beside them, boats sliced through the water with blinking red and green lights, while couples strolled the pier arm in arm. Quiet, romantic.

Perfect.

And light years more romantic than anything he'd ever done on a date. There was no hovering waiter, no softly playing instrumental music, no perfectly appointed dining room. It was simple, and nice. Nothing extra, nothing unnecessary.

It was as if Stace had read his mind, and given him something he didn't even know he wanted. Until he had it.

Stace gestured toward the wine. "Why don't you open that?"

He held up a finger. "Oh, you forgot one thing. A corkscrew."

Stace laughed. "We're dining on a server's salary, remember? That's a screw-top wine bottle."

He chuckled, then opened the bottle of Chardonnay and poured them each some. Stace unwrapped the cheese and bread, then held the loaf toward him. "Tear off a hunk, pair it with some cheese. It's Bohemian and—" She moaned in anticipation, and he wanted to grab her right then, and taste her, not the food, but then she smiled and the moment was gone. "And oh, so delicious that way."

He did as she instructed, and watched her do the same. The combination was a culinary delight, soft cheddar cheese melting on his tongue, with the rustic notes of the bread. He raised his plastic cup to hers. "To inventive dates."

"And flexible boyfriends." She clicked her glass against his, then sipped.

Riley shifted on the bench, a little closer to her. "Is that what I am? Your boyfriend?"

"Well, no, I didn't mean that. I was just being clever." She looked away, and the night hid whether she was embarrassed, or avoiding the subject.

"Why do you do that?" Riley asked.

"Do what?"

"Push me away every time I try to get close?"

She looked at him, green eyes wide, inquisitive. "Why do you try so hard to get close?"

"Touché." He had to admit, Stace Kettering was a woman who gave as good as she got. She was different from anyone he'd ever met before. Because she was...

Challenging.

Yes, that was the word. She challenged him, in a hundred different ways. To act better, to be more, and most of all, to be as honest with her as he wanted her to be with him.

He had dated dozens of women, but none had made him want to try so hard, to work so much to impress her, charm her.

Win her heart.

Why do you try so hard to get close?

He propped one ankle over the opposite knee, and leaned back on the bench. He didn't sip at the wine, didn't eat the food, just watched the dark arrowed shadows of boats making their way through the harbor. "I've never really been close to anyone. Or let anyone get that close to me."

One sentence, and it was probably the most honest one Riley McKenna had ever spoken in his whole life. He didn't know if it was the setting, or the woman beside him, or the wine, which he'd only had a sip of, but something made him want to open up, just a little.

"Why not?" Stace asked, her voice a quiet melody. Challenging him again, to open up even more.

He hesitated, but then realized that all that holding back, keeping himself to himself, had gotten him nowhere but in loud nightclubs with people he barely knew, and dates that had all the depth of a puddle. He used to think he enjoyed all that, because it put no ties on him, but in the last few weeks, he'd realized that lack of ties left him with a feeling of emptiness.

He'd perfected the art of avoiding heavy subjects, and now, it seemed like every one of those subjects he had avoided were weighing on his shoulders. What would it be like to lessen that load?

He'd done it already, in little steps, with Stace at her house, then in the pool, and finally, at the cemetery. In the process, he had started to find new dimensions to himself. Some he liked. Some he didn't. It was as if he was a pen-and-ink drawing and the closer he got to Stace, the more he added color and layers to that image.

"I guess that fear comes from losing my parents when I was so young," Riley said after a moment. "That kind of loss rocks your world in a way nothing else ever does."

She nodded. "I know what you mean. It leaves you—" she let out a breath "—vulnerable. I mean, I know I'm a grown-up now and I should be able to take care of myself, and I do, but when your parents are gone, it's like all of a sudden, the people who are supposed to watch out for you and warn you not to cross the street without looking aren't there."

He hadn't thought of it that way. He'd had his grandparents, and his older brothers, and there'd been advice aplenty from all of them. But none of them, no matter how much they loved him, had been his mother and father. "You're right. You can have all the surrogate parents in the world, but losing your own…it's different."

"We're orphans."

He let out a little laugh. "I'm a little old to be adopted."

"Me, too."

He drew her into him, his arm going around her shoulders. Riley bent to nuzzle a kiss into the top of her head. "Then I'll adopt you, Stace Kettering."

"You will?" She tossed him a grin. "I can be a handful."

"Me, too."

She curved into him, holding him as tight as he held her. "Then we'll adopt each other."

He let those words wash over him, and kept on holding her close. It was a fun fantasy to indulge, both of them needing someone else, and offering to be that for the other. "Will you read me stories at night?"

"I'm not very good at that. I put myself to sleep."

Riley laughed. "My father was like that. He worked really hard during the day, and my mom, who had had enough of three mischievous boys, always made my father do bedtime duty. He'd send the older two off to their room, then come see me. I was little, and always begging him for a story or two."

"What kind of stories?" Stace asked.

She was snuggled up against him, the food forgotten, the world a distant presence. It was nice…awfully nice.

"Adventure ones," Riley went on. "Like *Robinson Crusoe* and *The Swiss Family Robinson*. I liked anything where there was danger and weapons." He chuckled. "Typical boy, I guess."

"Jeremy was like that, too, when he was little. We worked our way through all the Hardy Boy mysteries one year. My sister was living with me, and I would read to Jeremy at night to get him to sleep."

"But did you ever fall asleep in the middle of the good parts?"

She thought for a second. "I don't think so."

"My dad did, all the time." Riley chuckled. "It didn't matter if the hero was about to be shot or the heroine was just kidnapped by train robbers. Dad would fall asleep at the point where I was on the edge of my seat with suspense. Drove me crazy. I couldn't wait for him to get home the next day and finish."

"Maybe he had an ulterior motive."

"Like what?"

"Maybe he wanted you to miss him. And be excited when he got home."

Riley considered that. Even though it had been over twenty years, he could remember his father walking through the door, and the three McKenna boys plowing into his chest, each clamoring for his attention. "We all hung on him like monkeys in a tree. He'd walk to the kitchen, with one or all of us hanging off his legs and arms."

She laughed. "I can picture that."

"But I was the youngest, the baby, you know, and he always propped me up on his arm. I think that made Finn and Brody jealous, but my dad said it was because they would have trampled me if he left me down on the floor." Riley smiled, and suddenly, the loss of his father and mother seemed to wash over him in a wave. Riley leaned forward, bracing his arms on his knees, and inhaled the salty tang of ocean air. "I...I wish he was still here."

Stace's hand went to his back. She rubbed gently, a comforting touch that told him she, of all the women in the world, understood. "I'm sorry, Riley."

He drew himself up, and her hand dropped away. "Yeah, me, too." He gathered the food and began to put it in the bag. "It's getting cold. Maybe we should get going."

"Uh...okay." She helped him pick up the rest of their meal. Riley tucked the bag under his arm, and they headed back up the dock and toward the car.

A part of him wanted to explain why he'd ended the conversation so fast, but the other part of him, the part that had won time and time again when it came to getting close to people, threw up the caution flag. Better to stay uninvolved, unattached, than to latch on to Stace and end up alone in the end. She was a woman who would see his opening up to her as commitment.

Yet, when he looked over at her as they drove back to his house, he wondered what it would be like to be committed to a woman like her. To know that she would be there, at the end of every single day, to greet him, hug him, kiss him.

Would every day be as sweet and delicious as that time on the pier? Or would he have a good time for a while, and then see it all taken away in the blink of an eye?

The ride passed quickly, and too soon, they pulled into the driveway of the guest house. The date was over.

A stone of disappointment sank in Riley's gut. "We're back."

"Yeah," she said.

"Do you, uh, want to go over and get Jeremy with me?"

"Sure. I want to thank your grandmother again, too."

Riley came around, opened her door, and waited for Stace to get out. When she rose, she brushed against him. The dark, quiet night wrapped around them like a cocoon and suddenly he didn't want the date to end. Didn't want them to go back to being coworkers. He wanted just a little bit more. Just tonight.

Riley wrapped an arm around her waist, and she shifted against him, let out a soft, enticing mew. Her chin went up, her green eyes met his, and everything inside him began to roar.

What was it about her that made him forget everything whenever she was in his arms? "I had a really nice time tonight," he said.

"Me, too."

"And I'm sorry for rushing you out of there. I just…" Didn't want to be serious anymore. Didn't want to continue with those weighty subjects. Now he wanted only to enjoy her. He offered her a grin, and then lowered his face to hers. She was centimeters away, so close he could feel the heat of her skin, catch the floral notes of her perfume. And the words he wanted to say went right out of his head. "Oh, Stace, you distract me."

She smiled, that intoxicating smile that was imprinted on his memory. "I'm not trying to."

He reached up and cupped her jaw. His thumbs traced over her bottom lip, and his heart stuttered. "You distract me just by standing there."

The smile widened. "You do the same to me. It's a

wonder I haven't poured a cup of coffee on myself. Or dropped an order on the floor every time you look at me or talk to me."

"There's no coffee here right now. No orders to fill. Nothing but us."

"I noticed." The words escaped her in a breath.

He knew he should pull back. Let her go. Go back to being friends and coworkers, and stop muddying the waters. But as he looked down into her eyes, he couldn't think of a single reason why that was a good idea. He closed the gap between them, let his arms drift down to her back, and pulled Stace Kettering into him until his lips met hers and the world stopped.

CHAPTER TEN

STACE Kettering was falling. Tumbling down, and down, and down, falling hard for Riley McKenna.

When he kissed her, the world came to a stop. She leaned into him, and fire ignited in the spaces where their bodies met. His hands roamed her back, sliding over her hips, her buttocks, and she pressed closer, held tighter.

God help her, but she wanted him. Now. In the worst possible way.

Riley drew back long enough to take a breath and nod toward the guest house. "Maybe Jeremy can wait a few minutes."

"Or a lot of minutes," she said. Who was this brazen woman, who made it clear she wanted a man? Who took his hand and ran headlong for the house like a love struck teenager? Who didn't think about the consequences, but just…desired?

Riley pressed Stace to the door, blindly fumbling to get the key in the lock, while he kept on kissing her. She grasped his shirt, wishing she could tug it off now, but then the door was open and they were tumbling into the house and rushing to get the door shut. In a few quick steps, they were at the sofa, and Riley was drawing her down onto his lap and her dress was hiking up over her thighs, leaving the skin deliciously bare to his touch, and she quit thinking.

His erection was hard against her, and she moaned into his mouth, shifting her position until he moaned, too. His hands tangled in her hair, hers went to his shirt, working the buttons until his skin was exposed to her touch. Breathless, she pulled back, and trailed kisses along his neck, over his shoulders, down his chest. Riley groaned, then hauled her back up, and kissed her so hard, so fast, her head spun.

His warm palms snaked under her dress with slow, easy, sensual moves. Every bit of skin he touched seemed to ignite, and Stace had to remind herself to breathe. Then he cupped her breasts through the lace of her bra, and she gasped. "Riley, oh, God, Riley. Oh—" She had no other words, no coherent thoughts.

"You are beautiful," he murmured against her skin, leaving her mouth long enough to trail kisses down her neck, over the soft jersey of her dress, then to the crest of her breasts. She arched against him, wanting more, wanting his mouth everywhere.

His fingers went to the clasp at her back. Hot anticipation filled her, driving a pounding, insistent need. How long had it been since she'd been touched? Kissed like this?

Then her gaze went to the glass patio doors. Her reflection shimmered back at her. Wanton, uninhibited—

Foolish.

How many times did she have to lose her head, before she got a clue? She scrambled off Riley's lap and pulled her dress down. Her lips were tender from his kisses, and her pulse thundered a protest in her head. "What do you want, Riley?"

He chuckled. "I'd think that was obvious. I want you,

Stace." He reached for her, caught her fingertips, and tugged her toward him.

But she remained resolute and stayed where she was. "I meant from this." She gestured between them. "Is this just one more notch in your belt, or do you want more?"

"I'm not looking to get married tonight." He let out a nervous laugh. "Come on, let's just enjoy what we have."

Hot tears rose in her eyes. She'd been so, so wrong about him. She'd let herself get distracted again by the messages she thought she was reading in a man's eyes. Once again, she'd read an ending that he wasn't even thinking. God, how could she be so stupid? "That's the trouble. We'll enjoy it for the night, but then when the morning comes, what do we have?"

"A really nice memory."

She shook her head, and willed the tears to stay at bay until she could get out of the room. "I want more than a memory," she said. "I want something that stays, that I can depend on. And you, Riley McKenna, are anything but dependable."

Then she ran out of the room, and shut her bedroom door so he wouldn't hear her crying.

Saturday morning dawned.

Unfortunately.

Stace had done her best to avoid Riley after their date. He'd gone to his grandmother's to retrieve Jeremy. She had taken the coward's way out while he was gone—and gone to bed. This morning, she'd headed out the door before Riley was even up, arriving at the diner before Frank. "You're in early," he'd said. "You do know we open later on Saturdays, don't you?"

"I'm too used to getting up early, I guess," Stace said. She avoided Frank's inquisitive gaze and got busy setting up the tables for the morning. As she did, she came across a newspaper tucked between the wall and one of the booths—probably a customer's, stuffed away and forgotten, and missed in the daily cleanup.

Stace tugged it out and turned to toss the week-old issue of the *Herald* into the trash. As she did, her gaze caught on a familiar image.

Riley. With another woman. Her skirt was hiked halfway to her knees, her head was thrown back in laughter, and her hands were on Riley's shoulders—with no mistaking they were together. Nausea rolled in Stace's stomach. She thrust the paper deep into the trash, then turned away.

That could have been her in that picture. Could have been Stace's image under the Playboy Finds A Good Time At Benefit Event headline. She'd come so close last night to falling for him.

For being another of a hundred women in his arms. Just like she had done before.

By the time Riley strolled in, a few minutes before they opened, she had herself firmly in work mode. No longer thinking about where those kisses could have gone last night.

Definitely not thinking about that. Not now, not ever.

A group of women doing a walking tour of the city came in right behind Riley. Stace took the table of eight, glad for the interruption. The morning continued like that, with a steady stream of customers.

A little after eleven, the diner slowed down, and Stace headed to the counter for a quick bite to eat. Frank slid a plate of pancakes over to her. "Heated up the syrup for you."

She smiled. "Thanks." She forked up a thick bite,

chewed, and swallowed. As she did, she noticed a flyer sitting on the counter. "Hey, what's that?"

Frank picked it up. "One of those travel club things. Bunch of old people running around the world."

"Sounds like fun."

Frank waved it off. "Eleanor Givens is always trying to talk me into going to Europe with her."

Stace grinned. Eleanor was in here every Saturday morning, one of the first customers of the day. She usually sat at the counter, and chatted with Frank the whole time. "I think that's because she likes you."

Frank waved the flyer again. "Nah."

"She's looking for a round-the-world travel buddy."

"She should look somewhere else. I don't much like her company." Frank grimaced. "Though I had an interesting conversation with Riley's grandmother the other day. Nice lady. And she likes to travel, too."

"You should invite her to Europe then. I bet she'd say yes."

"And what, leave this place? I'll be here till the day I die." Then his face crumpled. "Aw, Stace, I'm sorry, I didn't mean that."

"It's okay." Her smile wavered, then she brightened, and leaned toward the man she'd known nearly all her life. "You really need to take care of you, Frank, and stop worrying about me."

"I do."

She arched a brow. "So when are you retiring again?"

"Looking to get rid of me?"

"Looking for you to take one of those trips you talk about…and never take."

He shrugged, and got busy refilling a sugar dispenser. It was usually Stace's job, which meant Frank was avoiding the subject. "Traveling the world takes money. I have some savings, but I'm not exactly Rockefeller."

"Why don't you let me buy you out then?"

"We'll talk about that later."

She let out a gust. "You always say that, Frank."

The bell over the door rang, and Walter strode in, letting out his usual greeting of a grunt before heading for his favorite table. Before Stace could head to the booth, Walter waved over Riley.

Frank leaned close and lowered his voice. "Looks like Walter has a new favorite."

"Passing fancy."

Frank quirked a grin at her. "Is that what it is? A passing fancy?"

Stace waved at the corner booth, where Walter was chatting with Riley. Walter was nodding and moving his hands as he talked, animated customer now instead of grumpy older man. Whatever he was talking to Riley about, Walter was passionate about the topic. "You know Walter, he's always finding something new to complain about. He—"

"I didn't mean Walter. I meant you and Riley."

Stace toyed with her order pad. "There's nothing between me and Riley."

Frank let out a guffaw. "Yeah, right. I may be old, but I'm not blind, and there is something brewing between you two. Why, it's like the Morning Glory's own little soap opera."

"You are definitely imagining things." She slid off the stool and tucked her order pad back into the pocket of her apron. "I better go over there and make sure he's not riling Walter up."

Frank snorted. "Yep. That's exactly why you're going over there."

Stace ignored Frank. He had a tendency to play matchmaker with every man who expressed an interest in Stace. That was all that was. Frank's wishful thinking that she'd get married, settle down, and have a few kids he could spoil mercilessly.

She headed for the coffee station. The carafes were nearly empty, so she put on a new pot of both regular and decaf. She sensed Riley behind her before she heard him.

"Looked like a pretty serious conversation there with Frank," he said.

"It's nothing. Just the same-old, same-old, of me bugging him to retire." She tossed the used coffee grounds into the trash, then cleaned the area around the coffee station. "Once I get enough money saved, I want to buy out his half. Then he won't have any excuse not to travel the world." She sighed. "I just need business to pick up enough to afford that."

"Well, I think I can help with that. Remember the idea I was looking for? I thought—"

"I'm not getting any younger here. Can I get my coffee?" Walter called to Riley. *"Please?"*

Riley laughed. "Guess I'm rubbing off on Walter."

"You have a tendency to do that with people."

"What about you? Do I rub off on you?"

"You…made an impression."

He arched a brow. "A good one?"

"Keep Walter waiting too long and he won't leave you a tip." She had finished loading the coffee station, and turned away to rinse out the empty pots.

"Walter can wait for me to get your answer."

"He'll be waiting an awful long time then." She didn't want to talk to Riley. She wanted to avoid him and the images that picture had risen in her head, until Riley moved on to the next thing, the next woman. Surely she could keep from falling for the man, or at least, falling any more than she already had.

The man had all the permanence of chalk on the sidewalk. One good storm, and he'd disappear.

"You know," Riley said, unaware of Stace's thoughts—or her fervent wish that he would just go away—as he leaned against the counter while he waited on Walter's coffee to brew, "it's taken me a few days, but I finally realize why Walter looks so familiar to me."

"Oh, really?" Stupid coffeepot, which was probably older than Frank, had blinked off and refused to turn on. She fiddled with the switch, then reached behind and unplugged it, and replugged it into the wall. Still no response.

"It took me a while to put it together, but—" Riley gave the side of the coffee station a hard tap, and the machine leapt to life "—once I did, it gave me an idea."

"Hey, I don't have all day to wait for my coffee, you know." Walter's crabby voice carried through the diner again.

"One second, Walter. New coffee is brewing just for you." Riley shot Stace a grin. "What if I told you I had a way to turn Walter into the nicest customer you ever had? And also serve your goal of getting more business into this place. I'll need your help to pull it off, though."

"I don't know."

He paused to look at her as he poured the dark brew into a mug. "Just trust me. Please."

Trust him. That was where she got into trouble, every time. She'd trusted him on moving in to his guest house, and look where that had led. She'd trusted him on letting him work with her, and now she was forced to see him every day—until he gave up on this job and moved on to the next. She'd trusted him when he'd kissed her, and very nearly believed those kisses were real.

"Please," he whispered in her ear.

How she wanted to resist that deep baritone. But her heart quickened and her pulse leapt and a smile winged its way across her face, without her permission. "Okay."

As soon as they reached Walter's table, Riley plopped down the hot cup before him. "Good morning, Walter."

Walter snorted. "Don't try to cheer me up."

"Why not? It's a gorgeous day, and you're alive. Enough reason to celebrate, isn't it?"

He snorted again.

Riley leaned against the high back of the opposite seat. "You know, Walter, you'd think a guy who works with animals all day would be more...cheery."

Walter arched a brow, clearly surprised that Riley knew his occupation. Beside Riley, Stace held her own surprise in check. How had Riley learned that information? In all the time she'd served Walter, the only personal detail he'd shared was his addiction to kosher dill pickles.

"To me, animals are nicer than people," Walter said.

"That may very well be true," Riley said, then he slid into the booth opposite Walter, making enough room for Stace to join him. "But Stace and I have been thinking that it might be good to combine the two."

Walter sipped the hot coffee. "What do you mean?"

"You have a fundraiser coming up."

Now he had Walter's interest. The older man leaned back and propped an elbow on the banquette. "How do you know that?"

"My brother Finn has one of your dogs, a Golden named Heidi. Sweetest dog you've ever seen. She's a frequent guest at my grandmother's house, and Finn talks up the shelter every chance he gets."

"I agree," Stace said. "She's a lovely dog."

"Finn, as in Finn McKenna? He's one of our biggest supporters." Walter regarded Riley with new eyes. "You're his brother?"

"Yep."

Walter leaned forward. "And how exactly does that matter to me?"

"You need a place for your fundraiser. Finn mentioned that the shelter doesn't really have a good place to hold a big event, and your usual venue shut down unexpectedly last week. That leaves you high and dry, and probably scrambling for a location."

"We were planning on canceling." Walter scowled. "And yes, that has made me a little grumpy."

Riley smiled. "I wouldn't cancel just yet, not until you consider my idea."

Walter crossed his hands on the table. "I'm listening."

Stace glanced at Riley. What was he up to? "Me, too."

"You need something that will draw folks in, and you also need volunteers. I was thinking—" at this, Riley glanced at Stace "—maybe the Morning Glory would be a great place to hold it. The diner would get some publicity, there'd be food to lure people in, the shelter would get the bonus of a highly trafficked location, and on top of that, I think I could round up some extra volunteers to help with the dogs."

Walter scowled. "You can't have dogs in this place."

"You can on the outdoor patio," Stace said, leapfrogging onto Riley's train of thought. Why had she never thought to have events like this on the weekends? Using the Morning Glory for more than just a breakfast and lunch place could really boost sales and exposure. "The patio never gets used because we're a little understaffed right now. It's out back, but has street access."

"And if you held it on Tuesday afternoon, like you originally planned," Riley added, "you'd have all that traffic from the workers heading home."

When he paused, Stace leapt in again. "The diner is usually closed after lunch service, so if we're open for this event, we could bring in some business we normally don't have."

Walter mulled the idea. "You said you had volunteers."

"Stace knows someone who would love to design some posters for you, and I suspect, help with the animals, too." Riley's blue gaze held hers. "He's a bright kid, with a lot of artistic ability, and even better, he's got a lot of friends who would be good helpers."

Tears threatened the back of her eyes at Riley's thoughtfulness in including her nephew, a boy who was seeking approval, acceptance, purpose. It would be the perfect thing for Jeremy to be involved in. Something that would give him a positive outlet for his art. "Oh, yes. Definitely."

Walter drummed his fingers on the table. "Let me talk to my board, get back to you tomorrow."

"Sounds good." Riley and Stace slid out of the seat.

"In the meantime, I want some more coffee. Hot as you can make it. And don't make me wait all damned day this time." Walter went back to his paper, clearly done with today's human interaction.

Stace pulled Riley aside by the coffeepot. "How on earth did you come up with that idea?"

"I overheard Walter talking on his cell phone the other day. He was complaining about how he didn't have enough help for the fundraiser and the venue had let him down. Once I realized what fundraiser it was, I thought maybe there'd be a way to help. Then I thought the best way to help one is to help—" he grinned "—two."

"The shelter and the diner."

He nodded. "Hopefully it's a win-win all around."

"It's a brilliant idea." Riley's idea was exactly what both the shelter and the Morning Glory needed. "Thank you."

Riley's blue eyes met hers, and for a second she forgot that she wanted to stay away from him. Forgot that he might be good for the diner, but he was bad for her heart. "You know, for this to work, I'm going to need your help."

"My help? What am I going to do?"

"Convince Jeremy to do the posters, and help me with the marketing materials."

"I don't know anything about marketing materials." Stace handed Riley a clean mug, and he filled it with steaming hot coffee. "That's supposed to be your area."

"You know about this diner," he said. "Convince me why the Morning Glory is the best place on earth, or at least in the city of Boston, to eat. After that, we'll convince the world." He put up a hand. "You don't have to tell me now. Wait till lunch. We'll talk then. Okay?"

"Okay."

"Good. Then it's a date." Before she could respond, he was gone, headed to Walter's table with a fresh cup of coffee. She didn't want to have lunch with Riley. Or work on a project with him. She was trying to stay away from him, so her foolish body wouldn't betray her every time he was near. She glanced at the trash, and even though she could no longer see the image on the newspaper, she knew it was there. A reminder to redouble her resolve.

But as the morning and early afternoon passed, and Stace bustled around the diner, she found herself getting excited about the idea of the fundraiser. If the Morning Glory could turn the corner on profits, it might be enough to allow her to buy Frank out. Then she could finally take care of the man who had taken care of her for so many years.

It would, of course, mean putting her own life on hold again for a while, but at this rate, she was getting used to that. She'd done it for her sister, now for Jeremy, and soon, for Frank. She glanced around the diner that had been her father's dream, and heart. Maybe someday down the road there'd be time for Stace to fall in love, get married, have a family. Just not today.

Riley was across the room, talking to an elderly woman. He smiled, and the woman smiled in response. Infectious, that's what Riley was, and for a second, she envied the woman who had his attention. Then Stace shrugged off the emotion. He didn't want the same life she did, and wishing for a different ending would only leave her disappointed in the end.

Her cell phone buzzed in her pocket. Her tables didn't need anything for the moment, so Stace ducked out of the diner to take the call. The number was unfamiliar, and for a second, Stace's heart plummeted, sure that something had happened to Jeremy. "Hello?"

"Stace?" Lisa's voice. Wavering, unsure. So welcome after weeks of silence.

Still, Stace braced herself. If her sister was calling, it could only mean one thing—she needed money or a place to crash. How many times had they danced this dance? She loved her sister, but she couldn't be a refuge for Lisa, not anymore. It did nothing but give Lisa permission to keep on hurting herself, and that was something Stace could no longer watch. "Lisa, if you need money or a place to stay, I can't help you. You have to help yourself first."

"I'm doing that, Stace, really." The connection crackled and her voice echoed, sounding more like a payphone than a cell phone or regular landline. Had Lisa lost her cell again? Was she in some seedy neighborhood, waiting for rescue?

Again, Stace resisted the urge to help. "Good. I'm glad." She tried to work some enthusiasm into her voice. She had heard the same words a thousand times. Would this time stick? Or would Lisa break Jeremy's heart again?

"How's Jeremy?" Lisa asked.

"He's doing good. He got a scholarship to the Wilmont Academy and he's loving it there."

"He did?" Lisa's voice broke, with pride, with regret, Stace wasn't sure. "That's perfect for him. He's always loved to draw. I used to think he'd grow up to be an artist. Oh, he must be so happy."

"He's getting there," Stace said. He'd be happier if his mom was there and clean, but Stace didn't add that.

"I want to see him," Lisa said. "I miss him so much."

Now the anger did rise in Stace. She thought of all the times she had bailed out her sister. Given her money, food, a place to stay. Helped her raise her son. And then picked up the pieces when Lisa had left Jeremy behind. "You can't just do this, Lisa. You can't walk out of his life one day and walk back in the next. He's a kid. He needs stability. A mother he can depend on. And you haven't been any of those things."

"I love him."

Stace pressed a hand to her forehead. Damn, the words hurt, but they needed to be said. "Loving him means being a good mother. Instead of someone selfish enough to put drugs in front of their family. Get cleaned up, and maybe we can talk." The anger became a tide, built up over the past month, in every moment that Stace had had to comfort her nephew or fill in as surrogate mom. It should have been Lisa who'd dropped him off that day at the new school. Should have been Lisa making Jeremy pancakes and making sure he took his vitamins. "You dumped your own son in my lap after the car accident—"

"I'm sorry, Stace. That accident really shook me up and—"

"And you haven't spoken to any of us in a month." Stace sighed. She couldn't listen to the excuses, the pleas, anymore. "I love you but I can't do this anymore, Lisa. I really can't."

"Stace, I *am* better. You don't understand—"

But Stace had heard enough. Year after year, the same story, the same excuses. "Bye, Lisa." Then she hung up the phone and put it in her pocket. Her heart broke, and she wanted so badly to call Lisa back, to apologize, to smooth the waters like she had every time before. But then she thought of her nephew, of the heartbreak in his face the day his mother left, and knew she couldn't put Jeremy or herself through that anymore.

Riley poked his head out the diner door. "Hey, you okay?"

"Yeah. Just dealing with some…family stuff."

"Want to talk about it?"

She looked at Riley's tall frame, his broad shoulders, his hard chest, his soft blue eyes, and a part of her wanted so badly to curl into him and tell him everything. To let someone else share the burden for a while. "I'm okay."

He came outside, and waited for the door to shut before speaking. "You don't look okay."

"I handled it." Had she? All she'd done was hang up on her sister. She hadn't changed anything, not really.

He moved until his shadow draped over them both, like a cool blanket. "Why don't we talk for a little while?" He gestured toward the bench that sat outside the diner.

"We should get back to work."

"It's not a crime to rely on somebody else for a little while. You don't have to carry every burden by yourself, Stace."

"I'll be fine by myself," she said. "I always am."

Then she went back inside before she could give in to the temptation of Riley McKenna. Stace poured herself into work, which helped some to take her mind off of her sister. But not off of Riley.

She watched him from the corner of her eye, always, always aware of him just across the crowded room.

An hour later, the diner was deserted. Riley pulled two plates of burgers off the dividing wall between the kitchen and the diner, and brought them over to the booth where Stace had sat down. "Lunch is served."

She gave him a grateful smile. "Should I count the fries?"

"I already stole one of yours on the way over here. You can take it out of my pay."

She laughed, then heaped a generous portion of ketchup on the corner of her plate and began dipping and eating her fries. They melted like heaven in her mouth. The burger was amazing, as usual. "If I eat too many of these, you'll have to roll me home."

He laughed. "Maybe we'll become human bowling balls, and race down the street."

"Now, there's an advertisement for the food here." To punctuate the point, she downed another fry.

Riley leaned back in his seat and stretched. "If we're going to have that race, we'll have to do it before Wednesday."

"Why?" She swirled the last fry in the ketchup puddle.

"I put in my notice with Frank this morning. Turns out there's a big project over at McKenna Media, and they called me in to help with it."

"You got your old job back?" Disbelief tinged her words. He wasn't staying.

"I proved my grandmother's point. I got a job on my own, earned some income." Then he leaned forward and met her gaze. "You knew this was a temporary position for me. Frank's okay with it. He wished me well and everything. So what's wrong?"

"Are you happy there?"

He scoffed. "Who's happy in their job?"

"I am. It's hard work, yes, and it doesn't always pay well, but at the end of the day, I look around this place and think of all the people who have left here full, content, and happy, and that makes me feel full, contented, and happy. It started out as my father's dream, and somewhere along the way it became mine." Stace wrapped her hands around her glass of ice water. "Anyway, that's what I hope people feel when they're here."

"I think they do," he said. "Everybody but Walter anyway."

She laughed, then cursed Riley for making her laugh while he was also breaking her heart. "True."

Riley pushed his empty plate to the side, then pulled out a small notepad and pen. "Okay, now on to the reason for our lunch. To spread the word of the Morning

Glory's awesomeness to the city of Boston." He clicked the pen. "What do you think makes the Morning Glory special?"

"The burgers. The atmosphere. The service." She gave Riley a smile, but it was a weaker one than before. He was leaving, she needed to remember that.

"I meant to you, personally. Why is your heart in this place? Because it reminds you of your dad?"

In every corner, she could see a memory. Her father plopping her onto one of the counter stools, and spinning her in a circle. Sitting in a corner booth, doing her homework after school. Pushing a mop around that was bigger than her, just to help her dad at the end of the day. "Do you know where the name Morning Glory comes from?"

Riley shook his head.

"My dad used to call me Morning Glory. Whenever I woke up, he'd say, 'Good morning, glory,' as if the sun had just risen in front of him. My mother loved flowers, and I guess that's where it came from. He said I reminded him of the best parts of starting his day. So when he and Frank opened this place, they wanted that same atmosphere here." She glanced around the room, at the painted violet morning glories that ran along the ceiling, the bright blue seat cushions that had been there since the day they opened, and the pale yellow countertops that had served thousands of meals. "It's just a really special place to me."

"It's your life," Riley said.

She let out a long breath. "Yes, I suppose it is. There are days when the only thing I think about is this place and how to make it succeed."

"You know, if you changed a few things, that might help. Add free Wi-Fi, for instance, for all the businesspeople. Change out the paint color, switch up the menu to offer some healthier foods." He offered her a grin. "I may not have been the most useful employee at McKenna Media, but I did pick up some marketing ideas. Change isn't always a bad thing, you know." He squared up his silverware. "Maybe then the Morning Glory wouldn't consume your life. What do you think that has cost you?"

The conversation had taken a sudden detour, going down a road Stace never visited. After her sister's phone call earlier, the arrow hit especially deep. How much had all this cost her?

Too much.

But she'd be damned if she was going to tell Riley that. He was leaving and when he was gone, she had no doubt she'd be another distant memory in a mental crowd of blondes, brunettes, and redheads.

"It takes a lot to keep this place running," she said, instead of the truth, "but—"

"That's not what I meant. You've poured your whole self into this diner. And I bet that's come at a huge personal sacrifice."

"This doesn't help with marketing materials."

"No, but it helps me understand you."

She got to her feet. "You don't need to understand me. You just need to—" She cut off the words and turned away.

Riley grabbed her wrist and stopped her. "I need to do what?"

"Just do what you do best, Riley. And quit." Then she walked away before she let him see how much saying that had cost her.

CHAPTER ELEVEN

THE day of the rescue shelter's fundraiser dawned bright and sunny. Jeremy had moaned and groaned about helping, but in the end, he'd made three times the number of posters they needed, and was ready before Stace.

Riley had followed her request and stayed away. Stace had spent her free time swimming, logging lap after lap until exhaustion claimed her and she collapsed into bed at the end of the day. Riley spent the hours after work with Jeremy, creating posters and working on some "secret" project in the garage of Riley's grandmother's house. Whatever it was, the two of them had kept it from Stace. Her nephew had never been so excited about a project before, and for that, Stace was grateful to Riley. He'd lit a fire in her nephew. She could see the positive effects of that change in the way Jeremy held his head up, the way he talked, and most of all, the way he smiled.

But once Jeremy was in bed, Riley had headed out on the town. Stace would lie in her room, trying not to cry when she heard the front door shut and Riley's car start. She was sure she'd done the right thing in ending their relationship. Then why did it hurt so much?

"You're slow and Riley's not even out here yet,"

Jeremy said that morning when Stace entered the kitchen. "There are people waiting on us, you know."

Stace put a palm to her nephew's head. "Are you sick?"

"No." He laughed. "Not at all, Aunt Stace."

"Then why are you suddenly so responsible?" She perched a fist on her hip and eyed him. "Did my nephew get replaced by his alien pod twin?"

"I just…" Jeremy shrugged. "I really want this to go well. You know, 'cause it's for, like, abandoned animals."

Stace's heart constricted. She drew Jeremy into a hug. "I understand. I totally do."

Jeremy wrangled his way out of the embrace, but Stace could see a smile on his lips. As he headed out the door, he passed by their packed bags. The roofer was scheduled to finish up today. Once the fundraiser was over, she'd come back here, grab their bags, and return to the little house in Dorchester. She should have been relieved, but a part of her was sad.

Was it because she'd gotten used to living in this cozy little house? Or gotten used to being around Riley? That alone was a sign she needed to get back to her normal life—Riley would do nothing but break her heart in the end. He was leaving the diner tomorrow, replaced by Irene, who had found a babysitter and was anxious to get back to work. Riley would be gone, and before she knew it, hopefully he'd become a distant memory.

He'd made it clear, over and over, that he wasn't a guy who committed, and if there was one thing Stace had been all her life, it was committed. To the diner. To that house. To her family.

Hadn't he gone out again last night? It was probably why he was dragging a little this morning. Instead of waiting in the house to find out the answer, Stace waited outside for Riley, then the three of them headed over to the diner, taking Riley's car instead of the train, since traffic into the city was light in the mid-afternoon, and because Riley told her he had the "special project" in the back.

"Today should be busy," Riley said. "There was a write-up in the paper yesterday about it, and my brother said Walter's been talking it up to anyone who will listen."

"I bet you were hoping to end your last day on a less hectic note," she said.

"I don't mind working. Especially for a good cause." Riley rested his hands on the steering wheel. "This event has energized me. I'm excited about it."

"So excited you had to go out and celebrate last night. And the night before. And the night before that." She could have bit her tongue for saying what she did, for letting him know that she cared how he spent his time.

"It wasn't about that," Riley said. "When I went out, it was to—"

"I don't need an explanation. Let's just get through the day." She turned and kept her gaze on the road passing by her window. And the conversation ended.

By the time they arrived, Frank had already started cooking and Walter had his team in the back, setting up portable pens. Several volunteers wearing T-shirts emblazoned with the shelter's logo were unloading animals and setting up an adoption station.

A half dozen of Jeremy's new school friends had come by to help. Within moments, the nonchalant teenagers smiled and laughed as they interacted with the dogs and cats. Stace grinned at the sight of a burly football-player-type holding a shivering schnauzer, and talking softly to calm the little dog's jitters.

Stace and Riley headed into the Morning Glory, and returned with platters of fresh baked muffins and donuts, laying them out on tables beside steaming pots of coffee. They had priced them reasonably, and agreed to donate the profits to the rescue organization. Every person who took a treat got a small flyer advertising the Morning Glory's regular specials, and featuring Frank's award-winning burgers front and center.

As more and more people stopped by for the goodies and asked about the Morning Glory's menu, Stace had to admit that Riley had surprised her. He'd put together a successful event, in very little time, and she felt bad for giving him a hard time about going out. He had clearly spent a lot of his free time on planning the event and marketing it. When there was a lull in the activity, she slid over to where he was refilling the carafes. "You did great with this."

He shrugged. "I didn't do much. The shelter had a lot of the groundwork done already."

"The radio station is here, the TV station, too. And I think I see reporters from all the major papers. More pets have left here with new owners than I can count. Plus, you've got people buzzing about the Morning Glory in ways they never have before."

"That was the goal."

"It worked. And I'm sorry for giving you a hard time this morning."

"That's okay. Apology accepted."

"Good." She'd accomplished her purpose. She'd thanked him and she'd apologized. She should leave, and put some distance between herself and Riley before she was tempted into ignoring the warning bells in her head. Still, she lingered. "So, uh, where's this special project I've heard so much about?"

Riley glanced at Jeremy. The foot traffic had slowed, and only a couple of people milled around the adoption area. "Hey, Jeremy, do you think it's time?"

Jeremy grinned. "Yeah." The two walked around the other side of the building, while Stace waited by the table and nursed a cup of coffee. A few minutes later, they came back, each carrying the end of something long and covered by an old sheet.

Frank came up behind Stace. "What the hell is that?"

"A special project." She shrugged. "I don't know what, exactly. They kept the whole thing a secret from me."

Riley and Jeremy paused by Stace, tipped the item in their hands to one side, and stood it on its end. Then Riley stepped back and gestured to Jeremy. "You do the honors. You did the work."

Jeremy nodded, then tugged the sheet, revealing a tall, thin wooden curio stand, with turned spindles and a carved top. Sunlight bounced off the gleaming wood and its newly shellacked finish.

Stace stepped forward, running her finger over the shape forming the top. "Is that...?"

Jeremy raised one shoulder, let it drop. "It's supposed to be a bunch of morning glories."

She traced the outline of the trio of circular flowers and their blossoming bright centers. She could feel the ridges of the hand-working, the careful detail put into each one. "Oh, my goodness, they're beautiful."

"Pretty damned amazing, I think, kiddo," Frank said.

"It's supposed to be a shelf for you to put all those cups on," Jeremy said. "You know the ones you have in the house on your dresser?"

"My mother's teacups. Oh, Jeremy, that's so sweet." She pressed a hand to her mouth, while tears rushed to the back of her eyes. She lifted her gaze to Riley. "Thank you."

"Don't thank me. I made him do all the work." He thumbed toward Jeremy.

A measure of pride shone in Jeremy's eyes, then he dropped his gaze and toed at the ground. "Riley helped me. A lot."

"It's beautiful," she said again, and touched first one shelf, then the other. Already she could see the teacups seated there, proudly displayed as they always should have been. "I didn't know you knew how to do that."

"I didn't," Jeremy said. "But Riley did. He said it'd be a good thing for me to learn, because I like art and stuff, and this was art, but with wood." Jeremy ran a hand over the carved flowers. "It kinda is, isn't it?"

"It's a masterpiece is what it is," Frank said, clapping Jeremy on the back. "You did a good job, son."

"I agree. It *is* a masterpiece." Stace gave her nephew a big hug. For the first time, he didn't wriggle out of the embrace, and Stace marveled again at the positive changes Riley had brought into Jeremy's life. "I'm going to put this front and center in the house as soon as we get home tonight."

Home. Back to the little house in Dorchester. The thought saddened her—not because she didn't love that little house with all its flaws, the same house where she'd grown up, but because it would mean closing a chapter on her life. Maybe it was time to sell that house, to move on to something new. She glanced at her nephew, and decided it was time for all of them to try something new. "I think you did an incredible job, Jeremy."

"Thanks." Jeremy shifted from foot to foot, clearly uncomfortable with the praise. Then his eyes widened and he let out a gasp. "Mom?"

Stace's heart caught in her throat, and she hesitated a moment to pray, to hope, before she turned.

Lisa.

Her little sister stood on the sidelines, looking unsure, almost scared. And better than she had in five years. She had put on some weight and her hair was no longer a dyed carrot-red, but back to her natural blond color. Stace hesitated only a second, then closed the gap between them and put out her arms. "Hey, sis."

Lisa broke into tears, then dove into Stace's hug with a fierce, tight embrace. "Oh, God, I've missed you so much. You and Jeremy."

"Where have you been? You look terrific." She really did. Her face had lost that gaunt, drawn pallor. She looked alive, vibrant. Hope bloomed in Stace's chest. "You really look amazing, Lisa."

"Thanks." A watery smile filled Lisa's face. "I'm sorry I left without telling you where I went. I was so afraid that if I said anything, I'd jinx it, or I'd chicken out." She let out a long breath, and her smile wavered. "I went to rehab. Spent thirty days in, and now I'm enrolled in an outpatient program at a halfway house. I'm doing it this time, Stace. I really am." Lisa held up a chip that celebrated her thirty days of sobriety, clenching it as if it was a lifeline. Then she turned to her son, who stood a little to the side, not yet sure about his mother's return. "I can't miss one more day of your life, Jeremy, and I swear I won't. The day I left was a huge wake-up call for me. I almost killed my son that day because I was stupid and selfish and messed-up." Her voice caught on a sob, then she put a hand on Jeremy's shoulder, and the rest of her words poured out in a teary, heartfelt rush. "I don't ever want to be that mother again. I love you, Jeremy. I really do."

Then Jeremy stepped forward, moving slowly at first, then faster, until his arms were around his mother and she was crying onto his shoulder. His face reddened and tears brimmed in his eyes but the big, wide, growing smile on his face kept the tears at bay. Soon, all three of them were crying and hugging, with Lisa telling them in halting, excited sentences about the lessons she had learned and the changes she was going to make. For the first time in forever, Stace believed the change was real, lasting. Lisa had a long road ahead of her, but Stace had a feeling this time she was going to make it.

As Stace watched their reunion, a sad lump sank in her stomach. Jeremy was gone, Lisa was okay, and Stace was left...

Exactly where she'd been before. With her life on hold. How long would she keep on doing that?

Stace left Jeremy and Lisa to catch up, and returned to Riley and Frank. They were serving the last of the food to the shelter volunteers, who had begun loading up the remaining animals and cleaning up from the day. "Jeremy's mom?" Riley asked.

Stace nodded. "I guess it's true what they say."

"What's that?"

"Miracles can come true."

Riley's gaze met hers and held. "I think you're right. They can."

What did he mean by that? She wanted to ask, but didn't. He was leaving, after all, and the sooner she learned to let go, the better.

Frank cleared his throat. "Seems we're low on muffins. I better get back inside and get some more food for the troops." Frank headed into the Morning Glory, leaving Riley and Stace alone. Clearly, on purpose.

When Frank was gone, Stace turned back to the shelf.

"Was this your idea?" she asked, running a hand down the smooth surface of the shelf. It was as if Riley had read her mind. He'd created something that would hold her most precious mementos, one that featured her father's morning glories.

Why did he keep doing things that worked their way into her heart, even as she tried to forget him? "What made you build this, of all things?"

"You needed someplace strong and secure to put those teacups. Something better than a flimsy shelf in the bedroom."

"Well, now that I'll have a better roof, they should be safe." But was she safe? Had she fallen too far to be able to forget Riley after he left?

"Good. That's what I wanted." He placed a hand on the carving at the top. "I'm glad Jeremy enjoyed making it."

"He did. I think you inspired a new hobby in him." She cocked her head and studied Riley. "Who taught you?"

Riley pinched the flower at the center of the shelf, as if he could pluck it from its wooden home. But it didn't move, of course, and he finally released the faux flower. "My dad. That was our thing. We worked on all kinds of projects. Just before he died, we started building a tree house."

"That must have been fun."

"It was." His voice dropped into a quieter range as the memories flooded back. As he talked, Stace and he walked together to the corner of the building, far from the remaining people. "There was this woodpecker that would come and tap at the tree above our heads while we were working. Darn thing was there every single day. My dad called it the house mascot. He even built a little birdhouse and attached it to the tree house, so the woodpecker could stay." A soft smile stole over Riley's face at the memory. "Then my dad died. I went back to the tree house after the funeral, but the woodpecker wasn't there. I went back every single day, and tried to finish the tree house myself, thinking if I did, the woodpecker would come back. But he never did." Riley let out a low curse, then shook his head. "I stopped building things that day. Stopped…"

"Stopped what?"

"Stopped counting on things to be the same." He lifted his gaze to her and in his eyes, she saw the glimmer of unshed tears. "Nothing lasts, Stace, that's what I learned that day. *Nothing* lasts."

It all made sense in that moment. She saw in Riley the same fears that had plagued her. Who could have known that this man, from the other side of the city, the other side of the social coin, could be so similar to her?

"Oh, Riley." She led him over to the stoop at the back of the diner, and they sat on the cold concrete stub. "Do you know why I still live in that crappy house in Dorchester?"

"Because it's expensive as hell to buy a house in Boston?"

She laughed. "Well, there is that. But no, it's more…" She picked up a stick on the ground and peeled at the bark, stripping the thin piece of wood bare. "It's that I was afraid of the same thing as you. Nothing lasts, I told myself, but I thought that if I held on tight enough to what I had it would. I couldn't let go. I wanted things to stay the same, but I've realized the more I hold on to the same things and the same places, the more it keeps me stuck. Then the roof caved in—literally." She shook her head. "I have done the same thing every single day for eight years, Riley. I have gone to work at the Morning Glory, and gone home. Just like I did for all the years before that. And now today I finally realized why." She lifted her gaze to his, and this time, the tears pushed their way through, fat droplets puddling on her lap. "I was afraid to change. Afraid to take a risk. Afraid to be more, do more."

"Why?"

"Because then I could lose it all. And the only way I could keep my grip on everything I had left was to keep it all exactly the same. So I kept my dad's furniture and my mother's teacups and the same menu, and everything that had been as it was years ago. And guess what?"

He waited, letting her talk, letting her get it out.

"All it did was keep me glued in place. I didn't go to college, I didn't get married, I didn't have kids. I kept telling myself it was because I didn't have time, and maybe, yes, I didn't, but it was really because I was afraid of changing anything." She shook her head. "You were right about me. I let this place become my life. Then I saw my nephew, a boy who has just as much reason as me to try to control his world, embrace a change in school, in his hobbies, in his life, and I realized that change was good. This event, for instance, was the kind of thing I resisted for years because I thought it would destroy the spirit of the Morning Glory, but instead, it made it better. Stronger. It made the Morning Glory something more than it was before. And that's rewarding. It's not just a diner now, it's a part of the community. Because we changed." She met his blue gaze. "Because of you."

"All I had was the idea." He shrugged off the praise.

"Why do you do that? You were a major part of all of this, and you don't take any credit."

"Stace, I didn't do much."

"You did." Then she looked at him, really looked at him, and saw a mirror of herself. "And you know what? I think you're afraid, too."

"Me? No, not at all."

"You are. And that's why you keep running. From jobs. From responsibilities. From labels. From…me."

He looked away. "I'm not afraid of anything."

"Prove it. Take the biggest risk of your life, Riley." She got to her feet and tossed the stick onto the ground. It tumbled end over end into the shadows. "And stick to something. Really stick to it. Forever."

The shelter's fundraiser had been a success, on all fronts. Walter's face curved in something resembling a smile, and Frank strutted around the diner, beaming from ear to ear. "We should do more things like that," Frank said. "It shakes things up around here, and gets people talking."

Stace wrapped up the last of the muffins. Riley was outside, finishing the cleanup. She probably should have been helping him, but truly, she only wanted the day to be over. It was the last day Riley would be working here, and the last day she'd have to deal with the conflicting emotions that being around him awakened.

Riley hadn't followed after she'd issued the challenge. That told her everything she needed to know. Even as her heart shattered and tears threatened her eyes.

"I think it's time we did some things that got people talking," Stace said. Focus on work, on the diner, on things she could depend upon. "Maybe change up the menu. Give this place a new coat of paint."

Frank leaned back and crossed his arms over his chest. "Wow. Never thought I'd hear you say those words."

"I'm sorry, Frank." She put a hand on his arm. He had been a part of the Morning Glory since day one, and loved it as much as she did. How could she presume dramatic changes were okay? "Maybe we shouldn't change anything. Keep it just the way it's always been."

"Don't you dare," Frank said.

She arched a brow. "What?"

"I *want* you to change things. For this place, for you." He untied his apron and tossed it into the laundry bag. "And for me."

She dropped onto a counter stool, and sat the bag of muffins on her lap. "I've been trying to talk you into change for years." Doing it for someone else had clearly been easier than doing it for herself. But those days were over now. Change was in the air in Stace's life, too.

"I know you have." Frank said. "And I've just been waiting, Stace girl."

"For what?"

"For you to be okay." Frank's face softened, and he lowered himself onto the stool beside her. "It took some time, but now I think you're going to be just fine."

"I've always been fine."

"Nope. You've been pretending, and that ain't the same thing." His hand covered hers, so much bigger and warmer, and always, always there for her. "You've been spending the past eight years taking care of everyone but you. Telling me, and anyone who could listen, that you were fine, you didn't need any help. Then your roof got a big old hole in it, and you had to ask for help."

She let out a little laugh. "I guess literally, huh?"

"Yep." Frank gave her a grin. "Riley turned out to be good for you."

She scoffed. "He turned out to be exactly what I expected. Unreliable. He quit, remember?"

"Yep. And I'm fine with it. He's searching for his purpose. I don't know if he's found it yet, but he's a hundred steps closer than he was the day I hired him."

She shook her head. He didn't know the truth about Riley. "You always see the best in people, Frank."

"Maybe I just see the truth."

She considered that. "Maybe."

Frank reached into his back pocket, pulled out a piece of paper, and plopped it onto the counter between them. "You might want to take out a Help Wanted ad."

Stace picked up the paper, unfolded it, then raised her gaze to Frank's. "You're going? To Europe?"

"Yep. Eleanor talked me into it. Said she'd show me the sights." Frank arched a brow. "Though I think she's got her sights set on me."

Stace laughed. "What made you change your mind? I thought you wanted to wait."

"I *was* waiting. For you."

"Me?"

"For you to be ready for me to leave."

She laughed. "Frank, I'm a grown-up. I'll be fine. I'll miss you like crazy, but I'll be fine."

"I know that. I also know you've been wanting to buy me out for years now."

She put the brochure down. Its bright colors and bold headlines promised the trip of a lifetime, something Frank Simpson deserved. "I'm sorry, but I just don't have enough money yet. I've been saving like crazy, but—"

"Quit that." He grabbed her hand again. "You don't need to buy me out."

"Frank, how are you going to afford retirement? You need—"

"I don't need your money, Stace. Nor do I want it. I don't want you to buy me out. I want to keep on owning a little piece of the Morning Glory. I've been saving, too, you know. And waiting for you to ask me for help."

She shook her head. "Frank, you've done so much, I couldn't ask you for anything else."

"I'm your friend, Stace. Stop taking care of others all the time, and ask someone to take care of you once in a while. And guess what? If you ask me…" His light blue gaze and friendly smile met hers. "I'll be there."

She slid off the stool and wrapped him in a hug. "Oh, Frank, how can I ever repay you?"

"You can make this diner your own. It's not your dad's and mine anymore, it's *yours*. Change the colors, change the menu, change the name, I don't care. Make it your own, and then make it sing, like you always do."

Excitement bubbled inside her. She had no idea what she wanted to do with the Morning Glory, but just the thought of possibilities stirred her mental pot. She turned around, and saw changes in her mind. All these years, she'd resisted moving so much as a chair, but this new Stace, the one who had seen how a few changes could transform a life, a person, a neighborhood, she wanted to keep that momentum going, and let it snowball into a future she couldn't yet see.

"So you're really ready to travel the world?" she asked Frank.

"Yep." He tucked the brochure back into his pocket. "You know I never had kids of my own, but to me, you were always like a daughter."

"Aw, Frank." She hugged the burly chef a second time. "And you're like my second dad."

He drew her tight to him, and held her for a long time. Stace wasn't sure, but she thought she felt a teardrop onto her shoulder. Then Frank drew back, and swiped at his face. His teasing grin was back on his face before anyone could mistake him for getting emotional. "Well, it's time for me to go."

She held on one more time. Change was good, even if it sometimes hurt. She'd miss Frank. A lot. "I know."

"There was one more thing I was waiting for."

"What's that? A compliment from Walter?"

Frank chuckled. "That'd be way too much waiting for me." He paused and the teasing left his features. "No, I was waiting to be sure that you would have your own happy ending."

"I will. I'll be working on the diner and—"

"I meant with love. I wanted to wait to retire, until I knew you had met Mr. Right."

"I didn't—"

He put a finger under her chin, cutting off her protests. "You did. You just gotta believe it."

Riley walked into an empty house. No pancakes on the counter. No humming in the kitchen. No floral bags on the sink. Just Stace's bags by the door, waiting for her to pick them up in a little while. Soon, she'd be going back to her house for good.

Suddenly the thought of being here when she walked out of his life was too much. Riley headed across the lawn to his grandmother's house. A light burned in the morning room, and through the glass doors, he could see Mary, sitting in the same chair she always sat in, reading a book, with Heidi snoozing at her feet.

He slipped in through the French doors. "Hey, Gran."

Mary looked up and her face brightened. Heidi gave him a quick look then went back to her puppy dreams. "Riley. Come, sit down."

He did as she asked, thinking how odd it was to be back in the same spot as before. But this time, Riley had returned with a new attitude, a new purpose. Stace Kettering had had a lot to do with that. So had the changes he had made in his life. He'd just come from a meeting that had given him a whole new direction. One that sent a charge through him every time he thought about it.

He'd had a lot of time to think while he'd cleaned up from the fundraiser. He'd looked at all the people opening their hearts and homes to a pet. Taking on responsibility, commitment.

And looking happy as hell to do it. When had he last felt that happy?

When he'd nailed a bright blue tarp on Stace Kettering's roof while she watched and worried from below. Working at the diner, side by side with her, learning what a true work ethic was, and finding it was a whole lot more satisfying than he'd expected.

"I wanted to thank you," he said to his grandmother.

"For what?"

"For raising me. For loving me. And most of all, for kicking me out of the nest." He grinned. "I never would have realized what I wanted if you hadn't done that. You were a hundred percent right to do what you did and I appreciate it. That's why I'm going to…quit."

Mary arched a brow. "Quit?"

"I'm not going back to McKenna Media, Gran. I'm sorry. I know you were counting on a McKenna taking over when you retired, but that's not going to be me."

Mary leaned forward, smiling. "I would have loved to have one of my grandsons run the company when I stepped down, but I realize you all need to carve out your own niche in life. I'll promote someone or hire someone. It doesn't matter. What I care about is whether you and your brothers are happy."

Finn was. Brody had found his purpose. That left just Riley. "I'm working on it, Gran."

Worry creased her brow. "What are you going to do now, Riley?"

"Be just fine, Gran. Just fine." He rose out of his chair, gave his grandmother a kiss on the cheek, then headed back outside. To find the one thing he had really come home to find.

The water sluiced over her skin in a gentle caress as Stace made her way from one end of the pool to the other. She swam back and forth, back and forth, letting the laps ease her stress and clear her mind.

She'd come back to Riley's house alone—Jeremy and Lisa had gone out to talk and catch up—and found it empty. She should have grabbed her bags and left, but she couldn't resist one last dip in the pool. Each stroke numbed her thoughts a little more, but she suspected she could swim for a year and still not forget Riley McKenna.

Because she had fallen in love with him. Somewhere between the tarp on her roof and the shelf for her mother's teacups, she had fallen in love, and no matter how much she wished otherwise, she knew she'd never be able to excise him from her heart. Riley had made an indelible impression on her life.

There was a splash from behind her. Stace drew up, and planted her feet on the bottom. She wiped the water out of her eyes and turned to find Riley, standing beside her, still fully dressed—

And soaking wet.

"What are you doing here?" she asked. "In the pool? In your clothes?"

"Stopping you from leaving."

"I wasn't going anywhere yet. I stopped to take a swim." Then she realized this wasn't her property and she didn't have a right to the pool. Not anymore. "I'm sorry, I should have asked first."

"You're fine." He chuckled. "You can swim every day if you want."

"I won't make the journey over here from Dorchester." It was, in fact, the last time she'd ever be in this pool, and a part of her had just wanted to say goodbye. She turned toward the concrete steps. "Let me just get out of here and—"

He hauled her back. She slipped a little and collided with his chest. Riley wrapped an arm around her waist, and righted her again. But he didn't let go. "Stop running, Stace."

"I'm not." She lifted her gaze to his. "Okay, maybe I am."

"You are. Take it from me, the expert. I ran from anything that smacked of responsibility my whole life." He tipped her chin to his. "But no more. I finally found something worth staying for."

"What's that?"

A slow smile curved across his face. "You."

"If you're talking about the diner, I'll hire someone else. It'll be fine."

"I'm not talking about the diner. I know you'll be okay with that. And I think you could hire a monkey who could do a better job than me."

She laughed a little and shook her head. Those damned tears kept burning in the back of her eyes. "I think...you're going to be pretty irreplaceable, Riley."

"Just at the Morning Glory?"

She could have lied. Could have made up something flip. But Stace was tired of keeping her heart under lock and key. "No. For me, too."

The grin widened on Riley's face. "You have no idea how glad I am to hear that." He cupped her chin and let his thumb trace her jaw. "It took me a while, but I finally realized that being responsible, being committed, being dependable, wasn't some evil curse. It was a risk. One I had always been afraid to take. Then I met you, and Jeremy, and everything changed. First it was the lasagna, then it was the pancakes on the counter."

"Pancakes? What pancakes?" The water swirled around them, warm and gentle. The low hum of the filter provided a quiet undertow for their voices.

"The ones you left for Jeremy. I saw those, and I was jealous of a teenage boy whose aunt loved him enough to leave him pancakes in the morning. And I realized that the only way I was going to have pancakes on my counter was to open my heart."

"Is that what you want? For me to cook you breakfast?"

"No. I want to *have* breakfast with you every day. And lunch. And dinner. And go to bed with you and wake up with you." He paused and his blue eyes met hers. "I want to build a house and a future and a family with you, Stace. As soon as possible."

"Riley...I...I don't know what to say." Was he being truthful? Or was this a temporary phase? She wanted to believe him, wanted to take that leap, but a part of her was still screaming Caution.

"You don't have to say anything, Stace. Because I

love you, and if you aren't ready to love me, too, I can
wait." He dropped his arms to her waist, and hugged
her to him. "You know, I looked up morning glories.
They're a hardy flower. They grow fast, twining all over
whatever is near them. They're sturdy and dependable,
but they're shy, too. They open in the morning, and
then they close again at night. They look so delicate, but
they're strong as hell inside. Like you, Stace."

She shook her head. "I'm not—"

"You are. You're a waitress from Dorchester who
is the strongest woman I have ever met. The only one
who has ever made me want to be better than I was before. And the only woman I have ever truly fallen in
love with."

Her heart sang, and joy bloomed in her chest. "You...
you're in love with me?"

He nodded. "I am so damned in love with you that
it's all I think about. I wasn't going out at night to forget
you or to date someone else. I was going over to the office at McKenna Media to plan a marketing campaign
for that fundraiser that would knock your socks off. I
wanted to impress you, because I thought if I did..." He
paused and shook his head. "I thought maybe you'd fall
in love with me, too."

He'd done all that, just to win her heart. And here
she'd been thinking the worst. "You don't need to impress me for me to love you, Riley. You just needed to
put a tarp on my roof." She smiled at the memory of him
on her roof, drenched and determined. She'd thought her
life was falling apart that day, but in truth, it was just
beginning to get better. "I think I fell in love with you
that day. Or maybe it was the day in the cemetery. Or the
day you ballroom danced with me in a hallway. There
were a hundred moments when you stole my heart."

"And I'm never giving it back." He leaned down

and kissed her. A simple, sweet kiss this time, one that left her feeling loved and treasured. "I love you, Stace Kettering. And I want to marry you."

Marriage. The biggest risk of all. Binding her life to Riley's, depending on him to be there today, tomorrow, the next day. She thought of the Riley the media had depicted. Then she thought of the Riley she had met, and fallen in love with. The real Riley McKenna was the man who would do anything for the people he loved. She knew that now, to the very core of her being. "I want to marry you, too."

"Really? Oh, Stace." The smile exploded on his face and he hoisted her up to press another kiss to her lips, then lowered her to the water again. "How about we get married at the Morning Glory? I think it's time to build some happy memories in that diner."

This man knew her so well. Knew everything that made her tick. She leaned into him, pressed her head to his heart. "That sounds perfect."

"Good. We'll wait for Frank to come back from Europe. That should give me enough time to settle in at my new job."

"At the marketing agency?"

"Nope. At the Wilmont Academy." Riley grinned, and she could see pride and excitement shimmering in his eyes. "They needed someone to run an after-school program for at-risk kids. I'll be teaching the kids art and woodworking and whatever else gets them to open up and see there are other possibilities in their life than running away."

"That sounds perfect. For the kids, for you." Riley had the perfect personality for a program like that. Approachable, funny, and experienced in life's difficulties.

"Already got my first student. Jeremy." He grinned. "I think I've got a budding carpenter on my hands."

She thought of the days ahead, while all of them adjusted to Lisa's return. Jeremy would undoubtedly have rocky days. "He's going to need that male influence for a while."

"And I'm honored to be that for him."

They climbed out of the pool, hand in hand. Riley wrapped Stace in a towel, then hugged her to him. Warmth flooded her body, though she thought it was more from Riley than the terry cloth. She tilted her chin to kiss him. She loved this man and couldn't wait to see what the future brought for the two of them. Frank had been right—she had found Mr. Right. "Can I ask you something?"

"Anything."

"What was with you and ordering any old thing you wanted at the diner?"

"I did it because I knew what I liked and I wanted it." He trailed a finger down her nose. "Sort of like when I jumped in the pool to go after the woman I liked."

She laughed. "In other words, you're spoiled."

"*Was* spoiled. You have reformed me, Stace Kettering." He grinned. "More or less."

"Me? All I did was give you an apron."

He shook his head and his blue eyes caught hers. In that gaze, she saw love, joy and all the things she had craved in her life but never dared to hope she could have. "You've done a lot more than that. A lot more." Then he leaned down and kissed her and placed the only order either one of them wanted—one meal of forever, with a side of happy ending.

* * * * *

RETURN OF THE LAST MCKENNA

BY
SHIRLEY JUMP

To the most heroic military man I know—my husband,
who served his country, and has made me proud
to be his wife in a thousand different ways.
Not to mention, he's the kind of guy
who brings home cupcakes just
because I had a hard day.
He knows me well!

CHAPTER ONE

BRODY McKENNA checked his third sore throat of the morning, prescribed the same prescription as he had twice before—rest, fluids, acetaminophen—and tried to count his blessings. He had a dependable job as a family physician, a growing practice, and a close knit family living nearby. He'd returned from his time overseas none the worse for wear, and should have been excited to get back to his job.

He wasn't.

The six-year-old patient headed out the door, with a sugar-free lollipop and a less harried mother. As they left, Helen Maguire, the nurse who had been with him since day one, and with Doc Watkins for fifteen years before that, poked her head in the door. "That's the last patient of the morning," she said. A matronly figure in pink scrubs decorated with zoo animals, Mrs. Maguire had short gray hair and a smile for every patient, young or old. "We have an hour until it's time to start immunizations. And then later in the afternoon, we'll be doing sports physicals."

Brody's mind drifted away from his next appointment and the flurry of activity in his busy Newton office. His gaze swept the room, the jars of supplies, so easy to order and stock here in America, always on hand and ready for any emergency. Every bandage, every tongue depressor, every stethoscope, reminded him. Launched him back to a hot country and a dusty dirt floor hut short on supplies and even shorter on miracles.

"Doc? Did you hear me?" Mrs. Maguire asked.

"Oh, oh. Yes. Sorry." Brody washed his hands, then dried them and handed the chart to Helen. Focus on work, he told himself, not on a moment in the past that couldn't be changed. Or on a country on the other side of the world, to those people he couldn't save.

Especially not on that.

"Lots of colds going around," he said.

"It's that time of year."

"I think it's always that time of year."

Helen shrugged. "I think that's what I like about family practice. You can set your watch by the colds and flus and shots. It has a certain rhythm to it, don't you think?"

"I do." For a long time, Brody had thought he had the perfect life. A family practice for a family man.

Or at least, that had been the plan. Then the family had dissolved before it had a chance to form. By that time, Brody had already stepped into Doc Watkins's shoes. Walking away from a thriving practice would be insane, so he'd stayed. For a long time, he'd been happy. He liked the patients. Liked working with kids, liked seeing the families grow and change.

It was good work, and he took satisfaction in that, and had augmented it with volunteer time with different places over the years—a clinic in Alabama, a homeless shelter in Maine. When the opportunity to volunteer assisting the remaining military overseas arose, Brody had jumped at it.

For a month, he'd changed lives in Afghanistan, working side by side with other docs in a roving medical unit that visited villagers too poor to get to a doctor or hospital, with the American military along for protection.

Brody had thought he'd make a difference there, too. He had—just not in the way he wanted. And now he couldn't find peace, no matter where he turned.

"You okay, doc?" Mrs. Maguire asked.

"Fine." His gaze landed on the jars of supplies again. "Just distracted. I think I'll head out for lunch instead of eating at my desk."

And being around all these reminders.

"No problem. It'll do you good to take some time to enjoy the day." Mrs. Maguire smiled. "I find a little fresh air can make everything seem brighter."

Brody doubted the air would work any miracles for him, but maybe some space and distance would. Unfortunately, he had little of either. "I'll be back by one."

He stepped outside his office and into a warm, almost summer day. The temperatures still lingered in the high seventies, even though the calendar date read deep into September. Brody headed down the street, waving to the neighbors who flanked his Newton practice—Mr. Simon with his shoe repair shop, Mrs. Tipp with her art gallery and Milo, who had opened three different types of shops in the same location, like an entrepreneur with ADD.

Brody took the same path as he took most days when he walked during his lunch hour. He rarely ate, just walked from his office to the same destination and back. He'd done it so many times in the last few weeks, he half expected to see a worn river of footsteps down the center of the sidewalk.

Brody reached in his pocket as he rounded the corner. The paper was crinkled and worn, the edges beginning to fray, but the inked message had stayed clear.

> *Hey, Superman, take care of yourself and come home safe. People over here love and miss you. Especially me. Things just aren't the same without your goofy face around. Love you, Kate.*

Brody had held onto that card for a month now. He ran his hands over the letters now, and debated the same thing he'd had in his head for weeks. To fulfill Andrew's last wishes, or let it go?

He paused. His feet had taken him to the same destination as always. He stood under the bright red and white awning of Nora's Sweet Shop and debated again, the card firm in his grip.

> *Promise me, Doc. Promise me you'll go see her. Make sure she's okay. Make sure she's happy. But please, don't tell her what happened. She'll blame herself and Kate has suffered enough already.*

The promise had been easy to make a month ago. Harder to keep.

Brody fingered the card again. *Promise me.*

How many times had he made this journey and turned back instead of taking, literally, the next step?

If he returned to the thermometers and stethoscopes and bandages, though, would he ever find peace?

He knew that answer. No. He needed to do this. Step forward instead of back.

Brody took a deep breath, then opened the door and stepped inside the shop. The sweet scents of chocolate and vanilla drifted over him, while soft jazz music filled his ears. A glass case of cupcakes and chocolates sat at one end of the store while a bright rainbow of gift baskets lined the sides. A cake made out of cupcakes and decorated in bridal colors sat on a glass stand in a bay window. Along the top of the walls ran a border of dark pink writing trimmed with chocolate brown and a hand lettered script reading Nora's Sweet Shop. On the wall behind the counter, hung a framed spatula with the name of the shop carved in the handle.

"Just a minute!" a woman called from the back.

"No problem," Brody said, stuffing the card back into his pocket. "I'm just…"

Just what? Not browsing. Not looking for candy or cupcakes. And he sure as hell couldn't say the truth—

He'd come to this little shop in downtown Newton for forgiveness.

So instead he grabbed the first assembled basket of treats he saw and marched over to the counter. He was just pulling out his wallet when a slim brunette woman emerged from the back room.

"Hi, I'm Kate." She dried her hands on the front of her apron before proffering one for him to shake. "How can I help you?"

Kate Spencer. The owner of the shop, and the woman he'd thought of a hundred times in the past weeks. A woman he'd never met but heard enough about to write at least a couple chapters of her biography.

He took her hand, a steady, firm grip—and tried not to stare. All these weeks he'd held onto that card, he'd expected someone, well, someone like a young version of Mrs. Maguire. A motherly type with her hair in a bun, and an apron around her waist, and a hug ready for anyone she met. That was how Andrew had made his older sister sound. Loving, warm, dependable. Like a down comforter.

Not the thin, fit, dynamo who had hurried out of the back room, with a friendly smile on her face and her coffee colored hair in a sassy ponytail skewed a bit too far to the right. She had deep green eyes, full crimson lips and delicate, pretty features. Yet he saw shadows dusting the undersides of her eyes and a tension in her shoulders.

Brody opened his mouth to introduce himself, to fulfill his purpose for being here, but the words wouldn't get past his throat. "I...I...uh," he glanced down at the counter, at the cellophane package in his hands, "I wanted to get this."

"No problem. Is it for a special person?"

Brody's mind raced for an answer. "My, uh, grandmother. She loves chocolate."

"Your grandma?" Kate laughed, then spun the basket to face him. "You want me to, ah, change out this bow? To something a little more feminine? Unless your grandma is a big fan?"

He glanced down and noticed he'd chosen a basket with a Red Sox ribbon. The dark blue basket with red trim, filled with white foil wrapped chocolates shaped like baseballs and bats, couldn't be further from the type of thing his staid grandmother liked. He chuckled. "No, that'd be me. I've even got season tickets. When she does watch baseball, my grandma is strictly a Yankees fan, though you can't say that too loud in Boston."

Kate laughed, a light lyrical, happy sound. Again, Brody realized how far off his imaginings of her had been. "Well, Mr. Red Sox, let me make this more grandma friendly. Okay? And meanwhile, if you want to put a card with this, there are some on the counter over there."

"Thanks." He wandered over to the counter she'd indicated, and tugged out a card, then scribbled his name across it. That kept him from watching her and gave his brain a few minutes to adjust to the reality of Kate Spencer.

She was, in a word, beautiful. The kind of woman, on any other day, he might have asked out on a date. Friendly, sweet natured, with a ready smile and a teasing lilt to her words. Her smile had roused something in him the minute he saw her, and that surprised him. He hadn't expected to be attracted to her, not one bit.

He tried to find a way around to say what he had come to say. *Promise me.*

He'd practiced the words he needed to say in his head a hundred times, but now that the moment had arrived, they wouldn't come. It wasn't the kind of subject one could just dump in the middle of a business transaction, nor had he quite figured out how to fulfill Andrew's wishes without giving away why. He needed to lead up to it, somehow. Yeah, easier to climb Mt. Everest.

"So...how's business?" he asked.

"Pretty good. We've been growing every year since

we opened in 1953. Mondays are our only slow day of the week. Almost like a mini vacation, except at the beginning of the week."

"You make all the cupcakes and candy things yourself?"

She shook her head and laughed. "I couldn't. It's a lot of work. Nora's Sweet Shop has been a family business for many years, but…" she trailed off, seemed to look elsewhere for a second, then came back, "anyway, now I have a helper who's invaluable in the kitchen. Why, you applying?"

"Me? I'm all thumbs in the kitchen."

"That can be dangerous if there are knives involved." She grinned. "But seriously, baking is something you can learn. I never had formal training. Learned it all at my grandmother's knee. And if a hopeless case like me can grow up to be a baker, anyone can."

"Sounds like you love working here."

"I do. It's…therapeutic." The humor dimmed in her features, and her gaze again went to somewhere he couldn't see. He didn't have to be psychic to know why sadness had washed over her face. Because of choices Brody had made on the other side of the world.

Damn.

Brody cleared his throat. "Work can be good for the soul."

Or at least, that's what he told himself every time he walked into his practice. Ever since he'd returned from Afghanistan, though, he hadn't found that same satisfaction in his job as before. Maybe he just needed more time. That's what Mrs. Maguire said. Give it time, and it'll all get better.

"And what work do you do, that feeds your soul?"

She colored. "Sorry. That's a little personal. You don't have to answer. I was just curious."

"I'm a doctor," he said.

She leaned against the counter, one elbow on the glass, her body turned toward his. "That's a rewarding job. So much more so than baking. And not to mention, a lot more complicated than measuring out cupcake batter."

"Oh, I don't know about that," he said. "Your job looks pretty rewarding to me. I mean, you make people happy."

"It takes a lot of sugar to do that." She laughed. "But thank you. I try my best. Three generations of Spencers have been trying to do that here."

Brody's gaze drifted over the articles on the wall. Several contained accolades and positive reviews for the sweet shop, a third generation business that had enjoyed decades of raves, as evidenced by some of the framed, yellowed clippings. Brody paused when he got to the last article on the right. The page was creased on one side, as if someone had kept the paper in a book for a while before posting it on the wall. A picture of a handsome young man in uniform smiled out from the corner of the article.

SHOP OWNER'S BROTHER DIES IN AFGHANISTAN

Brody didn't have to read another word to write the ending. In an instant, he was back there, in that hot, dusty hut, praying and cursing, and praying and cursing some more, while he tried to pump life back into Andrew Spencer.

And failed.

Brody could still feel the young man's chest beneath his palms. A hard balloon, going up, going down, forced into moving by Brody's hands, but no breath escaping his lips. Andrew's eyes open, sightless, empty. His life ebbing away one second at a time, while Brody watched, helpless and frustrated. Powerless.

Damn. Damn.

No amount of time would heal that wound for Kate and her family. No amount of time would make that better. What had he been thinking? How could buying a basket ever ease the pain he'd caused Kate Spencer? What had Andrew been thinking, sending Brody here?

Brody's hand went to the card in his pocket again, but this time, the cardboard corners formed sharp barbs.

"Sir? Your basket is ready."

Brody whirled around. "My basket?"

Kate laughed and held it up. The arrangement sported a new pink and white bow and the sports-themed chocolates had been changed for ones shaped like flowers. "For grandma?"

"Oh, yeah, sure, thanks." He gestured toward the article on the wall. He knew he should let it go, but he'd made a promise, and somehow, he had to find a way to keep it. Maybe then he'd be able to sleep, to find peace, and to give some to Kate Spencer, too. "You had a brother in the war?"

A shadow dropped over her features. She fiddled with the pen on the counter. "Yeah. My little brother, Andrew. He died over there last month. We all thought he was safe because the big conflict was over, but there were still dangers around every corner."

"I'm sorry." So much sorrier than he could say. He wanted to step forward, but instead Brody lingered by the counter. All the words he'd practiced in his head seemed empty, inadequate. "That must have been tough."

"It has been. In a lot of ways. But I work, and I talk to him sometimes, and I get through it." She blushed. "That sounds crazy, I know."

"No, it doesn't. Not at all."

She smoothed a hand over the counter. "He used to work here. And I miss seeing him every day. He was the organized one in the family, and he'd be appalled at the condition of my office." She laughed, then nodded toward the basket. "Anyway, do you want to put your card with that?"

"Oh, yeah, sure." He handed Kate the message he'd scribbled to his grandmother and watched as she tucked the small paper inside the cellophane wrapper. Again, he tried to find the words he needed to say, and again, he failed. "I've, uh, never been to this place before. Lived in this neighborhood for a while and I've seen it often, but never stopped by."

"Well, thank you for coming and shopping at Nora's Sweet Shop." She gave the basket a friendly pat. "I hope your grandmother enjoys her treats."

"I'm sure she will." For the hundredth time he told himself to leave. And for the hundredth time, he didn't. "So if you're Kate, who's Nora?" He asked the question, even though he knew the answer. Andrew had talked about Nora's Sweet Shop often, and told Brody the entire story about its origins.

"Nora is my grandmother." A soft smile stole over Kate's face. "She opened this place right after my grandfather came home from the Korean War. He worked side by side with her here for sixty years before they both retired and gave the shop to my brother and me. She's the Nora in Nora's Sweet Shop and if you ask my grandfather, she's the sweet in his life."

"She's still alive?" Ever since Brody had met the jovial, brave soldier, he'd wondered what kind of people had raised a man like that. What kind of family surrounded him, supported him as he went off to defend the country.

"My grandparents are retired now," Kate said, "but they come by the shop all the time and still do some deliveries. My brother and I grew up around here, and we spent more time behind this counter than anywhere else. I think partly to help my grandparents, and partly to keep us out of trouble while my parents were working. We were mischievous when we were young," she said with a laugh, "and my brother Andrew served as my partner in crime. Back then...and also for years afterwards when we took over the shop from my grandma. He had the craziest ideas." She shook her head again. "Anyway, that's how a Kate ended up running Nora's."

Brody had heard the same story from Andrew. Both Spencer children had loved the little shop, and the indulgent grandparents who ran it. Andrew hadn't talked much about his parents, except to say they were divorced, but he had raved about his grandparents and his older sister.

It had been one of several things Brody had in common with the young soldier, and created a bond between the two of them almost from the first day they met. He'd understood that devotion to grandparents, and to siblings.

"My grandmother runs a family business, too. A marketing agency started by my grandfather years ago.

My brothers and I all went in different directions, so I think she's pinned her hopes on my cousin Alec for taking it over when she retires."

She cocked her head to one side and studied him, her gaze roaming over his suit, tie, the shiny dress shoes. A teasing smile played on her lips, danced in her eyes. Already he'd started to like Kate Spencer. Her sassy attitude, her friendly smile.

"And you, Mr. Red Sox ribbon, you are far from the business type, being a doctor?"

He chuckled. "Definitely."

"Well, should I ever feel faint," she pressed a hand to her chest and the smile widened, and something in Brody flipped inside out, "I know who to call."

For a second, he forgot his reason for being there. His gaze lingered on the hand on her chest, then drifted to the curve of her lips. "I'm right around the corner. Almost shouting distance."

"That's good to know." The smile again. "Really good."

The tension between them coiled tighter. The room warmed, and the traffic outside became a low, muted hum. Brody wished he was an ordinary customer, here on an ordinary reason. That he wasn't going to have to make that smile dim by telling her the truth.

Kate broke eye contact first. She jerked her attention to the register, her fingers hovering over the keys. "Goodness. I got so distracted by talking, I forgot to charge you."

"And I forgot to pay." Brody handed over a credit card. As he did, he noticed her hands. Long, delicate fingers tipped with no-nonsense nails. Pretty hands.

The kind that seemed like they'd have an easy, gentle touch.

She took the credit card, slid it through the register, pushed a few buttons, then waited for a receipt to print. She glanced down at his name as she handed him back the card. "Mr. McKenna, is it?"

He braced himself. Did she recognize the last name? But her smile remained friendly.

Yes, I'm Brody McKenna. The doctor who let your brother die.

Not the answer he wanted to give. Call him selfish, call him a coward, but for right now, he wanted only to see her smile again. He told himself it was because that was what Andrew had wanted, but really, Brody liked Kate's smile. A lot.

"Yes. But I prefer Brody." He scrawled his name across the receipt and slid it back to her.

"Well, thank you, Brody." His name slid off her tongue with an easy, sweet lilt. "I hope you return if you're in the neighborhood again."

"Thank you, Kate." He picked up his basket and headed for the door. As he pushed on the exit, he paused, turned back. He had come here for a reason, and had yet to fulfill even a tenth of that purpose. "Maybe someday I can return the favor."

"I didn't do anything special, just my job. If you want to return the favor, then tell all your friends to shop here and to call on us to help them celebrate special moments." And then, like a gift, she smiled at him again. "That'll be more than enough."

"No, it won't," he said, his voice low and quiet, then headed out the door.

CHAPTER TWO

WHAT had he been thinking?

He'd gone into that little shop planning...what?

To tell Kate the truth? That her little brother had charged him with making sure his sister was okay. That Brody was supposed to make sure she wasn't letting her grief overwhelm her, and that she was staying on track with her life, despite losing Andrew. Instead Brody had bought a basket of chocolates, and chickened out at the last minute. Damn.

"Tell me you're quiet because you're distracted by that pretty hostess over there," Riley said to Brody. The dim interior provided the perfect backdrop for the microbrewery/restaurant that had become their newest favorite stop for lunch. Brody had called Riley yesterday after his visit to Nora's Sweet Shop, and made plans for lunch today. That, he figured, would keep him from making another visit. And leaving without saying or doing what he'd gone there to do.

"Why are you mentioning the hostess?" Brody asked. "Aren't you getting married soon?"

"I am indeed. But that doesn't mean I can't keep my eye out for a pretty girl..." Riley leaned across the table and grinned, "for *you*. You're the last of the

McKenna boys who isn't married. Better pony up to the bar, brother, and join the club."

"No way. I've tried that—"

"You got engaged. Not married. Doesn't count. You came to the edge of the cliff and didn't jump."

"For good reason." Melissa had been more interested in the glamour of being a doctor's wife than in being *Brody's* wife. Once she'd realized he had opted for a small family practice instead of a lucrative practice like plastic surgery or cardiac care, she'd called off the engagement. She didn't want a man who spent his life "sacrificing," she'd said. No matter what Brody said or did, he couldn't fix their relationship and couldn't get it back on track. Brody's family dream had evaporated like a puddle on a summer day.

Brody picked up the menu and scanned the offerings. "How's work going?"

That drew more laughter from Riley. "Don't think I'm falling for that. You're changing the subject."

"You got me." Brody put up his hands. "I don't want to talk about the hostess or my love life or why I didn't get married. I want to visit with my little brother before he attaches the ball and chain to his ankle."

"No need for that. I'm head over heels in love with my wife to be." A goofy grin spread across Riley's face. "We're working out the final details for the wedding. Got the place—"

"The diner." A busy, quaint place in the heart of Boston where the former playboy Riley had worked for a few weeks when their grandmother had cut him off from the family pocketbook and told him to get a job and grow up. Now, a couple of months later, Riley had turned into a different man. Stace had brought out the best in Brody's little brother.

"Gran had a fit about us having the wedding at the Morning Glory, because she wanted us to get married at the Park Plaza, but Stace and I love that old diner, so it seemed only fitting we seal the deal there. Stace has her dress, though I am forbidden from seeing it until the wedding day. And you guys all have your suits—"

"Thank you again for not making me put on a tux."

Riley grinned. "You know me, Brody. I'd rather wear a horsehair shirt than a tux. Finn's the only formal one out of the three of us. He actually *wanted* a tux. Says I'm killing a tradition with the suit idea." Riley waved a hand in dismissal. "I'm sure Ellie will talk some sense into him. That wife of his has been the best thing ever for ol' stick in the mud Finn."

Brody shook his head. "I can't believe you're talking about wedding plans. You've changed, little brother."

"For the better, believe me. Meeting Stace made me change everything about myself, my life. And I'm glad it did." The waitress came by their table to take their orders. Riley opted to try the new Autumn Lager, while Brody stuck to water.

Riley raised a hand when a few of their mutual friends came in. Then he turned back to Brody. "Want me to invite them over to join us?"

Brody thought of the small talk they'd exchange, idle chatter about women, work and sports. "I don't feel much like company. Maybe another time."

"You okay?"

"I'm fine." Brody pushed his menu to the side of the table and avoided his brother's gaze.

"Sure you are. Brody, you're still struggling. You should talk about it."

The waitress dropped off their drinks. Brody thanked her, then took a long sip of the icy water. Talking about it hadn't done any good. He'd lost patients before, back when he was an intern, and in the last few years, seen a few patients die of heart disease and cancer, but this one had been different. Maybe because he'd lacked the tools so easy to obtain here.

Either way, Brody didn't want to discuss the loss of Andrew. Of the three McKennas, Brody kept the most inside. Maybe it came from being the middle brother, sandwiched between practical Finn and boisterous Riley. Or maybe it stemmed from his job—the good doctor trying to keep emotion out of the equation and relying on logic to make decisions. Or maybe it stemmed from something deeper.

Admitting he had failed. Doctors were the ones people relied on to fix it, make it better, and Brody hadn't done either.

"By the way," Brody said, "if you guys don't have a cake picked out yet for the wedding, there's this bakery down the street from my office that does cupcake wedding cakes. They had a display in the window. I thought it looked kind of cool. I know you and Stace are doing the unconventional thing, so maybe this would be a good fit."

"Changing the subject again?"

Brody grinned. "Doing my best."

"Okay. I get the hint. No, we don't have a cake decided on yet. We planned this whole thing pretty fast, because all I want to do is wake up next to Stace every day of my life." Riley grinned, then narrowed his eyes.

"Hey, since when do you bring dessert to a get-together? Or heck, offer anything other than a reminder to get my flu shot?"

Brody scowled. "I thought it'd be nice for you and Stace."

Riley leaned forward, studying his older brother's face. "Wait...did you say bakery? Is it the one owned by that guy's sister?"

"Yeah." Brody shrugged, concentrated on drinking his water. "It is. But that's not—"

"Oh." Riley paused a second. "Okay. I get it. Good idea."

"I'm just offering to help defray the costs of your wedding."

"Whatever spin you want to put on it is fine with me." Riley chuckled. "Stace talked about baking the cake herself, but she's so busy with the diner, and then planning this thing. Let me talk to Stace and see if that works for her. I'll do that right now, in fact."

"You don't have to—"

"I don't mind, Brody. Not one bit." Riley's face filled with sympathy. Riley knew very little about Brody's time in Afghanistan. A few facts, but no real details, and only because Riley had brought over a six-pack of beer to welcome Brody home, and by the third one, Brody had started talking. He'd told Riley one of the military guys who had died had been local, that he'd struck up a friendship with the man before he died. But that was all. Brody had hoped broaching the subject would be cathartic. Instead, in the morning he had a hangover and ten times more regrets.

Riley flipped out his cell phone and dialed. "How's the prettiest bride in Boston today?"

Brody heard Stace laugh on the other end. He turned away, watched the hum of activity in the restaurant. Waitstaff bustling back and forth, the bartender joking with a few regulars, the tables filling and emptying like tidal pools.

"Stace loves the idea," Riley said, closing the phone and tucking it back into his pocket. "She said to tell you our colors are—"

"Your colors?" Brody chuckled. "You have a color scheme there, Riley?"

A flush filled his younger brother's cheeks. "Hey, if it makes Stace happy, it makes me happy. Anyway, go for bright pink and purple. Morning glories, you know?"

Brody nodded. His brother had told him about the meaning behind the diner Stace owned. The one started years before by her father, and decorated with the flowers that he had said reminded him of his daughter. A sentimental gift to a daughter he'd loved very much. "That'll be nice."

"Yeah," Riley said, as a quiet smile stole across his face, "it will."

How Brody envied his brother that smile. The peace in his features. The happiness he wore like a comfortable shirt.

It was the same thing Brody had been searching for, and not finding. He'd thought maybe if he stopped by and talked to Kate, made a step toward the promise he'd made, it would help. If anything, it had stirred a need in him to do more, to do…something.

Hence, the cupcakes. Now that he'd opened his big mouth, he'd need to go back there and place the order.

Damn.

"So how is work going?" Brody said before Riley turned the conversation around again. His brother had started an after school program at the arts centered high school he'd once attended. For creative, energetic Riley, the job fit well.

"Awesome. The kids at the Wilmont Academy are loving the program. So much, we opened it up to other kids in the area. We're already talking about expanding it in size and number of schools."

"That's great." The waitress brought their food and laid a steaming platter of mini burgers and fries in front of Riley, a Waldorf salad in front of Brody.

"Why do you eat that crap?" Brody said. "You know what it's doing to your arteries. With our family history—"

Riley put up a hand. "I love you, Brody, I really do, but if you say anything about my fries, I'm going to have to hurt you."

"I just worry about you."

"And I appreciate it. I'll do an extra mile on the treadmill tonight if that makes you feel better."

"It does. Did you get your flu—"

Riley tick-tocked a finger. "Don't go all doctor on me. I'm out to lunch with my brother, and we're talking about my job. Okay?"

Brody grinned. "Okay."

As if to add an exclamation point to the conversation, Riley popped a fry into his mouth. "Things at Wilmont, like I said, are going great. We've got classes in woodworking, dance, film, you name it. They're filling up fast."

"That's great."

"Oh, yeah, before I forget. We're having a career day

next month and we're looking for people to speak to the kids about their jobs. Answer questions about education requirements, things like that." Riley fiddled with a fry. "Maybe you could come in and do a little presentation on going into medicine. You know, a day in the life of a doctor, that kind of thing."

Brody pushed his salad to the side, his appetite gone. "I don't think I'm the best person to talk about that."

Riley's blue eyes met his brother's. Old school rock music flowed from the sound system with a deep bass and steady beat. "You're the perfect one. You've got a variety of experiences and—"

"Just drop it. Okay?" He let out a curse and shook his head. Why had he called his brother? Why had he thought it would make things better? Hell, it had done the opposite. "I just want to get you some damned cupcakes. How many do you need?"

Riley sighed. He looked like he wanted to say something more but didn't. "There should be fifty guests. So whatever it takes to feed that many. We're keeping it small. I figure I've lived enough of my life in the limelight. I want this to be special. Just me and Stace, or as close as we can get to that."

Brody nodded. Tried not to let his envy for Riley's happiness show. First Finn, now Riley, settled down and making families. For a long time, Brody had traveled along that path, too. He'd dated Melissa for a couple years, and he'd thought they'd get married. Then just before he took over Doc Watkin's practice, he'd spent two weeks working for free in a clinic in Alabama, tending to people who fell into the gap between insurance and state aid. He'd been in the middle of stitching up a kid with a gaping leg wound when Melissa had called to tell him she was done, and moving on.

"Thanks," Brody said, getting to his feet and tossing some money onto the table. He turned away, shrugged into his jacket. "I'll let the baker know about the cupcakes."

"Brod?"

Brody turned back. "Yeah?"

"How are you? Really?"

Brody thought of the physicals and sore throats and aches and pains waiting for him back in his office. The patients expecting him to fix them, make them better. For a month, in Afghanistan, he'd thought he was doing just that, making a difference, until—

Until he'd watched the light die in Andrew Spencer's eyes.

"I thought I was fine," Brody said. "But I was wrong."

CHAPTER THREE

KATE stared at the pile of orders on her desk, the paperwork waiting to be done, but found her mind wandering to the handsome customer who had come in a couple days ago. The doctor with the Red Sox basket, who had been both friendly and...troubled. Yes, that was the word for it. She'd joked with him about spreading the word about the shop, told him it would be enough to repay her work on the basket, and he'd said—

No it won't.

Such an odd comment to leave her with. What on earth could he have meant? She hadn't done anything more for him than she'd do for any other customer. Changed a bow, added some feminine touches. It wasn't like she'd handed over a kidney or anything. Maybe she'd misheard him.

Kate gave up on the work and got to her feet, crossing to the window. She looked out over the alley that ran between her shop and the one next door, then down toward the street, busy with cars passing in a blur as people headed home after work. The sound system played music Kate didn't hear and the computer flashed messages of emails Kate didn't read.

Her mind strayed to Dr. Brody McKenna again. She

didn't know much about him, except that he was a Red Sox fan who'd been too distracted to notice the basket he'd picked out was more suited to a male than a female. Maybe he was one of those scattered professor types. Brilliant with medicine but clueless about real life.

She sighed, then turned away from the window. She had a hundred other priorities that didn't include daydreaming about a handsome doctor. She'd met two kinds of men in her life—lazy loafers who expected her to be their support system and driven career A-types who invested more in their jobs than their relationships.

Few heroes like Andrew, few men who lived every day with heart and passion. Until she met one like that, dating would run a distant second to a warm cup of coffee and a fresh from the oven cookie.

The shop door rang. Kate headed out front, working a smile to her face. It became a real smile when she saw her grandmother standing behind the counter, sneaking a red devil cupcake from under the glass dome. Kate put out her arms. "Grandma, what a nice surprise."

Nora laughed as she hugged her granddaughter. "It can't be that much of a surprise. I'm here almost every day for my sugar fix."

Kate released Grandma from the hug. "And I'm thrilled that you are."

Growing up, Kate had spent hours here after school, helping out in the shop and sneaking treats from under the very same glass dome. The sweet tooth came with the family dimples, she thought as she watched her grandmother peel the paper off the cupcake.

"Don't tell your grandfather I'm sneaking another cupcake," Nora warned, wagging a finger. "You know he thinks I'm already sweet enough."

"That's because he loves you."

Nora smiled at the mention of her husband. They had the kind of happy marriage so elusive to other people, and so valuable to those blessed with that gift. Unlike Kate's parents, who had turned fighting into a daily habit, Nora doted on her husband, always had, she said, and always would.

Nora popped a bite of cupcake in her mouth then looked around the shop. "How are things going here?"

"Busy."

"How's the hunt for a second location?"

Kate shrugged. "I haven't done much toward that yet."

"You had plans—"

"That was before, Grandma. Before..." She shook her head.

Nora laid a hand on Kate's shoulder. "I understand."

When Andrew had been alive, buying and opening new locations had been part of their business plan. But ever since he'd died, she'd had to work at keeping to that plan. Months ago, she'd found a spot for a second location in Weymouth, but had yet to visit it or run the numbers, all signs that she wasn't as enthused as she used to be.

Her grandmother smiled. "I like the idea of another Nora's Sweet Shop, but I worry about you, honey. If you want to take some time off, I'd be glad to step in and help. Your grandpa, too."

Kate looked at her eighty-three-year-old grandmother. She knew Nora would step in any time Kate asked her, but she wouldn't expect or ask that of Nora. "I know you would, and I appreciate that but I'm okay. You guys do enough for me making the daytime deliveries."

Nora waved that off. "It keeps us busy and gets us out of the house. You know we like tooling around town, stopping in to see the regular customers."

"You two deserve to enjoy your golden years, not spend them working over a hot oven. Besides, I'm doing fine, Grandma."

Nora brushed a strand of hair off Kate's face. "No you're not."

Kate nodded, then shook her head, and cursed the tears that rushed to her eyes. "I just…miss him."

She didn't add that she regretted, to the depth of her being, ever encouraging her brother to join the military. Maybe if she'd pushed him in another direction, or dismissed the idea of the military, he'd be here today.

Tears shimmered in Nora's eyes, too. She had doted on her grandson, and though she'd been proud of his military service, she had worried every minute of his deployment. "We all do. But he wouldn't want you to be sitting around, missing him. If there was one thing your brother did well, it was live his life. Remember the time he went parachuting off that mountain?"

Despite the tears, Kate smiled. Her brother had been a wild child, from the second he was born. He approached life head on—and never looked back. "And the time he skydived for the first time. Oh, and that crazy swim with the sharks trip he took." Kate shook her head. "He lived on the edge."

"While the rest of us stayed close to terra firma." Nora smiled. "But in the end, he always came back home."

"His heart was here."

"It was indeed," Nora said. "And he would want you to be happy, to celebrate your life, not bury it in work."

Before he left for Afghanistan, Andrew had tried to talk to her about the future. When he'd started on the what-ifs, she'd refused to listen, afraid of what might happen. Now, she regretted that choice. Maybe if she'd heard him out, she might have the secret to his risk taking. Something to urge her down the path they had planned for so long.

Andrew had soared the skies for the rest of them while the other Spencers offered caution, wisdom. She missed that about him, but knew she should also learn from him. Remember that life was short and to live every moment with gusto. Even if doing so seemed impossible some days. Kate swiped away the tears. "I'll try to remember that."

"Good." Nora patted her granddaughter on the shoulder. Then her gaze shifted to the picture window at the front of the shop. She nodded toward the door. "Ooh. Handsome man alert. Did you put on your lipstick?"

Kate laughed. Leave it to Nora to be sure her granddaughter was primped and ready should Mr. Right stride on by. Her grandmother lived in perpetual hope for great grandchildren that she could spoil ten times more than she'd spoiled her grandchildren. "Grandma, I'm not interested in dating right now."

"I think this guy will change your mind about that. Take a look."

The door opened and Brody McKenna strode inside. Kate's heart tripped a little. The doctor's piercing blue eyes zeroed in on hers, and the world dropped away.

She cleared her throat. "Back for another basket, Doctor?"

Way to go, Kate, establish it as a business only relationship. In the end, the best choice. Hadn't she watched her parents' marriage, started on a whim, with major differences in goals and values, disintegrate? She wanted a steady, dependable base, not a man who made her heart race and erased her common sense, regardless of the way Brody's lopsided smile and ocean blue eyes flipped a switch inside her.

"I just came by to thank you," he said. "The basket was a big hit. My grandmother sends her regards and her gratitude for the cherry chocolates. Especially those. In fact, I'm under strict orders to buy some more."

"Those are my favorites, too," Nora said. She leaned over the counter and put out a hand. "I'm Nora Spencer."

He smiled. "Ah, the famous Nora in Nora's Sweet Shop." He shook hands with her, and Kate swore she saw her eighty-three-year-old grandma blush. "Brody McKenna."

Nora arched a brow. "You're a *doctor,* you said?"

Kate wanted to elbow her grandmother but Nora had already stepped out of reach. Under the counter, she waved her hand, but Grandma ignored the hint.

"Yes, ma'am," Brody said. "I own a family practice right down the street from here. I took over for Doc Watkins."

"Oh, I remember him," Nora said. "Nice guy. Except for when he was losing at golf. Then he was grumpy. Every Wednesday, he played, so I learned never to make an appointment for first thing Thursday morning."

Brody chuckled. "Yep, you have him down to a tee."

Kate and her grandmother laughed at the pun. Then Nora tapped her chin, and studied Brody. "Wait... McKenna. Aren't you that doctor that volunteers all the time? Or something like that? I read about a charity your family heads up. Doctors and Borders or something like that."

"Medicine Across Borders." He shifted from foot to foot. "Yes, I'm involved in that. We travel the country and the world, providing volunteer medical help to people in need."

The name of the organization sounded familiar to Kate, but she figured maybe because she'd seen something in the news about it. Brody McKenna, however, seemed unnerved by talking about the group. His gaze darted to the right, and his posture tensed. Maybe he was one of those men who didn't like his charity work to be a big deal. A behind the scenes kind of guy.

Nora leaned in closer to him. "So tell me, Doctor McKenna, is there a Mrs. Doctor?"

"Grandma," Kate hissed. "Stop that." Still, Kate checked his left hand. No ring. The doctor was a single man. And she didn't care. At all.

Uh-huh.

"No, ma'am, there isn't a Mrs. Doctor," Brody said. "But I am here about a wedding that's in the near future."

Disappointment filled Kate. She told herself to quit those thoughts. She'd seen the man once for a few minutes and she didn't care if he married her next door neighbor or the Queen of England. For goodness sake, she'd turned into an emotional wreck today. And it was only Tuesday.

"I'd be glad to help you with that," she said, pulling out an order pad and a pen. "What do you need?"

"It's not for me. It's for my brother."

"Wonderful," Nora said. "In that case, we're even more glad to help you."

"Grandma, stop," Kate hissed again.

"It is nice to find such helpful and beautiful service in this city," Brody said with a smile.

Nora elbowed Kate. A little thrill ran through her at his words. Why did she care?

Darn those eyes of his.

"Oh, don't worry," Brody said. "I'm as far from getting married as a man can be. This is for my little brother, Riley. He's getting married next Saturday and it's a small, private affair, but I thought it would be nice to provide the dessert so his new bride doesn't have to cook it. She owns a diner in the city. Maybe you've heard of it. The Morning Glory."

"I've seen it before when I've been in the city," Kate said, stepping in with a change of subject before her grandmother found a way to turn a diner, a brother's wedding and a cupcake order into an opportunity for matchmaking. After all, hadn't Brody just said he had no interest in marriage? That screamed stay away, commitment-phobic bachelor. "Didn't the diner host an animal shelter thing a month ago?"

"It did. Went well. The diner's main chef is on a trip to Europe and they've got a new one filling in, but I think doing the dessert *and* the food might be a bit overwhelming for him. Plus it's a nice way for me to show my support for my brother and his new wife. As well as give some business to a local shop."

It all sounded plausible, but still, something about the story Brody told gave Kate pause. She couldn't put her finger on it. Why come here? To this shop? There were a hundred bakeries in the area, several dedicated to weddings. Why her shop?

She decided to stop looking a gift horse in the mouth.

She needed the income, and she'd be crazy to turn down the opportunity to get Nora's Sweet Shop name out there. Especially if she sthe tuck to the plan about expanding, every public event was an opportunity to spread the word, ease into new markets.

"You've come to the right place," Nora said, as if reading Kate's mind. "We've done lots of weddings."

"Yeah, I saw that cupcake thing you had in the window. My brother and his fiancé thought it'd be a great idea because they're having their wedding and reception at the diner. It's going to be more low-key than your traditional big cake and band kind of thing. They aren't your typical couple, either, and loved the idea of an atypical cake."

Kate thought a second while she tapped her pen on the order pad. "We could do a whole morning glory theme. Put faux flowers on top of the cupcakes and arrange them like a bouquet."

Brody nodded. "I like that. Great idea. And I know Stace—that's the bride—will love it, too. The diner is important to her."

The praise washed over Kate. She'd had dozens of customers rave about the shop's unique sweets. Why did this one man's—a stranger's—words affect her so? "How many people are we serving?"

"Uh, about fifty. I think that's what my brother said."

"Sounds great." She jotted some notes on the order pad, adding the details about the cupcakes, his name and the date of the event. Considering the number of orders already stacked up in her kitchen, adding his one into the mix would take some doing. Thank God she had her assistant Joanne to help. Joanne had the experience of ten bakers and had been with the shop for so many years, neither Kate or Nora could remember when she'd started.

"And what about a phone number?" Nora piped in. Kate shot her grandmother a glare, but Nora just smiled. "In case we need to get a hold of you."

Brody rattled off a number. "That's my office, which is where I usually am most days. Do you want my cell, too?"

"No," Kate said.

"Yes," Nora said. Louder.

Brody gave them the second number, then paused a second, like he wanted to say something else. He glanced across the room, at what, Kate wasn't sure. The cupcake display? The awards and accolades posted on the wall? "So, uh, thanks," he said, his attention swiveling back to her.

"You're welcome. And thank you for the order."

"You said spread the word." He shrugged and gave her a lopsided grin. "I did. I'm sorry it wasn't more."

She chuckled. "I appreciate all business that comes my way."

Again, he seemed to hesitate, but in the end, he just nodded toward her, said he'd call her if he thought of anything else, then headed out the door. Kate watched him go, even more intrigued than before. Why did this doctor keep her mind whirring?

"Why did you keep trying to fix us up?" Kate asked Nora when the door had shut behind Brody.

"Because he is a very handsome man and you are a very interested woman."

"I'm not at all."

"Coulda fooled me with those googly eyes."

Kate grabbed the order pad off the counter and

tucked the pen in her pocket. "My eyes are on one thing and one thing only. Keeping this shop running and sticking to the plan for expansion." Her gaze went to the article on the wall, the only one that truly mattered. To the plans she'd had, plans that seemed stalled on the ground, no matter how hard she tried to move them forward. "Because I promised I would."

Brody tried. He really did. He put in the hours, he smiled and joked, he filled out the charts, dispensed the prescriptions. But he still couldn't fit back into the shoes he'd left when he'd gone to Afghanistan. After all his other medical mission trips, he'd come back refreshed, ready to tackle his job with renewed enthusiasm. But not this time. And he knew why.

Because of Andrew Spencer.

Every day, Brody pulled the card out of his wallet, and kicked himself for not doing what he'd promised to do. Somehow, he had to find a way to start helping Kate Spencer. He'd seen the grief in her eyes, heard it in her voice. Andrew had asked Brody to make sure his sister moved on, followed her heart, and didn't let the loss of him weigh her down, and do it without telling her the truth. That he had been the one tending Andrew when he'd died.

She doesn't handle loss real well, Doc. She'll blame herself for encouraging me to go over here, and that'll just make her hurt more. Take care of her—

But don't tell her why you're doing it. I don't want her blaming herself or dwelling on the past. I want her eyes on the future. Encourage her to take a risk, to pursue her dreams. Don't let her spend one more second grieving or regretting.

When Brody had agreed, the promise had seemed easy. Check in on Kate Spencer, make sure she was okay, and maybe down the road, tell her about the incredible man her brother had been, and how Brody had known him. But now...

He couldn't seem to do any of the above.

Maybe if he wrote it down first, it would make the telling easier. He could take his time, find the words he needed.

The last patient of the day had left, as had Mrs. Maguire, and Brody sat in his office. His charts were done, which meant he could leave at any time. Head to his grandmother's for the weekly family dinner, or home to his empty apartment. Instead, he pulled out a sheet of blank paper, grabbed a pen, then propped the card up on his desk.

I never expected to bond with Andrew Spencer. To me, he was my guardian— and at times, a hindrance to the work I wanted to do, because he'd make me and the other doctors wait while he and his fellow troops cleared an area, double checked security, in short, protected our lives.

All I heard was a ticking clock of sick and dying people, but he was smarter than me, and reminded me time and again that if the doctors died, then the people surely would, too. That was Andrew Spencer—putting the good of all far ahead of the good of himself. He risked his life for us many times. But the last time—

Brody's cell rang, dancing across the oak surface of his desk. He considered letting it go to voicemail, but in the end answering the phone was easier than writing the letter. "Hello?"

"Dr. McKenna, this is Kate down at Nora's Sweet

Shop." Even over the phone, Kate's voice had the same sweet tone as in person. Brody liked the sound of her voice. Very much. Maybe too much. "I'm calling because there's a problem with your cupcake order. I…I can't fill it. My assistant had to go out of town today because her first grandchild came a little early, and that leaves me short-handed with a whole lot of orders, not to mention a huge one due tonight. Anyway, I took the liberty of calling another bakery in town and they said they'll be happy to take care of that for you. No extra charge, and I assure you their work is as good as mine."

Kate Spencer was in a bind. He could hear the stress in her voice, the tension stringing her words together. He thought of that card in his pocket, and of the promise he'd made to Andrew to help Kate. Now, it turned out that Brody's order had only added to her stress level.

"Anyway, let me give you the name and number of the other bakery," she said. "They're expecting your call, and have all my order notes."

Brody took down the number, jotting it on a Post-it beside the letter he'd been working on. His gaze skimmed the words he'd been writing again. *That was Andrew Spencer—putting the good of all far ahead of the good of himself.*

It was as if Andrew was nudging Brody from beyond the grave. Do something, you fool. You said you would. "Is there any way I can help?" Brody asked.

She laughed. "Unless you can come up with an experienced baker in thirty minutes who is free for the next few days, then no. But don't worry, we'll be fine. I do feel bad about the last minute notice on changing suppliers, but I assure you the other bakery will do a great job. Thanks again for the business, and please consider us in the future."

"In case I ever have another wedding to buy a cake for?"

"Well, you *are* a doctor," she said with a little laugh. "You know, most desirable kind of bachelor there is. God, I can't believe I said that. Something about being on the phone loosens my tongue to say stupid things." She exhaled. "I'm sorry."

"No, no, I'm flattered. Really. Most people who come to see me are complaining about something or other. It's nice to get a compliment once in a while."

She laughed again, a light lyrical sound that lit his heart. For the first time in days, it felt like sunshine had filled the room. "Well, good. I'm glad to brighten your day. Anyway, thanks again."

"Anytime." She was going to hang up, and his business with Kate Spencer would be through, unless he found a reason to buy a lot of chocolate filled baskets. He glanced again at the words on the page, but no brilliant way to keep her on the line came to mind.

"Thank you for understanding, Dr. McKenna." She said goodbye, then the connection ended. He stared at the phone and the number he'd written down for a long, long time. He read over his attempt at the letter, as half hearted as his attempts to keep his promise, then crumpled it into a ball and tossed it in the trash. Then he got his coat and headed out the door, walking fast.

Thirty minutes wasn't a lot of time to change a future, but Brody was sure going to try.

CHAPTER FOUR

WIND battered the small building and rain pattered against the windows of Nora's Sweet Shop. A fall storm, asserting its strength and warning of winter's imminent arrival. Kate sat at her desk, flipping through the thick stack of yellow order sheets.

She had two corporate orders. Three banquets. And now, the McKenna wedding—well, no, that one was safely in another bakery's hands. A lot of work for one bakery, never mind one person. On any other day, she'd be grateful for the influx of work. But today, it all just felt…overwhelming. She glanced over at the folder on her desk, filled with notes about expansions and new locations, then glanced away. That would have to be put on hold. For a long time.

Always before, baking had been her solace, the place where she could lose herself and find a sweet contentment that came from making something that would make people smile. But ever since Andrew's death, that passion for her job had wavered, disappearing from time to time like sunshine on a cloudy day.

Now, without her assistant on board, she knew getting the job done would take a Herculean effort. Best to just roll up her sleeves and get it done.

She glanced at the dark, angry sky. "I can't do this without you," she whispered to the storm above. Thunder rumbled disagreement. "We were supposed to expand this business together, take Nora's Sweet Shop to the masses. Remember? That's what you always said, Andrew. Now you're gone and I'm alone and trying like hell to stick to the plan. But…" she released a long, heavy sigh, "it's hard. So hard. I'm not the risk taker. I'm not the adventurer. You were. And now, the shop is in trouble and I…I need…help."

The bell over the door jingled. Kate jerked to her feet. For a second, she thought she'd round the corner and see Andrew, with his teasing grin and quick wit. Instead, she found the last answer she'd expect.

Brody McKenna.

He stomped off the rain on his shoes, swiped the worst of the wet from his hair, and offered her a sheepish smile, looking lost and sexy all at the same time. A part of her wanted to give him a good meal, a warm blanket, and a hug. She stopped that thought before it embedded itself in her mind. Dr. McKenna embodied dark, brooding, mysterious. A risk for a woman's heart if she'd ever seen one.

"Dr. McKenna, nice to see you again." She came out from behind the counter, cursing herself for smoothing at her hair and shirt as she did. "Did you have a problem with the other bakery?"

"No, no. I haven't even called them yet." He shifted his weight from foot to foot. The rain had darkened his lashes, and made his blue eyes seem even bluer. More like a tempestuous sea, rolling with secrets in its depths. "I, ah, stopped by to see if you had eaten."

She blinked. "If I had eaten?"

"I live near here and every night when I walk home, I see the light on." He took two steps closer. "Every morning when I leave for work, I see the light on in here." He took another two steps, then a few more, until he stood inches away from her, that deep blue ocean drawing her in, captivating her. "And it makes me wonder whether you ever go home or ever have time to have a decent meal."

"I…" She couldn't find a word to say. No one outside her immediate family had ever said anything like that to her. Worried that she'd eaten, worried that she worked too hard. Why did this man care? Was it just the doctor in him? Or something more? "I won't starve, believe me. I have a frozen meal in the back. I'll wolf it down between baking."

"That's not healthy."

She shrugged. "It's part of being a business owner. Take the bad with the good. And right now, the good is…well, a little harder to find." She didn't add that she planned on keeping herself busy in the kitchen because it kept her from thinking. From dwelling. From talking to people who were no longer here.

Brody leaned against the counter, his height giving him at least a foot's advantage over her. For a second, she wondered what it would be like to lean into that height, to put her head against his broad chest, to tell him her troubles and share her burdens.

Then she got a grip and shook her head. He was asking her about her eating habits, chiding her about working too much. Not offering to be her confidante. Or anything more.

"Listen, I eat alone way too often," he said. "Like

you, I work a lot more hours than I probably should and end up trading healthy food for fast food."

She laughed. "Doctor, heal thyself?"

"Yeah, something like that. So why don't we eat together, and then you can get back to baking or whatever it is you're doing here. It's a blustery night, the kind when you need a warm meal and some good company. Not something packaged and processed."

Damn, that sounded good. Tempting. Comforting. Perfect.

Despite her reservations, a smile stole across Kate's face. "And are you the good company?"

"That you'll have to decide for yourself." He grinned. "My head nurse thinks I'm a pain in the neck, but my grandmother sings my praises."

She laughed. "Isn't that what grandmothers are supposed to do?"

"I do believe that's Chapter One in the Good Grandma Handbook."

Kate laughed again. Her stomach let out a rumble at the thought of a real meal. Twice a week she went to Nora's for dinner, but the rest of her meals were consumed on the run. Quick bites between filling baking pans and spreading icing. Brody had a point about her diet being far from healthy. "Well, I am hungry."

"Me, too. And I don't know about you, but I…I don't want to eat alone tonight."

She thought of the gray sky, the stormy rumbles from the clouds and the conversations she'd had with her dead brother. "Me, either," Kate said softly.

Brody thumbed to the east. "There's a great little place down the street. The Cast Iron Skillet. Have you been there?"

The rumble in her stomach became a full-out roar. "I ate there a couple times after they first opened. They have an amazing cast iron chicken. Drizzled with garlic butter and served with mashed sweet potatoes. Okay, now I'm salivating."

"Then drool with me and let's get a table."

Drool with him? She was already drooling over him. Temptation coiled inside her. Damn those blue eyes of his.

She hesitated for a fraction of a second, then decided the work had waited this long, it could wait a little longer. She wasn't being much use in the kitchen right now anyway, and couldn't seem to get on track. Not to mention, she couldn't remember the last time she'd had a meal that hadn't come from the microwave. She grabbed her jacket and purse from under the counter, then her umbrella from the stand by the door. "Here," she said, handing it to him, "let's be smart before we go out in the rain."

But as Kate left the shop and turned the lock in the door, she had to wonder if letting the handsome doctor talk her into a dinner that sounded a lot like a date was smart. At all.

The food met its promise, but Brody didn't notice. He'd been captivated by Kate Spencer from the day he met her, and the more time he spent with her, the more intrigued he became. What had started as a way to get to know the person whom Andrew had raved about, the one who had written that card to her brother and sent Andrew so many care packages he'd joked he could have opened a store, had become something more. Something bigger.

Something Brody danced around in his mind but knew would lead to trouble. He was here to fulfill a promise, not fall for Andrew's sister.

Kate took a deep drink of her ice water then stretched her shoulders. She'd already devoured half her dinner, which told Brody he'd made the right decision in inviting her out. Like him, he suspected she spent more time worrying about others than about herself.

For the tenth time he wondered what had spurred him to invite her to dinner, when he'd gone over to the shop tonight to just check in on her, ask her how business was going, and somehow direct the conversation to expansions. Drop a few words in her ear about what a good idea that would be then be on his way, mission accomplished. Once again, his intentions and actions had gone in different directions. Maybe because he was having trouble seeing how to make those intentions work.

"I forgot…what kind of medicine do you practice?" she asked, as she forked up a bite of chicken. The restaurant's casual ambience, created by earth tone décor and cozy booths, had drawn dozens of couples and several families. The murmur of conversation rose and fell like a wave.

"Family practice," Brody said. "I see kids with runny noses. Parents with back aches. I've administered more flu shots than I can count, and taped up more sprained ankles than the folks at Ace bandage."

She laughed. "That must be rewarding."

"It is. I've gotten to know a lot of people over the years, their families, too, and it's nice to be a part of helping them live their lives to the fullest. When they take my advice, of course." He grinned.

"Stubborn patients who keep on eating fast food and surfing the sofa?"

He nodded. "All things in moderation, I tell them. Honestly, most of my job is just about…listening."

"How so?"

"Patients, by and large, know the right things to do. Sometimes, they just want someone to hear them say they're worried about the chances of having a heart attack, or scared about a cancer diagnosis. They want someone to—"

"Care."

"Exactly. And my job is to do that then try to fix whatever ails them." Which he'd done here, many times, but when it had counted—

He hadn't fixed Andrew, not at all. He'd done his best, and he'd failed.

"Where did you start out? I mean, residency." Kate's question drew Brody back to the present.

"Mass General's ER. That's a crazy job, especially in Boston. You never know what's going to come through the door. It was exciting and vibrant and…insane. At the end of the day, I could have slept for a week." He chuckled. "The total opposite of a family practice in a lot of ways. Not to say I don't have my share of emergencies, but it's less hectic. I have more time with my patients in family practice, which is nice."

"I have a cousin in Detroit who works in the ER. I don't think he's been off for a single holiday."

"That's life in the ER, that's for sure." Brody got a taste of that ER life every time he went on a medical mission trips and again in Afghanistan. "That's one of the perks Doc Watkins told me about when I took over the practice. There are days when all those runny noses can get a bit predictable, but by and large, I really enjoy my work."

"Same with cupcakes. Decorated one, decorated a thousand." She laughed. "Though I do like to experiment with different flavors and toppings. And the chocolates—those leave lots of room for creativity."

"Do you ever want to step out of the box, and do something totally different?"

"I have plans to." She fiddled with her fork. "My brother and I always wanted to expand Nora's Sweet Shop, to take it national, maybe even start franchising. Andrew was the one with the big, risky ideas. I'm a little more cautious, but when he talked, I signed on for the ride. He was so enthusiastic, that he got me excited about the idea, too."

"And have you expanded yet?" Brody crossed his hands in front of him, his dinner forgotten. Here was what he had come here to discuss, though he got the feeling it wasn't a subject Kate really liked visiting.

She shook her head. "I've thought about it. Even found a property in Weymouth that I saw online, but…" Kate sighed, "ever since Andrew died, it's been hard to get enthusiastic about the idea again. I know he'd want me to push forward but…it's hard."

Guilt weighed heavy on Brody's shoulders. Maybe if he'd been a better doctor, if he'd found a way to save Andrew, her brother would be here now, and Kate wouldn't be debating about opening another location. She'd be celebrating with Andrew.

Promise me.

Andrew had asked him to watch out for his little sister, to make sure she was moving on, living her life. Taking her to dinner was part of that, Brody supposed, but he knew Andrew had meant more than a platter of chicken Alfredo and some breadsticks.

"You should expand anyway. Your brother would want you to," Brody said, wondering if she knew how true that was. "And if it's a matter of financing, I can help if you want."

She laughed. "You? What do you know about franchising or opening new locations?"

"Uh…nothing. But I think it sounds like a great idea and if you need financial backing—" Was that what he was going to do? Throw money at the problem and send it away? "—then I am more than happy to provide that."

"You hardly know me. Why would you give me money, just like that? And how can you afford it?"

"I'm a McKenna, and part of being a McKenna means having money. I inherited quite a lot when my parents died, and my grandparents were good investors. Even after paying for medical school and my own practice, I've been left with more than I know what to do with." He leaned forward, wishing he had the magic words he needed. "I've tasted your cupcakes and chocolates. That's a business worth backing."

"Well, I appreciate the offer, but…"

"But what?"

"I'm not ready for expanding or any kind of a big change yet." She toyed with the fork some more. "Maybe down the road." She raised her gaze to his. Green eyes wide, looking to him for answers, support. "I think part of it is fear of the unknown, you know? Andrew was good at that, just leaping and looking afterwards. I'm one of those people who has to peek behind the curtains a few times before I do anything." She twirled some noodles onto her fork. "I'm the one in the back of the scenes, not out there leading the charge."

He watched her take a bite, swallow, then reach for her water. Every time he saw her, he saw the memory of her brother. They had similar coloring—dark brown hair, deep green eyes, high cheekbones. Andrew had been taller than Kate, tanned from his time in the desert. But Brody could still see so much of the brave young man in his younger sister.

A part of Brody wanted to leave, to head away from those reminders. To bury those days in Afghanistan and his regrets deep, so deep he would never remember them, never have them pop up and send him off-kilter again.

Except that would be the coward's way out, and Brody refused to take that path.

"I used to be that way, too," he said. "Afraid of the unknown. Then I went on my first medical mission trip, and it cured the scare in me."

"How?"

"You get dropped into a new place, with new people and new equipment, and you have to sink or swim. If you sink, then other people get hurt. So I had no choice but to buck up and get over my worries that I wouldn't be a good enough doctor."

But had he been a good enough doctor? Sure he'd helped people in Alabama, Alaska, Costa Rica, even here in Newton, MA, but when it came down to a moment that mattered, a moment when death waited outside the door, he hadn't been good enough after all. He had tried his best and he had failed.

Medical school had taught him over and over again that sometimes, people just die. Maybe that was true, or maybe it was just that the wrong doctor had been in charge that day. He had rethought every action of that day a hundred times, questioned every decision, and retraced his steps. But in the end, it didn't matter because no matter how much he did the day over in his head, it wouldn't bring Andrew back.

"I think just taking care of people like you do, and giving back on those trips you take, is brave enough," she said.

"I don't know about that. It's my job and I just try to do the best I can." Would he ever be brave enough to take on another mission? Or spend the rest of his life afraid of regretting his mistakes?

"My whole family has always been the kind that believes in giving to others," Kate said. "From bringing food to the shelters to donating to good causes, to giving people who need a second chance a job. That's easy, if you ask me. But doing what you do, going to a strange city or country and caring for people…that takes guts."

"There are others who do far gutsier jobs than I," he said. "They're the ones to admire, not me."

"I don't know. You've worked the ER at Mass General." She laughed. "That takes some courage, too."

He had no desire to sit here and discuss courage and himself in the same sentence. He'd come here to keep a promise, and knew he couldn't leave until he did. "Courage is also about going after your dreams, which is what I think you should do. Open that new location." He placed his hand on the table, so close he could have touched her with a breath of movement. "My offer to back you stands, so just know whenever you need me, I'll be there."

"You barely know me," she said again.

"What I know looks like a very good investment."

Her cheeks filled with pink, and she glanced away. "Well, thank you. I'll let you know if I move forward."

Damn. She didn't sound any more enthused about the idea now than she had before.

The other diners chatted and ate, filling the small restaurant with the music of clanking forks and clinking glasses. Waiters bustled to and fro, silent black clad shadows.

"I forgot to get more of those chocolates my grandmother wanted when I was at the shop the other day. She wanted me to also tell you that she liked those chocolate leaves you had in the basket," he said, keeping the topic neutral. Away from the hard stuff. "She said they were so realistic, she almost didn't want to eat them."

The pink in her cheeks deepened to red. "Thank you."

"Don't be embarrassed, Kate. It's clear you enjoy your work by how good the finished product turns out."

"I'm just not used to being the one in the spotlight. For years, I was the one in the back, baking. My grandmother was the face of Nora's for a long time, then Andrew and now…"

"You."

She smiled. "Me."

"You make a good face for the company. Sweet, like the baked treats." The words were out before he could stop them. Damn.

"Keep saying things like that, Dr. McKenna, and I'll never stop blushing." She grinned, then grabbed another breadstick from the basket.

"I wouldn't complain." What the hell was he doing? Flirting with her? He cleared his throat and got back to the reason for being here—a reason that eluded him more and more every minute. "It sounds like you enjoy your job a great deal."

"I do. Except when there's a huge stack of orders and I'm short on help. And…" She glanced at her watch. "Oh, darn, I almost forgot I have a delivery to make tonight." She pushed her plate to the side and got to her feet. "Thanks for dinner, but I have to go."

He rose and tossed some money onto the bill. "Let me walk you back."

She smiled. "It's only a couple blocks to the shop. I'm fine by myself."

"A gentleman never lets a lady walk home alone. My grandfather drilled that into me."

"A gentleman, huh?" The smile widened and her gaze assessed him. "Well, I wouldn't want you to disappoint your grandfather."

They headed out the door, back into the rain. Brody unfurled the umbrella over them, and matched his pace to Kate's fast walk. He noted the shadows under her eyes. From working hard, maybe too hard. She was doing exactly what Andrew had predicted—spending her days baking and wearing herself into the ground. Not taking care of herself. Hence the microwave dinners and shadows under her eyes. "Do you make many deliveries yourself?"

She shook her head. "My grandparents make the daytime deliveries—they enjoy getting out and seeing folks in the neighborhood, but they don't like to drive at night, so I handle those. I don't mind, but when I've been working all day…well, it can make for some long days."

"You need not one assistant, but a whole army of them."

She laughed. "I agree. And as soon as Joanne gets back and I have some time to run an ad and do some interviews, I'll be hiring, so I don't end up in this boat again."

They had reached the shop. Brody waited while she unlocked the door and let them inside. He set the wet umbrella by the door. Kate turned toward him. "Thanks for walking me back."

"No problem."

"And, I'm really sorry about having to send you to another bakery for the cupcake order. If there was a way to fit that in my schedule, believe me I would. I just had too many existing orders and not enough time." She grinned and put her hands up. "There's only one me."

"You could get a temp," he said. "I've hired them when my nurse is on vacation. And during busy seasons."

She waved that suggestion off. "Trying to find someone trained in cooking and willing to work just those few days…it's almost more work to do that than it is to just handle it myself. And right now, my time is so limited, I can't imagine adding to my To Do list."

She reminded Brody of himself when he had been an intern in medical school, burning the candle at both ends, and sometimes from the middle, too. "How are you going to get all the orders done? And make deliveries and do paperwork and all the stuff that goes with owning your own business?"

"Working hard. Working long hours. I do most of the baking after the shop closes, which means for very long nights sometimes." She shrugged. "I've done it before. I can do it again."

He saw the tension in her face, the shadows under her eyes, the weight of so much responsibility on her shoulders. Andrew had told him, in that long, long conversation that had lingered long into the night while Brody prayed and medicine failed, that his sister had poured her whole life into the shop, giving up dates, parties with friends, everything, to keep it running when the economy was down, and get it strong enough to take on the next challenge of expansion. Baking made her happy, especially during the tumultuous years of their childhood and after their parents' divorce, Andrew had said, and seeing his older sister happy had become Andrew's top mission. The business had meant as much to Andrew as it did to Kate. Andrew would never let it falter, even for a few days.

Nor would he want Brody to just keep throwing words at the problem. He had tasked Brody with making sure Kate moved forward, found that happiness again. That meant doing what Brody did best—digging in with both hands.

"What if I helped you?" Brody said.

"You?" She laughed as she crossed the room and flipped on a light. "Didn't you tell me you're all thumbs in the kitchen?"

"Well, yeah, but I can measure out doses." The urge to help her, to do something other than buy a damned basket of chocolates, washed over him in a wave. She wouldn't let him back her next location, and he didn't know enough to just go out there and buy one for her, but he could take up some of the slack for her. He followed her into the back room. "I'm sure I can measure flour and sugar and…whatever. And if I can take the temperature of a patient, I can add stuff to an oven. I may not have the best handwriting in the world—"

At that, she laughed.

"But I can handle putting some flowers on some cupcakes."

"I appreciate the offer, but I'm sure you're busy with your practice, and this would be a heck of a job to just jump into. I'll be fine." She had pulled a paper off the wall and read it over. The order that needed to be delivered, he surmised. At night, maybe to a less than desirable neighborhood, alone.

A thick stack of orders were tacked to the wall, waiting to be filled after she did this one. Piles of bakery supplies lined the far counter. Sacks of flour and sugar, tubs of something labeled fondant. A huge work load for anyone. Not to mention someone still reeling from a big personal loss.

Once again the urge to walk away, to distance himself from this reminder of his greatest mistake, roared inside him. If he did this, he'd be around Kate for hours at a time. At some point, the subject of her brother would come up. How long did he think he could go before the truth about why he was here came out?

Promise me.

Damned if he'd let her struggle here on her own. Andrew wouldn't want that.

Once she was stronger, ready for the rest, he would tell her how he had come to be in her shop that day. Andrew had warned Brody that his sister looked tough, a cover for a fragile heart, and cautioned him against telling Kate the truth. Brody suspected Andrew did on his deathbed what he'd done all his life—protected the sister he loved so much.

And now he'd given Brody that job. He'd deal with the rest when he had to, but for now, there was Kate and Kate needed help. He took a step closer. "Let me help you, at least with the delivery, and if we work well together, then maybe I can help you in here, too."

"I don't know. I—"

"It'll only be for a few days, you said so yourself. And I'll work for free. We can get that cupcake order done for my brother and I can be the hero of the wedding." He grinned. "Just let me help. I'll feel better if I do."

She leaned closer, her green eyes capturing his. "Why?"

"Because you need the help. And I...I need something to occupy my nights."

"Why?"

He could have thrown off some flippant answer. Something about being single and bored, or a workaholic who needed more to do, but instead, his gaze went to the far corner of the room, where a sister had pinned up an article about a brother who'd given his all, and the words came from deep in Brody's heart. Not the whole truth, but something far closer than he'd said up until now. "I'm working through some stuff. And I just need something to...take my mind off it, until I find the best way to handle it."

She worried her bottom lip, assessing him. "Okay, we'll start with the delivery. It's a simple one, just getting those cupcakes," she pointed to a stack of boxes on the counter, "over to a local place for a party they're having tonight."

"Okay." He hefted the boxes into his arms, careful to keep them level, then followed Kate out the back door and over to a van she had parked in the alley between her shop and the one next door. The words Nora's Sweet Shop reflected off the white panels in a bright pink script. Kate slid open the side door, and he loaded the boxes on racks inside the van.

She climbed into the driver's seat and waited for him to get in on the passenger's side. "Before we go, I better warn you, that this place can be a little...rowdy."

"Rowdy? In Newton?"

"Sort of. You'll see." She put the vehicle in gear, a bemused smile on her face. He liked her profile, the way the streetlights illuminated her delicate features.

They headed down the street, bumping over a few potholes. Kate drove with caution, keeping one eye on the road and one on the cargo in the back. He kept quiet, allowing her to concentrate on the still congested city roads. A few turns, and then they pulled into the parking lot of the Golden Ages Rest Home.

"A rowdy rest home?" He arched a brow.

She just grinned, then parked the van, got out and slid open the side door. "I hope you wore your dancing shoes."

"My what? Why?"

But Kate didn't explain. He grabbed several of the boxes and followed her into the building. Strains of perky jazz music filled the foyer. No Grandma's basement decorations here. The rest home sported cream and cranberry colored furnishings offset by a light oak wood floor and a chandelier that cast sparkling light over the space. A petite gray haired lady rushed forward when Kate entered. "I'm so glad you're here. The natives were getting restless." She placed a hand on Kate's arm. "Thank you so much for helping us out again. You are an angel."

Kate hefted the boxes. "An angel with dessert to the rescue! I'm always more than happy to help you all out, Mrs. White."

The older lady waved the last words off. "You know that calling me Mrs. White makes me feel as old as my grandmother. Call me Tabitha, Kate, and you'll keep me young at heart."

Kate laughed. "Of course, Tabitha. How could I forget that?"

"Maybe you're getting a little old, too, my dear," Tabitha said, with a grin. She beckoned them to follow. They headed down the hall and into a room decked out for a party.

A pulsing disco ball hung from the ceiling, casting the darkened room in a rainbow of lights. Couches had been pushed against the walls, but few people sat on them. Jazz music pulsed from the sound system, while couples and groups of seniors danced to the tunes, some on their own, some using walkers and canes as partners. On the far wall, sat a table laden with food and drinks, and a wide open space waiting for dessert.

A tall elderly man with a full head of thick white hair and twinkling blue eyes, came up to Kate as soon as she entered the room. "Miss Kate, are you here to give me that promised dance?"

"Of course, Mr. Roberts." She rose to her toes and bussed a kiss onto his cheek. "Let me get dessert set up and I'll be ready to tango."

"Glad to hear it. Oh, and I see you brought a partner for Mrs. Williams." The man nodded toward Brody. "I didn't know you had another brother."

"Oh, he's not my brother."

"A beau?" Mr. Roberts grinned and shot a wink at Brody. "That's wonderful, Miss Kate. You deserve a man who will treat you right." He eyed Brody. "You *are* going to treat her right, aren't you?"

Brody sputtered for an answer, but Kate saved him by putting a hand between the men. "Oh, no, Brody's not a beau. Just a…friend."

Friend. The kiss of death between a man and a woman, Brody thought. But really, did he want anything more? Brody wanted to help Kate, not be her boyfriend.

Yet the thought of them having nothing more than a cordial relationship left him with a sense of disappointment. A war between what he wanted and what he should have brewed in his chest. He opted for the should have. Help her through this bump in her business, make sure she got back on track, that she was happy and secure again, then go back to his life. No more. No less.

"What, are you nuts, boy? This woman is a catch and a half. If I was thirty, okay," Mr. Roberts winked, "fifty years younger, I'd marry her myself."

"Mr. Roberts, you are an incorrigible flirt."

"Keeps me young." He grinned. "And keeps the ladies around here on their toes."

"Speaking of people on their toes," Kate said, "I better get dessert on the table before dinner is served."

She and Brody headed across the room, and started loading the cupcakes onto the waiting trays. A flock of eager and hungry partygoers lingered to the side, waiting for them to finish. Several people greeted Kate by name, and raved about her cupcakes. When she and

Brody were done, they stowed the empty boxes under the table, and stepped to the side.

"Tabitha wasn't kidding." Brody glanced around the room. "People are dying for those cupcakes. I think if we waited any longer, you'd have had a riot on your hands."

Kate laughed. "It's that way every month. I donate dessert for the Senior Shindig, and people are always already lined up to get one, sometimes before I even get here."

"That's because everyone here loves your desserts, and you," Brody said.

She brushed the bangs off her forehead and watched the residents shimmy to a fifties be-bop tune. "This place has always had a tender spot in my heart. Bringing the dessert for their events has sort of become a family tradition. When Andrew and I were kids, my grandparents used to bake for them. My great grandparents, Nora's parents, lived here, and from the beginning, the shop donated treats. On the weekends, Andrew and I would help deliver the cupcakes. The residents got to know us and we got to know them. We've cried when people have passed away, celebrated when they hit milestones, and helped them weather storms whenever we could."

"Weather storms?"

She leaned against the wall, while her gaze scanned the room. "This place was started by a husband and wife team who wanted to provide a low-cost but really nice option for retirees who needed a caring place to live. Because of that, it's faced some financial challenges, so my brother and I followed in my grandparent's footsteps, and over the years, we donated our time and talents to help them out. As a result, a lot of these residents are…well, friends. Sort of an extended family."

All in keeping with the jovial, caring hero that Brody had met in Afghanistan. A young man who would put his life in front of another's without thinking twice. Kate possessed those same admirable traits. Brody's esteem for her rose several notches, and so, too, did his connection with her. He could see some of the same spirit that had driven him into medicine, shining in her eyes as she took in the room. Kate was what Brody's grandmother would call a "good soul," the kind of woman who put others ahead of herself. "So you're not just the baker, but the dance partner as well?"

She laughed. "I like coming here. The residents remind me of what's important and what I get to look forward to."

"You're looking forward to the days of walkers and canes and wheelchairs?"

"In a way, yes. I mean, look at them." She waved toward the people around them. "These truly are their golden years. These are people who are happy and content with who they are. They've achieved their goals, realized their dreams, for the most part, and now they want to enjoy their lives. If a red devil cupcake can help in that a little bit, I'm more than happy to bake a few dozen."

"But doesn't that put you behind on your other work?"

"Some work," Kate said, her voice soft while she watched the crowd of people move about the room, "pays so much more than money. That's what Andrew always said, and it's true."

"I agree." Brody watched the happy faces of the residents as they greeted Kate, complimented the cupcakes. "That's how I feel about working in medicine. It's not about the money—and the medical mission work is all volunteer, so there's no money there at all, it's about the return on my time. The satisfaction at the end of the day is—"

"Priceless." She turned to him and smiled. "Then that's something we have in common."

He could feel the thread extending in the space between them, interlocking him more and more every minute with Kate Spencer. "It is indeed."

They were bonding, he realized, doing the very thing he had told himself not to do. But a part of Brody couldn't resist this intriguing woman who blushed at compliments and gave of her heart to so many around her.

Mr. Roberts stepped up to Kate and put out his arm. Just as she put her hand on the older man's arm, the perky elderly woman who had greeted them at the door sidled up to Brody. "Care to dance, young man? I hope you know the foxtrot."

"Be careful." Kate laid a hand on Brody's. "Tabitha can cut a rug better than Ginger Rogers."

"Now don't say that, Kate," the other lady said. "You'll scare off my dancing partner."

"I'm not much of a dancer." Brody offered up a sheepish grin. "That's my brother Riley's department."

"You're young and you have your original hips," Tabitha said. "That's good enough for me. Come on, honey, let's show those young kids we can outdance them." She took his hand and led him to the floor, followed by Kate and Mr. Roberts. The music shifted to a slow paced waltz, and Brody put out a hand and an arm to Tabitha. The older lady slipped into the space with a very young giggle, and they were off, stepping around the room with ease.

He tried to keep his attention on the chatty woman in his arms, but Brody's gaze kept straying to Kate. She laughed at something Mr. Roberts said, her head thrown back, that wild mane of rich dark brown hair cascading down her shoulders, swinging across his back, begging to be touched. Her lithe body swung from step to step, a sure sign she'd danced dozens of times before. As she danced a circle with Mr. Roberts, the people in the room said hello, thanked her for the cupcakes, and each one received a kind word or a friendly smile in return.

Too often, Brody had seen business people who cared about dollars and cents, not about people. Kate had that unique combination of heart and grace, coupled with killer baking skills. He admired that about her. He admired a lot about her, in fact.

Mr. Roberts swung Kate over to the space beside Brody, then sent a wink Tabitha's way. "Hey, Tabby, isn't it partner *change* time?"

"Partner change time?" The other woman gave him a blank look, paused, then a slow, knowing nod. "Oh, yes, of course. Partner change time. Thanks for the dance, kiddo." She stepped out of Brody's arms and into Mr. Roberts's, leaving Kate standing on the floor.

She laughed and watched the older couple spin away. "Not exactly subtle, are they?"

"About as subtle as a bull horn." Until that moment, Brody hadn't realized how much he had been waiting for an opportunity to dance with Kate. To feel her in his arms, instead of watching her in another's. This woman had intrigued him, captivated him, and even as he told himself this was a *bad idea* on a hundred levels, he put out his arms. "Shall we, partner?"

"I think we shall." She stepped into the circle created by his embrace, and they began to move together to the music. The big band sounds swirled in the air around them, as other couples whooshed back and forth in a flurry of colors and low conversations.

As they danced, the other people in the room disappeared, the lights narrowed their focus, and every ounce of Kate's attention honed in on Brody. She could have been dancing on the moon and wouldn't have noticed a thirty-foot crater underfoot. Her heart beat in rhythm with the steps, and her body tuned to his hand pressed to the small of her back, the warmth of his palm against hers, the way his dark woodsy cologne wrapped around them in a tempting cloud. She could see the slight five o'clock shadow on his chin, watch the movement of his lips with each breath, and she wondered how it would feel if he kissed her.

Working through some stuff.

That was what he had given as his reason for wanting to help her. Kate wanted to ask, to probe, to find out what had caused the shadows in his eyes. What he wasn't telling her—and what had been in all those odd comments that he'd never explained. But Kate Simpson didn't want anyone asking about the shadows in her own eyes, so she sure as heck wasn't going to ask about his.

And that meant not letting one dance distract her, or wrap her in a spell. She'd stick to business only. Period.

"Thank you again for dinner and for helping me with the delivery tonight," she said.

"I wasn't a bad cupcake transporter?" he asked as he turned her to the right, exerting a slight bit of pressure to help her move. How she wanted to lean into that touch, but she didn't.

She knew better than to try to step up and solve another man's problems. To be the shoulder he cried on, the heart he leaned on, only to leave her alone in the end when he returned to his busy life. How many times had she seen her mother crying, alone? How many times had she heard their fights, watched the destruction of their marriage a little at a time? She'd come close herself to repeating that mistake with her last boyfriend, and had no intentions of doing that again.

"Not bad at all," she said.

"Thanks." He chuckled. "It's always nice to have a back up career, should there ever be a sudden need for cupcake transportation throughout the greater Massachusetts area."

She laughed. The song had come to an end, and they broke apart, and made their way to where the parquet met carpet, carving out a corner of the room for themselves, apart from the others. Despite her reservations, and her determination to keep things platonic, she liked Brody. Liked spending time with him. He had a wit that could coax a laugh out of her on her worst day, a smile that made her forget her stress, and eyes that inspired all kind of other thoughts that had nothing to do with work.

It might not be so bad to have him around, particularly when the days got long and her thoughts drifted toward Andrew, and she found herself ready to cry. Her brother, she knew, wouldn't want her to do that, but getting past the loss was far from easy.

Easier, though, when Brody was around, she'd found. Maybe it wouldn't be so bad to have him in her kitchen for a time. "If you want to learn the baking business,

I'd be a fool to turn down free help. Especially sort of experienced free help."

Brody nodded toward Mr. Roberts and Tabitha, who were watching from the sidelines. Tabitha sent up a little wave. "I do come with the recommendations of Tabitha. Wait, that was just for my dancing skills. Is there a lot of call for dancing in your bakery?"

"Not so much, but I'm sure we can figure something out." She put out her hand. "Just remember—in the cup-cake operating room, I'm the one in charge."

"Yes, ma'am." He grinned, then took her hand and when they shook, the warm connection sent a tremor through Kate's veins.

She dropped his hand and vowed that no matter what, the only thing she'd be cooking up in her kitchen over the next few days was dessert. Not a relationship with a handsome doctor. She could see in his eyes, in those shadows and in his soft words, that he needed someone.

And the one thing Kate vowed never to be again was the kind of person who filled that gap. To be a tempo-rary pillow before the man returned to his driven life and discarded her like a forgotten towel on the floor. Because her heart was already scarred and one more blow would surely damage it forever.

CHAPTER FIVE

THE logistics of Brody's plan required more finesse than negotiating a peace treaty. A busy family practice doctor couldn't just up and walk out of the office to bake cupcakes. He'd told Mrs. Maguire he needed a bit of breathing room. "Just to get back into the swing of things," he'd said. "It's been a big change coming back from being overseas."

She'd put a hand on his shoulder, her brown eyes filled with kindness. "I understand. You take care of you and I'll take care of the schedule."

In a matter of hours, she'd managed to free half his days for the coming week. Brody made a mental note to send Mrs. Maguire a big box of chocolates and a gift certificate to her favorite restaurant. Maybe two gift certificates.

The day brightened as the sun began its journey to the other side of the sky. Odd how the same sun that warmed Boston's streets created an oven in Afghanistan. And how the same sun that shone over a quiet neighborhood street could shine over a war zone peppered with the wounded and the dead.

The dead—like Andrew Spencer. Cut down before he'd lived a fraction of his life.

Guilt washed over Brody, teemed in his chest. He'd done all he could, but still, it never seemed he'd done enough. Had he missed something? Forgotten something? Taken too few risks—

Or too many?

The what ifs had plagued Brody ever since Andrew's last stuttering breath. They'd been a heavy blanket on his shoulders as he'd boarded a plane to return to his family, knowing another plane had brought Andrew home to his family, stowed in a wooden casket in the cargo hold.

He could still see Andrew's wide green eyes, trusting Brody, hoping that Brody would pull off an eleventh hour miracle. Then trust had given way to fear, as the reality hit home. All the while, Brody battled death, tending to Andrew, then to the other wounded soldiers, assessing wounds based on survivability, and making his priorities off that grim reality.

Those who would die no matter what were put to the end of the list. While those who had a chance were helped first. Brody and the other doctor with him had worked on the others, knowing Andrew's chances...

Brody cursed as he drew up short outside the cupcake shop. Why had he agreed to do this? And why would Andrew pick him, the doctor who had tended him until his last breath, to watch over Kate? The task loomed like a mountain, impossible.

Inside the building, Kate crossed into his line of vision. She saw him outside and shot him a wave. Today, she had her hair up in a clip that poufed the back in a riot of curls. The style accented her delicate features, drew attention to her emerald eyes.

Maybe not impossible, just tough as hell. As he

watched Kate, he decided no matter what mountain faced him, it would be worth the climb.

Brody opened the door and stepped inside. Sweet scents of vanilla, chocolate, berry, wrapped around him like a calorie laden blanket. "Damn, it smells good in here."

"Thanks." Kate smiled. "If you ask me, it smells like temptation on a stick. Working here makes staying on any kind of diet impossible."

His gaze traveled over her lithe frame. She had on a V-necked black T-shirt emblazoned with the shop's logo and a pair of body hugging jeans. Tempting was exactly the word he'd use, too. "I'd say you're doing just fine in that department."

Had he just flirted with her? What the hell was he thinking?

A pale pink flush filled her cheeks, and the smile widened. "Well, thank you again." Her eyes lit with a tease. She wagged a finger at him. "But don't think you're getting out of dishes just because you complimented me."

"Damn," Brody said, then grinned. "And here I thought you'd go easy on me."

"And why would I do that?"

"Because of my charming good looks and great bedside manner, of course."

She laughed. "That might work with the nurses, but I'll have you know, I am a tough taskmaster."

He closed the gap between them, and his gaze dropped to her lips. Desire warred with his common sense. "How tough?"

"Very." She took a breath, and her chest rose, fell. "Very tough."

The urge to kiss her roared inside him. If there was one woman on this planet Brody shouldn't date, it was her. Already, he'd gotten too close, gotten too involved, when he had promised to help her, not fall for her.

Damn. Holding back the truth only made it worse. Everything in Brody, all the practical, logical, deal with the facts sides of him, wanted to tell Kate who he was. But Andrew had been firm—

Don't tell her. I don't want her to dwell on what happened to me or to blame herself for suggesting I enlist. I want her to move forward.

Telling her, Andrew had said, would leave Kate hurting, in pain again. That was the last thing Brody wanted to bring to Kate Spencer's life—more hurt and pain. He was here to make her laugh, not cry.

"Here." Kate thrust a bright pink apron between them. "Sorry I don't have any in more manly colors."

"This'll be fine." He slipped it over his head. "Reminds me of med school when one of my roommates did the laundry one week and washed the lab coats with a red sweatshirt. We were all pink for a while."

Kate laughed. "My brother said the pink made him look approachable to the ladies."

"I'll keep that in mind."

"Though, I have to say, Andrew was one of the most manly men I've ever known. When the war started, he told me he wanted to make a difference. So I said he should…" She shook her head and her eyes misted. "He joined the National Guard, and really took to the job. Everything Andrew did, he gave a hundred and ten percent."

Brody swallowed hard. "I'm sorry for your loss."

Such inadequate words. He'd said them many times

over the years of being a doctor, but never had they run more hollow than right now. Maybe because he knew Andrew, and knew that loss didn't even begin to describe the hole now left in the world.

"It's okay. I've always wondered and wished…" She shook her head again and bit her lip. "Anyway, he died doing what he loved. And although I miss him every single day, I'm proud of him." She swiped at her eyes, and let out a long breath. "Now let's to get to work so he can be proud of me, too."

Brody followed her into the kitchen in the back. Stainless steel countertops and machines gleamed under the bright lights. Here, the sweet scents were stronger, a tempting perfume filling the space. "So, where do we start? With Riley and Stace's cupcakes?"

"Not yet. We'll be making those closer to the date of the wedding, so they'll be fresh. Right now, we have another cupcake order to complete." She pointed to a huge sack on the floor. "You offered to be the muscle, so let's see how much muscle you have. I need five pounds in that mixer there."

He lifted the heavy bag, then gave her a blank look. "Do I just dump the whole thing in?"

She laughed. "No. Weigh it in that container on the scale, then when I tell you, you're going to add it, a little at a time." She dropped sticks of butter into the mixing bowl, then added sugar and turned on the beaters. "Have you ever cooked anything before?"

"Does making grilled cheese with an iron count?" He grinned. "Old college trick. Some wax paper from a cereal box, a loaf of bread, a package of cheese and an iron, and dinner is done."

"All I can say is thank God you went into medicine

instead of the restaurant industry." She added eggs, one at a time, keeping the beaters whirring until the mixture blended into a pale yellow ribbon. She crossed to Brody and added the rest of the dry ingredients to the flour. "Now remember, add a little at a time, otherwise the flour will go everywhere and we'll get covered. I'm baking cupcakes, not you and me."

Heat flushed her face. What was that? You and me? *Focus, Kate, focus.*

So she did, concentrating on the recipe instead of on Brody McKenna. And the reasons why he was here. Why he had cut his schedule in half to help her. And why work with her, of all the people in the city of Boston?

A few minutes later, the two of them scooped the batter into cupcake liners, then popped the trays into the oven. Kate started melting some chocolate, then laying out molds for the candy orders. "We'll pour these, then make the pink flowers that go with them. By then the cupcakes should be cooled and ready to frost. If you want to start the buttercream frosting, I'll get the ingredients out for you. Frosting is pretty simple. Dump and mix."

"That I can handle." He shot her a lopsided grin, then he paused and stepped forward. The streetlights glimmered outside, casting a golden glow over the counter under the window. The city's busy hum had dropped to a whisper. The storm had broken, and from time to time, a night bird called out.

Kate's gaze met Brody's. He had the bluest eyes she'd ever seen. A color as rich and true as the ocean. Eyes that studied her and analyzed her, and made her heart trip.

What the heck was she doing here?

Because right now it didn't feel like baking cup-cakes. At all.

"You're good at this," he said.

"Thanks."

"I can make a huge mess just heating up restaurant takeout. But you…" he gestured toward the kitchen counters, "you manage to keep this place clean from start to finish."

The flush returned to her cheeks. "Oh, I'm not that neat. You should see my bookshelves and my closets." Had she just invited him to her apartment? If she danced any closer to the edge, she'd fall over—and fall for Mr. Wrong. She wanted steady, dependable, quiet, not a man who turned her insides into Jell-o and sent a riot of de-sire roaring through her whenever he smiled.

"I didn't say you were that neat," he said, and the grin played again on his lips, "because you, uh, have some flour…"

He reached out a finger, slid it down her cheek. A warm, slight touch. Sexy in its innocence. She drew in a breath, held it. "Right there," he finished.

"Thank you." The words were a whisper. Her heart hammered in her chest.

"Anytime." His voice dropped, low, husky, tempting.

His hand lingered against her cheek for a long, dark second. Was he going to kiss her? Did she want him to?

Then the oven timer beeped and broke the spell. She stepped back. "We…we should get back to work."

"Yeah." Those blue eyes locked on hers. "We wouldn't want anything to get burned."

"No. We wouldn't." She grabbed a pair of potholders and turned toward the oven before she could question whether he was talking about cupcakes—or them. She opened the oven, took out the trays and laid them on the counter to cool for a minute before she could remove the cupcakes and set them on racks.

Brody stood to the side, watching her. "You go a million miles a minute here. No wonder you never have time to eat."

"There are days when it's slow." Then she looked at the list of orders clipped to the board against the wall and laughed. "Though I have to admit, there aren't too many of those. Thank goodness."

"Admit it. You're just as Type A as I am."

She bristled. "I'm as far from Type A as you get."

"You run your own business, work too many hours, dig in and get the work done regardless of the obstacles in your way." He flicked out fingers to emphasize his list. "That defines Type A to me."

"You've got me all wrong." She turned away, and started taking the cupcakes out of the pans. Just as she'd thought. He'd admitted he was the exact kind of career focused man she tried to avoid. The kind who swept a woman off her feet, then left her in the dust when his job called. "My father was type A-plus. He worked every second he could. Took on extra shifts because he was convinced no other surgeon could do as good a job as he could."

"Your father was a doctor, too?"

"Yes. So that means I know the type. Come home at the end of the day, dump an emotional load on the family dinner table, then leave again when it's time for play practice or violin lessons. That is *not* me." How could he see her in that same light? She had a life, a world outside this bakery. Her gaze dropped to the cupcakes before her. Didn't she? "At all."

"Not all doctors are the same. And even so, being driven isn't always a bad thing, you know," he said. "That's the kind of trait that encourages you to do things like expand the business, open new locations."

"You're here to help, Dr. McKenna, not analyze me or my life choices." Suddenly he seemed much closer than when he'd been touching her a moment ago. She didn't need anyone to hold a magnifying glass to her life, or her choices. Because when they did that, all she could see was mistakes. "I'd appreciate it if you stuck to mixing dough and left the personal issues to the side. You stay out of my personal life and I'll stay out of yours. I'm sure you don't want me analyzing why you're working here instead of taking care of patients."

He stared at her for a long moment. His jaw worked, then he let out a long breath. "Yeah, I agree. Keeping this impersonal is best for both of us."

"Agreed." She should have been relieved that he agreed. Then why did a stone of disappointment weigh on her chest? She stowed the baked cupcakes in the refrigerator then removed her apron and laid it over a chair. "We're done here tonight."

"Yeah," he said quietly. "We are."

That couldn't have gone worse if he'd lit a flame to the night and set it ablaze. Regret filled Brody the next morning, heavy and thick. He sat in a booth at the Morning Glory, thinking for a man intending to do the right thing, he kept going in the wrong direction.

"Hey, Brody, how you doing?" Stace plopped a coffee cup before him and filled it to the brim with steaming java.

"Great, now that I have some coffee." He grinned. "How about you? Getting nervous about the wedding?"

She cast a glance toward Riley across the room, talking to one of the other customers. Riley caught his fiancé looking at him and gave her a wide smile. "How can I be nervous when I'm marrying the man of my dreams?"

Jealousy flickered in Brody. Finn had Ellie, and wore the same goofy smile as Riley every day. His two brothers had found that elusive gift of true love. To Brody, a man who measured everything in doses and scientific facts, it seemed an anomaly worthy of Haley's Comet.

The door to the diner opened, and instead of his older brother striding in, as Brody had expected, his grandmother entered. Stace went over and greeted her, followed by Riley. Mary said hello, then headed straight for Brody's table.

Mary McKenna wasn't the kind of woman to make social calls. Even as she eased out of her position at the helm of McKenna Media and groomed her grandnephew Alec to take the top spot, she spent her days with purpose. There were lists and appointments, tasks and goals. So when she slid into the seat opposite him, he knew she hadn't come by to chit-chat.

"Gran, nice to see you." He rose, and pressed a kiss to her cheek.

"Brody. I missed you at dinner the other night." It was an admonishment more than anything else. His seventy-eight-year-old grandmother, Brody knew, worried about him, and that meant she liked to see him regularly so she could be sure he wasn't wallowing away in a dark corner.

"Working late. Sorry."

"Working late...baking?"

"How'd you know that's where I was?"

"Your brothers are worse than magpies, the way they talk." A smile crossed her face. "Riley said you missed your regular lunch with him and when he asked Mrs. Maguire where you were, she said you were making cupcakes. He told Finn, and Finn told me."

His brothers. He should have known. Finn and Riley had found their happily ever afters and seemed to be on a two-man mission to make sure Brody did the same. They'd done everything short of bring him on a blind date shotgun wedding. Brody rolled his eyes. "I wish my brothers would stay out of my life."

"They only interfere because they love you." She pressed a hand to his cheek. "And so do I."

His grandmother had been a second mother to him for so long, there were days it seemed like it had always been just his grandparents and the McKenna boys. They'd been a rock in a turbulent childhood for all three boys, and stayed that way long after the McKennas graduated college, moved out on their own and became adults. After her husband's death three years ago, Mary had taken over the full time running of McKenna Media, but still doted on her grandsons with a firm but loving touch.

Brody's gaze softened, and he covered his grandmother's hand with his own. "I love you, too, Gran."

"And thank you for following up with my doctor this morning. You know you don't have to do that."

"I just worry about you, Gran. Wanted to make sure he covered all the bases."

"You do enough worrying for five doctors." She gave

his hand a squeeze. "I'm fine. Just suffering from a little old age."

He chuckled. "Glad to hear it."

Stace brought over a cup. "Some coffee, Mrs. M?"

"Goodness, no, dear. I'll slosh out of here if I drink any more." She pressed a hand to the belly of her pale gray suit. "But thank you."

"No problem. Let me know if you want to order anything." Stace headed off to another table.

"I like that girl," Mary said. "Sassy, strong, smart, and most of all, perfect for Riley." She returned her attention to Brody. "I just suffered through a long, excruciating meeting with the head of Medicine Across Borders. That's why I came by today. Finn is meeting me here in a second, so we can chat about the group."

His eldest brother had become more involved with the McKenna Foundation's overseas mission work after he'd married Ellie and adopted Jiao, an orphan from China. He'd been instrumental in organizing fundraisers and getting the word out.

"Was Larry at the meeting?" Brody asked. The assistant director had gone on his own mission a few weeks prior. Brody had always liked the older man, who had dedicated his life to the charity. Both Brody and Larry had a special place in their hearts for Medicine Across Borders because it took what he and other doctors did in the United States and multiplied it around the world.

"No, he's still in Haiti. It's been rough, he said." Gran sighed. "He lost a few patients last week. One of them a child, and it hit him hard. He said he wished that you were there because you're the best doctor he knows."

Brody shook his head. "Larry doesn't need me."

"I don't know about that," Gran said. "Larry talked to

me about that time you worked that clinic in Alabama. He said you changed those people's lives. They raised enough money to hire a second doctor after you left, and the mortality rate there has dropped significantly, in part because of those diabetes and heart disease awareness programs you started."

"I just did my job."

"You don't give yourself enough credit," Gran said. "You always were the one who worried too much and made it your personal mission to fix everything. Ah, Brody, you don't have to take so much on your shoulders."

"I'm not doing that, Gran."

"You do it and you don't even realize it. You protect the family, you protect your patients, and I suspect you're even protecting that pretty bakery owner. Sometimes, people have to face their worst fears and face the worst possible outcome in order to learn and grow. Protecting them can do them a disservice." She read his face, and let out a sigh. "You disagree, but maybe you'll think about it. Anyway, Larry said to say hello to you. He should be home in about a month. He says there's still a lot of need for basic medical care in Haiti, but he's making a dent, one patient at a time."

Brody listened to his grandmother's news about the charity, but his mind kept drifting to Kate Spencer. He had dodged her question, and dodged an opportunity to tell her the truth. Why?

He knew why. Because he was starting to like her. As much as he'd told himself he had no right to get involved with her, and no room in his life for a relationship right now, he had started to fall for her. She was sweet and funny and despite everything, upbeat and cheery. She was like a daisy in the middle of a lawn that had filled with weeds.

And if he told her—

It would devastate her. She'd relive her brother's death, hold herself responsible for him being there.

Maybe his grandmother had a point. Maybe in protecting her, he was hurting her more.

"Brody? Did you hear me?" his grandmother asked.

"Huh? Uh…sorry. My mind drifted for a second. What'd you say, Gran?"

"I asked if you would deliver the speech for the fundraiser next week. I realize it's short notice, but Dr. Granville broke his leg skiing in Switzerland and won't even be stateside again in time."

"Gran, you know I hate speeches. And hate tuxes even more."

Finn slid into the booth beside his brother. "You and Riley, couple of tux-phobics. What is wrong with the two of you?"

"We're not as uptight as you, hence our more casual formal wear," Brody quipped.

"Nah, you're not as debonair as me." Finn jiggled his tie. "My wife says I make this look sexy."

Brody laughed. "She's biased."

"She is indeed." The same smile that had been on Stace and Riley's faces winged its way across Finn's. Gran sat across from the boys, pleasure lighting her eyes. The whole family was in some kind of happiness time warp. Brody rolled his eyes.

Riley plopped onto the seat beside Gran. "What'd I miss?"

"The hard work." Finn shot him a grin.

"Hey, I've matured. Become a taxpayer, a fiancé *and* a responsible adult, all at the same time."

Brody arched a brow. "You have two of the three. Bummer on the third."

Mary let out an exasperated sigh. "You boys still act like children. My goodness. Celebrate with each other, not tease each other."

Riley pressed a kiss to his grandmother's cheek. "If we did that, we'd have no fun at all, Gran. Besides, Finn and Brody are big boys. They can take whatever I can dish out."

"And deliver it back to you with a second helping," Finn said.

Mary just shook her head, and smiled. "Well as much as I would love to sit here and chat all day with you boys, I do need to get back to the office. So, Brody, will you do the keynote? I think it will do the attendees good to hear about the experiences of someone who actually went overseas and helped people."

Brody swallowed hard. "No one wants to hear what I went through."

His grandmother leaned forward and covered his hand with her own. "You need to talk about it. Maybe if you did—"

"It wouldn't change anything." He shook his head and bit back a curse. "I can't."

His brothers cast him sympathetic looks. "If it helps, we'll sit in the audience and heckle you," Riley joked. "Or just give you a thumbs-up."

Brody shook his head.

"Think about it." Gran got to her feet. Her eyes were kind as she looked down at Brody. "Promise me you'll think about it."

"I will." He intended to do no such thing. But he'd never say that to Gran. He could see the worry in her features, and refused to add to her burdens. He'd find another reason to back out, and line up another speaker for her. That way, she wouldn't be in a bind and he wouldn't be stuck delivering a speech. Maybe Finn would do it for him. "I'll be fine, Gran. And I'll be at the next family dinner."

"Good. And since Riley will be on his honeymoon—"

"Basking on the beach with my beautiful new wife," Riley put in.

"—and we'll have room at the table, I want you to make sure you bring that bakery owner. No excuses."

"Gran, I don't think that's a good idea."

"I want to thank her in person for those chocolates. So don't forget. Sunday afternoon at two. Oh, and when she comes to dinner, tell her to bring more of those chocolates. An old lady needs to have at least one vice, and I've decided mine will be those chocolates." Gran winked, then headed out of the Morning Glory.

Brody tossed some singles on the table for his coffee and started to get to his feet. Finn put a hand on his arm. "I gotta get back to the office."

"You have a minute. I haven't seen you in a while, Brody. And you know, you look like crap."

"Hey!"

"I mean it in the nicest way possible," Finn said.

"He does," Riley added. "Or as nice as Finn can be."

Finn scowled at Riley, then went on. "If you ask me, you've been stewing too much and talking too little. You're a proactive guy, Brody. One who gets in there and makes it right. If you want my advice—"

"I don't." He brushed off Finn's touch. "Thanks for the concern, but I'm doing fine on my own."

"Are you?" Finn asked.

Brody didn't answer. Instead he headed out of the diner. As he did, he realized Finn had a point. Buying a basket of chocolates, bringing cupcakes to a retirement home and adding flour to a mix were not proactive events. None of them were, in fact, in keeping with the kind of thing he normally did. Brody McKenna was a hands-on guy, in a hands-on industry. And until he found something that let him do that, he knew he wouldn't be able to fulfill Andrew's last wishes, or get Kate Spencer moving forward.

And in the process, find a little peace for himself.

CHAPTER SIX

Two days later

HE'D last seen Kate two days ago. And yet, she hadn't been out of his mind once in all that time. He'd come so close to kissing her that night in her shop—too close. He'd called her on Friday, making up an excuse about not being able to help that night, then spent the evening with a bottle of Merlot and a lot of junk TV.

Hadn't changed anything. He still thought about her too much, still worried about her, and still didn't see a way out of the web he'd woven. Finn had been right— he needed a proactive approach to the problem. One that did not involve kissing her.

Brody slipped on a pair of shorts, an old T, and his running shoes, then grabbed his iPod and headed out into the fall sunshine. Most mornings, he had just enough time to run the three mile circuit around his own neighborhood, but on Saturdays, his appointments started later in the morning, which left him extra time to extend his run to the picturesque Chestnut Hill Reservoir.

Dozens of runners, walkers and dog owners strolled the park, greeting the regulars with friendly waves and quick conversations. Late summer flowers peeked through the still green foliage, while the water glistened under the rising sun, twinkling back at him as Brody made the 1.6-mile loop. The sandy packed path was soft under his feet, and soon he slipped into the rhythm of running, oblivious to anyone around him.

He rounded a bend, turning into a gentle breeze skipping over the surface of the water. Ahead of him, Brody spotted a familiar figure.

Kate.

She'd pulled her dark brown hair into a ponytail, and she'd traded her usual jeans and T-shirt for silky navy shorts and a Red Cross T-shirt. Her legs were long and lean, the muscles flexing with each step. She had good form, a steady pace, all signs she ran often. Working off those cupcakes, he presumed. He smiled to himself.

Damn she looked good. Enticing. For the thousandth time, he wished he had kissed her back in the bakery. The magnet of attraction drew him to her again and again. Hunger—yes, that was the word for it—hunger to know her better, to see her more, brewed inside him.

Brody increased his pace until he drew up alongside Kate. "I owe you an apology."

She tugged an earphone out of her ear and glanced over at him. Her skin glistened in the sun. "Brody. I didn't even see you, sorry. I get into a zone when I'm running and don't notice anything around me."

"Me, too." But he had noticed her. He had a feeling no matter what he was doing, he'd be distracted by Kate Spencer. "I wanted to apologize for the other night. You're right. I have no business telling you how to run your life."

She slowed her pace a bit and exhaled. "You might

have been a teensy bit right. I do tend to put in more time at work than I should. And yes, sometimes use work to avoid the hard stuff."

"I can relate to that. Though, sometimes work can be therapeutic."

"True. Or it can be an avoidance technique. Whichever it is, I've got plenty of it to keep me busy." She chuckled. "I appreciate the apology."

He shot her a grin. "You sure you don't want to say anything more? Bash me a bit? Because this is a prime opportunity to get me back by telling me everything I'm doing wrong."

"Oh, I would, but I'm trying to save my breath for running."

He laughed at that. They settled into a comfortable mutual rhythm of running, their steps matching one another as they rounded the sparkling waters of the reservoir. Geese honked as they flew overhead, their bodies forming a perfect V. Brody and Kate neared an empty bench, and slowed their pace.

"I've never seen you running here before," Kate said when they stopped, her words peppered with gasps as she drew in several deep breaths. She propped a leg on one end of the bench and bent forward to stretch.

He did the same on the other end, trying not to watch her. And failing. "During the week, I don't have enough time to make it over here. Most days, I do a quick jog through my neighborhood and then get to work. I run here on the weekends."

"And weekends are my busy time for deliveries, so I get most of my longer runs in during the week." She bent over to stretch her hamstrings, and Brody reminded himself again to be a gentleman and not stare at the creamy length of her legs.

Instead he propped his foot against a nearby post and stretched his calves. Still his gaze stole over to Kate several times, watching as she bent this way and that, working out the lactic acid in her legs.

Beautiful. Absolutely beautiful woman.

And absolutely off limits.

Kate got to her feet, and opened her mouth to say something, then stopped. Her eyes misted, and she turned away. Her body tensed and the good humor left her. Brody's gaze followed where hers had gone.

A dark-haired man in an ARMY T-shirt ran past them, pounding the pavement at a fast clip. He had the crew cut and honed build that spoke of current military service. The close resemblance to Andrew caused a stutter in Brody's chest. Kate paled, and exhaled a long breath.

"Hey," he laid a hand on her shoulder, "you okay?"

"Yeah. That guy over there just looked so much like my brother that for a second I thought…" She shook her head and tried a smile, but it fell flat. "Andrew's gone. Sometimes I forget that. And when I remember…"

"It hurts like hell."

"Yeah." She sighed. "It does."

"Here, sit down for a minute." Brody waved toward the bench, and waited for her to take a seat. In these unguarded moments, Brody got a peek beneath the layers of Kate's grief.

Take care of my sister, Andrew had said. *Don't let her wallow in grief. Make sure she's happy. Living her life.*

"Thank you," she said.

"I'm sorry," Brody said. "I know that's so inadequate when you're hurting, but I am sorry." The words sat miles away from the true depth of his regret. He watched emotions flicker across her face, and wrestled with what more to say. A thousand times, he'd had to counsel patients, offer advice. And now, when it counted, he froze.

He knew why. Because he'd started to care about her, had allowed his heart to get tangled.

"Have you ever lost someone you were close to?" Kate asked.

Brody picked a leaf off a low-lying branch near the bench and shredded it as he spoke. "My parents."

"Your parents died? Both of them?"

He nodded. "When I was eight. Car accident. The whole thing was sudden and unexpected." And tough as hell. He hadn't talked about that loss in so long, but there were times, like now, when it hit him all over again.

"You were only eight? Oh, God, that's awful."

"I had my brothers, which made a difference, but yeah, it was still tough." He let out a long breath, and suddenly, he was there again, sandwiched on that overstuffed ugly floral couch in the living room between Finn and Riley while his grandfather delivered the news. Finn, the stoic one, seeming to grow up in an instant, while Riley fidgeted, too young to know better. Brody had stared straight ahead, trying to fit the words into some kind of logical sense, and failing. "I remember when my grandfather told me. It was like my whole world caved in, one wall at a time. Everything I knew was gone, like that." He snapped his fingers. "My grandparents took me and my brothers in. They did their best, but it's never the same as having your mom and dad around, you know?"

"Yeah." She watched the geese settle on the grass across from them, and waddle fat bodies toward the water. "I spent most of my childhood with my grandparents. My parents fought all the time, and Andrew and I hung out in the bakery. To escape, I guess. Then, finally, they got divorced when I was in high school. My dad moved to Florida and my mom moved to Maine, and Andrew and I stayed here with our grandparents. That's part of why Andrew and I were so close. And my grandparents, too. We formed our own little family here."

Andrew had told him that Kate had taken the divorce hard. That she'd been heartbroken at the breakup of the family, as fractured as it was. Andrew had taken it on his shoulders to cheer up his sister, to keep her from dwelling on the major changes in her life. He could see in Kate's face that it still affected her, even after all these years. A childhood interrupted, just like his. "I'm glad you had each other," he said. "Like my brothers and I had each other."

"Yeah. But I don't have him anymore now, do I?" She cursed, let out a long breath, then turned to Brody. "It was my fault, you know." Her eyes filled with tears, and everything in Brody wanted to head off what was coming. "I was the one that encouraged him to sign up. He kept talking about wanting to make a difference, wanting to change lives, and he was such an adventurer, you know? It just seemed perfect. I thought the war was over, how dangerous could it be?" She shook her head and bit her lip. "I shouldn't have said anything. I should have—"

She cursed. Brody ached to tell her the truth, but how could he do that without adding to her pain? Recount the story of Andrew's death, and his part in that moment, and see her go through that loss all over again. He bit his tongue and listened instead.

"A part of me feels like…" at this her eyes misted again, and Brody wanted to both hold her and run for the hills, "if I hadn't encouraged him, if I had told him to become a hiking instructor or skydiver or something instead, he'd be here today."

He put a hand on her shoulder. "Kate. It's not your fault. Your brother loved—"

"My brother died because of me, don't you see that?" Tears streamed down her cheeks, and she swiped them away with a quick, hard movement. "I'm the one that encouraged him, pushed him. If I never said a word, he'd be here today and I'd…"

He reached for her hand. "You'd what?"

She exhaled, a long, slow breath. "I'd forgive myself."

Brody's heart ached for her. How he knew that pain. That guilt. "You can't blame yourself, Kate. People do what they want to do. Andrew was an adult. If he didn't want to join, he would have told you. You said yourself he loved his job."

She shook her head. "Every day, I live with that regret. Every day, I wish I could take the words back. I go to work and I stand there, and I wish I could do it over. It's like I'm standing in cement, and no matter how hard I try, I can't pick my feet up again." Pain etched Kate's features. Brody saw now why Andrew had been so adamant about protecting his sister. She did blame herself, and the worst thing Brody could do was add to that burden.

I don't want her blaming herself or dwelling on the past. I want her eyes on the future. Encourage her to take a risk, to pursue her dreams. Don't let her spend one more second grieving or regretting.

Andrew's words came back to him. Somehow, Brody needed to find a way to redirect Kate's emotional rudder.

She sat for a moment, then shifted in her seat to face him. "Before the soldiers even knocked on my door, I knew. I fell apart right then, a sobbing messy puddle on the floor. That pain," she exhaled a long, shaky breath, "that pain was excruciating. As if someone had ripped out my heart right in front of me." She drew her knees up to her chest, and hugged her arms around her shins. "What if I'd said 'be careful' one more time, or told him I loved him again? Would it have ended differently?"

"I think you did everything you could. Sometimes… these things just happen." Every instinct in him wanted to make this better for her, to ease her pain. And somehow do it without violating the promise he had made. "When I was in med school, I lost a patient. I'd seen him a couple times before, and had gotten to know him during the time I was working there."

It was a story Brody had never fully told before. The words halted in his throat, but he pushed them forward. He had promised to help Kate, and maybe, just maybe, knowing she wasn't alone would do that. "He loved to walk the city," Brody went on. "But he was legally blind, and in a city that busy…"

"Accidents happened."

Brody nodded. "Construction projects springing up

out of nowhere create obstacles that he couldn't see or anticipate. He had a cane, and was thinking about getting a guide dog, when he was hit by a car."

"Oh, Brody. That's awful."

"He was just crossing the street. One of those senseless deaths that shouldn't happen." Brody sighed and shook his head. "I tried so hard to keep that man alive. So damned hard. I kept pushing on his chest, up, down, up, down, yelling at him to hold, to keep trying, don't die on me—"

At some point he'd stopped talking about the patient in Boston. His mind had gone back to that dusty hut in Afghanistan, to a moment that could have been a carbon copy of the one at Mass General. Young man, cut down in the prime of his life, and Brody, powerless to prevent his death.

"It was too late," Brody went on, his voice low, hoarse. In that instant, he didn't see the pedestrian hit by a car, he saw Andrew's eyes again. So like Kate's. Wide, trusting, believing the doctor tending to his wounds would know what to do. So sure that Brody could save his life. "It's in your hands, doc," Andrew had said. He'd given Brody his life—

And Brody had let him down.

Brody heard the choppers in his head, the pounding of the rotors, the shouting of the other soldiers. Heard himself calling out to the other doctors, asking for supplies they didn't have. Too many wounded at one time, too few resources, and too few miracles available. Brody flexed his palms, but he could still feel Andrew's chest beneath his hands. The furious pumping to try to bring him back, and the silent, still response.

"They had to stop me from doing CPR," Brody said.

The other doctor, pulling him off, telling him it was too late. There was no hope. "I just...I wanted him to live so bad, but it wasn't enough. Not enough at all."

Now her hand covered his, sympathetic, understanding. "Oh, Brody, I'm so sorry."

On the other side of the reservoir, Brody saw the gray flash of the soldier's T-shirt moving down the path. Guilt and regret settled hard and bitter in Brody's stomach. Did he want to see Kate living with that the rest of her life?

He wasn't here to assuage his own pain. He was here to help her with hers.

"How did you..." she took a breath, let it out again, "how did you get past that loss?"

"For a long time, I blamed myself," Brody said, his mind drifting back to those difficult days in med school. "For a while, I thought I should do something else, something outside of medicine. I felt so damned guilty, like you do."

She nodded, mute.

"He was always joking, that patient of mine. It got so that I even kidded him about walking the streets of Boston, told him to keep an eye out. He thought that was the funniest damned thing he ever heard. It became a running joke between us. He'd thank me for stitching him up and joke that he'd be back for another appointment next week. I did the same thing you did, Kate, I blamed myself. What if I didn't joke with him? What if I'd lectured him about being careful?" He tossed the remains of the leaf onto the ground and turned to her. "For weeks, I was stuck, like you. Then I realized I wasn't doing myself, or his memory, any good." His gaze swept over Kate's delicate features. He thought of all she had told him in the last few days, and of what Finn had said. Do something proactive. That was what Brody had done all those years ago, and what Kate needed to do now. "I ended up going down to city hall and petitioning them for an audio crosswalk at the intersection where my patient was hit. The kind that beeps, warns people with vision problems. It might have been too late for him, but it wasn't for the next person. Doing that helped me a lot. It made me move forward."

"That's what I need to do." She sighed. "Someday."

Then he knew how he could help her. How he could get her out of that self-imposed cement. Something bigger, better than baking cupcakes and delivering desserts. "How do you feel about taking a trip to Weymouth this afternoon?"

"Weymouth? Why?"

"Let's go look at that location you were considering. See if it's good enough for another Nora's Sweet Shop."

"Oh, Brody, I can't—"

"Can't? Or won't? I'll be done with patients at three, and last I checked, the sign on the door said you close at three. I'd say that's a sign we should go. Do something proactive, Kate, and maybe..." his hand covered hers, "maybe then you can move forward again."

She studied him for a second then a smile curved across her face. "You're not going to let me say no, are you?"

"Not on your life."

"Okay. Meet me at the shop at three. I'll give the realtor a call this morning."

He got to his feet, put out a hand and hauled her to her feet, too. Now she stood close, so close, a strong breeze would have brought them together. His thoughts swirled around the sweet temptation of Kate Spencer. Her emerald eyes, her beautiful smile, her slender frame. And then to her lips, parted slightly, as if begging him to kiss them. How he wanted to, and oh how he shouldn't. "Then it's a date."

A date.

Kate pondered those words all day while she worked. Joanne had called and said she'd be tied up for a few more days with her daughter. "She's finding out a new baby is a lot more exhausting than she thought," Joanne said, "and my son-in-law couldn't take any more time off from work to help her. Are you sure you're going to be okay without me?"

"I have temporary help," Kate said. "You just enjoy that new grandbaby." She and Joanne chatted a bit more about the new baby, then Kate hung up. She glanced at the clock, saw the hands slowly marking time until Brody arrived.

Nerves fluttered in her stomach. Crazy. He might have used the word *date,* but that didn't mean he meant it. They were going to look at a piece of real estate, for goodness' sake, not go dancing.

That word conjured up the memory of dancing with Brody, of being in his strong, capable arms, pressed to his broad, muscled chest. He'd had a sure step, a confident swing, and when she'd been in his arms, she'd felt—

Safe. Treasured.

Nope, nope, nope. Her goal today involved real estate, not potential husbands.

Still, a part of her really liked Brody. He'd told her not all doctors were the same, and the more she got to know him, the more she wondered if he was that one rare animal in the room. Could this man who volunteered in needy areas, who'd taken the time to help a stressed out baker, could he be the one for her? Or too good to be true?

The last thing she wanted to do was repeat her mother's mistakes and rush into a relationship that was doomed from the start, then spend the rest of her life fighting to make it into something it could never be. Better to be cautious, to find a quiet, gentle man. Not one who sent her heart into overdrive.

Easier said than done.

Kate fussed with her hair. Checked her lipstick twice. Rethought her choice of a skirt instead of jeans at least a dozen times. Ever since she'd met Brody, her mind had been working against her resolve to business only. First peppering her dreams with images of him, then flashing to his smile, his eyes, at the oddest times. She was hooked, and hooked but good.

A little after one, the bell over the door rang, and Kate had to force herself not to break out in a huge smile when Brody walked into the shop. "You're here early. I thought you said you wouldn't be over until three."

"My one o'clock appointment canceled, and I had an hour until the next one, so I thought I'd stop by and see how you were doing."

Thoughtful. Sweet. Because he liked her? "It's been a busy day."

"Too busy for lunch?" He held up a bag from a local sub shop.

She snatched it out of his hands. "Bless you. I was about to eat the fixtures." She glanced up at him, trying to read the intent behind his blue eyes. "You're always taking care of me."

"I'm trying to, Kate." His gaze met hers and held.

"Well, thank you." The intensity in his eyes rocked her, and she turned on her heel, heading for the kitchen, rather than deal with the simmering tension between them.

He followed her out back and sat across from her while she ate.

She finished up the sandwich. "Thank you again. I don't think I've ever eaten that fast in my life. And one more healthy meal from Doctor McKenna. This is becoming a habit."

"All part of the service, ma'am." He grinned. "Besides, it'll be on my bill."

She laughed. "Well maybe I should charge you for cupcakes consumed."

"Who me?" He snatched one of the miniature ones she'd just frosted, and popped it in his mouth. "I don't know what you're talking about. Show me the evidence."

"I'll do better than that." She wagged a finger at him. "I'll make you work harder next time we're in this kitchen."

He glanced around the room, at the stacks of orders on the counter, the tubs of supplies waiting by the mixer. "If you want, we can tackle whatever is on your To Do list after we see that property today."

"That would make for a really long day. Wouldn't that interfere with your plans?"

"Plans?"

A flush filled her cheeks. She got to her feet, and tossed her trash into the bin. "Well, it's Saturday and

I didn't want to assume you didn't have…" *Push the words out, Kate, you'll never know unless you ask,* "a date or anything."

"I don't have a date." He came over to her, lowered the apron to the counter. "Not tonight."

"What about tomorrow night?" Who was this forward woman? Hadn't she vowed a thousand times not to get involved with a man like him? To be cautious, look for someone who didn't inspire her to run off to the nearest bedroom? But a part of her wondered if Brody was different, if the risk in falling for him would end in the kind of love story her grandparents had enjoyed. And that part wanted to get that answer. Very, very badly.

"Not tomorrow night, either. I'm not dating anyone right now." He reached up a hand and captured the end of her ponytail, letting it slide through his fingers. She inhaled the dark woodsy scent of his cologne. "In fact, I don't even have a date for my own brother's wedding."

"That's too bad. Especially if there's dancing." A smile curved across her face. "I bet Tabitha is free."

"I'd much rather take someone closer to my own age. Someone who could use a night off." He twirled the end of her hair around his finger, his blue eyes locked on hers. "Someone like you."

Her heart hammered in her chest. Her pulse tripped. She reminded herself—twice—to breathe. "Are you asking me on a real date, Brody McKenna?"

"I am indeed."

Now the smile she'd been trying to hold back did wing its way across her face. Her heart sputtered, then soared. "Then I accept."

"Good." His hands took hers, and he pulled her to

him. "You know, I haven't been able to stop thinking about you all day. I would be talking to a patient, and end up thinking about you. Or I'd be trying to write up my notes, and think about you. I even called poor Mrs. Maguire Kate today instead of Helen."

"Because of my cupcakes?"

He traced a finger along her face, down her jaw, over her lips. She breathed, and when her lips parted, his finger lingered on her lower lip. Tempting. "Because of your smile. Because of your eyes. Because of the way you make me hope and dream of things I…well, I hadn't wanted before. You…you're not what I expected."

Another odd comment. Brody McKenna seemed full of them. The man had more dimensions than a layer cake. "What you expected?" She laughed. "It seems my reputation has preceded me, if you had expectations." She lifted her jaw to his, sassy, teasing. "Have other people been talking about me and saying I'm this boring old fuddy duddy who does nothing but work?"

"That's not it."

"Then what expectations did you have? Because you seem to have a heck of a bead on everything about me. As if you knew me before you met me."

The humor dropped from his face, and he took a step back, releasing her hands. He turned away, facing the wall where she had hung the plaques and reviews of the shop. "I'm not…not who you think I am, Kate."

"Not a doctor?" She grinned. "Don't tell me you're actually a nurse."

"No, no, it's not that. It's—"

A ding sounded from the oven. "Oh, the cupcakes are done. I have to get them out of the oven or they'll burn." Kate pivoted to take the trays of baked cupcakes out of the oven and set them on the racks to cool. "God, what a busy day. Good thing you're taking me to Weymouth this afternoon, or I'd be liable to work until I passed out. In case you haven't noticed, I'm still working on the prioritizing thing. Like learning to add a little fun into my day and keep my eye on the bigger goal."

"Which is?"

She placed her hands on the counter and glanced out the window at the clear blue sky. "Continue the legacy my grandparents started, while learning not to waste a second of my life on grief. Someone gave me some advice about that today, and I'm still trying to take it in." She gave Brody a watery smile. "I'm working on it anyway."

"Good." Brody handed her another batch ready to go, then helped her load liners and batter into the next set of cupcake pans.

"So, what'd you want to tell me?" she asked. "What did you mean when you said you're not who I think you are?"

He gave her that grin she was beginning to know as well as her own. "Well, first, that I'm not a baker, not by any stretch."

"That I noticed." She sensed shadows lurking behind Brody's words, like secret passages that led to parts of himself he'd closed off. She wanted to quiz him, wanted to press him, but the cupcakes were waiting to be frosted, and the orders were piled up, and time was of the essence if she hoped to get out of here on time. So Kate let it drop for now, intending to come back to serious topics when they had more time.

Kate added a pink fondant flower to the top of one of the baked treats. "I used to send care packages to

Andrew's unit overseas, and one time, I sent him a whole batch of cookies with pink flowers on top, as a joke. He said they were the best damned thing he and the guys ever ate, and asked me to send more. So I did. Pink and blue and purple flowers. He said it was like a garden exploded when he opened the box." She laughed, then shook her head, as the laugh turned to tears. "Oh, damn. See what I mean? I'm trying, but I'm not doing so good at the last one. I miss him. God, do I miss him."

Brody turned to her at the same time she turned to him. He gathered her to his chest, and she let the tears fall. She'd promised herself she'd never again rely on a man, never fall fast and hard, but Brody seemed different. Like the kind of man she could trust. Lean into. Depend upon.

Then like a wave, the loss of her brother hit her all over again. He was gone, and she'd never again see his smile or hear him tease her, or look for treasures in the yard. He was gone...and she was here, without him.

"Andrew was the strong one, you know? When our parents got divorced, he was the one who told me it'd all be okay. He was the one who dragged me down to the bakery day after day. He saved me." She shook her head, tears smearing into the cotton of his shirt. "I don't know what I would have done without him. And I don't know what I'll do without him now."

"You'll go on, and put one foot in front of the other. Because he would want that."

She raised her gaze to Brody's. Damn. This man read her like a book. "He would."

"He'd want you to keep running this shop and keep your family's legacy going. He'd want you to go look at that location this afternoon, and move toward the future. He wouldn't want you to stand around and cry for him."

"You talk like you know him." She swiped at her face. "That's exactly what Andrew would say. Actually, he'd say it far more direct and with far more colorful language." She laughed, and the sorrow that had gripped her began to ease a bit. "I wish you had met him. He was an amazing man."

"I feel like I have met him," Brody said quietly. "He's in every part of this shop and everything you do and... it's like he's here with us."

"It is." She bit her lip and nodded. "Thank you for lunch, for being here, for cheering me up."

"Kate—" The clock on the wall chimed quarter to the hour, at the same time Brody's cell phone began to vibrate. "Damn. My time's up. I have to get back to the office for the last couple of appointments." He pressed a kiss to her lips, then cupped her jaw. "I'll be back. And we'll talk then, okay?"

"I can't wait." And as she watched Brody McKenna leave, Kate thought there was nothing closer to the truth than that.

She was beginning to fall for the doctor, and fall hard.

CHAPTER SEVEN

ONE hour later, true to his word, Brody returned to the shop. The sight of him caused a hitch in Kate's breath. "You're on time," she said. "Quite impressive for a doctor."

He chuckled. "That's a pet peeve of mine. I hate to be late, for anything, and I work hard to make sure my practice runs on time. Makes for happier patients—"

"And a happier doctor."

"That, too." He swung his car keys around his finger. "You ready? I thought I'd drive, so you could concentrate on the building and neighborhood."

Thoughtful. Nice. Again. Did the man like her, or just see a pity case?

And why did she keep wondering about that?

"I won't turn that offer down." She tucked her apron behind the counter then headed out of the shop behind him, locking the door as she left. At the curb, Brody opened the passenger side door of an older Jeep, its dark green paint a little worse for wear. "What, no Mercedes?"

"I told you. I'm not the typical doctor. This is the car that got me through my college years, and I've had it so long, it's part of the family." He shrugged. "Whether

I can afford a Mercedes or not isn't the point. I don't need a sixty thousand dollar piece of metal to prove I'm successful. I'd rather let my patients speak to that."

"You are different," she said. "In a good way." She got into the Jeep, and waited while Brody came around to the driver's side. Every time Kate thought she had him pigeonholed, he added another dimension to his character. Maybe she'd misjudged him. Seen him through jaded eyes. Every minute she spent with him, Brody McKenna came closer to the kind of man she thought didn't exist.

Still, she suspected Brody McKenna kept a part of himself back. She wasn't sure what it was, or why he was keeping himself distanced from her, but she knew better than to try to force a bridge when there was only a rope across the river between them. If he was interested, he'd open up, and if he didn't...

She didn't need to fall for a mystery. Her mother had made that mistake, and she refused to do the same.

"So, tell me about this property." Brody put the Jeep in gear—a stick shift, which impressed Kate a little more—and pulled away from the curb.

"It's a thousand square feet, which is pretty much the same size I have now, and it's on a corner lot, beside a coffee shop and a florist. Busy location, with a lot of foot traffic."

"Sounds perfect. And like the kind of location that would let you do some partnering and cross-marketing with your neighbors." He flashed her a grin. "Sometimes I listened when my grandparents talked about work."

Kate laughed. "We'll see. I've looked at it online, and talked to the realtor a few weeks back, but this is my first in-person visit. Sometimes what you get in person isn't as good as the advertisement."

"Sort of like online dating, huh?"

"Speaking from personal experience, Doctor?" Curiosity about Brody's dating past sparked inside her. What had kept such an eligible, smart, handsome man from marrying? Was he really that gun-shy or had he been burned before, like her?

"Nope, can't say I've ever tried that," he said. "I'm old-fashioned. I like to meet people, see if there's a connection, and then take the next step."

"You said you came close to settling down before. What happened to that connection?"

Brody sighed. "Melissa and I got engaged right out of college, then I went on my first medical mission trip, and she broke up with me while I was gone."

"She did? Why?"

"She expected that being a doctor's wife meant shopping on Fifth Avenue and vacationing in Italy, not visiting third world countries to treat malaria and set broken bones. And, I was distant, and didn't put in the time I should have with the relationship." He sighed. "I tried to fix things, but I was too late."

"And that burned you forever on the idea of love?"

"That and…a few other things. I guess at a certain point, I gave up on finding someone who shared my goals."

She chuckled. "Now you sound like me. Two jaded souls. Destined for…"

"What?" he asked.

"I don't know. You tell me."

He raised and lowered a shoulder, a grin playing on

his lips. "Last I checked, psychic abilities weren't on my résumé."

She laughed. "No fair. You can't go all mysterious on me."

"Me? Mysterious? I'm as easy to read as a prescription."

That made her laugh even harder. "Written in a doctor's handwriting? That makes it illegible."

"I never said figuring me out would be easy." He grinned.

"Oh, I agree. You are far from easy to decipher. You're a Sphinx with a stethoscope." Kate sat back against the seat, wondering about this other side of her that being around Brody encouraged. She didn't trade flirty repartee with men. She worked hard, kept her nose to the grindstone, and yes came up for air once in a while to go on a date. But never had she met a man who made her exchange...

Banter.

Or met a man who made her blush like a schoolgirl. A man who made butterflies flutter in her stomach. A man who made her begin to dream again of things she'd given up on long ago. Not like this, she hadn't. A part of her threw up a huge Caution side while another part craved more.

The whole ride to Weymouth went like that, the two of them exchanging barbs, always with a hint of flirting on the side. The sun shone bright, and Brody had the windows down, letting in a nice fresh breeze. When they turned off on the Route 18 exit, disappointment filled Kate as they neared their destination.

A few minutes later—and after getting turned around once—they pulled in front of the location, a cute little storefront smack dab in a part of Weymouth dubbed Columbian Square. From the historic homes bordering the square to the old style storefronts, Kate could see vestiges of Weymouth's historic roots. Across the street from the shop sat the Cameo Theater, an old-style movie house that harkened back to the days of Model T cars. "Quaint, isn't it?"

"It looks perfect for a second Nora's." Brody came around and opened her door then the two of them headed for the storefront. People walked along the sidewalk, popping in and out of shops, chatting and enjoying the warm fall day. Traffic slowed at the stop signs, drivers casting quick glances at the shop wares before continuing on their way.

A wiry dark-haired man came hustling down the street, a packet of papers under one arm, a briefcase in the opposite hand. He extended his free hand as he came upon Kate and Brody. "Hello, hello. You must be Miss…Spencer? Here about the building?"

"Kate Spencer." She shook with the other man. "Owner of Nora's Sweet Shop in Newton. Thank you for meeting me today."

"No problem." He turned to Brody and shook. "I'm Bill Taylor." He turned and unlocked the door, then led them inside. "Nora's Sweet Shop, you said? Sounds like just the thing for our little community. We have lots of shops here that can compliment a bakery. And with the hospital around the corner, there's always a demand for gift baskets and the like."

As Bill talked about square footage and lighting, Kate took the time to look around, to imagine a counter here, a display there. The shop had housed a deli before, and the kitchen would need minimal changes to meet Kate's needs. All in all, the shop had the space and equipment to house another Nora's, not to mention a prime location.

"Looks perfect," Brody said to Kate. "Not that I'm an expert in these kinds of things, but it sure seems ideal to me."

"It is perfect. Right town, right space, right location."

"And right for you now?" Bill asked, already reaching into his stash of papers for an offer sheet.

Kate looked around. Nerves threatened to choke her. Brody had told her to be proactive, but now that the moment to take that step forward had arrived, she stalled. "I, um, I don't know. I need some time to think about it." She thanked Bill for his time, promised to call the realtor with any other questions, then headed out to the car. Brody opened her door, then climbed in the driver's seat.

"Why didn't you make an offer?" he asked. "I thought you said that place was perfect."

"I just don't think now is the right time to be adding locations." She watched the storefront grow smaller as the Jeep headed down the street. A mixture of disappointment and relief washed over her. Disappointment that she'd let the location go. Relief that she didn't have to tackle a major task like a second location. Maybe next month. Or the month after. Maybe she'd wait till spring when the weather improved, and people spent more time strolling the streets. Valid reasons? Or stall tactics?

"Do you want to talk about it?" Brody asked.

No, she didn't, but Brody had driven her here and deserved an answer. Maybe if she got her reservations out on the table, the worries would ease.

"It's scary to take that next step, you know?" she

said. "And I'm just not sure that I'm ready for it. I mean, adding a second location splits me in two, and I have my hands full with the Newton location as it is."

"Your assistant will be back soon, and you talked about hiring others, so that will free up your time," he pointed out. "I agree that the next step is scary as hell. You could fail, or you could succeed. But you won't know either unless you try."

She watched the streets of Weymouth pass by outside the window. Neat houses in neat rows, flanked by businesses on either side. A bustling, growing community, one that seemed much like Newton. One that could support a Nora's Sweet Shop, if she dared to make the attempt.

Fail...or succeed. Either prospect sent a shiver of worry down her spine. She turned to Brody. "How did you do it?"

Brody flipped on the directional, then merged onto the interstate. His gaze remained on the road, his hand shifting the gear as they accelerated and entered the fray of automobiles. "Do what?"

"Take those risks, fly to other cities, other countries, and step into a strange environment? How did you know it would work out?"

"I didn't. I had to trust in my skills as a doctor. And sometimes, I succeeded. And sometimes," he let out a long, low breath, "I failed."

"That's what I'm most afraid of, I guess. Andrew was the risk taker, the one who would go all in on everything from poker to tic-tac-toe." She fiddled with the strap on her purse. Andrew had traveled the world, leapt out of airplanes, climbed mountains. While all her life, Kate had stayed in the same town, worked in the same business, seen the same people, baked the same things. "I know he'd want me to do it, but…"

"You're afraid of letting him down."

"Yeah." She sighed. "And myself. And my grandmother. And all those people who love Nora's Sweet Shop."

"I can relate to that. When someone gives you a huge responsibility, it can be scary. You worry about whether you are up to the task. Whether you'll fulfill their wishes, the way they wanted. Whether…you're doing the right thing at all." Little traffic filled the highway, few people traveling in or out of the city on a fall Saturday afternoon. "Maybe you should wait then. Give it a little time."

"Maybe." Or maybe she should throw caution to the wind, as Andrew had done, and just go for it. Leap off the edge and trust the winds to carry her.

As the miles clicked by and the city drew closer, Kate realized she didn't want the day to end. Brody had been good company, and joking with him on the way out here had brightened her day, eased the tension in her shoulders. Whenever she spent time with him, he had the same effect. He made her forget, made her think about the day ahead, rather than the past.

She liked him, as a friend, and as something more, something she wanted to explore, taste. She wondered about the things he kept to himself, wondered how it fit with the man she'd gotten to know. "I'm not sure what your plan is for today, but if you're free, I'd like to invite you over for dinner. Nothing too fancy, because I'm not exactly cook of the year, but it'll be edible, I promise."

"I've tasted your cupcakes. You can definitely cook."

"Bake, not cook. They're two different sciences. I'm

great with things that are exact and precise, but with cooking, a lot of it is a pinch of this, a dash of that, and it gets me all flustered." She shook her head. "Don't even ask me about the Thanksgiving turkey debacle."

He laughed. "Now that I'd like to see. You flustered."

"You'll see that, and the parts of my life that aren't so organized." Inviting him over meant opening a door to herself. She hadn't done that in a long, long time. She thought of her brother, and how he approached his days with a what's-the-worst-that-could-happen attitude, and decided she'd take a cue from Andrew, and dance a little closer to the edge of danger.

"You'll be shattering my image of you as the perfect woman, you know," Brody said.

She pivoted in her seat. "You think I'm the perfect woman?"

He turned toward her, but his eyes remained unreadable behind dark sunglasses. "I think you're pretty damned amazing."

Her face heated, and a smile winged across her face. Her heart skipped, as if she'd been rocketed back to middle school and the cute boy in math class had dropped a note on her desk. "Amazing, huh? You're not so bad yourself, Doctor."

"Well, there's a rousing endorsement." He laughed. "I'll have to add that to my online dating profile."

She gave him a coy smile. "I can't be throwing out compliments left and right at you. You could get a swelled head."

"I doubt that's going to happen. I have my brothers to remind me that I can still be a dork sometimes."

"You? A dork? I don't think so." She took in the sharp line of his jaw, his tousled dark hair, his defined, strong hands. The last word she'd use to describe Brody was *dork*. Sexy, mysterious, intriguing, tempting…

A hundred other words came to mind when she looked at Brody McKenna.

"Hey, don't underestimate me. I read medical journals in my spare time. And watch operation shows on TV. I've never been in the cool kids clique." He grinned.

She waved that off. "That's overrated if you ask me."

He grinned. "Oh, were you in the cool kids group?"

"I was a cheerleader." She shrugged. "Membership came with the pom-poms."

"You were a cheerleader?" A grin quirked up on one side of his face. "You do know that when you tell a man that, it gives him ideas?"

"Does it help to know I was terrible at it?"

He thought a second. "Ummm…nope."

"Well, just don't ask me to rah-rah and we'll get along just fine."

"Even if I say please?"

"Even if you say please." She laughed, but still a simmering sexual tension filled the car, rife with the innuendos and unspoken desires hanging between them. Maybe later, she'd explore a little of that with Brody McKenna. Take a chance for once, and let the man not just into her house, but into her heart.

They neared her exit, and she gave Brody directions. In a few minutes, he had reached the driveway of her townhome. "Home sweet home," he said, and shut off the engine. The Jeep clicked a few times, then fell silent.

Nerves bubbled inside her. She'd invited men into her home before, but this time seemed different. Because she'd started to like Brody—a lot? Because being around an enticing man like Brody embodied taking a risk?

Either way, the few steps it took to get from the driveway to the front door seemed to last forever. She unlocked the door, then flicked on the hall light and stepped inside, with Brody following. "Can I get you something to drink?"

"Sure."

"Um, beer, water, soda?"

He opted for water. She filled two glasses, then led him to the small sunroom at the back of her townhouse. Screened in the summer, shuttered in the winter, the room offered large windows and a fabulous peek of the outdoors. "This is my favorite room. It's not very big, but it has a fabulous view." She waved toward the picture windows, and the thick copse of woods that ran along the back of the property. She'd hung birdfeeders on several of the trees when she first moved in, which provided a constant flurry of winged activity.

Brody sat on an overstuffed floral patterned love-seat, a tall man on a feminine couch. Somehow, Brody made it work. "I can see why you love it," he said. "It's hard to get something like this so close to the city, with woods and everything. Sitting here must be a nice way for you to unwind."

"It is. I've spent many an afternoon or evening out here, reading a book or just listening to music and watching the birds. It's…"

"Calming," Brody said.

"Yes. Very." Except with Brody in the room, calm didn't describe the riot of awareness rocketing through her. Her mind went back to that almost kiss the other day. For the hundredth time, she wished they'd finished what they'd started.

Who was Brody McKenna? Between the flirting and the compliments and the help in the bakery, he seemed interested in her, but when it came to moving things to the next level, he backed away instead. Was she misreading him?

"When I was in. . ." he stopped, started again, "overseas, we stopped in this tiny village for several days. It sat in this little oasis, a valley of sorts, nestled between several mountain ranges." As he spoke, she had the feeling in his mind, he'd gone to that destination, and his voice softened with the memory. "Not many places over there had trees, but this one did. The room where I stayed looked out over a stone wall and a field, all shadowed by the majesty of the mountains. When the sun rose, it painted an exquisite picture. Gold washing over purple, then over green, like unrolling a blanket of yellow. It was simple and beautiful."

"It sounds it."

"The days there were long, and tough." He ran a hand through his hair and sighed. "Some days, that mountain range restored my sanity, brought me back to reality. To what mattered."

"My brother talked about something similar. He said that every day he spent in Afghanistan, he made it a point to find something beautiful wherever he went. And when things got tough, he'd just focus on that one beautiful thing, and it would remind him of home and why he was there."

"Those moments brought him peace?"

"I think they did." She looked at Brody McKenna and saw a man who needed that same kind of peace.

He carried a load of troubles on his shoulders. What troubles, she wasn't sure, but she suspected it stemmed from a recent tragic event. Maybe she could help him find a little solace, or if nothing else, show him she understood. He was trying to do that for her, and the least she could do was the same.

Kate got to her feet, and crossed to a cedar box that sat on the shelf. All this time, the box had sat, closed, waiting for her to be ready. To open it, to share the contents, to tell the story. She realized as she carried the small wooden container back to the loveseat, that for a month, she'd put her emotions on a back burner. She'd done that long enough.

"I want to show you something." Kate settled herself beside Brody, and opened the lid. "I haven't shown this to anyone, except my grandmother." She pulled out a trio of velvet boxes, and laid them on the coffee table. "Andrew's medals, given posthumously. Odd word, isn't that? Posthumously. Like it was funny afterwards or something." She shook her head, then reached into the box, and withdrew another item. "The flag from his funeral." She placed the triangular folded item on the table, giving it one lingering touch then reached inside one more time. "And the four leaf clover necklace he wore. He called it his good luck charm."

Brody remembered.

In that moment, he was back in the first village they'd stayed in, sitting outside, watching the sun go down behind the mountains. Andrew sat beside him, fingering the necklace. The clover had caught the last of the sun's rays, bouncing them off like an aura. Brody had asked Andrew about the emblem, and that conversation had built the beginnings of a friendship between the two men.

The memory sent a rush of emotion through Brody. He glanced at the necklace in Kate's hand. The explosion had chipped off one corner, twisted another, doing the same damage to the jewelry as it had done inside Andrew's body. He could see Andrew all over again, lying on the ground, torn apart by the blast, while his friends lay nearby. Blood mingled with fear, and Brody and the other doctor with him rushing to try and save them all. Knowing at least one would die before the day ended.

Brody's throat grew thick, his eyes burned. "You okay?" Kate asked, placing a hand on his arm. Her comforting him, when he should be the one comforting her.

"Yeah." A lie. He hadn't been okay in a long time, and the necklace brought back all the reasons why. "My father used to have a four leaf clover necktie. He wore it whenever he called on a new client." Brody had shared the same story with Andrew, all those weeks ago and sharing it now with Kate was like being back there on that porch while the sun sent the world a goodnight kiss. "One of us inherited the tie when my father died. Finn, I think. We're Irish, so you know the four-leaf clover superstition is alive and well."

"Andrew just liked them. When we were kids, we spent an entire afternoon, combing the yard, looking for one." She ran her thumb over the four heart shapes that converged to form the trademark leaves. "We never found one, but we tried our best."

"Maybe that's because luck isn't something you find. It's something you...create."

"True." She gave the necklace one last touch then

lowered it to the table, one link at a time. "That's why I don't want to open another location. Because I'm afraid that..."

When she didn't go on, he turned to her, took one of her hands in his and waited until her gaze met his. "Afraid of what?"

"Afraid that I'll be as unlucky as Andrew." The truth sat there, cold, stark. "That I'll take a risk and I'll fail, and I'll..." Her hand ran over the folded surface of the flag, "Let him down. Let myself down."

"You're smart, Kate. Talented as hell. And you have something that people love and enjoy. That's a recipe for success." He closed her palm over the charm. "With or without a good luck charm, you're going to do just fine."

"I hope you're right." She gave him a watery smile. "There are days when it's hard to find that view, and focus on the good."

"I know what you mean. I don't think I've seen that view in a long, long time."

She gave the box a loving touch then raised her gaze to Brody's. "I shared all this with you because I wanted you to know that I understand what it's like to need that one little thing that restores your sanity, gets you back on track. I don't know what's bothering you, but it's clear something is weighing heavy on your shoulders." She picked up the necklace and dropped it into Brody's palm. "I want you to have this. Let it be your view, Brody. It worked for Andrew, and I'm sure it'll work for you."

The gold weighed heavy in his palm. "I...I can't take this, Kate."

"But—"

Brody glanced at the medals, the flag, lying on the

table, and knew he could delay this no longer. Kate deserved to know the truth, even if it hurt. Even if it went against her brother's wishes. Maybe Andrew was wrong. Maybe his sister could handle more than he'd thought.

"Kate, there's something I want to tell you." Against Brody's hip, his cell phone began to ring, the distinctive trilling tone that meant his service was trying to reach him. Routine calls, like appointment changes, were routed to voicemail, but emergencies went straight to Brody's cell. He cursed under his breath. "I have to get this."

He flipped out the phone, and answered it. In seconds, the operator relayed the information—one of his patients had landed in the hospital a few minutes ago with heart attack symptoms. The cardiac team wanted the primary care physician's input before proceeding. "I'll be right there." He closed the phone and put it back in the holster. "I'm sorry. I have to go."

"Duty calls?"

He nodded. "It's an emergency. Listen, I'll catch up with you tomorrow, okay?"

"I can't. My grandparents and I are going up to Maine for the day to visit my mom. How about Monday?"

"I'll be there." Even though he dreaded the conversation he needed to have with her, a part of him couldn't wait to see her again. Today had been fun, and brought an unexpected lightness to his heart. He craved more of that.

Craved more of Kate.

"You'll be there on Monday, with your apron on?" She gave him a teasing wink.

He chuckled. "Of course. I'm starting to see it as the

next best fashion accessory. What all the cool docs will be wearing this winter."

She led him to the door, then paused and put a hand on his arm. Her gentle touch warmed his skin. "Brody?"

"Yeah?"

"Thank you for today. You made me laugh, and you made me forget, and it was…wonderful." A smile curved across her face, this one a sweet, easy smile. "I needed that. A lot."

All Andrew Spencer had wanted was his older sister's happiness. Brody had done his best to ensure that, and to ensure she followed the path she'd been on before she lost her brother. A win in that column, but a loss in the other, where the truth lay. And complicating the equation—

Brody liked Kate Spencer. A lot. He wanted more, wanted to make her his. Wanted to take her in his arms and kiss her until neither of them could see straight. To do that, he had to start them off on the right foot—

And tell her why he had walked into her shop that first day. Was she ready to hear the truth? Or would it set her back even more?

His phone buzzed a second time, reminding him the patient came first. Before what Brody wanted, before what Brody craved. And that meant any relationship with Kate Spencer fell far down the line from the promise Brody had made in that dusty hut.

CHAPTER EIGHT

THE Morning Glory Diner promised good home cooked meals according to the sign in the window and the delicious scents emanating every time someone opened the door. Kate stepped inside, and opted for a table by the window. The flowers of the namesake ringed the bright diner's walls and decorated everything from the menus to the napkin holders. The counters were a soft pale yellow, the seats a deep navy blue, which offset the border of violet morning glories well.

A smiling blonde came over and greeted Kate. Her nametag read Stace, but somehow Kate would have pegged her for a McKenna fiancé without it. She had the kind of bright, happy personality that seemed to fit with what Kate knew of the McKenna men so far. "Welcome to the Morning Glory," Stace said. "Can I get you some coffee?"

"Sure." Kate put out her hand. "And if you have a sec, I'd love to chat with you. I'm Kate and I'm making your wedding cupcakes this week."

"Kate, how nice to finally meet you in person." The other woman smiled. "Brody told us about you. And so did Riley's grandmother. She said you made amazing chocolates."

"Thank you." Brody had been talking about her. At first, it flattered her, then she realized it made sense. He'd hired her to make Stace's wedding cake, after all, and giving her business a plug would be part of that. Kate had been puzzling over Brody's words from Saturday all weekend. Something troubled him, but what it was, she didn't know. He'd left the necklace behind, right next to a whole lot of unanswered questions.

"Listen, I need to get a couple orders on the tables, but then I should have a few minutes to sit and chat. I'll bring us coffee." Stace cast a glance toward the clock on the wall. "And knowing my husband-to-be, he'll be walking in those doors in about thirty seconds for his omelet fix, so you can meet Riley, too."

"Sounds great." Kate gave Stace a smile.

A few seconds later, the door opened and a man who looked like a younger version of Brody strode inside, straight to Stace. He took her in his arms, gave her a quick dip that had her laughing, then a longer kiss that had her blushing. She gave him a gentle swat, then gestured in Kate's direction.

Riley crossed the room, a wide smile on his face. He slid into the opposite seat and put out a hand. "Riley McKenna. The youngest and cutest McKenna brother— and you can tell Brody I said so."

Kate laughed and shook hands with Riley. She liked him from the start. "Nice to meet you. Kate Spencer, owner of Nora's Sweet Shop."

"So you're the one that has my brother all distracted. The man doesn't know if he's coming or going lately."

Had he said that? Been talking about her? "Brody and I are just working together. He's helping me out while my assistant is out of town."

"Well, for Brody it's more than some baking and measuring. The man can't stop talking about you." Riley leaned across the table. "He's smitten, I'd say. Though if you tell him I said that, I'll deny it."

Kate put up her hands. "Brody and I are not dating—" well, Saturday had been kind of a date, and the tension between them spoke of something more than friendship "—I'm not sure he's interested in me that way." Because despite the day they'd spent together, the flirting and the jokes, he kept taking two steps forward, one step back. The mixed signals confused her, and as much as she'd told Riley and Stace she'd come here to get more details for their wedding cake, she knew the truth. She'd stopped in to pump those who knew Brody best for more information. Something to help her solve the puzzle of the enigmatic Brody McKenna.

"Tell me," Riley said, "is Brody there pretty much every day?"

"Well, yes, but—"

"Is he doing nice things like opening the door for you?"

"Well, yes, but—"

"And is he finding excuses to run into you when he doesn't have to be there?"

"Well, yes, but—"

"Then he's interested. Trust me, Brody doesn't waste his time on things that don't matter to him. If he's around you all the time, he's interested. Not to mention, he manages to bring up your name about... oh, a hundred times in conversation."

Stace slid into the booth beside Riley and handed Kate a cup of coffee. "You talking about Brody?"

"Yup. And how the middle brother is the last to learn

that a good woman is the secret to happiness." Riley pressed a kiss to Stace's cheek. "It's always the smart ones that are the dumbest."

"I agree with that." Stace gave him a gentle nudge, then turned to Kate. "Riley was just as bad as Brody. Kept on pretending he didn't have any interest in me. And meanwhile, he was drooling behind my back."

Riley feigned horror. "I was not. That was Finn with Ellie."

Kate laughed. "Brody mentioned him a few times."

"The first to fall and get married, and he surprised the hell out of all of us by eloping. He's got one kid already, another on the way. By taking the plunge, he blazed the trail for the rest of us." Riley chuckled. "And this weekend, it'll be my turn. I can't wait."

Stace beamed at him. "Neither can I." Riley slipped his arm behind Stace and drew her a little closer, a little tighter.

Kate dug a notepad out of her purse. "While I have you two here, I wanted to ask you some questions about the cupcakes. Brody gave me information, but—"

"He's a guy and they aren't big on details, right?" Stace said. "Whatever Brody told you, though, is probably just fine. I'm the least fussy person you'll ever meet. Just make them edible and pretty and I'll be happy."

"Because all you want to do is marry me, right?" Riley said.

"No. All I want to do is gorge on cupcakes." She laughed. "Okay, and marry you."

Riley swiped a hand across his forehead. "Phew. You had me worried there for a minute. I thought the wedding was all an elaborate plot for dessert."

"Oh, it is," Stace said with a grin. "And you're the dessert I'm getting."

The two of them embodied happiness. Kate envied them a bit. No, a lot. Would she ever meet a man who would love her that much? "I'm not sure my cupcakes can live up to that," she said with a smile.

"I'm sure they'll be all that and more. I heard all about your chocolates from Mary at dinner last week."

"A family dinner that Brody skipped," Riley said. "I heard it was because he was working with you."

"I'm sorry, if I had known he should have been at a family dinner—"

Riley put up a hand to stop her. "It was no big deal, really. Honestly, we're all glad Brody started working with you. It's been good for him."

Stace nodded. Concern filled both their faces. "Be patient with Brody. He's been through a lot."

Did that explain the distance he maintained? The way he pulled back every time they got close? What could possibly be that bad that he felt he couldn't tell her?

"He told me his parents died." Kate shook her head. "I meant yours, Riley. I'm sorry about that."

"Thanks, but that isn't what troubles Brody these days. He's been through something…traumatic. In the recent past." Riley exchanged a glance with Stace.

Something Brody hadn't shared. The big thing he kept dancing around, then dropping? Hurt roared inside Kate. She had sat there with him and poured her heart out, sharing her deepest fears, and he had yet to do the same. Why?

"He said he's working with me because it helps him

get his mind off things," Kate said. "I'm glad that baking can do that for him."

And that he can avoid the hard topics yet coax them out of me.

"Brody hates to cook," Riley said with a laugh. "Like seriously runs the other way if someone turns on the oven. He's a takeout only man."

"Then why would he offer to help me?"

Again, Riley and Stace exchanged a glance and again, Kate got the feeling there was something— something big—they weren't telling her. "You need to ask him about that," Riley said. "Just know that if Brody is there doing the thing he hates the most in the world, there is a really, really big reason for him doing so."

"Bigger than your wedding?" Kate asked.

Riley thought a second. "Brody's not there for our wedding. He's there because—" Stace laid a hand on Riley's arm and he cut off the sentence. "Brody's a good man," Riley said instead. "And he's trying his damnedest to do the right thing. So before you judge him, think about that. And give him the benefit of the doubt."

Thursday afternoon, Brody sat in his office, surrounded by charts he needed to finish up and notes he should be reviewing, and ignored it all. He'd come so close to telling Kate the truth on Saturday, but at the last minute, chickened out, using the emergency as an excuse to get out of there. And in the days since, he'd found one excuse after another to avoid the bakery. Instead, he'd gone for long, hard, punishing runs that hadn't solved a damned thing.

The problem? He liked Kate. Liked her a lot. And he knew if he wanted a future with her, then he had to start being honest. Trust that she could handle the information, and not be worse for knowing it.

Andrew's concerns continued to nag in the back of Brody's head, though. Who would know her better than her brother? Maybe Andrew was right to protect her, or maybe he didn't realize his sister's strength.

How well did Brody know her, though, after only a couple weeks? Better than her own flesh and blood?

Mrs. Maguire gave his door a soft knock, and came inside. "Do you need anything else before I leave, Doctor?"

"No, thanks, Mrs. Maguire." His head nurse had been a model of efficiency this week, and kept him on track despite his uncharacteristic lack of attention to his practice. She'd noticed, and mentioned it a few times. He'd attributed his inattentiveness to exhaustion, an excuse that didn't work, given he'd worked half days all week.

She lingered in the doorway, then came inside and put a hand on the back of his visitor's chair but didn't sit. "I've noticed you've been troubled lately, Doc." He put up a hand to argue, but she cut him off. "Can I give you some advice? The same advice Doc Watkins gave me one day?"

Concern etched her features. Working side by side with him for years had given Mrs. Maguire an insight into what made Brody tick. Maybe she'd share something that could take the edge off his emotions, give him a way to find his direction again. "Sure."

She swung around to the front of the chair and eased into it. "Did I ever tell you about my daughter, Sharon?"

"Just that she's married and given you two, no, three grandchildren to spoil." Every day it seemed Mrs.

Maguire put out a new picture of one of the three kids on her desk. Or a new drawing colored with thick crayons, and marked with love for Grandma. The kids lived a couple towns over, and Brody knew Mrs. Maguire devoted every spare minute to seeing them.

A smile curved across Mrs. Maguire's face. "She has indeed. But for a time there, I didn't think she was going to do anything with her life, anything except die."

As far as he could remember, Mrs. Maguire had only shared the good news about her family, never any kind of troubles beyond the typical colds or restaurant meltdowns. "I didn't know that. What happened?"

"This was before your time, and back when it was just me and Doc Watkins. As a single mom, I juggled everything—work, school, soccer matches. Sharon felt neglected, I think. When she got to high school, she made a lot of bad choices. Fell in with the wrong crowd. Pot led to coke, led to crack. In those days, crack ran rampant." She shook her head. "I thought I was going to lose her. I did everything I could to try to keep her safe. Console her, stay home with her, whatever it took to keep her on track. But nothing worked. One day at a time, I watched my baby die."

"Oh, Mrs. Maguire, I'm so sorry." He couldn't imagine the stress on her shoulders during those days, coupled with working full-time and paying the bills.

"And here I was, a nurse. The kind of person who should know better, you know? I kept trying to fix it, like putting a band-aid on a cut, but it wasn't a cut, it was a hemorrhage, and she didn't want the help."

"What did you do?"

"I came in here one day and I cried to Doc Watkins. Told him I had to quit so I could take care of my baby.

I was going to devote myself full time to trying to fix Sharon. And you know what he told me?"

Brody shook his head.

"He said if I quit, it would be the worst thing I could do. Well, he said more than that, and a whole lot more colorfully than I would. You know Doc Watkins. He was nothing if not direct."

Brody chuckled. "I remember."

Mrs. Maguire crossed her hands in her lap and dropped her gaze to her fingers. "Back then, there wasn't a lot of that fanciness about enabling and co-dependency, but that's what it was. I just didn't see it. All I saw was that I was protecting my daughter, helping her. Doc gave me the number of a great rehab. Told me to drop her off and drive away. I did, but damn, I didn't want to. She was crying and screaming and calling me names, then begging me to come back in the same breath. I had to shut the windows, turn the rearview mirror, so I wouldn't give in." Tears filled the older woman's eyes at the memory, and she leaned forward, grabbed a tissue from the box on his desk, and dabbed at her face. "I left her there. Hardest damned thing I ever did in my life, and also the best. Three months later, she came out clean. Moved to Brookline, got herself a job in a dress shop, and after a year or so, met the man that became her husband."

"I'm glad that all worked out." He'd admired Mrs. Maguire before, but his esteem for her increased ten-fold. The woman sitting across from him possessed an incredible inner strength. "You must have been so worried."

"I was, but more than that, I was beating myself up for not fixing it. It took me a long time to realize that some things are out of my hands. I couldn't make her come clean. I couldn't make her want it; she had to want it for herself. Just because I have medical training doesn't make me a miracle worker." She crumpled the tissue into her fist, then leaned forward. "Most of all, I had to learn that sometimes, you just have to cut yourself some slack. You and me both."

"I try, Mrs. Maguire. I really do."

"No, you don't. I've seen your face ever since you got back from Afghanistan. Whatever happened over there, you are blaming yourself for and now that weight has become an albatross around your neck." She put up a hand. "Now I don't know the whole story, and I might be just talking out of my hat, but all I can say is that I have been in shoes similar to yours, and if you put your faith in others, and stop beating yourself up for what you can't control, what you couldn't fix, it'll all work out. You are a doctor, and you're used to fixing, bandaging. Not everything can be fixed. Some things just have to be." She got to her feet, and smoothed a hand down her jacket. "I've said my piece, and I'll let you be. I'm not trying to tell you what to do, Dr. McKenna, just trying to offer you a solution. Take it if you want." She gave him a kind smile, then left the room.

Brody got to his feet and went to the window. He looked out at the busy streets of Newton, beginning to fill with cars now that the clock had ticked past five. For the next few hours, it would be bumper to bumper with people trying to get home to their lives, their homes, their families. They would sit around the table and talk about their days, and few, if any, would realize just how lucky they were to be together.

He thought of Mrs. Maguire and her daughter, and

how close his head nurse had come to losing her only child. He thought of albatrosses and choices, and after a long time, he pulled out the card, read it over for the millionth time, then tucked it back into his wallet. It was time he told Kate the real story about her brother.

And let the chips fall where they may after that.

CHAPTER NINE

Kate had baked and decorated, frosted and sugared.
But it hadn't been enough to make her forget what Riley
and Stace had said. Or to put Brody McKenna out of
her mind.

Because she'd started to like him. He kept his cards
close to his chest—heck, hidden inside his chest—but
every once in a while, the other side of Brody peeked
out. A playful, sweet side. Like when they'd danced together at the rest home. When he'd dug in and started
baking, even wearing the pink apron. At the same time,
he showed this dimension of caring. Like the kind of
man a woman could lean against, depend upon. Even if
being around him stirred her in a way she hadn't been
stirred before.

Would it be worth it to take the risk and fall in love
with him? Or would she be burned by a man who was
keeping part of himself hidden? She'd seen her mother
do it time and again with her father. Giving, giving,
giving, and never receiving his full heart in return.
Would Brody be the same? Would she be repeating
her mother's mistakes?

Her conversation with Riley and Stace had only
stirred the pot. What had Brody been hiding behind

those blue eyes? The flame of Brody McKenna drew her again and again. She needed to exercise caution— or she'd get burned.

"Somebody's got a lot on her mind."

Kate jerked her head up and looked at her grandmother. "Huh?"

"You just turned that rose into a radish." She pointed at the red clump of buttercream on top of the cupcake.

"Oh, no." She swiped the ruined decoration off, then set down the piping bag. "I guess I am a little distracted."

"And I know why." Nora hefted a heavy tub of frosting onto the counter and started to peel off the lid.

"Grandma, quit that!" Kate said, sliding in to finish the job before her grandmother hurt herself. "No helping."

"You need the help. I have the experience. Let me give you a hand."

Kate sighed. She knew her grandmother. She wouldn't give up. "Okay. If you promise to take it easy, and sit down while you work, can you frost those cupcakes over there?"

Nora laughed. "You sound like you're the grandmother and I'm the granddaughter."

"Just watching out for my favorite grandma." Kate slid a stool over to the counter, then plopped a platter of red devil cupcakes and a piping bag of cream cheese frosting in front of her grandmother. She laid a hand on Nora's shoulder. "Thanks, Grandma."

Nora took Kate's hand and gave it a squeeze. "Anytime, sweetie. I love this place almost as much as I love you."

"Ditto." She grinned, then dipped her head to focus

on assembling the order she'd been working on. Maybe talking about work would keep her from thinking about Brody. "By the way, I looked at that second location the other day."

"You did? What'd you think of it?"

"It was…perfect. In this quaint little town square in Weymouth, across the street from an old-fashioned movie theater. There's a florist and a café nearby, and a hospital right down the street."

"I don't think it gets much better than that," Nora said. "Did you make an offer?"

"Not yet."

"What are you waiting for?"

Kate shrugged, then threw up her hands. "I don't know. A sign? A big, blinking, this is the right decision to make sign."

Nora laughed. "Life never gives us those. If it did, every choice we make would be easy as pie."

"True."

Nora laid a hand on her granddaughter's shoulder. "You'll know the right answer when the time comes. Meanwhile, you have a big night tonight. Are you ready?"

Kate glanced down at the dress she'd put on, the heels she'd brought to work just for tonight. "As ready as I'll ever be. If I just stick with the desserts, I'll be fine. Either way, I'm packing tissues in my purse."

Her grandmother gave her a quick hug. "Such a smart, practical girl. No wonder I'm so proud of you."

The bell over the door rang, and Kate turned to go out to the shop when she heard Brody's voice call out a hello. Her heart tripped, and a smile curved across her face. Not thinking about Brody had worked for, oh, five seconds.

"Hmm…and you wonder why you're distracted," Nora said. "I think the reason just walked in."

"It has nothing to do with him," Kate whispered. "Nothing at all."

"Mmm, hmm." Nora drew a little frosting heart on the stainless steel counter. Kate swiped the romantic symbol onto her finger and plopped the sweet treat in her mouth before Brody walked in and saw it.

Damn. Every time she saw Brody McKenna, she forgot to breathe. He had on a suit jacket with his shirt and tie today, and he looked so handsome she could have fainted. "Hi," she said, because her brain wouldn't process any other words.

"Hi, yourself." He started to shrug out of the jacket. He had a tall, lean body, defined in all the right places. His muscles rippled under the pressed cotton of his shirt, and she wondered what he'd look like bare-chested. She'd seen him in a T-shirt and shorts and that had been a delicious sight that had lingered in her mind. What would he look like, wet from the shower? Fresh out of bed in the morning? In the dark of night, slipping under the sheets?

Damn. Why did this man affect her so?

"Uh, you might want to keep that on," she said, putting up a hand to stop him. "I have another delivery tonight. I forgot to tell you earlier. If you don't mind helping me, there'll be a free dinner in it for you."

"A free dinner? One that doesn't come out of a microwave or a drive-through? Who can turn down that offer?" He grinned, then entered the kitchen.

Her stomach flipped, her heart tripped, and she knew

why her thoughts lingered on him whenever they were apart. That smile. And those eyes. And everything else about him. In that second, she decided she'd take the risk, open her heart.

"Hello, Mrs. Spencer," he said to Kate's grandmother.

"Why hello, Dr. McKenna. So nice to see you again."

"You, too, ma'am."

"Why, would you look at the time?" Nora said. She took off her apron, and laid it beside the piping bag. "I completely forgot I promised your grandfather I'd go out with him for the early birds dinner special tonight. I better go." She shrugged into her coat. "You two can handle this alone, can't you?"

She laid a slight emphasis on the word "alone" and gave her granddaughter a knowing smile. Behind Brody's back, she drew a heart in the air and pointed at Kate. "Oh, and, Brody," Nora said, "I'd love to have you over for Wednesday night dinner at our house next week."

"I'd be honored, Mrs. Spencer. Thank you."

"Good. I'll see you at six. Kate knows the address." She gave her granddaughter a smile. "Maybe she'll even drive you."

Kate had no doubt her grandmother would drive over and pick up Brody herself if her granddaughter didn't. Matchmaker Nora at work again. Andrew had had some of those tendencies himself, always telling Kate he'd keep an eye out for the perfect man for his amazing sister.

"Do you need me to bring anything?" Brody asked.

"Aren't you sweet? No, nothing at all. Just bring yourself." Nora shot Kate another smile of approval for Brody. He'd racked up several brownie points and had clearly moved to the top of Nora's list. "That'll be enough."

Nora headed out the door. Kate wished the floor would open up and swallow her but it didn't. Or a customer would come in and save her from the awkward silence. None did. Or the sky would fall and create a distraction—

None of that happened. Instead, the room became a warm, tight space of just her. And Brody. Her gaze roamed over him. Desire pulsed in her veins. He wore a half smile, and in an odd way, that turned her on more than a full smile. She wanted to feel his hard chest beneath her palms, but most of all, she wanted to kiss him.

Why had he yet to make a move in that direction? Brody didn't strike her as the shy type. She had read attraction between them, she was sure of it. What was holding him back from pushing this further?

She watched him loading the finished cupcakes into boxes, and read tension in his shoulders, a distance in his words, his smile. She kept on talking, filling the room with endless chatter, if only to keep from asking the obvious question—

What's wrong?

They worked together for several minutes, exchanging small talk about their days. The whole thing seemed so ordinary, smacking of a domestic life with Brody. She could imagine a future like this—her coming home from the shop, sitting across the dinner table from him, and talking about everything, and nothing at all. Like ordinary couples with ordinary lives.

Already, that told her that her heart had connected

with him. A lot. She was falling for him. But the falling felt nice, like tumbling into a warm pool.

As much as she wanted to linger in that pool, she held back, because she sensed a reservation in Brody. Maybe he didn't feel the same way. Maybe he did, as though it was moving too fast. Or maybe she had read him wrong. And she could be making the mistake of a lifetime.

"There, that's the last one," she said, sandwiching the last cupcake in the container. She closed the lid and handed it to Brody. He stacked them together, then gave her a grin.

"Another job done."

"Yep." Joanne would be back Saturday, and then her afternoons of working with Brody would come to an end. Already, she could see that finish line, and it saddened her. She'd gotten used to having him here.

"I'm sorry about my grandmother earlier," Kate said, "but you don't have to go to dinner if you don't want." Her roundabout way of saying *if you aren't interested in me, here's your out.*

"I'd love to go. Your grandmother didn't bother me at all by asking me over. I think there's something in a grandmother's DNA that makes them bound and determined to matchmake," Brody said. "When I saw mine a few days ago, she said the same thing. That I should bring you to the next family dinner, which in case I get in trouble for not inviting you, is at Mary McKenna's house in Newton, on Sunday at two. She's just a few blocks north of here."

Kate laughed. "Seems like our grandmothers are determined to bring us together."

"Mine heard glowing reports from Riley about how

nice you were. And that got her wheels turning, thinking that you and I…" His voice trailed off.

"Yeah, my grandmother, too." Kate let out a nervous
laugh. She brushed at her hair. Damn. She was acting
like a schoolgirl. Her face heated under Brody's lingering gaze. She turned away to grab a spoon and moved
too fast, unnerved by the tension, by the unanswered
questions. Did he like her? Or not?

As she pivoted, her arm bumped the bowl, and sent
it tumbling onto the floor. When it hit the concrete, the
violet frosting in the bowl splattered upward, and outward, spreading in a burst of color on Brody's shirt and
his suit jacket. "Oh no! I'm sorry."

"No problem. I've had worse on my shirt. Especially
during flu season." He slipped off the jacket, then, just
like in her fantasy, he began to undo the buttons. Her
heart skipped a beat, and nearly stopped when he peeled
apart the panels of his shirt and revealed, a lean, muscled chest.

Oh. My. God. Kate opened her mouth. Closed it
again. "Uh…I can get you a T-shirt. If you don't mind
one that says Nora's Sweet Shop."

"Better to wear the words than the actual sweets."
Brody grinned.

Kate spun away before she reached out and ran a
hand down his chest. Or worse. Like threw him onto
the stainless steel counter and ravaged his body. She
grabbed a T-shirt from the glass case out front and
brought it back with her. "At least this is brown, instead of pink like the aprons."

"It's almost manly. Thanks."

"Anytime." And anytime he wanted to take his shirt

off in her presence, he could. But she didn't say that, either.

He moved closer, standing inches away now, that broad chest so close she could feel the heat against her own skin. "Do you, uh, want to give it to me?"

Way to go, Kate, hold the man's shirt hostage.

"Oh. Oh, yes. I'm sorry. I…got distracted." She inhaled, and caught the woodsy scent of his cologne. Dark, mysterious, like wandering a forest in the middle of the night.

"Distracted by what?"

"You." There. The truth hung there, in plain sight. "You distract me, Brody McKenna."

"I don't mean to." He reached up a hand and cupped her jaw. His hand was big, strong, yet gentle against her skin. "I keep telling myself not to do this, not to take things further, but then every time I leave here, all I do is think about you. And when I'm near you, all I can do is think about kissing you."

"Really?" She swallowed. "But…"

"But what?"

"But…you haven't."

A smile curved across his face. Slow, sexy. "No, I haven't. And maybe it's time I remedied that."

"Maybe it is."

"Do you want me to kiss you, Kate?"

"Yes." She exhaled. "Yes, I do."

"Good." He leaned in, winnowing the gap between them until a fraction of space separated them. Her pulse rumbled like thunder and a craving for Brody grew inside her until the world disappeared.

She watched the gold flecks dance in his eyes. Her heart stuttered, stopped, stuttered again.

"Ah, Kate…" he said, her name a harsh whisper, then he closed the space and kissed her.

His lips were hard against hers at first, a strong, wild kiss, like a sudden summer storm. His hands tangled in her hair, and he pulled her to him, tight against his chest. She curved into Brody, heat racing through her body, charging up her spine. Her hands worked against his back, feeling the ripple of the muscles she had fantasized about. The warm expanse of his skin, the hard places of his body. He plundered her mouth, his tongue dancing hot and furious with hers.

She couldn't think. Couldn't breathe. Couldn't move. Desire pounded a hard rhythm in her body, and for a long, long second she forgot where she was. She only knew Brody was kissing her and it was the sexiest, most exquisite experience of her life. She shifted against him, pressing her pelvis to his erection, wanting more, wanting—

Brody broke away. He cursed and spun toward the window. "I'm sorry, Kate. I shouldn't have done that. I wasn't thinking. I…"

She laid a hand on his bare shoulder and waited until he'd pivoted back to face her. "It's okay, Brody. I wanted that as much as you did."

"I know, but…I need to talk to you before we take this any further."

The clock chimed the half hour. She cursed the timing. "Can it wait? We have to get going before we're late. Already, with the traffic and set up time, we're likely to barely make it there before the event starts."

"Yeah, it can wait." He drew the T-shirt over his head, and she bit back a sigh of disappointment. "A little while, but not too long, okay?"

"Sounds serious." She grinned. "You're not giving me a fatal diagnosis, Doctor, are you?"

"No, no." He fiddled with the stack of orders on the counter beside him. "Just something I've been meaning to tell you."

"Okay." She lifted the boxes of cupcakes, then placed them in his arms. Curiosity piqued inside her but she had to concentrate on work for now. Like he said, they'd talk later. "We'd better head out now or we'll be late."

"If you don't mind, we can stop by my office. I keep an extra shirt and tie there, for accidents just like this."

"Sure." He helped her load the cupcakes into the van, repeating what they had done two nights before, with her driving, him sitting in the passenger's seat. They drove the few blocks to his office, and Kate waited in the van while he went inside and traded the T-shirt for a clean shirt and suit jacket. When he returned, she put the van in gear.

Brody glanced over at her. "You look beautiful."

"Thank you." She smoothed a hand over the black jersey fabric of the sweetheart neckline dress she'd chosen. "This is a special event."

"Big one for Nora's Sweet Shop?"

"You could say that." She paused. "Really, it's a big one for me."

"Sounds important."

"It is. It's a way of thanking the people who have been there for me when I needed them." She glanced over at him. "It's a thank you for the troops."

He tensed beside her. Whatever he'd been holding back seemed to be bubbling under the surface. Why?

"Is something bothering you?" she asked.

He glanced out the window, as they headed out of

Newton and into the city, against the flow of outgoing traffic. Horns honked. Lights flashed. But Kate's attention stayed on Brody.

"Yes and no," he said after a while.

"You want to talk about it?"

He didn't say anything for a long time, so long she thought he hadn't heard the question. Finally, he let out a breath. "I've been wrestling with something for some time now and I know I need to talk about it, but…" he shook his head, "doing so is a lot harder than I expected." He paused again, and she waited for him to continue. "The last medical mission trip I took was really difficult. I lost a patient, and it's been haunting me."

"Oh, Brody, I'm sorry."

"I made a promise to the patient, one I'm not so sure I can keep anymore. He didn't want me to say what happened to him. He just wanted me to encourage someone very close to him to focus on the future, not on what happened in the past, and I just don't know if that's the right thing to do." Brody hesitated again and then looked at her. "If it were you, what would you want?"

She thought about her answer. "I don't know. A part of me feels like I've just started moving forward, and knowing more, or going back there would be like the day I found out. I just…don't want to go there again. I'm just getting out of that cement, you know?"

"So you're saying it would be better not to know?"

"For me, for now…that's what I'd want. Maybe down the road, it would be easier."

"Thanks for the advice. I'll keep that in mind." He turned to the window, and watched the world go by, a clear sign the subject was closed.

The sun had started to set, casting a golden lake over the rippling green waters of Boston Harbor, and twinkling halos over every skyscraper.

"The city is amazing, isn't it?" Kate said. "Every winter, I say I want to move and open up a location in Florida or Hawaii, or any place that doesn't get snow. But there's just something about Boston, something... magical, that I love. No matter where I go, my heart will always be here."

"I feel the same way. I've traveled all over the country, seen a lot of the world, and there's still nothing like Boston. I love it here, for all its faults...and traffic."

Kate laughed. "Yeah, the traffic is one thing I can do without. My grandparents don't mind it. They say it gives them extra alone time in the car. They're old romantics that way."

"They sound it." Brody glanced out the window, watching the city go by in a blur of buildings. "I guess everyone hopes to find a true love like that, the kind that can last a lifetime. I know my grandparents were like that. My parents, not so much. They fought all the time. Then they'd make up, and it'd be fiery in a different way. I think they were two opposite souls, who just couldn't let go of each other."

"Sometimes the fireworks are good." Though for her parents, attraction hadn't been enough to sustain their marriage. They'd been too different to make it work, too infatuated to slow down and think before they tied the knot.

Still, fireworks summed up what had been going on inside her ever since she'd met Brody. And every time he smiled at her. Or touched her. And, oh, yes, when he kissed her.

Fireworks. Bottle rockets—no, Roman candles—of desire, launching in her chest. Fireworks alone didn't create a relationship, and she needed to remember that.

Brody had turned his attention on her, and it took all her effort to keep her eyes on the road and not on him. "Is that what you're looking for? The fireworks and happiness, even in a traffic jam?"

She sighed. "I gave up on that a long time ago. My parents were like yours. All fireworks, no substance. I guess watching their marriage disintegrate made me lose faith in ever finding Mr. Right."

"And who is your Mr. Right?"

"Why, are you applying for the job?" She cast him a grin, pretending the question was a joke. But after that kiss, a part of her hoped like hell the answer was yes.

"Can't do that if I don't know the qualifications." He grinned. "I could be all wrong for you."

"Could be." Or he could be all right. She didn't know yet, but a part of her really wanted to find out. "I guess my brother is the one I hold up as the ideal for all the men I meet. Andrew was smart, and funny, and driven, and above all, a hero. The kind of man who was true to those he loved, loyal to everyone he knew, and braver than anyone in the world. You could count on him to be honest, to be the one you depended on, rather than him depending on you."

"He sounds like the perfect guy."

She laughed. "Oh, he was far from perfect, believe me. There was a time when we were little, like nine and seven. He and I were fighting over a toy, and he slugged me, hard. My eye swelled up, my cheek turned purple, and he felt so bad, he carried me to my grandmother, and stood over me for hours, changing out the ice pack and worrying like a new mother. He got in a lot of trouble that day, and for years, would tell me how bad he felt about it. I, of course, being the evil older sister, milked that injury for all I could."

Brody laughed. "I know that trick. Riley and I have given Finn a hard time and taken him on a guilt trip more than once."

"I've met Riley and I can see that about him. He seems like he was…mischievous as a child."

Brody laughed. "He still is."

"What's Finn like?"

"The total opposite of Riley. Finn is an architect, all straight lines and organizational charts, although marrying Ellie and adopting a child has loosened him up a lot. Riley runs an after school program at Wilmont Academy. He was the slowest to grow up, but he's making us all proud now."

"And you, of course, being a doctor who also volunteers his time to help the needy. You must make them all proud, too."

His gaze went to the window again. For a long time, he was silent, just watching the traffic go by, the houses yield to skyscrapers. "Some days I think I do. Other days…not so much."

He didn't elaborate and she didn't press. Once again, Brody had closed a door between them, and Kate reminded herself she didn't need a man like that. At its heart, this wasn't a relationship, it was a business deal. He was helping her and in exchange, he'd get the cupcakes for Riley's wedding. Fireworks or not, if there was no substance, there wasn't anything to build on.

Then why did she care what troubles lay behind those blue eyes? Why did she keep pressing for more?

Because she sensed something good, deep inside of Brody. Something worth fighting for.

"So, who's your ideal Mrs. Right?" she asked, up-ending her own vow to stay neutral. She exited the highway, and came to stop at a red light. A sign for her and Brody? "The perfect doctor's wife with the gloves and pillbox hat?"

"Lord, no, that would drive me nuts." He chuckled. "I'm not that formal. Ever. I like women who are... natural."

"As in no makeup, wearing sandals and T-shirts?" The light turned green, and Kate accelerated again.

"As in they act like themselves all the time. I hate when people act one way but feel the opposite. I don't like secrets or surprises."

"Me, too. If you asked me my relationship deal-breaker, it would be dishonesty. I can't stand being lied to. Have the courage to tell me the truth, or don't waste my time." She flicked on her directional, then pulled into the hotel's parking garage. The van bumped over a speed strip. Kate cast a quick glance at the cargo, but nothing had moved. "If you want people who are true to their word and to those they care about, then you've come to the right place tonight."

Brody didn't say much as they pulled the boxes out of the van, then loaded them onto a cart and headed up the to the third floor in the hotel elevator. Once inside the ballroom, a hotel staffer directed Kate to the ban-quet table, telling her to set up dessert on the far corner.

She glanced at Brody several times, but the easy banter between them had disappeared. Had she said something wrong? Or was he still thinking about the patient he had lost?

"We only have a few minutes before everyone arrives, so we need to hurry," she said. They worked out an assembly line of sorts, with Brody handing Kate the cupcakes while she laid them on tiered trays she had brought with her.

"Red, white and blue?" he said, noting the arrangement of the desserts. "It almost looks like you've made flags."

"I did." She pointed to the array of cupcakes, set in the familiar pattern of the flag for the USA. Then she drew in a deep breath. Tonight would be difficult, no doubt, but the cause was a worthy one, and Kate vowed to suck it up and not cry. "Okay. Here they come."

The ballroom doors opened and dozens of men and women in uniform strode into the ballroom, chatting in low tones as the band took up the stage and began to play "America the Beautiful." The room filled with a sea of green and camouflage, flanked by bright flags on either end.

"I haven't seen these people in a long time. I'm so nervous and excited."

"I thought you said it was a thank you," Brody said.

"It is." She leaned in and lowered her voice. "For the members of Andrew's unit, along with several other units from Massachusetts who returned to the States in the last few weeks. It was originally supposed to be a retirement party for the top ranking general in the area, but the general put up his own money and paid to have a party for the troops instead. So it mushroomed into this big event. They came to me for the cupcakes because they knew my brother had…" She bit her lip and shook her head. She would not cry tonight. Would not. "Well, that he didn't come home."

The troops settled into chairs that ringed tables decorated with patriotic colors. An honor guard marched in, raised the flag, and the whole room stood at attention to sing "The Star Spangled Banner."

"There are members of Andrew's unit here tonight?" Brody hung back behind the banquet tables with Kate, his stomach riding his throat.

"Yes. I can't wait to introduce you to them."

Introduce him? The thought hit Brody in the chest like an anvil. Kate had said the one thing she couldn't abide was someone who didn't tell the truth. All Brody had done since he met her was lie. Lie about who he was. Lie about why he was in her shop. Lie about his volunteer work. He'd done it because it had been Andrew's last request, but now...

Now he wasn't sure it had been the right decision. How could he expect her to move forward, to look to the future, if Brody was holding a key to her past in his hands?

"These are the true heroes," she whispered to Brody. Tears filled her eyes, while she watched the general take the stage and thank the brave men and women who had given their lives in defense of their country. "The people who risked everything for those back home."

Brody had thought he was doing the right thing by not telling Kate about Andrew's death, but he'd been wrong. The woman beside him was no daisy. She was as strong as an oak tree, and the time had come for him to tell her the truth. He'd be there to help her through it, and she would be okay. He'd make sure of it.

The general finished his speech, then began introducing the vendors who had donated their time and products to the event. "And I'd also like to introduce

Miss Kate Spencer, owner of Nora's Sweet Shop. She lost her brother, Andrew, in Afghanistan last month. A tragic accident, that occurred while Andrew and members of his team were accompanying a medical team helping local villagers. Kate, come on up here." The general waved to her.

She hesitated. "I don't know if I'm ready for this," she whispered. She spun toward Brody. "Go with me? At least until the stage?"

"Of course." He took her hand, and they walked across the room and over to the stage. Kate gave Brody a smile, then climbed the few steps and crossed to the podium. "Thank you, General Martin. I'm afraid you've given me too much credit. I didn't do anything but make cupcakes. It's all of you who made the sacrifices and gave of yourselves. I hope these desserts thank you, at least in some tiny measure, for all you have done. I know my brother was proud to be in the National Guard, but not as proud as I was to call him my brother."

A roar of applause and hearty agreement went up from the crowd. Kate gave them all a smile, then climbed back down the stairs and took Brody's hand again. "Thank you."

"You did great." She'd been poised and brief, and delivered a speech that touched people with a few words. He'd never seen another woman who could do so much, and touch so many, so easily.

Damn, he liked her. A lot.

And because he did, he would tell her who he really was, and what had happened in that dusty hut, and pray it all worked out. In his practice, he'd seen a thousand times that the truth gave patients power. To make their own decisions, to handle a diagnosis. Kate needed that, and Brody was done waiting to give it to her.

"I'm just glad I got through it without crying." She smiled again, but this time her eyes shimmered. "It's still hard to talk about him sometimes."

"I understand. More than you know." He led her through the crowd and toward the banquet tables. Maybe they could slip out for a few minutes and he could talk to her. Or maybe it would be better to wait until they had left, and they could find a quiet place to talk alone.

Along the way, several troops got to their feet to offer condolences, and thank-yous for the cupcakes. Brody's feet sputtered to a stop when a familiar face rose to greet Kate. "Hey, Kate. Nice to see you again."

"Artie! Oh my gosh, it's been so long since I've seen you!" She let go of Brody's hand and gave the tall man a big hug. "How have you been?"

Artie Gavins, one of the other men in Andrew's unit. Brody forgot what his job had been, but he knew his face. He'd bandaged it the same day that Andrew had died. A serious man, who the others had dubbed "Straight Line" because he rarely cracked a smile. Andrew said Artie kept them all on track, but had also respected the other man's common sense approach.

"Fine, just fine," Artie said. Then his gaze traveled past Kate, and landed on Brody. It took him a second, but Brody could see him making the connection in his brain, processing the man in the suit jacket and tie, and connected him with the doctor in a khaki coat and jeans that he'd known last month. "Doc? Wow, I can't believe it's you. Hell, I almost didn't recognize you all dressed up and wearing a suit and tie."

Brody put out his hand and shook with the other man. "Good to see you, too."

And it was. There'd been so many wounded that day, so many to tend to. Seeing one of the men as hearty and hale as ever, gave Brody more reward than any paycheck ever could.

Still, he prayed Artie wouldn't say anything else. Brody didn't want Kate to find out who he was like this. He wanted time to explain it to her, time to get the words right, and here, in a public place, among all these people, wasn't the right place or time. "We, uh, better get back to the dessert table," he said to Kate. "I think we forgot to unload one of the boxes."

"Oh, yes, we need to get that done. Wouldn't want anyone to miss out on dessert." She gave Artie's shoulder a squeeze. "We'll catch up later."

"We will. Nice to see you, Kate, Doc." Artie took his seat again.

Brody hurried through the rest of the crowd with Kate, and back over to the banquet table. He wanted to pull Kate aside, but they were pinned in by the banquet tables and people were already lining up for food. No discreet way to duck out of the room.

"I didn't know you knew Artie," she said. "What a small world. How did you meet him?"

"He was...my patient once." Brody cast a glance down the long white tableclothed space. The hungry crowd was closing the gap between the chicken cordon bleu and dessert.

"Wow, and you remember him? That's pretty impressive, Doc."

"There are certain patients I never forget." Understatement of the year. "Listen, can we get out of here? I really want to talk to you."

"I can't leave. I promised the general I'd stay and eat with the troops. Plus, I'd love to catch up with Andrew's unit. It makes me feel closer to him. Why don't you stay? I promise, none of them bite." She grinned.

"I...I can't. I..." How could he explain it? The gap had closed, and the diners were now ten feet away. In that crowd was Artie, and most like Sully and Richards, the other two who had been on that mission with Andrew, also wounded, also part of the mad rush between Brody and the other doctor to save lives. "I...I need to talk to you, Kate."

She put a hand on his arm "Are you okay? You look...pale."

He glanced at the troops heading toward them, then at the woman who had just talked about the one army man who wouldn't be coming home, and the guilt hit him again in a wave so hard, he had to take a breath before he spoke again. "No, I'm not okay. Not at all."

"What is it?"

Andrew's last words rushed over Brody. *Don't tell her. She'll only grieve more.*

But that bequest warred with everything Brody knew to be true. A patient couldn't mend if they were in the dark about their ailment. Kate's heart was hurting her, and keeping the truth from her even one second longer wasn't going to help her heal. No amount of cupcake baking or location scouting could do what the simple truth could.

He was standing in a room with the bravest people in the world, and standing across from one of the bravest women he had ever met. He was doing her a disservice by keeping this tucked inside one minute longer. "Remember I told you about that patient I lost when I was on the medical mission?"

"Uh-huh." She pivoted a cupcake to the right, straightened another, until the frostings were aligned and the colors made straight lines in the flag design.

"That patient was someone you know."

She jerked her head up. "Someone I know?"

The hungry troops had reached the cupcakes. They exclaimed over the design as they selected one and moved on. "We need to go somewhere private, Kate."

"What, now?"

"Yes. It can't wait any longer. In fact, what I have to tell you shouldn't have waited as long as it has."

"Kate, I've saved a seat at the head table for you," the general said. "Come on and join me for dinner."

She glanced at Brody then back at the general. "I will, sir. Can you give me one second, please?"

The general nodded. "Take all the time you need."

She grabbed Brody's hand and they scooted along the wall, and out of the ballroom. Kate glanced back at the room as the doors shut. "I only have a minute, Brody."

He reached into his pocket and pulled out his wallet. Then he withdrew the card he had carried for so long and handed it to her. A parade of emotions washed over her face. Confusion, shock, hurt.

"How…how did you get this?" she asked.

The moment had come, and dread rumbled in Brody's gut. How he wished he didn't have to tell her this, didn't have to watch the happiness dim in her eyes. "Artie knows me…because I was his doctor."

"You said that."

"I was his doctor in Afghanistan. In fact, I treated several of the troops in that room."

"Wait. You were in Afghanistan? When?"

He let out a long breath. "I was part of a medical team that was going from village to village, helping provide care to people too poor or too far from a doctor, and also tending to those who had been injured because of the war. A National Guard unit had been dispatched to serve as protection for us because it was still a dangerous area." He met her gaze. "It was Andrew's unit, Kate."

"I don't understand. How did you know my brother? Is that how you got my card?"

"Remember that town I told you about? The one with the mountain range? We were there for several days and while we were, Andrew received one of your care packages."

She clutched the card tighter, her face pale. "I sent him those baskets every week, like clockwork. Lord only knows how the military got them to him, but they did."

"He loved those baskets." Brody chuckled a little at the memory of big, strong Andrew, as happy as a kid on Christmas when he received a box from home. He'd handed out cupcakes to all, boasting about his sister as he did. "I know he kidded you about them, but he kept every card, and talked about you all the time. When I met you, I felt like I already knew you."

"He talked about me?"

He nodded. "He was a good guy, your brother. Really good. It was probably a boring detail, just going from town to town with a couple doctors, but he treated it like the most important mission he had ever been on."

A smile wavered on her face. "That was Andrew. His whole life was about taking care of other people."

"He did a good job at it," Brody said.

"That still doesn't explain why *you* have the card I sent him."

Brody let out a long breath. He crossed to the brick wall and laid his palm against the cold, hard stone. The words stuck in his throat, churned with bile in his gut, but still he pressed forward. "I got to know your brother while he was with our group. We talked a lot. We had a lot in common, you know, both being from around here, and both being Red Sox fans and…"

"That's good. I'm glad he made a friend." Her voice broke a little.

"He was my friend," Brody said, turning to Kate. "I need you to know that. I cared about him a lot. And I wanted to save him. So badly, I really did."

"What do you mean?"

In the room behind them, the party rolled on. Someone laughed at a joke, and the band shifted into a pop song. Forks clanked, voices hummed.

Brody bit his lip. Damn. "All he ever talked about was you, and this shop, and getting back here to help his family out. He loved all of you very much, and he wanted nothing more than to see a chain of Nora's Sweet Shops someday. He told me you'd be scared to death to do it alone, but I should encourage you to go after your dreams. He worried about you. Worried that you'd get scared, or be too overwhelmed by his death, to keep going forward." Brody swallowed hard. Forced the words out. "He wanted me to make sure you did that. It was his dying wish."

"You…you were with him when he died?"

Brody nodded. He wanted to look away when he said the next part, but Kate deserved the truth, deserved the unvarnished, painful as hell truth. So he met her gaze, and said it. "I was his doctor."

"His doctor?" She pressed a hand to her forehead. "When were you going to tell me?"

"I tried to. A thousand times. But I didn't…" He sighed. "I didn't want to hurt you."

"You took care of him?"

"He was badly injured, and so were several other guys. That blast…it hurt them all. Some worse than others. The second doctor on the team was overwhelmed, less experienced, and there was a lot to deal with, all at once. It was chaos, Kate, sheer chaos. I did my best, believe me, but his injuries were too severe."

The words hung in the air between them for a long, long time. He watched her process them, her eyes going wide with disbelief, then filling with tears, then narrowing with anger. "You…why didn't you save him? What kind of doctor are you?"

"I tried, Kate, I tried. But you've got to understand, we were in the middle of nowhere, and our supplies were low. We'd just come from a village that had a lot of wounded and sick people, and we were on our way to the rendezvous spot for a resupply, when Andrew's truck went over the IED. All of them were hurt, and we had to try to help everyone, all at the same time. We did our best, but Andrew was badly injured. There was nothing I could do for him."

"Did he…" She bit her lip, swiped at the tears on her cheeks. "Did he suffer?"

People asked that question and never wanted the truth. They never wanted to know that their loved one had been in pain, or lingered with a mortal wound. They wanted death to be quick, painless, as simple as closing your eyes. "He wasn't in any pain," Brody said, which was the truth. The one thing they'd had in good supply was painkillers. "And we talked a lot during his last hours."

"Hours? He suffered for *hours?* Why…why didn't you get more help? Call in a helicopter? Do something… else? Why did you…let him die?"

"I didn't let him, Kate. I did everything I could."

"But it wasn't enough, was it?" She shook her head, then glanced down at the card. When she raised her gaze to his, those emerald eyes had gone stone cold. "And so you came here, came to me, on what, a mercy mission? Take care of the grieving older sister?"

"It wasn't like that. I—"

"I don't care anymore, Brody. I don't care what you intended or what you meant. You let my brother die and then you stood in my shop and watched me cry and never said a word." She flung the card at him. It pinged off Brody's chest and tumbled to the carpeting. "Stay away from me. I'm not your pity case anymore."

Then she turned on her heel and headed back into the ballroom. The door shut, and Kate was gone.

CHAPTER TEN

BRODY stood beside his brother and watched Riley and Stace pledge till death do us part, with ridiculous, happy smiles all over their faces. Frank, Stace's head chef, longtime friend and business partner, watched from his seat, tears streaming down his face. Gran sat beside Frank, dabbing at her pale blue eyes. Stace's sister and nephew sat on the other side of Frank, beaming like proud parents.

The wedding had been simple, the service lasting just a few minutes, with Brody and Finn serving as ushers. Finn had been best man, and gave Riley a hug of congratulations when he handed the youngest McKenna the rings. As soon as the minister pronounced them man and wife, Jiao, Finn and Ellie's adopted daughter who had served as flower girl, scooted out of her mother's arms, and scattered more rose petals on the altar. The guests laughed, and Jiao ducked back behind her mother again. Ellie chuckled, and wrapped a protective arm around the small dark-haired girl.

The minister introduced Mr. and Mrs. McKenna, then Riley and Stace turned toward the small crowd of guests, hand in hand. Applause and cheers went up, and the couple headed down the makeshift aisle in the center of the diner, while guests showered them with rose petals and Jiao brought up the rear, scattering flowers in their wake.

Throughout the wedding, Brody had forced himself to keep his attention on the front of the room. Not to turn back and see if Kate was one of the guests seated in the diner. But now, as Riley and Stace walked away, his gaze scanned the crowd, searching for long brown hair, deep green eyes.

Disappointment sunk like a stone in his gut. She wasn't here.

He'd hoped, even though he had heard the finality in her voice, but still he'd hoped that she would change her mind. His heart kept looking for her, kept hoping to see her when there was a flash of dark brown hair or the sound of laughter.

The band began playing, and several waitstaff hurried in to move the seating around to accommodate a dance floor in the center of the diner. The cupcakes had been delivered early this morning, probably part of Kate's plan to avoid him. Before Brody arrived, she'd stacked them on a towering stack of circular plates, decorated with fresh flowers and strands of iridescent pearls, like a real wedding cake. As always, Kate had surpassed expectations. The guests oohed and aahed, and Riley pointed to Brody. "Don't tell us, tell my brother over there. I believe he made each one himself."

"It wasn't me," Brody said, "it was all the work of—"

The door opened. Kate strode inside. She had her hair up in a loose bun, with tendrils tickling along her jaw. She wore a pale blue dress that floated above her knees in a swishy bell, and floral heels that accented her legs, curved her calves. Brody reminded himself to breathe.

He couldn't dare to hope for forgiveness for lying to her for so long, regardless of how many times he'd apologized. But a part of him was damned glad to see her, and wishing anyway.

"Thank that beautiful woman there." He pointed at Kate. "Kate Spencer, the owner of Nora's Sweet Shop, which makes amazing cupcakes and chocolates."

Several guests swarmed Kate, singing her praises over the floral decorated cupcakes. She thanked them, the admiration causing her to blush. After a while, she broke away from the group, accepting a glass of champagne from a passing waiter. She chatted with Ellie while Brody watched and wished she was talking to him.

Riley strode over to Brody. "I see your baker is here. You going to ask her to dance?"

"She's not my anything." She never had been, really. The relationship he'd built with her had been built on a lie, and everyone knew a castle constructed on sand would never last.

Riley arched a brow. "What happened?"

"I told her about Afghanistan. That I was the doctor with her brother when he died. And that her brother had asked me to watch out for her."

"How'd that go?"

Brody scowled at his little brother. "How do you think?"

"I'm glad you finally talked about it, Brody."

"Yeah, well, I'm not. Now I've lost her, and all because I was trying to do the right thing."

Riley clapped a hand on Brody's shoulder. "Remember

when you and me tricked Finn into seeing Ellie, with that old bait and switch we did with the bagels?"

"Yeah." Brody watched Kate across the room. Stace had moved on to greet other guests and now Kate stood away from the crowd, sipping her champagne, and watching the guests. Avoiding all eye contact with him.

"You need to do the same thing, and find a way to get that pretty girl to talk to you again."

"She doesn't want to see me."

"Did you ask her?"

"Of course not. I just assumed—"

Riley let out a gust. "Geez, Brody, now I'm the expert in relationships in this family? If that's the case, then you'd better check the sky, because I think pigs are flying. You don't assume, brother, you go find out. You have to get in there and take a shot before you can score."

Brody arched a brow. "Did you just tell me to score?"

"Hey, I may be grown up and responsible and married now," he sent a wave over to Stace, "but I'm not perfect." Riley gave Brody a nudge. "Now go over there and take a chance. The woman really likes you. Lord only knows why, but she does." He grinned. "So don't let her get away, or Finn and I will have to take charge."

Riley joined his wife. Brody waved off the waiter's offer of champagne and threaded his way through the tables and chairs until he reached Kate. Up close, she looked a hundred times more beautiful. With her hair up, he could see the delicate curve of her neck, the tiny diamond earrings in her lobes. He caught the scent of vanilla and cinnamon, and a bone deep ache to hold her rushed through his veins.

Brody headed over to her. "Can we talk?"

"I think we've talked all we need to," Kate said, her tone short, cold. "Our business is concluded, and I've found out who you really are. What else is there to discuss?" She raised her eyes to him. Hurt and disappointment pooled in those emerald depths.

"Kate, let me explain."

"Why? What are you going to tell me that's going to change anything?"

"Just hear me out. Please. Five minutes, that's all I ask."

She bit her lip, considering. "Fine. Five minutes."

A start. Right now, Brody would take any start he could get.

"Let's get out of here, okay?" He led her through the diner, into the kitchen, then out the back door and into the alley that ran behind the Morning Glory. He propped the back door open with a rock, then turned to Kate. The sun danced off her hair, shining on those tempting curls, and it was all he could do not to take her in his arms. "I'm sorry for not telling you who I was right off the bat. I was wrong."

She shook her head, tears welling in her eyes. "You should have told me."

"I know. You're right." If he could have done it differently, he would have. All this time, he'd thought he was doing the right thing, but he hadn't been. Looking at Kate now, at the hurt in her face, he wished he could start over. "That last conversation I had with Andrew, when he knew he was dying, he asked only one thing of me."

She raised her gaze to his. "What?"

"That I make sure you were okay. That you were moving forward with your life. He said he was afraid you'd be stuck in your grief. He begged me not to tell you the truth because he was afraid it would make things worse for you."

"Worse? How can knowing the truth make it worse?"

Brody wanted to reach for Kate, but he held back. "He was afraid you would blame yourself all over again. He said you told him that if anything ever happened to him, you'd feel responsible."

She nodded. "I did say that. And he was right. If I hadn't—"

"The last thing he wanted was for you to think you were the reason he was over there." Brody reached for Kate's hand. "Andrew loved his job, and he loved you. He didn't join the military because of you, he joined because he was doing what he does best."

"What's that?"

"Protecting the people he loves. He was doing it then, and he's been doing it ever since he died, through me." Brody let go of Kate's hand and dropped onto the concrete stoop to face a few self truths. "I can relate, because that's what I've done all my life. I've protected my family. Protected myself. I nag my grandmother about getting checkups, harass my brothers about annual physicals. I take care of those around me, because if I do, I can…"

"Prevent another tragedy."

"Yeah. Or at least that was my plan. I thought I went into medicine to change people's lives," he said, "but in reality, I did it to change my own. When my parents died, I remember thinking how powerless I felt. One minute they were here, the next they were gone. I didn't have any say in it. I didn't have any control over it."

"You were eight, Brody. There was nothing you could do."

"Try telling that to an eight-year-old whose world just turned inside out. I became a doctor, I think partly as a way to change that history. You know, save someone else's loved ones and do it often enough, and it would make up for my loss. But it never did. I kept thinking if I could find the right prescription, make the right diagnosis, it would be enough. Change a life, in some small way. And most of all, control the risks, as best I could."

"And thus control the outcome."

He nodded. "But then I went to Afghanistan and realized that sometimes you have to let people take risks. If your brother hadn't been the one in the lead, if he and his team hadn't hit that bomb, it would have hit us. And those villagers would have died. He gave his life for us, because that was his job. He protected us, by risking himself."

She bit her lip. "That was Andrew. He did it all his life."

"You once called him a true hero, and I agree. He was an example for the rest of us to live up to," Brody said. "When that patient of mine at Mass General died, I had to go and tell the family. It was my first notification and the attending thought it would be a good idea for me to learn how. The whole thing was...agonizing. Horrible. The patient's sister was there, and his mother and father, and all I remember seeing was the grief in their eyes. I knew I was causing it, by my words, and I couldn't stop it, because it was the truth. There was no going back and bringing that man back to life. Or bringing him back to his family."

"But you're a doctor. You deal with life and death

every day. Why was this any different?" She took two steps closer and bent her knees until they were eye level. "I *deserved* to know, Brody. You lied to me, over and over again. Why would you do that? To me? Why couldn't you—"

"Because he was my *friend,* damn it!" The last words ripped from Brody's throat, leaving him hoarse. All those weeks he'd spent overseas with Andrew by his side, he'd imagined the two of them meeting up again in Newton, sitting down to watch the game, have a few beers, trading stories about their time in the Middle East. He'd never expected that a bright, sunny morning in the middle of fall would be the day Andrew Spencer, that vibrant, strong young man, would breathe his last breath. "I watched my friend die and it tore me apart. It was like I was losing a brother. I kicked myself for every decision, every moment. I wanted to go back and undo it, to change the course of destiny, and I couldn't. I couldn't do it, Kate, no matter how much I wanted to." He ran a hand through his hair. "I thought it was hard losing that first patient, but at least there, I had all the tools I needed, all the medical staff I could want. The best hospital, the best tests. When he died, I knew I had done everything I could. But when Andrew died—" Brody cursed and turned away.

"What about when Andrew died?"

Brody was back there again. The heat of the Middle East a powerful, shimmering wall. At every turn, the smell of poverty, desperation, lost hope. "We were in this tiny little dirt floor hut in the middle of nowhere. Hours from a hospital. There was me and one other in-experienced doctor, and that was it. No X-ray machines. No operating rooms. No specialists on call. We'd just come from a village that had a lot of sick and wounded people, and our supplies were low. If I'd been in a hospital, I could have hooked him up to a machine. I could have bought him some time. I could have..." He cursed again. The ground blurred before him.

"Changed the ending?"

Brody closed his eyes and drew in a long, deep breath. All these weeks, the what ifs had plagued him. He'd replayed the entire day a hundred times in his mind, but in the end, always came to the same conclusion. The one ending that in his heart he couldn't accept, even though he knew it was the only one. No matter how many hospitals or experts had been on the scene of that explosion, the outcome would have been the same. Sometimes, people just died. And it sucked, plain and simple. "No. He had deep internal injuries from that bomb. The best hospital in the world would have only been able to do one thing." He lifted his gaze to Kate's. "Buy him more time."

"To do what?" Kate asked. "To suffer?"

"To say goodbye."

And there, Brody realized, lay the crux of what had dogged him all these weeks. What had kept him from sleeping. What had laid guilt on his shoulders like a two-ton wall. "I wanted him to have time to talk to you. The cell service where we were was non-existent, and I kept hoping he'd get well enough that we could transport or that a signal would magically appear. I just wanted Andrew to have time to tell his family he loved them. I didn't want to be his messenger, damn it, I wanted him to talk to his family himself. He tried to hold on, he really did, I could hear the helicopters in the distance and I kept hoping, and praying, and trying to keep him alive." Brody's voice broke, and he raised his gaze to her. "But I couldn't fix this, Kate. I...couldn't. I failed and I'm sorry, Kate. I'm so, so sorry."

She buried her face in her hands. Her shoulders shook with her tears, and Brody got to his feet, wrapped an arm around Kate and drew her to him. She tensed, then finally leaned against him. She cried for a long time, Brody doing nothing more than holding her and running a hand down her back and whispering the same thing over and over again. *I'm sorry.*

He could have said it a thousand times and never felt like it was enough. Finally, her tears eased, and so too did the stiffness in her body, the tension in her features. She drew back, the dark green lakes of her eyes still brimming. "Don't you understand, Brody?" she said. "My brother did say goodbye to me and did tell me he loved me. He did it through you."

Perhaps. But had Brody done all he could have to ensure Andrew's final message had been delivered? "The only thing I could do afterwards was fulfill his last wishes. It wasn't enough, but it was all I had, and for a friend like Andrew, I couldn't let him down again. I wasn't a very good messenger. I should have..." he threw up his hands, "done more."

"Sometimes you do all you can and you accept that it's enough. You said something like that to me just the other day. Remember?"

He could hear the band playing inside, music celebrating a new beginning, a new life, while outside in the alley, he and Kate were discussing a loss and trying like hell to move forward with their own lives.

"I'm a doctor," he said. "I'm supposed to heal people. It's in the Hippocratic Oath, for God's sake. Do no harm. And I did harm by treating him in the middle of nowhere, in a place that didn't have everything I needed. I did him harm by not giving him the time to say good-bye." He cursed and shook his head. "I did my best, and I fell short. Maybe I'm not the doctor I thought I was."

"Let me ask you something." She laid a hand on his. "What would have happened to my brother if you hadn't been there? If he'd been alone and that bomb went off?"

"He'd have suffered. It would have been long and slow, and painful." A horrible, undeserved end for a hero like Andrew.

"And you eased that pain, didn't you?" Kate asked.

"Yes. We had plenty of painkillers."

"I meant you eased that pain by talking to him. By making him forget what was happening. He didn't suf-fer because he had you. A friend, when he needed one most." She held Brody's hand tight in her own, her touch a soothing balm for his tortured thoughts. "Thank you for being with him. Thank you for taking care of him. Thank you for making it easier for him."

The words came from Kate's heart. She didn't blame him. She'd absolved him. "He cared about you deeply. I wish I could have brought him home to you."

Tears spilled from her eyes. "I do, too."

His entire goal for the last few weeks had been to help her move forward, to help her go after her dreams, and even if she never spoke to him again after today, he wanted to know she was at least driving down that path and he had done what Andrew asked of him. Then he could take satisfaction in that. He told himself it would be enough. "You have to move forward, Kate. Rent that building. Expand the business. The one thing Andrew wanted more than anything was for you to be happy.

For you to go after your dreams. We stood in that shop in Weymouth and I could see in your eyes that you wanted to take that chance, but in the end, you walked away. You've stood still for weeks, Kate, instead of taking the leap."

"I wasn't the risk taker. That was Andrew. And without him—" She shook her head. "I can't do it. Nora's Sweet Shop is doing just fine where it is. I don't need to expand."

"Because you're afraid of failure."

"I'm done." She turned away. "I didn't come here for you to tell me what I'm doing wrong with my life."

"You're just going to run away? Because the conversation got tough?"

"I'm not doing that, Brody." She pressed a finger into his chest. "You are. Quit telling me how to change my life until you have the courage to change your own." She crossed to the door and jerked it open.

She was about to leave, and he knew, as well as he knew his own name, that he would never see her again if he let her go now. He had done what he always did—protect, worry, dispense advice and medicine—and had been too afraid to do the same for himself.

Doctor, heal thyself, she'd joked.

How true that was.

If he didn't change now, he'd lose everything that mattered. Brody was tired of losing what was important to him. Not one more day, not one more minute, would he live afraid of the risks ahead. Afraid of loss. Afraid of being out of control.

"Kate, wait." He let out a gust. She lingered at the door, half here, half gone. "We're two of a kind, aren't we? Both in fields that require us to take a chance every day, and both of us too scared to do that. You would think I wouldn't be, because I've seen risk and loss firsthand, felt it under my hands, heard it in the slowing beep of a heart rate. But I am. I'm scared as hell to lose a patient. And scared as hell to lose you."

"Me? Why?"

"Because you're the first woman I've ever met who has shown me my faults and dared me to face them. You're right about me. About my need to fix everything. I think it's part of why I do the medical missions. It wasn't enough to change lives here. I needed to do it in other towns, other countries. And I thought I was doing just fine." Now the words that he had always kept to himself, the tight leash he had held on his emotions, uncoiled, and the sentences spilled out in a fast waterfall. "Until I went to Afghanistan. There, I was stuck in the middle of nowhere with a dying man and a roomful of wounded. Not enough time, not enough supplies, not enough medicine in the world to save everyone. Medicine couldn't save him, and all I could do was watch him die." Brody ran a hand over his face. "I have been scared, all this time, of not having control over the situation. Of exactly what happened with your brother." He took in Kate's delicate features, her wide green eyes. In the past few weeks, she had changed him in dozens of ways, by encouraging him to step out his normal world. He wanted more of that. More of her. And that meant changing, right this second. "I'm done being afraid of risk, Kate. It's kept me from doing what truly makes me happy."

"Like what?"

"Like expanding the medical missions to be bigger, to take on new challenges. Like doing more to change the lives of the people here in Newton. And most of all," he paused, "like falling in love."

"Falling in love? You have?"

"A long time ago." As he said the words, he realized they were true. "I think I fell in love with you before I even met you."

She shook her head. "That's impossible. How could you do that?"

"Andrew and I talked about you all the time. Whenever we were between towns, or between shifts, we talked. He told me all about the shop and your grandmother, and you." Brody grinned. "He made you sound like Mother Theresa and Santa Claus, all rolled into one."

And finally, Kate laughed and Brody saw a bit of her fire return. "I'm not that nice or that altruistic."

"He thought you were. And the more he talked, the more I saw you through his eyes. I saw you in the care packages you sent. In the notes you wrote. In the memories he shared. And I thought, damn, what would it be like to have someone love me that much?" He took her hands in his and held tight. "It took me over a month to work up the courage to walk into your shop. I would walk down there every day during my lunch break, and after I got done for the day, and every time I would turn around. Partly because I was dreading telling you who I was and why I was there, and partly because I was afraid I'd meet you and you wouldn't be what I imagined."

"I wouldn't live up to the hype?"

He smiled. "Something like that. But then I met you, and you were all Andrew said, and more. You were kind and funny and smart and beautiful. Very beautiful." He closed the gap between them and took both her hands in his. "More than I deserved. More than I ever hoped."

"Brody—"

"You knocked me off my feet so badly that first day, I didn't even realize I picked out a sports basket for my grandmother, who is as far from a sports fan as you can get. All I knew was that I wanted to talk to you, wanted to get to know you. And…" He let out a breath, and faced the last bit of truth. That for all these years, he had held back from love, protecting his own heart, because of one failure. Which had cost him true happiness. No more. "I want more of that, Kate. I want you. In my life now and for always."

She shook her head and broke away from him. "Brody, I can't do this right now. I'm supposed to be at the wedding, and so are you, and—"

He reached for her again, this time cupping her face with his hands. "Take a risk with me, Kate."

Her eyes grew wide, and her cheeks flushed. "I…I can't." She shook her head. "You need to quit believing in the impossible, Brody McKenna, and look at the facts. We're not meant to be together. We started out on a lie, and you can't build anything from that. Nothing except goodbye."

Then she headed back inside. The door slammed shut with a loud bang that echoed in the alley for a long, long time.

CHAPTER ELEVEN

THE ruined cupcakes sat on the counter, mocking Kate. Distracted and out of sorts, she'd burned two batches this morning. She'd thought coming in on a Sunday would allow her to get caught up, but it had only put her further behind. When Joanne had come in to help, Kate almost burst into tears with relief. "I hate to abandon you on your first day back," she said to Joanne, "but I really need to get some air. I think I'll go for a run."

"Go, go. I'll be fine. Besides, your grandmother is due to stop by for her daily sugar fix. She'll keep me company."

Kate tossed her apron to the side and headed out to the front of the store. Just as she did, Nora entered, making a beeline for the cupcake display. She placed a small box on the counter beside her, then lifted the glass dome. "Good morning, granddaughter."

"Good morning." She pressed a kiss to Nora's cheek. "How are you?"

"Just fine, just fine, or I will be when I get my daily cupcake." Nora's hand hovered over the red devil, then the peanut butter banana, then the chocolate cherry. "Off to see the cute doctor?"

"No. I'm just heading out for a run."

"Well, before you go, maybe you should open this package. I found it on the doorstep when I came in." Nora settled on the chocolate cherry, and replaced the glass dome. She leaned against the counter, peeled off the paper wrapping and took a bite. "Amazing. As always."

"That package is for me?" Kate grabbed a box cutter from under the counter. Maybe she'd ordered something for the shop and forgotten. She slipped the knife under the tape, and as she peeled it off, she realized the box had no stamp, no delivery confirmation tag. And it was Sunday, a day no service delivered. "You just found it out front?"

"Yup." Nora took another bite, and smiled. "Delicious. Sometimes the best and sweetest one is the one you missed, in your rush to make a choice. Don't you think?"

Kate peeled up one flap, then the other. She reached into the cardboard container and pulled out a small black velvet box. A card had been attached to the top, and she opened that first.

Sometimes all you need is a little luck before you leap.
—Brody

"What do you have there?" Nora asked.

"I don't know." Kate pried open the hinged lid of the box, and let out a gasp when she saw the contents. A four leaf clover, a real one, encased in a glass dome, and attached to a heart shaped charm, dangling from a wide silver ring. A keychain, waiting for keys.

"That man knows you well," Nora said.

"He does. But—"

Nora laid a hand on Kate's shoulder, cutting off her words. "Before you go spouting off all the reasons why you shouldn't love him, let me ask you something. Did I ever tell you the story of who named the shop?"

Kate nodded. "Yeah, but tell it again. It's my favorite."

A soft smile stole across Nora's face as she talked. "When we were first married, your grandfather knew how much I wanted to open a little shop like this, but I was young and had a child on the way and a husband going off to war, and the whole idea just scared the pants off me. The day he left, I woke up and found a spatula on my pillow. Tied up with a bow. He'd carved Nora's Sweet Shop into the handle. Did it by hand, with a pocketknife I gave him for his birthday. He told me the sweetest thing I could ever do for him was to go after my dreams. And I did. I never regretted it, not for a second. I've been so proud to see you and Andrew take up the reins and carry that dream forward." Nora put a hand on Kate's. "Now it's your turn to run with the ball and carry it the rest of the way. To take Nora's to new heights."

"I'm scared, Grandma." Kate ran her hands over the silver ring. "What if I fail?"

"Just by having the courage to go after your dreams, you've already won, my dear." She drew her granddaughter into a long, tight hug. "And no matter what, I'll be here to support you."

Kate fingered the charm, then lifted her gaze to the newspaper article on the wall. Andrew seemed to be smiling his support from across the room. He would want her to do this. To move forward, and as Brody had said, quit standing still. "Thanks, Grandma."

"You're welcome. Now go for that run, and clear your head. I'll stay here and," she lifted the glass dome and snagged a peanut butter banana cupcake this time, "guard the cupcakes."

Kate laughed. She slipped the keychain into her pocket then headed out the door. A few minutes later, she had stopped at her townhouse, changed her clothes, and started toward the reservoir. The Sunday morning sunshine warmed her, and she found herself slipping into the rhythm and peace of running.

Her mind drifted to Brody and she found herself looking for him, hoping to see him running, too. The keychain bounced in her pocket, a reminder of his gift. A little luck to encourage her to take a risk.

A risk like opening a second location?

A risk like…

Opening her heart?

She rounded the bend of the reservoir, startling a flock of pigeons. They burst into flight, with a chatter of wings. The contingent of pigeons circled away, opting for greener pastures, while several settled back onto the ground in Kate's wake. She watched the ones in flight, their squat bodies becoming sleek gray missiles against the sunny fall sky.

Her steps slowed. She glanced to her right, and saw two paths. One that led toward home. One that led another direction. The opposite from the one she'd always taken. Kate drew in a breath and started running again.

The smell of braised beef filled the kitchen of Mary McKenna's Newton house. Finn, Ellie and Jiao stood in the sunroom and talked with Mary, while Brody hung back in the library and pretended to look for a book he had no intention of reading.

His attempt to show Kate he cared, that he supported her, had gone bust. He'd dropped off the package early this morning, tempted to deliver it in person, but not sure what kind of reception he'd get. After the way things had ended yesterday, he wasn't sure she ever wanted to see him again. Still, he couldn't get her out of his mind, no matter how hard he tried.

"Come join us, Brody," Ellie said to her brother-in-law. "Your grandmother's about to open a bottle of that '92 Merlot you like." She rubbed a hand over her stomach. "Though I'm sticking to apple juice for a while."

Brody waved off the offer. "I'm not in a wine mood tonight. I'll be out shortly."

Ellie sighed and leaned against the doorjamb. "You McKenna men are all the same." A soft smile stole across her face. "Stubborn, determined and impossible."

"Hey. How's that supposed to make me feel better?"

"It's not." Ellie pushed off from the door and crossed to Finn. Her pregnancy had just started to show, giving her a tiny bit of a curve to her belly. "Those are the qualities I love the most in Finn. He's like a bulldog, only cuter."

Brody laughed. "I don't know about the cute part."

"I heard what you did." Ellie paused before him. She took the book in his hands away and shoved it back on the bookshelf. "Both in Afghanistan and with Kate. I think you did the right thing."

He shook his head. "I lost her in the end. How is that the right thing?"

"You were doing what all three of you do. Protecting

her. Taking care of her. She'll realize that and come around."

"I hope so."

"She will." Ellie laid a hand on Brody's arm, the loving support of a sister-in-law who had already become an indelible part of the McKenna family tree. "And it'll all work out. A wise man once told me that the smart man lets the woman he loves go, so that when she returns, it'll be because she truly loves him." She poked a finger at his chest. "That smart man was you. That day in the coffee shop, remember?"

"I do." He and Riley had dragged Finn down there and surprised him with Ellie, all in hopes of spurring the two to work it out. Which, clearly, they had. "Thank you, Ellie."

"You're welcome."

"You're a smart woman," Brody said.

She laughed. "Well, be sure to tell Finn that."

"I think he already knows."

Ellie smiled, the same private smile that Brody had seen on Riley, Stace and Finn. The smile of someone deeply in love and happy as hell.

She gave his arm a gentle tug. "Come on, Brody, have a glass of wine with your family and have a little faith that it will all be okay."

He headed out of the library and into the hall with Ellie. "You do know I'm a doctor, right? Faith is a hard commodity to come by in a world of tests and logic."

"I know. But you're also an Irishman and if anyone trusts in luck and faith, it should be you." She gave him a grin, then stepped away and waved toward the front door.

Brody turned. Kate stood in the doorway, wearing a

T-shirt, shorts and running shoes. A fine sheen of sweat glistened on her skin. To Brody, she'd never looked more beautiful or desirable. He caught his breath.

"I'm sorry for just showing up, but…" she bit her lip and gave him a tentative version of a smile, "does that offer for a family dinner still stand?"

Joy burst in his heart and he closed the distance between them in a few short strides. "Yes, every Sunday. Two on the dot," he said, then let out a gust. "Oh, God, Kate, I wasn't sure I'd see you again."

"I got the package." She reached in her pocket and held up the keychain. It tick-tocked back and forth on her finger. "Thank you."

"You're welcome."

She turned it over in her palm, and dropped her gaze to the small green leaves. "When I got it, my first instinct was to do what I've always done. To run from the risk and the fear. And I literally did just that."

"I can tell." He grinned. "But you still look sexy, even after a run."

"I thought running would help me forget," she said, "but all I did was look for you. At every turn, at every stop. I didn't want to run around the reservoir. I wanted to run to you, Brody. And so…"

"You did." If happiness were a meter, Brody's would shoot off the charts. "I'm glad."

"You were right. I was scared. When I was a kid, I was the one who had to be the steady rudder for Andrew. And he worried about me. The two of us, taking care of each other. Our parents fought all the time and it was just…chaos. I didn't want my little brother to worry or get scared, so I became the practical, dependable one. I let him dream big, and I kept my feet firmly on the ground. Then when he died, it shook me badly. So I did what I do best, and kept those feet cemented in place. I thought if I did everything the same, no surprises, no risks, I wouldn't have to experience that kind of loss or pain again. But I was wrong. Because in the end, it cost me you."

"I'm still here, Kate." He brushed a tendril of hair off her forehead. "And I always will be."

"When you told me you'd fallen in love with me, all I could see was this big cliff and you standing beside it, asking me to jump with you. I got scared and I ran, instead of doing what I should have done."

"Which was…?"

She smiled and winnowed the gap between them, lifted her arms to wrap around his neck and raised on her tiptoes. She pressed a kiss to his lips, then drew back. "That."

"Much better than walking away." He tightened his hold on her, then kissed her back. God, he loved this woman. Loved her smile. Loved her smarts. Loved everything about her. "Much, much better."

"I got scared, because I fell in love with you, too. I found a hundred reasons not to be with you, because I couldn't believe that a man like you really existed. One who could light fireworks inside me and at the same time understand my deepest needs." She tangled her fingers in his hair and her eyes shimmered with emotion. "A real hero."

He glanced away. "That's not me."

"It is." She drew his face around until he faced her again. "You saved my brother. And you saved me. You put everyone else ahead of you and you took the risks no one else wanted to take. That's a hero to me."

He still disagreed about the real hero here, but if the woman he loved saw him as one, he wouldn't argue. To Brody, Kate was the heroic one, determined and smart, the one who had saved him from an empty life. He cupped her jaw, and ran a thumb along her chin. "I love you, Kate Spencer."

A smile burst across her face, bright as the sun. "I love you, too, Brody. I think I fell for you the minute you brought that silly basket up to the counter for your grandmother."

He chuckled. "I was too distracted by you to make a smart buying decision."

"Good thing." She grinned. She held up the key ring again. "You know, there's only one thing this ring needs now."

"What?"

"Keys to a second location. As soon as I get home, I'm calling that realtor. There will be a Nora's in every town, or at least a lot of them." She laughed.

"And I'm thinking of taking on a partner for the practice, so I can keep treating people here in Newton, but also step up my mission work."

She smiled. "Both of us, taking risks."

"Together. The best way to do it."

She laid her head against his chest. "I agree, Brody. I agree."

"The best choice I ever made was that basket. And... you." His heart, no his entire world, were complete now with Kate in his arms. He could see their future ahead, one where she brought smiles to people everywhere there was a Nora's Sweet Shop, and he healed the sick and wounded in far-flung places. There would be some compromises ahead, making both her business and his mission trips work, but Brody had no doubt they'd find a way because in the end, he and Kate had the same core values. The same goals. To create a world full of heroes. And he couldn't wait another minute to start on that path. "I meant what I said. I want to spend the rest of my life with you. Will you marry me, Kate?"

She drew in a deep breath, then exhaled it with a smile. "Yes, I will, Brody."

A burst of applause sounded from behind them. Brody turned to find Finn and Ellie, flanked by his grandmother and Jiao, all clapping and beaming their approval. "I only have one thing to say," Finn said, crossing to his middle brother. "It's about damned time."

Brody laughed. "Always direct and to the point, Finn."

Finn drew Kate into a hug, so tight she squeaked. "Welcome to the family, Kate. The McKennas are a rowdy bunch, so be prepared."

"For what?" Kate asked.

"For the happiest time of your life." He clapped Brody on the shoulder, offered the two of them congratulations, then headed for the dining room. "Now let's eat."

* * * * *

MILLS & BOON®
By Request

RELIVE THE ROMANCE WITH THE BEST OF THE BEST

A sneak peek at next month's titles...

In stores from 20th November 2015:

- **Scandal in the Spotlight** – Lucy King, Kimberly Lang & Anne Oliver

- **His Forbidden Conquest** – Kate Hardy, Aimee Carson & Kate Hoffmann

In stores from 4th December 2015:

- **Propositioned by the Prince** – Jennifer Lewis

- **A Diamond for Christmas** – Susan Meier, Scarlet Wilson & Patricia Thayer

Available at WHSmith, Tesco, Asda, Eason, Amazon and Apple

Just can't wait?
Buy our books online a month before they hit the shops!
visit www.millsandboon.co.uk

These books are also available in eBook format!

1115/05